Crossroads

Peri Jean Mace Ghost Thrillers #7

Copyright © 2017 Catie Rhodes.

All rights reserved.

Published by: Long Roads and Dark Ends Press

Cover artwork by Book Cover Corner

Content Editing by Word Webber Press

Copy Editing by Julie Glover

Proofreading by Deborah Digrispino

ISBN Ebook: 978-1-947462-14-4

ISBN Print: 978-1-947462-15-1

First Printing, 2017

Rhodes, Catie.

Crossroads/ Catie Rhodes. — 1st ed.

Visit the author website: www.catierhodes.com

SERIES LIST

Forever Road (Book #1)

Black Opal (Book #2)

Rocks & Gravel (Book #3)

Rest Stop (Book #4)

Forbidden Highway (Book #5)

Rear View: Prequel (Book #6)

Crossroads (Book #7)

Dead End (Book #8)

Dark Traveler (Book #9)

Wrong Turn (Book #10)

Last Exit (Book #11)

CROSSROADS

PERI JEAN MACE GHOST THRILLERS #7

CATIE RHODES

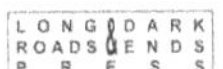

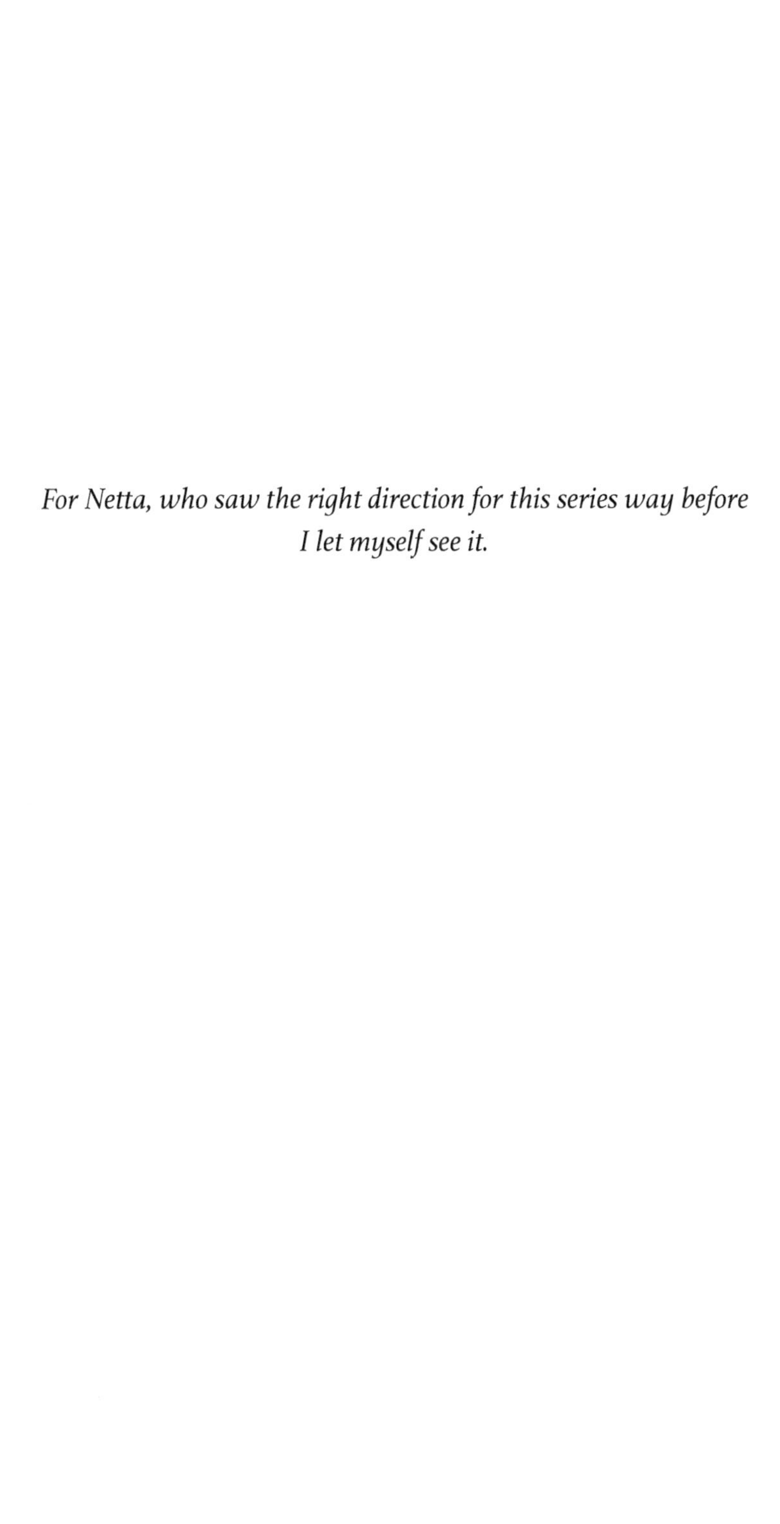

*For Netta, who saw the right direction for this series way before
I let myself see it.*

1

———

THE RESTAURANT BUZZED around me as early morning patrons filled the space, hungry for a dose of greasy breakfast. The salty tang of frying bacon mixed with the dark smell of brewing coffee made my stomach growl under normal circumstances. Today, sour acid burned my guts.

He's late. I shoved the thought away and stared out into the parking lot. No new cars had come since the last time I'd looked sixty seconds ago.

Late February chill radiated from the huge window. I cupped my half-full coffee mug between my hands and hunched my shoulders. Sitting alone at a big table in a busy restaurant qualified for a championship medal in loserdom. I checked the clock on my cellphone and squirmed.

My great-uncle Cecil was now fifteen minutes late. My cheeks heated at the idea of being stood up. Cecil had been friendly and welcoming when I'd tracked him down in Livingston, Texas two months earlier. But then he'd proceeded to ignore my phone calls. The only communication I'd had from him consisted of a postcard showing a beach somewhere in Florida. On the back Cecil had written, *Hey, Peri Jean! My favorite place in the world!* in his scratchy old man's scrawl. It took me almost a week to remember I'd never given Cecil my address.

The call asking if I wanted to meet for breakfast had come late the night before, and Cecil had sounded in a rush with people talking in the background. Had I come to the wrong place? This was a popular chain in the Houston area. I racked my memory, calling up Cecil's papery voice, remembering the street name he'd said. No, this was the right location.

My shirt, one I wore for client meetings, itched at the seams. I tried to scratch without looking like I was feeling myself up. The itch migrated just out of my reach. A crack in the restaurant's vinyl booth seat bit into my leg through my black slacks. Why had I decided to dress up? This was stupid. I was stupid.

I checked my cellphone one more time. Twenty minutes late now. Cecil wasn't coming. From now on, I wouldn't answer his calls—fuck wanting to know more about my family. I'd learn about the origins of my growing power, or not, on my own. I tried to catch the waitress's eye to signal for my check.

The woman stood with her back to me, talking to a table full of men dressed in jeans and work shirts. She laughed at something, throwing her head back, flirting with them for better tips. Great.

My black opal pendant pinged on my chest, signaling

the presence of magic. I turned my attention back to the parking lot in time to watch my great-uncle get out of a four-door pickup. He finger-combed his thinning dark hair back and, smiling, said something to someone still inside the truck.

He'd brought others with him? My heart thudded harder. Now I'd have to impress not only Cecil but also whoever was with him. I wasn't sure I could pull it off. All the ways I could screw up danced merrily through my head. I saw myself spilling coffee, getting food caught in my teeth, or just saying the wrong thing.

"Ma'am?" A voice interrupted my increasingly dark thoughts. "Can you help me?"

I turned away from the window. My visitor, a girl a few years my junior, wore a black tank top, the straps of her turquoise bra visible. Chill bumps covered her arms.

Her wide, tear-filled eyes locked on mine. "I was sitting in this booth earlier. My fiancé and I left, and I realized I've lost my engagement ring." She held up one hand and pointed to her third finger.

"Let's see if it's here." I stood from the booth and began searching through the crevices of the seat, most of my attention on the four-door truck in the parking lot. A young blonde woman had gotten out. Someone inside handed her a baby boy with black curls who was just big enough to start walking. He immediately began kicking for her to let him down. She set him on the parking lot's asphalt but gripped his hand. Another adult-sized arm reached out of the truck, this one masculine. Someone tapped my arm.

"You see it?" A tear spilled out of one eye and tracked down the girl's cheek. She swiped at it, her lips trembling. "Me and Will just got engaged last night. We came here for an early breakfast to celebrate. Got home and didn't have the ring."

I re-doubled my efforts, even kneeling to look under the table, but saw nothing other than dirt, trash, and a dropped French fry. I stood and shook my head at her. "I'm sorry."

She dug in her bag, took out an envelope, and scribbled something on it. I took my attention off her and watched the front door. Cecil walked in, spotting me immediately. The young woman, now holding onto two small children for dear life, crowded in behind him. A man I recognized as my cousin Finn entered the restaurant behind them, a blonde on his arm. A hostess spoke to them. Cecil pointed at me and then gestured to the children. She nodded, grabbed two kiddie chairs, and followed them.

The girl with the missing ring set the envelope on my table. "Will said the ring cost him one month's salary, so I'm willing to offer a $500 reward. If you find it, call this number."

Please leave now. I couldn't say those words out loud, so I nodded, pretty sure she'd never see the ring again.

Cecil and his entourage were halfway across the restaurant. My black opal gave another ping, probably in response to the supernatural gifts they shared with me. My shoulders cranked higher, and my heart tried to jackhammer its way out of my chest.

The missing ring girl followed my gaze, eyes widening. She mumbled her thanks and hurried away. Before I had time to analyze the weird encounter, Cecil was close enough to hold out his arms to me.

I went to him, and we hugged. He held me at arm's length and put one chilly hand on each side of my face. He smiled, his dentures catching the harsh overhead lights. "You remind me so much of my sister."

The well of loss, the one that came and went since the death of my beloved Memaw, opened up. I swallowed against it. My cousin Finn, thin-faced and handsome in an anemic way, pushed around Cecil and wrapped his arms around me. He'd been so busy in December we barely had a chance to speak, but our connection went all the way back to the night I got my raven tattoo when I was eighteen.

The blonde had taken Cecil's arm. She stared straight ahead at nothing in particular. And I saw she was young. Really young. Both girls were. What the hell were they doing with Cecil, who had to be in his eighties, and Finn, who was within a few years of my age?

Cecil pulled her toward me. "This is my daughter, Jadine. My wife and I adopted her as an infant."

That made sense. Jadine held out one hand, a smile curving her shapely lips, eyes still not meeting mine. It hit me then. Jadine was blind. I took her warm, slim hand in mine and gave it a shake. "Good to meet you."

"I'm the one told Papaw to call you." Her voice was soft and melodious as wind chimes on a fall day. "I saw you in a dream, sitting in our motor home."

"Jadine's got a touch of the sight." Cecil smiled. "Some-times her visions warn us about things. Sometimes they remind us to do things—like call and have breakfast with you."

Everybody laughed. I joined in, but hesitantly. Cecil said Jadine was his daughter. Why did she call him Papaw? I'd never heard of someone calling their father Papaw.

Finn pushed the girl-woman holding a toddler on one hip and a barely walking baby on the other hip toward me. "This here's my wife, Dillon."

Dillon pushed the toddler at her husband and extended the hand it freed up. Dark-haired and thin, Dillon had more freckles than anybody I'd ever met, other than Hannah Kessler. Makeup covered most of the freckles on her face, but little reddish dots covered her hands and the part of her chest visible above the neckline of her shirt. The two of us shook. Dillon's grip ground my bones together. I returned her squeeze because I don't take shit off anybody. Dillon's lips curved.

"I think I'm gonna like you." She had more of a drawl than I did, and her words ran together. She didn't look any older up close. She looked younger. Twenty-two tops. I did the math. She must've been a teenager when she and Finn got together.

Finn, busy putting his son and daughter in their special chairs, took care to be gentle and patient, speaking to each child and giving them kisses on their heads. They responded to his touch with smiles.

The little girl leaned around him to stare at me. She had the same dark eyes as Finn, Cecil, and I have. Something in the depths of them caught my attention, pulled at my emotions.

"Zora," she yelled at me.

"My oldest." Dillon slid into the booth. "She's a ringtail tooter. My boy is Zander. He's kinda quiet. We wanted Z names 'cuz it's unusual..." She trailed off, maybe realizing Zora mesmerized me. I stuttered a compliment on the names, which were unique and nice, and kept staring at Zora.

She didn't look like our family other than the brown eyes. Her mahogany colored hair curled into cunning ringlets, which looked to be the same texture as Dillon's. The brutal Texas sun would probably burn and freckle her velvety skin into oblivion. Then she'd be a near carbon copy of her mother. Nothing wrong there. Dillon was cute as a label on a beer bottle. But there was something familiar in the little girl's eyes. "She's beautiful," I murmured.

"Gonna sit down?" Finn motioned for me to get into the booth first so he could sit by his children. I startled, so intent on staring at Zora I'd almost forgotten everybody else. I obeyed and scooted all the way to the wall, leaning against the cold window.

The waitress came over, and we ordered. My jaw dropped when I heard the lavish amounts of food my family ordered. Enough for ten people, let alone five. Memaw had always been so conservative with our money.

"I'm sorry I haven't been in touch," Cecil said as soon as the waitress left.

I pulled my gaze off Zora's. There was something so familiar about her. I couldn't quite place it.

"Hope you didn't take offense." Cecil added.

I shook my head to indicate it was okay, although his silence had confused and hurt me.

"We have a little community of sorts. There are strict rules about who gets brought in." Cecil and Finn exchanged a long look.

Finn's dark eyes flashed with mischief. "You showing up like you did in December ruffled some feathers. They got onto Papaw something fierce."

I opened my mouth to apologize but was struck again by Finn calling Cecil Papaw. Finn was Cecil's nephew. His grandmother had been one of Cecil's sisters, just like Memaw. Weird.

Cecil smiled at whatever he saw on my face. "What is it? You can ask us anything."

"Both Jadine and Finn have called you Papaw." I tried to think of a way to word the question without being rude.

They all laughed, but Cecil spoke. "All the family calls me Papaw. I want you to do it, too, when it feels right." He smiled. "Which I hope it does, soon. This is such a big, important day." He gestured at the group gathered around the table. "This right here is the last of our family." Cecil's eyes misted, and he swallowed hard. He reached for my hand. I let him take it.

"I really hope I didn't cause y'all too many problems showing up like I did," I said, remembering what Finn said about the other members of their community giving Cecil the dickens over it.

"Fuck anybody who doesn't want you." Dillon raised her brows, creating a fan of wrinkles on her forehead. That fair, freckled skin would only look young a few more years. Poor thing. "'Cuz we do."

Finn chuckled and touched his fingers to his temple, reminding me so much of my father and my uncle Jesse it almost hurt. Was this what Daddy would have looked like had he lived into his thirties?

"What happened to everybody?" I glanced around the table. "When I got my tattoo, there seemed to be quite a few of you."

The table went quiet, glances I couldn't quite read exchanged.

"Bad luck, more or less." Cecil stared at his hands. "My sister Ruth, your memaw's twin, died of cancer. Same thing happened to her son, who was Finn's father."

I glanced at Finn. I remembered meeting both his father and his mother all those years ago.

"My mother couldn't stand the idea of life without Pops." Finn's thin lips were set in a grim line. "My sister, Mindy, married a guy from France and moved there. But my sister, Lottie, she disappeared. We think somebody bad got her."

"My first wife and two children died in a plane crash in the sixties." Cecil stared at his hands, and I regretted bringing all this up. "I didn't remarry for years. Then I met Shelly and fell in love again. We have Jadine together."

The waitress brought plate after plate of food to the table. I was glad for the interruption, realizing I'd brought up a sad subject. Everyone dug into their food. Plates were passed, samples offered. My stomach, sour from nerves, kept me from enjoying any of it. Cecil and the rest of my family ate heartily, but they barely made a dent in all the food they ordered.

Feeling the weight of someone's gaze on me, I raised my head and found Zora staring. I smiled. She smiled back. My black opal pinged, and I put my hand to my chest. The magic, the strong magic anyway, came from her. Was that what felt so familiar? I watched her, thinking about it. No. There was something else. I still couldn't put my finger on it.

The waitress approached, check in hand. "Need anything else?" She stared at all the uneaten food.

"Nope." Dillon held out her hand for the check.

I half stood and reached for the check. "No. I've got it." And I was willing. For the first time in my life, I had money to spare.

Dillon snatched the check and tucked it under her plate. She winked at me.

What did that mean? Butterflies and Valkyries swam in my stomach. Memaw always told me these people were cons. Was I about to get into the middle of some weird eat-and-run scene? I squirmed at the idea of calling Griff and Mysti from the police station.

Finn tugged my sleeve. "When we came in, there was a woman talking to you. What did she want?"

"She'd lost her engagement ring." I pulled the envelope with her contact information on it out of my pocket and showed it to them. "She offered me a five hundred dollar reward."

Everybody at the table, including Jadine, burst out laughing. Zora clapped her hands and shouted along. Zander watched with big, solemn eyes and stuck his thumb in his mouth. Dillon stopped howling long enough to reach over and take it out. She handed him a part of a syrup-doused waffle in trade.

Cecil leaned across the table and winked at Finn. "Where's her partner, boy?"

Finn leaned back and surveyed the restaurant, finger-tips drumming on the table, eyes narrowed. The fingers stopped drumming. "Lady by herself over there. Short, soccer mom hair. Expensive bag."

We all stared at her.

"They thought Peri Jean here was a good mark until we rescued her." Finn patted my arm. "Easier to get somebody by themselves to do something stupid, you know? But now Soccer Mom is focused on that older dude with the gold watch. The one eating at the counter?" The man sat hunched over a newspaper, one finger hooked through the handle of a coffee mug. "She's getting ready to play it... right now." Finn softly snapped his fingers, and Soccer Mom stood like magic. She walked over to the man with the fancy watch and dropped something on the floor. Then she clapped her hands to her cheeks and gasped. Soccer Mom had to tap the man's shoulder to get his attention. She pointed to whatever she'd thrown on the floor. The man bent and picked up a piece of jewelry.

"What's going on?" I directed the question to no one and everyone at the same time.

"It's an old scam, but a good one." Cecil grinned. "It

takes a two-person team. The first person identifies a mark and tells him she lost her ring or some other expensive item and says she'll offer a reward. You met her already. The second person on the team, your Soccer Mom, finds the ring within sight of the mark." Cecil gestured to the man and woman. They had their heads together, intent on each other. "The mark already has the contact information of the girl who supposedly lost the ring. He'll say she's offering a reward." As Cecil spoke, the man pulled an envelope just like mine out of his pocket and showed it to Soccer Mom. She checked her cellphone and shook her head, pointing at the exit.

"But Soccer Mom has an appointment she just has to get to." Finn said the words with feeling, dark eyes glinting. "Now she's going to offer to let the guy buy her out of the reward. How much did you say the reward was?"

"Five hundred dollars." I watched the scene, mesmerized.

"Soccer Mom'll offer to let him keep the ring and collect the reward for, say, two hundred fifty dollars." Cecil sat up straight, smiling at the transaction. Sure enough, the man pulled out his wallet and peeled off some bills.

"But, see, he's going to find out that number on the envelope doesn't work." Finn fake pouted. "And when he takes the ring to a pawn shop, he'll find out it's costume jewelry."

Soccer Mom handed her mark the ring, shook his hand, and headed for the door.

"Aren't we going to stop her?" I tried to stand.

Finn put his hand on my shoulder and pushed me back down. "No, we're going to…"

The waitress appeared at the table, blocking our view. "I can take that check whenever you're ready."

Dillon moved her arm to cover the edge of the check. "We done paid our bill." She made her voice sound high, bewildered, and incredibly young. She stared into the waitress's face. "I give you a hundred and a twenty. Told you to keep the change."

The waitress's face went blank. She blinked twice and slowly nodded. "Sure. Sure, I remember. Y'all have a nice day."

"Time to go." Cecil stood and helped Jadine out of the booth. Finn and Dillon each grabbed a kid and took off for the door. I stumbled after them, feeling dirty and dishonest. Our meal would probably come out of that poor woman's paycheck. And we allowed that man to get conned. I followed Cecil and the rest of my family to their monstrous pickup and watched them load up, much more hurriedly than they'd arrived. I pulled my car keys from my purse and shifted foot to foot.

Dillon turned to me once her kids were inside the truck. "The persuasion on that waitress won't wear off for another hour or so. She ain't gonna run out all hollering and shit."

"But we still have to go." Finn pulled me into a quick hug. "Those two women with their rings been running their scam all night, and that one lady has several thousand dollars in her car. We gonna get that money."

Jadine leaned out the passenger window. "She's about

to get a flat tire. She'll call her partner then. We'll have to hurry if we're going to catch her alone."

Finn climbed into the back of the truck, and Dillon shoved a slip of paper at me. On it were written several phone numbers, each with a name after. "This is Finn, me, and Jadine. You call or text anytime. Jadine's got one of them special phones that reads the texts to her."

"Y'all aren't going to rob that woman, are you?" I reached into my pocket and felt for my antacids, found my cigarettes instead, and lit one. It did little to calm my jangling nerves.

"You saw me in that restaurant." Dillon leveled her gaze on mine. "You think I need to force anybody to give me anything?"

Obviously, she and I had different definitions of rob. Best to drop it.

"Oh, in that vision I mentioned." Jadine waved her hand at me.

"Yes?" I answered out loud so she'd know I was paying attention since she couldn't see me nod.

"You were getting into a horse-drawn carriage. I got a real bad feeling." She paused and frowned. "I'm not sure what it meant. Sometimes the stuff I see is symbolic—"

"Wrap it up." Finn snapped his fingers.

"Just don't get in any carriages." Jadine held out her pale hand. I took it and squeezed.

"Thank you." I stood on my tiptoes to see Cecil. We exchanged a smile, and he blew me a kiss.

"See you soon, baby." He peeled out of his parking place before I had time to answer.

I watched them cut off another car getting out of the parking lot. The driver laid on his horn. Cecil's window lowered, and the old man's fist popped out. He flipped the other driver the bird and pumped it for emphasis.

Holy guacamole. What had I gotten myself into? Not paying for breakfast. Robbing another criminal. Despite what Dillon said, that's what they were headed off to do. Memaw would have had an absolute shit fit over all this.

I got into my car and caught a glimpse of myself in the rearview mirror. My eyes glowed like dark fire. I shivered from the excitement. What was the matter with me? Hadn't I learned anything from Memaw? Sure I had. Family was everything. And what was left of mine accepted me. They wanted something to do with me. I let out a cackle.

My cellphone dinged. It was Mysti reminding me we had an appointment. I got in my own hurry.

2

An hour later, I stood in a strange kid's bedroom, shocked that Griffin Reed, my boss, had allowed a teenage boy to hire us. This damn kid should have been in school.

I wrinkled my nose against the smell of dirty socks and glanced at Mysti Whitebyrd, my friend and mentor. She held a lace hanky to her face. Griff frowned at me, silently asking what my problem was. I shook my head and turned my attention back to the pimple-faced teenager whose socks smelled like Satan's foot cheese.

"We moved here last year. Soon as I told my friends, they were all telling me how my house would probably be haunted." His name was Travis, and he spoke directly to my tits, gaze sometimes wandering to the tattoos on my arms or the heavy silver rings on my fingers. I wanted to snap my fingers at the kid and point at my eyes. Griff would have my ass if I did.

"Why's that?" I dipped my head, trying to make eye contact. My skin crawled from his staring. I knew teenage boys had to learn how to act decent in public like the rest of us, but this one needed special training. Like a quick shot of my cowboy boot to his nuts.

"Back in olden times, like plantations and slaves times, a whole bunch of murders took place right near here. Like a serial killer. You know?" The kid stopped staring at my chest long enough to check my face, make sure I was following. I nodded.

"Do you think that has anything to do with what you're experiencing now?" Griff wandered around the room, frowning at the filth.

"Not at first, no. Sure, I saw a few weird things out in the woods, like signs of people maybe devil worshipping." Because anything unfamiliar is always devil worship. "But then I met Neecie and things got out of control." Travis extended one grubby finger to the tattoo peeking out of my shirt's neckline. "Hey, is that real?"

"Don't touch me." I pushed his hand away. Travis dropped his gaze back to my tits. "Let's just stick to what you've experienced. Who's Neecie, and how did the two of you make things worse?"

"Neecie's, like, older." He raised his eyebrows at me. "She's got her own place and everything. We met at Dragon's Daze. She ignored me until she found out where I live."

"And then?" Mysti came to stand beside me, arms crossed protectively over her bosom. She cocked her head and watched Travis.

"She came over one weekend my parents were gone, stayed all weekend, if you know what I mean." He glanced at my face to make sure I was listening. I gave him a weak smile, wondering what kind of grown woman would fool around with this little weenie. "We had a séance with an Ouija board."

Griff winced. "Not a great thing to do."

"We didn't make contact with any spirits, but the next week, in the middle of the night, I saw the carriage." Gooseflesh rose on his smooth arms, and he gave them a vigorous rub.

Jadine's talk about her vision rushed to the forefront of my mind. "What a minute. A carriage? Like with horses?"

"It came every night. It would just stop at the curb of the house, and the door would open." This time Travis stared straight into my face.

Jadine said her visions were sometimes symbolic, but the carriage must have been real. Why would I get into a ghost carriage? Maybe the message was for Travis. He began talking again before I could pass it on.

"You remember what I was telling you about the serial killer from the olden days?" Travis glanced at Mysti and Griff, including them. "People from around here call him the Coachman. Legend goes the Coachman went around in a carriage trolling for people to kill. Kids. Legend says if you get in the Coachman's carriage, you'll never come back."

A chill crept up my back. Something was off here. I'd felt the presence as soon as I got out of Griff's SUV. It hung over the neighborhood like toxic smog. Having Travis's story entwine with Jadine's vision spooked me even worse. "You stayed away from the carriage, didn't you?"

"Well…" Travis's gaze slid off my boobs and to the matted, beige carpet. "I *think* I did. But this one night, I dreamed I went down to the door and opened it, and there was this man there. Dressed, you know, like olden times."

Olden times, indeed. I tried not to shake my head and almost made it.

"Night after that, I heard the voice. It came from my closet. It said, 'Traviiiiiiis.'" He lowered his voice to a growl. "Then there was, like, this chuckle. The next day, Ash Mettlin disappeared."

"And you think that had something to do with the haunting?" Mysti glanced at me, disbelief clear on her face.

"What if Ash got into the carriage? She was a few years younger than me." Travis hunched his shoulders.

A dark shadow passed by Travis's bedroom door. Something was in this house, something nastier than what I'd felt outside. I let my consciousness sink deep until it found Priscilla Herrera's mantle, the gasoline behind my magical power. It sent prickles all over my body. The black opal heated to nearly unbearable levels, and my vision changed. It sharpened to the point that things vibrated. Something brushed against my consciousness and sent a shiver down my back.

The spirit entered the room and perched in one corner. The translucent man wore the clothes Travis had described as "olden." He crossed his arms over his chest and glared at me.

Brad, Mysti's brother and another employee of Griff's private investigations business, stepped into the room, his face pale and shiny with sweat. Mysti raised her eyebrows in silent question. He nodded and wiped at the back of his neck. The initial cleansing of the outer rooms was done. No wonder the ghost came in here.

Mysti nodded at me. "Time to start this rodeo."

"Has the spirit tried to make any further contact with you?" I knelt on the floor, unzipped the backpack holding my spelling supplies, and dug in it without looking at Travis. Maybe he'd come close to the truth without me staring at him.

"Sometimes there's a dark shadow behind me in the mirror." Travis knelt next to me and peered into my backpack. "And I have nightmares. Awful nightmares." He reached for something in my backpack, and I slapped his hand.

I took out what I'd need for the banishment spell. Salt. Sage. White candles. My athame. I glanced at Mysti. "You doing this with me?"

She shook her head, smiling a little. "I'm assisting today." Brad picked up the candles and began placing them in a circle around me. Travis tried to leave the circle, and Brad stopped him. "You invited the spirit here. You're going to have to tell it you want it gone."

"But I didn't think...I mean, isn't this stuff sort of risky?"

"You've got to be kidding me." Griff rolled his head back until it touched his shoulders. "You had a séance with a hot, older woman in here, and now you're too chicken to undo the damage?"

I snorted and stopped Brad's progress with the candles long enough to roll up the rug covering the wood floor.

Brad nodded his approval, picked up the candles, and began walking his sunwise circle again.

"What're you doing?" Travis's eyes bugged out. Made him look like a frog, if frogs had zits.

"Making a circle," I snapped. "Which I wouldn't have to do if you hadn't had a funky monkey sex séance with Neecie. By the way, did she offer to help you clean up this mess?"

"She quit answering my calls." Travis's face flamed.

"Figures." I closed my eyes and reached for the mantle. The familiar buzz filled me, but it felt thin. I drew back, puzzled. The mantle had never let me down before. It always provided enough magic to achieve my means. I pulled at the power, reached for more. It didn't come. All I had was what I had. It would have to work. I took a deep breath and let the power bloom inside me.

Everything came to life. The slight humidity in the small room felt big as drops of rain on my skin. The wood beneath my feet sent earth magic, leftover from when it was part of a tree, through the bones of my feet. Even the flames from the candles sent off little sparks of magic. A slight breeze crept over my skin. Brad finished lighting candles and came to stand next to me.

"The elements are here," I breathed. "Are you ready?"

"Y-y-yes." Brad's breath came in near pants. The thrum of his heart in his chest was as clear to my ears as the gentle winter sunlight streaming in through the window.

I pulled the earth magic into me. The room hazed over with a greenish cast. Athame in hand, I walked to the first candle and began my chant.

"Elements of wind, fire, earth, and water
I, of the ancient blood, gather your power
I maiden, mother, and crone—all and none—circle around
Seeking blessings and protection, on this sacred ground
Circle of light
Dance of the moon
Burn white and bright
Protect all living souls in this room."

I stopped where I'd started and raised my arms over my head. The tide of power rose in me, surging through. The candles burned harder, hissing and popping. Travis mumbled something, and Brad told him to shut up.

"Spirits in this house, I call you to me." The closet door blasted open and slammed against the wall. The bed shook. The radio came on and blared some stupid sounding crap. The flat screen TV flicked on, a shadow standing in the static. Travis screamed like a girl. I ignored his outburst and spoke to him in a firm voice. "Travis, you have to tell it to go. Tell it there's a better place waiting for it. Tell it to trust me."

"S-s-spirits, you can't stay. Trust this lady to send you to a better place." Travis's voice cracked and went up several octaves. I glanced at him to find him at the edge of the circle. Brad had a death grip on his arm.

"You go out, you lose the protection we have here." Brad strained against the younger man's terror.

"Spirits, go back the way you came to find peace." Wind kicked up. Papers flew around the room. Books slid across the floor. The spirit still hovered in the corner of the ceiling, as though it was waiting for something. Tiredness crept through my body, an ache in my bones. I wiped sweat off my forehead and glanced at the door. Mysti and Griff stood there holding bundles of sage. Mysti raised her eyebrows at me.

I gathered the last of my energy and grabbed at the spirit. We met, and his wrongness, the sliminess of his evil, settled over me. I siphoned more magic and felt it run out. Fear chilled my blood. I tried again and got nothing more than a weak flutter of energy. *No. How can this be?* I concentrated so hard I shook. The mantle's energy hovered just out of my reach. To hell with it. I'd just have to keep fighting. I grabbed a handful of salt and tossed it at the spot in the corner of the room. "By the powers of earth, air, wind, and fire, I command you to leave this room. You cannot be invited back by anybody but me."

A rending sound filled the room. Pressure whined in my ears. I tossed another handful of salt at the spirit, so weak I could barely lift my arm. I had to end this thing. "Go now." I pulled on the power of the mantle and got nothing.

Next to me Travis began to laugh. It started out as snorts and snickers but evolved into booming chuckles. The boy turned to me, eyes gone wild and insane. Fear beat its wings inside me, desperate to escape the thing I'd foolishly invited into my circle. The spirit rushed out of Travis and at me, dark and formless, the only identifiable feature a mouth yawning open, ready to eat me up in one gulp.

I tried to gather my strength, to repel it, but I was too weak and tired. It hit me like a hammer between the eyes.

———

Darkness spread over my vision, pulling me down deep, into the part of myself where I never went, to the dark places I kept bottled up and hidden. I hit bottom and opened my eyes.

A sea of curious yet impassive faces hovered, staring down at me. I heard their voices but didn't understand a one of their words. They could have been speaking a foreign language. Their white coats blended with the light and the smell of sterility and pain. Desperate sweat broke out all over my body.

"You've got to calm down, Peri Jean," said the woman with her hair drawn into such a tight bun it elongated her eyes. "We can't help you if you can't quit screaming."

"I want my momma. I want someone to call my momma." My voice, high and childish, pushed a tide adrenaline through me. A wild horse of fear strained in my chest. This was wrong, all of it wrong. I already did this. I already lived through this. *Why am I here again?*

"We're going to have to sedate you if you can't calm down." The man had a tuft of gray hair sticking out of the collar of his shirt. His face, square and plain, leaned toward me. He attempted a smile, but his eyes flashed with something else. Impatience? Anger?

I opened my mouth to explain I didn't belong here, to tell them I was an adult, I knew the law, and they couldn't hold me. Instead the childish voice came out. "Momma! Help me! Please come get me. I'll be a good girl this time."

A dark figure rose behind the doctors, the features of

the ghost from Travis's room slowly taking form. He straightened the ascot at the neck of his bright white shirt and parted the shining white sea of lab coats to lean over me. His breath smelled like rotting leaves and dead flowers.

"Your mother isn't coming. Nobody is. You're not worth it." A syringe appeared between his thick fingers, its needle sharp and long, a drop of clear liquid clinging to its tip.

I tried to wrench control of my mind back from this ghost. He shouldn't have been able to manipulate me like this. But he pushed the needle toward me, and I lost it screaming, "No, no, no." The shot they gave me at the mental hospital had made me float. The ghosts of the place had hovered over me, jeering into my face. "Not again, no."

The needle plunged into my arm with a sharp sting, and I drifted away and floated down a hallway of nightmare images, distorted and wavering and dizzying, their pull magnetic.

Through a doorway with a cracked and tilted frame, my mother slit my father's throat, her eyes glittering with venomous hate. He fell to his knees, hands uselessly pressing against the gaping wound. He turned his head in my direction and stared at me, his eyes gone black and pupil-less. I clapped my hand over my mouth and ran.

Through another doorway, the body of my cousin Rae lay spread out and used up on a camper table, her eyes glazed and still. She jumped and blinked, then rolled her eyes to stare at me. Her dry, cracked lips moved, and her voice sounded like something moving in a grave. "They'll get you in the end, cousin. Might as well give up now. Just close your eyes and give up." She smiled, and her teeth were smeared with blood. I screamed and ran into the next horror.

A long empty hallway appeared before me. Red and white streamers, the Gaslight City school colors, waved from the walls. Distant music made its way to me. I recognized the song from my senior prom.

Steps slow, I drifted toward the entrance to the gymnasium, dread cutting at me. Another scene I didn't want to see. I tried to stop, but my feet kept right on taking steps. At the doors, I tried holding my hands tight to my sides. One drifted out on its own accord and pushed open the door. Bodies moved around, some dancing, some talking.

I floated toward the table in the back, knowing what I'd find. Chase Fischer, the love of my life, sat with the girl who stole him from me. She giggled as I approached. Chase turned to me and smiled. Smoke rose from his tuxedo, drifting lazily to the ceiling. Then the garment burst into flames.

Chase acted as though nothing was the matter as the skin on his face rippled, parched, and broke open. He said, "We're waiting for you down here. Just let go. Let it happen." He repeated himself once, then again. His voice sped up, getting higher and higher until his words degenerated into an unintelligible shriek. The skin peeled off his body, leaving nothing but a blackened skeleton. Next to him, Felicia clutched her sides and convulsed with mirth.

I backed away from them, my heart an aching throb in my chest. My arms ached with blood rushing through them. I tripped on something and fell. I hurtled through a black expanse and came into a room where someone with a thick, flat accent ranted endlessly. Lights cast a dim glow, and my vision faded in. But I didn't need to see the ranter to recognize Michael Gage's voice.

We sat in the secret room off his study in the Mace House. It smelled like cigarette smoke and cheap perfume. Gage looked the same way he did after the final time we tangled. Blood flowed from his ears and nose. The whites of his eyes glowed red. He shuffled toward me, holding out one hand. "It's you and me, baby. You can't run. I'm always here, ready to play. Why don't you take off your clothes?"

"Peri Jean? Fight. Do not let this happen." Mysti's voice shook the wood-paneled walls and made the light fixture vibrate. "I'm here. We're going to get the ghost out of you. He's trying to trick you. Do you hear me?"

I did hear her, but my mind closed off and drifted away, the way it sometimes did when I dreamed. The scene with Michael Gage dissolved. I woke up in a place I thought I'd forgotten.

The mildewy smell of dirty carpet filled my senses. Nasty fibers tickled my nose. My abdomen cramped, shooting threads of pain down my thighs. I wanted to get up, to at least lie on my beat-up couch, but I couldn't move. All I could do was hold my hands laced over my belly where my ex-husband had kicked me before he stormed out, still screaming about the money he'd come for. A bolt of pain shot through me, this cramp worse than all the others, and a wetness bloomed between my legs.

"Peri Jean?" Mysti's voice came from the bathroom.

"Can you still hear me? Oh shit, Griff. I think she's given up, let this thing have her."

My eyes snapped open. I raised my head and surveyed the wreckage of the apartment I'd rented after my husband and I split up. The door to the tiny, cockroach-infested bedroom swung open, hinges groaning.

The dark shadow strolled out of the bedroom and came to stand over me. He made a clicking sound inside his mouth and pouted. "Such a hard, sad life. Let me make it better." He leaned toward me and opened his mouth. His stench enveloped me.

I recoiled but was too weak to escape. Something inside me flip-flopped. A hum I recognized as the mantle's power stuttered through me. The tips of my fingers and the skin on my face tingled and grew numb, like a vital blood vein was blocked or a plugged drain was backing up. An uncomfortable feeling of fullness swelled my insides. Then my magic began to work its way out. It came from my mouth in a thick thread and passed into the ghost's open mouth. Deep inside, pain awoke, throbbing in the side of my neck. For some reason, the image of a funnel overflowing came to mind. A bright flash of pain jolted through me, like something had ripped.

I snapped to attention. This sorry son of a bitch was taking away my power. No way. Not if I had any fight left. I pulled myself together enough to let out a howl in the face of the spirit. Its force shoved him backward. I rolled onto my knees and pulled myself to a standing position using the back of the old, plaid couch I'd wanted to lie on a few seconds earlier when I thought I was dying. The dark spirit made a gesture with one hand, and a wave of black shot out at me. It hit me in the chest and knocked me to the floor. My clarity slipped away.

I smelled the damp earth, the medicinal smell of pines, and my own sweat. My hand hurt where it had been cut so my blood could be used against me. My magic blood. Something, some idea of what I should do, scratched at my consciousness, trying to get out. I tried to zero in on it, but a familiar voice interrupted me.

"Open your eyes, you worthless piece of shit." I'd always recognize my mother's voice, no matter how long I went without hearing it.

I did what she said before I could think better of it. Dirt covered her hair and filled her empty eye sockets. Something, some creature, writhed between her parted lips.

"Someone who kills her own mother doesn't have a chance at redemption. Doesn't deserve a chance." She came closer. Things moved under her skin. I winced away, pressing my back against the tree, its sharp bark biting into my skin. "But you can make things different. Do something good for once in your life. All you have to do is give up."

Jadine appeared next to my dead mother, eyes fixed on me, seeing me. "Peri Jean, girl, you gotta go back. You hear me?"

I managed to nod at her.

"Just listen for the real world. That's how you get out of a bad vision." She gave my shoulder a gentle shake.

"Get out, blind girl." The ascot-wearing ghost's roar of rage came from all around me.

Jadine winked out of sight.

I tried to do what she'd said and listened hard for the real world. *Tap tap tap.* The sound almost wasn't there. I focused on it. A window appeared between two huge pine trees. Glass sheeted down to fill it. On the other side of the glass perched my raven. While I watched, he pecked the glass.

My vision whirled and changed again. I was on my back, lying on a bed, with people leaning over me. I breathed in, expecting to smell hospital grade cleaner but instead smelled dirty socks. Griff's face, shiny with sweat, came into focus. Eyes wild and frantic, he held something under my nose. I winced away from it.

"Peri Jean?" Mysti leaned into my face. "That you?"

Bright light flashed in my vision, and a syringe with a long needle appeared in Mysti's hand. I yelped and struggled against the arms holding me down.

The mantle rose up, wild and out of control, its power burning my veins, screaming through me. I pushed at the extra entity inside me and felt him lodge deeper. My breath came too fast, in dry pants, and my head swam with the surplus oxygen.

Tap tap tap. Tap tap tap.

"Let the fucking bird in," I screamed.

Griff snapped his attention off me and stared at the window, mouth opening at the shining black raven perched on the sill.

"Let it in, Griff." My voice was deeper, womanly in a way men wrote songs about, and the way I said words had changed into something more lilting.

Griff hurried to the window and struggled to open it. It

came up with an ugly screech. The raven brushed past Griff, hitting him in the face with its wings. He staggered backward and sat hard on a clothes hamper. It gave a loud crack and crumbled under his weight. The raven flew at me and landed on my chest.

Caw. Caw Caw.

The magic burning inside my skin, pushing out sour sweat, knew his words. *Open your mouth and let me pull it out.*

I opened my mouth as wide as I could, and the bird leaned his beak into it. The entity inside me hooked razor-tipped claws into my soul, ripping and tearing. My scream rose and twisted with that of the dark entity. The pain bloomed as the raven pulled on the spirit.

A male voice, one I recognized as my tormenter, bayed like a dog at the moon, mad and wild. The raven leaned forward and tried again. The spirit tightened its hold, but the raven kept pulling until it ripped through my soul, my psyche, whatever it held on to. My jaw stretched wide, aching as the raven pulled out the bad spirit. It came out as a worm of smoke and dark shadow, writhing against the bright sunlight.

"Spirit, I banish you from this house, bind you from doing harm." Mysti threw salt at the swirling mass of shadow. It writhed like a slug. "Never force your way into another living body." She threw salt again.

Laughter boomed through the room. My skin stiffened and broke out in gooseflesh.

"You don't control me, witch." The voice boomed against my eardrums, hurting them. The mirror in the glass bureau broke, shattering outward, the shards peppering me, cutting my skin. The room shook, ceiling fan swaying. The mattress underneath me rippled as something thick and long slithered through it.

I grabbed Mysti and used her to pull myself off the bed. She dragged me away from it, teeth chattering. Brad stepped between us and the spirit, clutching something in one fist.

The raven flapped its wings, pulling hard against the spirit. It looked the same way birds looked on windy days. Making all the effort in the world but going nowhere.

Brad uncapped whatever he held in his hand and pitched it on the spirit. The entity let out one last howl, and the raven towed it through the window and outside.

"This isn't over, Peri Jean Mace. You're mine." A deafening crash echoed through the house. Outside, car alarms began blaring.

Travis, the kid who'd gotten more than he bargained for, ran out of the room and came back seconds later. "Every piece of glass in this house is broken. You people did it. I want my money back."

"No refunds," Griff snapped. He grabbed our belongings and motioned the rest of us to leave.

"Bullshit." Travis stood in the door to his bedroom, blocking our exit.

Griff used one arm to shove him aside. "Next time, don't contact spirits. You're the one who brought that thing here. It's your fault."

Travis didn't try to fight, but he yelled at us all the way out to our car. He threatened to call the cops, threatened to sue us, threatened to write a bad review online. Brad helped me into the backseat of Griff's new SUV and slid in beside me. Mysti and Griff got in the front. We left with Travis still standing in the driveway yelling, car alarms blaring all around him.

"Think he'll recommend us to his friends?" I managed to croak. Everybody laughed, everybody but me. That bad spirit told me he'd be back. Would he? Could he?

Jadine. Had she really been there? My cellphone buzzed with a text message. An unfamiliar number appeared on my screen with two words beneath it. *You ok?*

Had to be her. I tapped out my reply. *Yes and thank you.*

A freaky end to a fucked-up day.

3

I JERKED AWAKE, my room dark and my heart pounding. *Where did my day go?* Then I remembered stumbling up the stairs, legs weak with fatigue, kicking off my shoes, and climbing under my department store quilt.

I pushed off the quilt and got out of bed, shoving the house slippers Brad gave me for Christmas onto my feet. My hours-long nap had chased away the blinding fatigue the Coachman's ghost left in me.

The memory of what he'd done, how he'd controlled me came roaring back. I shivered and crossed my arms over my chest. This was the first time a ghost had tried to possess me. I'd failed to stop him.

No matter how much I learned about myself and this power I had, something always lurked in the shadows, ready to let me know how unprepared I was for the hidden world of the supernatural. What if I had been alone? Would I be walking around with the Coachman control-ling me right now?

The smell of something tangy drifted under my closed door. It was Griff's turn to cook, so probably chili. The temperature was supposed to drop below thirty tonight. The weather in the Houston area was warmer than the northern part of East Texas, but we still had cool nights.

My stomach rumbled. I thought about when I last ate and remembered picking at my breakfast that morning, nervous about impressing my family. I'd had nothing else all day except cigarettes, water, and coffee. I snuck down the stairs, still shy about joining Griff and Mysti for supper, even after a few months of living with them. I came into the kitchen the back way.

Sure enough Griff stood at the gas-powered stove, stirring something in a big pot. He wore sweats, but his feet were bare on the gray stone floor. He set his stirring spoon down on the granite counter. I walked the rest of the way into the kitchen.

"Mysti'll have your ass." I grabbed the spoon rest out of the dishwasher, put his spoon in it, and wiped up the chili juice.

"It's my house. I'll ruin the astronomically expensive counters if I want to." Griff raised one black eyebrow at me. "Your nap help?"

The embarrassment heated my face, and I shrugged. "There enough chili for me to eat too?"

"Peri Jean, please stop asking if you can eat meals here. When it's your turn to buy groceries, you buy groceries for all of us to eat. When you cook, you cook enough for all four of us." He took three bowls out of the cabinet and set them on the countertop. "If you're hungry, you eat. Understand?"

I got out silverware and napkins and began setting the table. "Where's Mysti?"

"She had a phone call to make. And Bradley had a date, so she ironed his shirt for him."

I quit setting the table and made eye contact with Griff through the pass-through window separating the kitchen from the dining room. He rolled his eyes. I nodded in agreement. Mysti's spoiling of her baby brother drove us both crazy.

"Chili? Again?" Mysti came out of the study, sweeping her robe around her. "I hope it's not as hot as the last batch."

"Ring of fire, baby, ring of fire." Griff brought in the drinks. Beer for him. Water for me. Something odd and unpronounceable for Mysti. I brought the chili in and set it on a pot holder in the center of the table. We filled our bowls.

"You feel okay, Peri Jean?" Mysti stared at my face. "You've got those dark circles again."

"The sleep did me good." I took a few bites of chili and rehearsed what I wanted to say. "Look, I'm sorry things got so out of control."

"Stop." Mysti held up her spoon. "It's I who should apologize to you. I never should have left you and Brad to get rid of that spirit. I saw how big it was but never imagined it would possess you."

"My fault." I put a handful of corn chips in my chili.

"To hell with fault. I want to know what he did to you."

Griff's thick brows wrinkled into a frown. "You were crying, saying names of people who weren't in the room, begging someone to stop kicking you."

My scalp tingled as sweat broke out over it. I didn't want Griff and Mysti knowing all that stuff. Without going into detail, I told them the spirit had taken me through my darkest times and used them to weaken me. I shivered as I explained how he'd sucked away my strength.

"What are you saying he did?" Mysti stopped eating and stared at me.

"There was this light that came out of my mouth and into his." I set my spoon in my half-empty bowl. "It made me feel so weak and tired."

"Was he taking her power?" Griff, spoon held aloft, stared across the table at Mysti.

Her brows bunched together in a frown. "How am I supposed to know?"

We finished our meal in silence, all of us lost in thought. Mysti and I did the dishes while Griff took out the trash. I wiped chili spatters off the counter and expensive cabinets while Mysti quickly swept the floors. We had our homey routine down pat. The only weird part was the way I was a third wheel in Griff and Mysti's home. Both insisted I stay as long as I needed.

I wanted to strike out on my own but hadn't yet hit on where I wanted to go. Griff and Mysti's home was in The Woodlands. Right down the road, huge apartment complexes lined both sides of I-45. All of them advertised move-in specials, but they weren't for me. They seemed more like hives of buzzing activity than the safe harbor of home. Did anybody consider this place, with all its lights and noise, home?

"Let's go into the living room and talk about what happened tonight." Mysti's voice broke into my thoughts. She put the broom away and motioned me to follow her. Dread spread through me. Mysti and Griff wouldn't call a meeting for shits and grins. I shuffled into the living room and fell into one of the huge recliners, the same way I approached Memaw's lectures as a teenager.

Mysti sat on the couch with Griff. He set his laptop and files aside and joined hands with her. My worry kicked up a notch. She said, "Do you remember what the ghost said to you right before he left?"

"That he'd be back." The chili sat in my stomach like a lump of cold grease. I stifled a sour burp.

"He called your full name." Griff grimaced. "Remember?"

I nodded. Something about knowing someone's full name moved around in the back of my mind. I chased it down and tackled it. "And full names have power."

"A full name gives someone dominion over another." Griff laced his fingers. "So yes, they have plenty of power."

"While the ghost—what did that kid call him? The Coachman?" Mysti nodded and took a deep breath. "While the Coachman was inside you, he likely got way more than your full name. He probably created footholds inside you to ease his return."

"In a perfect world, we'd know the Coachman's full name." Griff picked up his yellow legal pad, and I saw it was covered with scribbles. "Use it to turn the tables on him. But since we don't have that right now…"

Mysti raised her hand. "I've made an alternate plan. Remember the first day we met, and I talked to you about how powerful the magic already inside you was?"

I thought back to the day, to the excitement on Mysti's face, despite the ordeal she'd been through. She'd offered to mentor me right then. I nodded.

"Every witch has talents. One of mine—one I got from Petunia Leblanc's mantle—is the ability to see inside others." She waited for me to digest what she said before she continued. "At a glance I could see the depth of your magical abilities. Once you took on Priscilla Herrera's mantle…" She smiled and shook her head. "No ghost should have been able to even think about possessing you. I want to understand why that happened."

My chest tightened, and worry set in. "What do you expect to find?"

"Our work together lets me see both your victories and your frustrations." She paused, her face tightening. I wanted to yell at her to spit it out but didn't quite dare. "I've sensed an unevenness in your abilities. Today's events make me suspect there's more to it than inexperience. I want to see if I can figure out what's wrong."

So this had turned into something wrong with me. Of course. Would there ever come a time when everything went as it should? When I was just normal? "What if I don't want to know?"

Griff shook his head. "That'd be crazy. The Coachman's

coming back. He's had a taste of your power. He's going to want more. This is your only chance to put up a real fight."

I gave up. This was going to happen whether we argued about it for five minutes or we argued all night. "How much does it hurt?" Magic had a price. It often wasn't fun.

"The strain is more on me than you. In order to really see inside a person, I have to work myself into a deeply meditative, almost trancelike, state." She stared at me, vulnerability naked on her face. There was something she wasn't telling me, wouldn't tell me even if I asked.

A chill worked its way through my body.

"Do I have your permission to scan you?" She tried to smile. "Please?"

I nodded even though I wanted to say no. Anything to figure out a way to fight this new threat.

———

GRIFF'S HOUSE had a split floor plan with the master bedroom on the ground floor and the other bedrooms on the upper floor. Separating the two upstairs bedrooms was a den of sorts. It opened onto a balcony overlooking the living room. At the back of this den was a small, separate room. Mysti called it her witch room and rarely invited guests inside. This was only my second visit.

From the ceiling hung drying herbs. Piles of books sat in every corner. A huge wooden shelf with ornate carvings on its frame took up a whole wall. Jars of mystery potions sat next to totems and charms that made my skin crawl.

Mysti pulled a roll of fabric from the bottom shelf. "This is a bedroll. I'd like you to lie on it while I do this. I'll be kneeling on this." She held up an oblong cushion.

I nodded and helped her unroll the rough, dark green canvas on the floor and knelt on it while I watched her prepare.

She first lit a bundle of sage. Using a tiny gold key, she unlocked a matching padlock hanging from the hasp of a rosewood box carved with symbols unfamiliar to me. From it she drew a velvet pouch. She upended the pouch into her cupped hand. I strained to see what she kept under lock and key.

"This is seer quartz." She held out her hand so I could take a look at the egg-shaped stone, polished so that it was clear with a cloud of topaz running through. I reached out one finger, and she drew the stone away. "I'm the only one who touches it. If you want, we'll see about getting one for you."

I drew back my hand. Mysti had given me a couple of crystals, but I hadn't used them much. Her magic and mine were different. I wasn't sure how the crystals fit into what I could do. But I found myself drawn to her seer quartz. Maybe I would get my own.

"Go ahead and lie down. Try to relax." She tried to smile, which she did a lot, but this time her lips only quirked a little. "I'm going to go into my trance now. I need you to be as quiet as possible."

I lay down on the mat, apprehension sour in my mouth.

"And, Peri Jean? Whatever you see needs to stay here,

okay?" She watched me until I nodded, unfamiliar worry lines etched into her forehead.

Mysti knelt on the pillow and lowered her head, curly hair falling into her face. From her came a whispered chant. I tried to make out the words but caught only snatches. "Eyes that can see, hands that can touch, fill me with the power of the old ones." Over and over again.

The sage smoke filled my senses, and I tried to relax. Not knowing what to expect made it hard. I never trusted things to be okay. I always prepared for the worst, never realizing until the horror had ended that things would be as they would be. My reactions and actions had little consequence in the big picture.

Mysti stopped chanting. I slitted my eyes open. She raised her head. White orbs, with no pupils or irises, had taken the place of her normally golden brown eyes, widening them, making them bug out. She held the crystal over me, and the topaz cloud inside began to move like the sage smoke across the room. A beam of amber colored light came from the crystal and shot into me. It cut a path of fire to my center. My chest began to ache.

The black opal around my neck heated at the magical intrusion. Mysti jerked as its magic touched her. Her lips moved, this time silently. I couldn't hear or understand what she said.

The glow from the crystal grew brighter, burning my eyes the way a bright light will after sleep. The fire inside me intensified. I clenched my teeth against it, determined to let Mysti finish what she'd started. I didn't want to repeat this exercise.

Mysti's head lay back against her shoulders. A golden glow formed around her. Her hands holding the crystal had changed shape, their fingers thinning and lengthening. The nails were sharp and pointed, silver and shiny. My heart picked up speed. I looked away to calm myself.

The burning inside me lessened by degrees. Mysti's hands dropped to her lap, and she slumped. Her sides heaved with her hard breathing. She raised her head. Her eyes were normal again. I glanced at her hands to find them normal again too.

"You saw?" Expression guarded, her gaze roamed over my face.

I nodded. The tide of fear still roared through me. I steeled myself to it. Mysti accepted me for what I was, and I'd accept her for what she was. Even though I had no idea how to classify what I'd just seen.

"I got it with 'Tunia's mantle. Brad saw it first." Her face stiffened.

I snorted. The first guffaw nearly choked me, and I sat up, picturing the horror on Brad's face, imagining his wimpy reaction to seeing his sister turn into some kind of monster. Mysti sat watching me for several seconds, face still and serious. I clapped one hand over my mouth. It did little to staunch my laugher. She joined in. We laughed until she had flopped over on her hip and held her sides. Sides aching, laughter still hissing from me, I slapped the floor. Tears streamed from her eyes.

"You going to tell me what you saw inside me?" Then a thought came to me. "Or is it too bad?"

"Let's get this cleaned up and talk." She stood, replaced

the crystal in its velvet pouch, and locked it away. I helped her roll the bedroll and stow it on the bottom shelf. We put away everything else we'd used, went into the den, and sat on Mysti's couch from her house in Tyler.

It was an ugly old thing. Every cushion sagged in the middle, and the fabric was stained from years of Brad's careless messes. But it was ten times more comfortable than Griff's stiff new leather couch downstairs. Mysti curled her legs under her, and I did the same. Mysti bit her lip and frowned.

"What's the bad news?" Anxiety closed like a vise over my chest.

"Unfortunately, there's quite a bit of it. Let me start by showing you something new." Mysti took a hematite from her pocket and sat it on the scarred coffee table from her Tyler house.

So this is yet another teaching session. Does she ever leave her teacher hat in the drawer? I leaned forward, trying to concentrate even though I didn't want this. I just wanted to know what was wrong and how to fix it.

"Each of us special ones has a magical core. That's where the great creator saw fit to put all our magical ability." She held up the hematite to let me know it represented my magical core. "When you took on Priscilla Herrera's mantle, it should have absorbed into your magical core and become one with what you are." She snatched a tissue out of the box on the coffee table and shaped it around the hematite. "That's not what I saw inside you. Instead there was a layer of something like scar tissue surrounding your magical core."

"Scar tissue?" I tried to make sense of it and couldn't quite get there.

"The scar tissue was made up of all the trauma you've suffered. The deepest, most impenetrable layers were things that happened to you as a child. Your father's murder. Your mother's abandoning you to a mental hospital. And other stuff." She chewed the corner of her lip.

Other stuff. Like the way my ex-husband kicked me until I miscarried our child? Or maybe some forgotten wound, one buried so deep I couldn't even think of it right now. Humiliation pricked at the mask I wore each day to protect myself. I stared at my legs.

"Sisters like us have neither secrets nor shame." Mysti cupped my chin and made me look at her. "I trust you with what you saw here. Can you trust me with what I saw?"

I turned my face away. The idea of her seeing those awful things, knowing about the horrors of my life, made me feel dirty. But Mysti was the only person who could help right then. I nodded.

She pulled me into one of her hugs and released me. "On top of the scar tissue was the mantle, unable to completely absorb into your magical core."

I began shaking my head. "That doesn't make sense. After I took on the mantle, I could do things I couldn't before." Like read spilled guts the same way some fortunetellers read tea leaves. Like see the magic vibrating in every living thing and hear the hum of it within the earth.

Mysti nodded and rearranged the tissue around the hematite so it looked like a wasp's nest with a hole at the bottom. "There's a crack in the scar tissue, so this really thin line of the mantle was able to seep through and get to your magical center. Otherwise, you taking on the mantle would have never worked at all." She scooped the hematite back into one pocket, wadded the tissue, and put it in her other pocket. She let out a deep breath.

"You haven't told me all of it, have you?" It was a redundant question. Mysti wore her dread like an uncomfortable pair of shoes.

She shook her head, gaze fixed on the carpet. "A spell caused that scar tissue to form and set it into place." She shifted. "The mantle should have dissolved the spell. But it's so entwined with you, like an organ almost. I think it must have been put there not long after your birth." She sucked in a lungful of air and let it out in a trembling breath. "Have I told you every witch's magic has a unique signature? My gift of seeing inside people makes it almost like a second face, easily identifiable."

The subject change threw me. I stared at her, mouth open, barely able to shake my head.

"The spell causing the scar tissue has a signature very similar to the signature of your magic. Someone related to you put this spell on you." Her shoulders relaxed. She'd told me all of it.

The information sank in with a thud. A million questions came from the reverberations. Who? Why?

"My advice is for you to call your great-uncle Cecil." Mysti searched my face. I could almost read her thoughts. She would know the betrayal I was feeling right about now. Cecil'd already had two chances to tell me about this spell and didn't. Of course not. Cecil was a con artist. Information like this probably came at a steep price. And I hadn't quite paid it. I'd show him. I lowered my head, gritting my teeth. Mysti shook my arm. "Don't let your temper blow this out of proportion, not until you have all the facts."

I flopped back on the couch and crossed my arms over my chest. "Can't you just remove the spell?"

Mysti made a face. She didn't like to claim any kind of shortcoming. "A spell like this is delicate. Done wrong, I could turn you into an amnesiac, maybe even a vegetable. That's why I want you to talk calmly with Cecil. He may know the reverse spell."

Griff stepped into the room holding a stack of files. "I'm a million kinds of wrong, but I've been standing on the staircase listening." Mysti threw her head back and rolled her eyes. Griff glanced at her and flushed. "Peri Jean, I don't want you calling Cecil or going into that wolf den for advice."

4

————

GRIFF SAT on the couch and scooted around like a bug had crawled up his butt crack. He clutched his stack of manila folders in both hands and turned his head away from me. If he was embarrassed about anything, it was having to admit he'd been nosing around again. The man snooped no matter where we went, no matter whose stuff if was. It was like some kind of compulsion. I caught him going through my things within a week of moving into his house. He'd apologized, promised it wouldn't happen again. But here he was with a file of information about my family.

I could already guess most of it. This morning's breakfast had bleached my rose colored glasses. My family did what they wanted. "Another time maybe."

Griff's gaze turned cold and direct. I tried not to squirm. I knew The Look and its intended effect. The time I spent dating a cop taught me all about it. Now it pissed me off. How dare Griff snoop around and expect me to reward him for it? I pushed my anger back, tried to calm down, and concentrated on Griff's and Mysti's scents. Mysti wore the same lotion Memaw had used. Griff used some fruity smelling tonic on his black hair to make it shine. These two people cared about me. They took me into their home when mine burned down. They did everything in their power to make me feel welcome. My irritation faded.

"Look, Memaw never spared the truth when it came to my uncle Cecil. She said he and the whole family were a bunch of cons." I tried to smile and hoped it worked a little. "Whatever you've got in that folder doesn't change the fact that I need their help right now."

"But don't you want to know what you're walking into?" Griff still gave me The Look, only now it held a healthy dose of suspicion. It was like he knew I'd seen something. "Don't you want to know some provable facts?"

I turned to see Mysti's reaction. Her normally placid face was creased into a frown. She played with the pendant she wore, a tiny crystal ball set in silver.

"What do you think, Mistress Mysti?" I said my pet name for her jokingly, unnerved at seeing her so serious.

"I wish I had known Griff had reservations before I told you to call Cecil." Her frown deepened. "Part of me thinks you may not be all that put off. And that worries me."

Another tide of irritation surged through me. I wasn't going to get out of here without listening to what Griff had to say. "Fine. Show me."

Griff opened the folder. "Let's start with the recent stuff. You found your family at a carnival in Livingston in late December. Do you remember what you told me puzzled you about that night?"

"How big a hurry they were in to get their stuff packed up and leave." It was hard to keep the impatience out of my voice. "We drove almost all the way to Houston before we stopped at a truck stop. Then after Cecil and I talked for a while, a man came in and said they had to go right then." After what I went through to find them, I expected more. The memory of Finn kissing my cheek, promising to catch up later returned, and with it something else. Finn told me not to go back to Livingston. I had a feeling I was about to find out why.

Griff nodded. "Did you meet a girl named Dillon this morning? She's your cousin Finn's wife, even though she's too young for him by about a decade."

Oh, good gravy. If whatever made them run had something to do with Dillon, I could only imagine what it entailed. I closed my eyes and wished this would go away.

"Her legal name is Dillon Worley Gregg. But she goes by a dozen others. Your family probably had to beat feet out of Livingston because Dillon got caught stealing both Internet and cable from the park. She must have bribed a worker to hook it up for her. They couldn't really figure out how she did it."

I knew exactly how she'd done it. She'd just asked.

Griff opened his file and read from it. "Right after your family left Livingston, the RV park had a security breach. All the guest credit card information on their computer was compromised. The owner of the RV park said they never could find any proof your family had something to do with it or they'd have pressed charges. Your family always seems to get out in time, like one of them knows when the jig is up."

Griff stopped reading and studied my face. My laughter shriveled in my throat. This wasn't funny. Memaw taught me people who did stuff like this were no good. But I had a problem. I liked the people I'd met this morning, wanted to know them better. I reminded myself I might change my mind after I learned how I got the spell that caused the scar tissue. I nodded for Griff to continue.

"When you left your family at the Cozy Corner Truck Stop, they drove on to a little beach town in southeast Florida. It's a yearly trip for them." That must have been where Cecil sent the postcard from. "They winter in a dumpy RV park right next door to a crummy tourist trap with mini-golf and other crap designed to separate you from your money." Griff turned a page.

"What do they do at the tourist place?" The question popped out despite me knowing I needed to keep my mouth shut and let Griff talk himself out.

"Same sort of thing you found them doing at the carnival." Griff took his gaze off the file and turned to me. "They came back from Florida earlier this year because a woman who travels with them, a Danielle Michalk, was suspected of pickpocketing." Griff turned several pages in the file. "Something that minor might have faded away, but a guy turned up beaten to death in the tourist trap. His rap sheet implied he was a fence."

Beaten to death. That went beyond petty cons. It was some downright ugly shit.

Griff leafed through his file. He held up a blurry

picture of a tall blonde walking on a street. She had a silver cane extended in front of her. "Met her yet?"

I pressed my lips together and tried to ignore the defensiveness sparking in my brain.

"This chick doesn't exist on paper. Cop who questioned her about the murder wrote her name down as Jadine Gregson. Wasn't Gregson the name your memaw used as her maiden name?" Griff paused, waiting for an answer. I managed to nod. "Jadine had an ID with that name on it, but there's no record of her birth, her going to school, anything. God only knows where she came from or how she ended up with them. Cop who talked to her said she read his fortune. Told him he'd be a father this year. Said his wife announced she was pregnant that day."

I turned my face away from the picture, not wanting to tell give Griff any more information than he had. Instead I thought about how Jadine could see into the future. That's how they knew the engagement ring con artist would have a flat and where she'd have it. They worked together as a team, a pretty nasty one. Had I underestimated my family? But my daddy had wanted me to grow up among them at the time of his murder. Maybe Daddy had been wrong. Maybe I didn't belong with them. If so, where did I belong?

"Let's talk about some older stuff." Griff closed the file he held and picked up another. "Your great-uncle Cecil. He did federal time in the 1970s for tax evasion."

I swallowed hard and pictured my skinny old uncle ordering pecan syrup on his pancakes. Heard him asking me to call him Papaw. Could I picture him not paying his taxes?

Yes. Did it matter to me? The question made something squirm inside me. It was the same feeling I got around the Six Gun Revolutionaries. They made their own laws, exacted their own justice. I hadn't cared as much as I thought I would.

"Your cousin Finlay Gregg, who goes by Finn, was under indictment for theft." Griff turned to me, a half smile on his face. "This was about ten years ago. The story I got was he became friendly with a middle-aged widow and systematically cleaned out most of the money her husband left her."

"What happened?" I liked Finn, knew he stole stuff. We first met because he tried to steal my watch. But he'd left someone completely broke?

"He avoided prison. The woman ended up dropping charges after her house burned." Something passed behind Griff's eyes as he stared at me. Sadness made his features droop. "I'll stop when you're ready."

"No. Go ahead and tell me all of it." I wanted this to be the last conversation Griff and I had about this but guessed it wouldn't. A stray thought hit me. What if this subject marked the beginning of the end of my friendship with Griff? I didn't want that at all.

"I mentioned Dillon Worley Gregg earlier."

"I know exactly who you're talking about." My mind helpfully supplied a picture of Dillon telling the waitress we'd already paid the huge bill for our lavish breakfast.

"This lifestyle is nothing new to her. Dillon was born into a mid-level crime family out of Alabama. She's a chip off the old block, got a rap sheet a mile long. Extortion. Hot checks. Selling stolen items." Griff closed the file and chewed his lip.

"What?" My body tensed. Whatever else Griff had must be pretty bad.

"Dillon was a suspect in a murder when she was seventeen." Griff swallowed hard. "Her brother, Trigger Worley, got jammed up in a murder beef. Girl who was the only witness turned up drowned in her car. She'd run off in a river."

"How'd she get out of it?" I knew exactly how Dillon had done the murder. *We done paid our bill. I give you a hundred and a twenty. Told you to keep the change.* The knowledge should have made my blood run cold. But I, too, had killed to save someone I loved.

"No evidence. All they had was Dillon had mouthed off that the girl was going to get shut up."

Griff turned a few more pages. "Shelly Montesano. Know her?" He held up a picture of a sixtyish blonde who looked damn good for her age.

I remembered Cecil mentioning a Shelly. "Cecil's wife. She's out of state right now, visiting family."

"She's not his wife. They're not married. But they've been together thirty years. She's your garden variety grifter, but her first husband was a bank robber." Griff showed me a picture of a man lying in a pool of blood, eyes wide and staring straight ahead. "Shelly started having an affair with Cecil. Her husband went to rob a bank one day, and the cops were waiting on him. Said they got an anonymous tip."

Griff stared at me a long time, his gaze hot as a sunny

day at the tail end of summer. "I bet I know what you're thinking." He winked at me, the good old boy sharing a joke with a pretty girl. "None of this is so bad. There's probably a good explanation for all of it."

"The guy being beaten to death in Florida sounds pretty bad." I imagined the number of blows it would take, when the victim would stop feeling the blows, and shivered. Then I wondered what he'd done to instigate it. *Where did that come from? I'm not like this. Yet,* whispered a chilly voice in my head. A rash of chill bumps appeared on my bare arms.

"So you recognize it's serious, then. Maybe you're thinking none of it can touch you." Griff's voice was overly bright. It was starting to piss me off. "Or maybe you don't much care? Your connections with the Six Gun Revolutionaries and Tubby Tubman make me think you're no stranger to breaking the law. Maybe you think this is where you belong. Is one of those close?"

The heat rushed up my back again, prickling, making my skin itch. My memory played back times I'd done things outside the law, things I could go to prison, maybe to Texas's death row, for doing.

"Hmm?" Griff raised his thick brows.

"I don't know." Problem was, I did know, and I knew Griff would never understand. I wanted the chance to be part of something, of some place where I, Peri Jean Mace, belonged. Mattered.

"If you're around them when they commit one of these crimes, and you know about it, Texas law says you can face the same charges and sentencing they do." Griff sounded the way my cop ex-boyfriend had all the times he lectured me. The budding anger in my gut went ahead and blossomed into a big pile of nasty.

"I know that." I spun to face Griff, ignoring Mysti's groan from the other side of me. "You don't always follow the law to the letter, Mr. Do-Right. And you sure as hell don't protest when I help you break the law."

"The difference is I help people." Griff's voice raised.

"Maybe my family thinks they're helping too." I didn't believe this, not for a second. My family did what they did to help themselves. But I knew just from living that every family is its own society all by itself with different rules and norms. I wanted to find out how this one worked, find out if it was, indeed, where I belonged.

Griff snorted. "Go sell it to somebody who can't tell when you're lying."

"Did you just call me a fucking liar?" I jumped off the couch, ready to fight with Griff, even though I knew I'd lose, even though I loved him like family.

"If the name fits—" Griff shouted. My cellphone ringing cut off his angry words.

"It's Cecil," I said and answered. "Uncle Cecil?"

Cecil laughed. "Honey, go on and call me Papaw like everyone else. There any chance you'd come see me tonight?" My great-uncle sounded like he was smiling. "Jadine spoke with me about what happened earlier. I think we need to talk."

That ain't all we need to talk about. "Sure. I can come see you." What had happened to strangers coming into their camp being a big deal? I'd bet a crisp hundred-dollar bill they hadn't gotten it straightened out.

"I'm not interrupting anything, am I?" Now Cecil sounded like he was holding back laughter.

"No, sir. Just talking with my roommates." I had an eye fight with Griff as I spoke to Cecil. "I'll put on some warm clothes and leave in the next ten minutes."

"That isn't Griffin Reed you're talking about, is it?" Cecil sounded even more cheerful.

"Yes, sir." The blood drained out of my head and rushed through my body, driven by a tide of adrenaline. How had Cecil known who I lived with? We'd never talked about that.

"You give Mr. Reed my regards. Tell him I am so appreciative he took my sweet niece in, despite all the history between us." He chuckled. My mind raced. What history? How did they know each other? "Ask him if he shares his daddy's fondness for rolling the bones."

My cheeks tingled. I didn't answer Cecil. I was too busy trying not to pass out. I sat back down on the couch next to Griff.

"Go on, Peri Jean." Cecil's voice firmed. "Tell him what I said."

I did. I repeated Cecil's exact words to Griff. His face stilled. Beads of sweat popped out on his forehead. He leaned close to speak into the phone. "Let's understand each other, Mr. Gregson. Or Gregg. Or Gregory. Or whoever you are this week. If you cause Peri Jean harm, I'll be on you like a dump truck full of shit."

Cecil's laugh rang over the cellphone. "Tell him I said, 'Fair enough.'"

I did it, never feeling more like a bystander caught in the crossfire between rival gangs than I did right then.

"Peri Jean, Finn and Dillon want to have a campfire and roast marshmallows. Would you be a dear and bring some?" Cecil's voice changed as though he'd flipped a switch. Gone was the menacing old buzzard. The sweet old uncle was back for more fun and games.

I couldn't answer at first. I didn't know how to shift gears that fast.

"Peri Jean, honey?" Cecil prompted.

"Yes, sir. Just the marshmallows? Or graham crackers and chocolate too?" My voice cracked on the last word. A rivulet of sweat tickled down my side.

"Oh, s'mores are a wonderful idea. Get it all." Cecil's voice lowered. "Now I've got some information about what happened to you this afternoon, about what got into you. Come quickly." He hung up.

What was he going to say when I told him about the scar tissue and the spell? Didn't matter. It had to come up. I shoved the cellphone into my pocket and hung my head. I didn't want to face Griff after the way I'd talked to him. I shouldn't have let myself get angry. I was the one who insisted he tell me. I turned to him, trying to formulate a proper apology. Griff stood from the couch and hugged me before I could speak. His cologne made me want to sneeze, but I wrapped my arms around him and squeezed, the whole time wondering what went on between Griff and Cecil.

"I'm sorry," I whispered. "You're just trying to help."

"I am." He let go of me. "But you're seeking a meaning to ascribe to your life. Who am I to assume these people aren't it?"

I turned to Mysti, searching for anger or signs of rejection. Mouth turned down, eyes wet, she just looked sad.

"We don't want to lose you." She pressed her lips together. "They're going to spirit you away."

"I don't think it'll come to that." I tried to laugh and choked. I stared into Griff's handsome face. "Not now that I know who I'm dancing with. Thank you for the warning."

He nodded and patted my shoulder.

"What's the deal between you and Cecil? He do you wrong on something?" The words tasted sour in my mouth, but I couldn't stand not asking.

Griff shook his head. "Too painful to talk about. Okay?"

"No problem." I got up to walk out, more curious than ever but knowing I could ask no more. Mysti grabbed me in a fierce hug. The smell of sage incense clung to her hair. I hugged her back. I walked out to my car with the feeling I was forgetting something important, but I couldn't figure out what.

———

MY TOYOTA SEDAN's built-in GPS offered two possible routes to the address Cecil gave me. I traced both routes with my finger and let out a surprised grunt. This went right back to the area where Travis lived. Griff, his constant hurry the driving force in his life, had chosen the fastest route up the freeway. I chose the route he didn't take, and the GPS started telling me how to get out of Griff's neighborhood. I rolled my eyes and lit a cigarette, conveniently forgetting I had needed GPS to find the freeway as few as three weeks ago.

I picked up the snacks at a convenience store at the mouth of Griff's subdivision and took the freeway several miles north, terrified the car behind me was going to mount my little Toyota and mate with it. The potholed back roads of Montgomery County came as a welcome relief. The streetlights flashed by less and less often until the lights glowing behind the dashboard were my only company.

The tension in my neck loosened. Thoughts of how I wanted to handle telling Cecil about the spell that Mysti saw inside me climbed over each other, begging for attention. It would probably be best to listen first to what Jadine had to say. She'd saved my skinny behind earlier, and she might have some insight on how to get rid of the Coachman for good. His going away needed to happen, and soon.

But eventually I'd have to tell Cecil what Mysti saw inside me. I didn't look forward to that conversation. Cecil might get defensive, refuse to talk. He and Memaw'd had some sort of rift between them that never healed. He could also lie. That thought lit a little flicker of anger. Cecil better not try to fool with me.

What would I do if he did? I didn't have a way to leverage the information out of him unless I used my gifts to scare it out of him. That might kill him. Sometimes me getting fancy with my magic bore a close resemblance to a monkey running around with a grenade launcher.

Then there was the beef between Griff and Cecil. Why didn't he tell me before? A chilly voice spoke over chatter running through my head. *Because Cecil might have never followed up with you. Griff didn't want to strain your friendship.* But he did spill the beans. Spill? What Griff had done was more like projectile vomiting. He wanted to keep me away from my family. He might have wanted to protect me. Or he might have wanted to deprive Cecil of having a relationship with me. The animosity between those two could have lit a bonfire.

Whatever Griff's motivation, his revelations had merit. People who did bad things tended to make the wrong folks mad. Sometimes they got mashed flatter than a cow turd underneath a tractor wheel. I had to be careful or I'd get squashed right along with them.

I stopped on some railroad tracks to stare at the bright orb of moon chasing the rails off into the darkness. The road to the unknown. Story of my life. The thick banks of pine trees framing the railroad tracks contrasted sharply with the flat, concrete wasteland I'd lived in for the past few months. I couldn't believe I hadn't seen any of this when we went to Travis's house. The trees, the silence, and the solitude felt almost like home. *Almost.* I smiled in spite of the snake's nest of nerves writhing in my stomach. I pressed the accelerator and eased forward.

"Destination is on the right," the dull voice from the GPS intoned. I slowed to a crawl, not sure what I was looking for. The headlights flashed on a faded sign reading Woodsy Haven RV Park. *Is this it?*

I turned into the driveway and stopped at a metal gate barring my way. Cecil hadn't mentioned a gate. Maybe I was at the wrong place. I stared at the sign. No. The address on the sign matched the one Cecil gave me. A silhouette fluttered in front of my headlights. Orev, my raven familiar, landed on the gatepost. He leaned forward. I didn't have to hear to know he was cawing at me.

Orev wasn't a nocturnal creature. He only came out at night if he had good reason. Had he come to warn me? I touched the magic of my black opal necklace and reached out to my familiar. The crackling feel of his spirit, which lived within mine, filled my mind. It wasn't distress that brought him here. He thought he could help. With what? I tried to send the question to the bird, but he closed himself off to me.

A small pair of headlights cut through the darkness on the other side of the gate. I disconnected from Orev and got out of my car, chest tight with apprehension. The gate slowly swung open. The headlights drew closer and passed under a floodlight. A golf cart? A skinny figure sat in the driver's seat. I recognized Cecil's posture before I made out his face. He drew alongside me and showed me the straight line of his dentures. "Welcome to Sanctuary."

What's Sanctuary? Before I could voice my question, Orev cawed from the fencepost.

"See you got your podna with you." Cecil watched the raven, something close to awe on his face.

"He thought he could help." I stared past my uncle and

into the darkened campground. Lights glowed on white sand paths through the maze of campers and motor homes, most with lights glowing from behind their windows. The smell of someone cooking on an outdoor grill drifted out. The chili I'd eaten at Griff and Mysti's sat greasily in my stomach.

"See that parking lot over there?" Cecil pointed at a dirt lot in front of a portable building with a sign that said Check In Here. "Park your car and ride up to my RV in the cart."

I did as Cecil said and joined him in the golf cart, the bag holding the marshmallows and other treats rattling against my chest. The silence of the cold night closed around us. Somewhere nearby, a deer snorted. The light sound of its hoofs hitting the dirt drummed and then faded as it ran for safety. Maybe I should have been doing the same thing. The golf cart whirred to life, and I understood it was too late.

Cecil drove us up a hill and toward a stretch of woods running behind the RV park. Two rows of campers and RVs sat off to the side, separate from the rest of the park. We rattled over a wooden bridge and across a drainage pond and passed a large white sign reading Sanctuary in black, blocky letters.

"So what's Sanctuary?" I held on too tight to the edge of my seat. "The sign out front said Woodsy Haven."

"Sanctuary is the community my parents created after the death of their youngest son, my brother Raymond." Cecil's thin voice got even more so, a tremor shaking the edges of his words. I remembered who Raymond was.

Memaw told me she left home after he died because her parents' lifestyle caused his death.

Cecil drove us past the RVs on Sanctuary's little hill. A few of the blinds peeked open, dim lights streaking into the darkness. The stares from behind those blinds felt heavy with curiosity. Cecil stopped in front of a tour-bus-sized motor home with slide-out extensions on both sides and cut the golf cart's engine. He faced me. "Sanctuary is wherever me and my people happen to be at any given moment. It's a haven for all of us outsiders and castoffs. This RV park, Woodsy Haven, is our home base, so to speak. We take a rest here each year."

Orev, wings flapping fast as he slowed, perched on the charcoal grill. He cawed a couple of times and flew into a tall pine tree next to the RV. Again, Cecil watched the bird as though it held the answers to life.

"I remember the day those things quit coming around," he muttered. "Learned later it was the day you were born." He climbed out of the golf cart. "Lemme show you something."

He slipped off his jacket, threw it on the golf cart's seat, and unbuttoned the sleeve of his shirt. Unease worked its way through my body as Cecil shoved up his shirtsleeve. He tapped a faded tattoo on his forearm. "Just like yours. We wear these to remember it's us against the world. The bond of our blood is above all others." He grabbed his coat and put it back on, bleak eyes fixed on my face. "Understand?"

I managed to nod and follow him inside, my insides shaking from the weird display.

5

———

THE SMELL of coffee and cigarettes greeted me, along with a blast from the noisy heating unit. Newspapers and magazines littered the gray and white patterned, vinyl tile floor around a cream-colored leather recliner. Just like a real home. Across from the recliner sat a matching couch with a crocheted granny square afghan, like the kind Memaw sometimes made, draped over the back. On the couch sat Jadine, hands folded in her lap.

"Bet you didn't expect to see me again so soon." Jadine had those full sensuous lips romance novels rhapsodized over. Now they quirked into a mischievous smile. She patted the couch next to her. Cecil took the bag of chocolate, graham crackers, and marshmallows from me and gave me a light push toward Jadine.

"Show her your raven," Cecil said to his adopted daughter as I joined her on the couch.

Jadine obediently pulled off her cardigan and tapped her arm. I stared at her raven. It was in the same position as mine, but Jadine's wore a top hat. In one claw, the raven held a watch with no numbers or hands.

Cecil put one gnarled hand on my shoulder and squeezed. "We all carry this mark. All for one. One for all. Regardless of what Mr. Reed had to say about us, you're—"

"What happened between you and Griff?" Seemed like as good a time as any to bring it up. The curiosity itched like the kind of rash you didn't want to tell anybody about.

Cecil shook his head. "That's Mr. Reed's story to tell. All I'll say is he had a hard childhood. Grew up in abject poverty. That does something to you." He leaned down so our eyes met. "The reason I had Jadine show her raven mark, the reason I showed you mine, is I want you to understand you're at home among us. You can trust us."

Between Griff's revelations and what I'd seen them do with my own eyes, I was beginning to feel like I'd stepped into some black and white noir film from the forties. The urge to get the hell out of this place slammed into me, raging like a bull loose from his pen. *They've got information I need.* I took a deep breath and let it out slowly. I could do this.

"Thanks for saving me today, girl." I patted Jadine's shoulder. "Not sure what would have happened had you not shown up."

"Didn't have a choice." She whipped her head side to side. "I got insomnia. By the afternoon, I need a nap. Soon as I dozed off, there you were."

I stared at her, lost.

"Jadine has a bit of clairvoyance, but her real talent is dream-walking." Cecil sat down in the recliner and turned it to face us. "No sight in the waking world, but she sees in dreams."

"You did see me." I remembered the recognition on her face, the way her eyes had tracked movement.

She smiled. "That thing that had ahold of you is strong. He..." She turned toward Cecil.

"Go on, tell her." He nodded even though his adopted daughter couldn't see.

Tell me what?

"He offered me sight in the waking world if I helped him." A pulse beat steady in Jadine's milky smooth throat.

"Help him what?" The Coachman's ghost tried to possess me, but what was his ultimate goal?

"He wouldn't let me see that. But I want to show you what he did let me see, to let me know the extent of his power. " Jadine leaned close to me. "Can you sleep now?"

I sat motionless and speechless. How would she show me anything? I'd never heard of anybody planting visions or memories in someone else's head. Who was I kidding? Before today, I'd never even realized people could walk into other people's dreams. Didn't matter. I was too keyed up to sleep. "I slept all afternoon."

Cecil pulled a brown bottle from his pocket. Something rattled inside. "This'll knock you right out. You really need to understand who you're fighting."

"Can't you just tell me?" I asked Jadine.

"I think you need to see. There's no way I can do it justice." She wouldn't budge. I could see it in the set of her shoulders.

Caw. Caw. Caw. Orev's call came from outside the RV. Something began to tap on the metal door.

Jadine turned toward the door first. Cecil rotated his recliner to stare at the door.

Caw. Caw. Caw. Tap, tap, tap.

Orev's thoughts came to me as they always did, bright with impulse and simplicity.

"He wants in." I continued sitting on the couch. Mysti wouldn't let the bird in her house. She worried he'd crap everywhere.

Cecil, however, stood and took the few steps to the door. With one shaking hand, he opened it. Orev hopped inside and made a beeline for the shelf near my head. He leaned close and cawed softly into my ear. Though we shared no language, I knew what to do. I took off my black opal necklace.

"Orev is my familiar." We shared more than just a psychic link. Orev and I shared a life force. "He thinks the three of us can have a sort of psychic conference call, where I'll be able to see your vision. Only thing is, you'll have to touch Orev."

"Is he going to bite me?" Jadine lifted one hand off her lap and hesitantly reached out.

"If he does, I'll bite him." The bird's sharp gaze fixed on mine. I knew incredulity when I saw it. "Orev won't bite. He suggested this."

The bird let out a soft caw. I held out the black opal necklace to him. He took the chain in his odd, curved beak and dropped it over his feet. The black opal magnified its owner's power. Right now, Orev needed it more than I did.

The bird cawed again, and I placed one of Jadine's hands on his back. I put my hand over hers. Cecil's chair creaked, and he leaned forward, his brow creased, eyes hard with anticipation.

Magic charged the air. It danced over my skin like static electricity, standing the hairs on end. I glanced at Jadine to see a light halo around her head where some of her hair had actually raised. I counted to four as I inhaled and four on the exhale.

"Find Orev's magic." My voice had deepened, taken on a languid, slow pattern. "It's already inside you. Just search for the thread."

Jadine's eyes squeezed shut as she concentrated. Her body jerked as she connected to the magic. The static of Orev's thoughts, mostly images and sounds, filled my mind but then dimmed.

"Is this it?" Jadine's voice boomed in my head.

"You don't have to yell. And yes. Just relax and show me what you want me to see." My muscles felt heavy and warm, as though I really were sleeping. Had Orev simply put us to sleep? Before I could ponder the idea, Jadine's mind took hold of mine. My vision blacked out. Panic gripped my chest, crushing all the breath out of me, and I felt myself moving to a different time and place.

The smell of wet rock fills my nostrils. A few seconds later, the plop of water dripping on rock further grounds me. My eyes adjust. Candlelight casts more shadows than creates light, but it is easy to see the room's jagged rock walls. Where are we? A cave? A castle?

A man stands with his back to us, a paintbrush held aloft.

He paints several broad strokes. The dark paint streaks and runs.

A hand closes around mine, and Jadine's presence surrounds me. I cannot see her so much as feel her. The smell of blood hits me. The marks on the walls aren't paint. They are made with blood. I move closer, and my foot scrapes against the rock floor and splashes in some standing water.

The man spins around. The Coachman. Alive and well. "Who is it?" The Coachman raises a lantern and peers into darkness. "Is it he whom I seek?" He takes a knife from his belt and approaches another lump of black cloth. "I call to Darkness, the darkness that gathers in shadow, the darkness from which men hide. I call to Darkness all powerful."

Shadows gather in the corner. Something with no face and goat horns on its head steps forward, hoofs clicking on the stone floor. "It is I. He who walks behind the light. Make your sacrifice and state your petition."

The Coachman whips open the black cloth. Little legs kick and small arms flail. A tiny voice babbles.

A baby. No. My skin crawls. Next to me, Jadine whimpers. What does this guy plan to do with a baby? I think I know and don't want to know what I think I know.

The Coachman swings the knife down. The baby shrieks, but only for a second. Its cry ends in a wet gurgle. The candles flare, the same way they do for me when a spell works. I clamp a hand over my mouth to keep from screaming.

The Coachman moves to a rock with a gold object on it. With one blood-soaked hand, he draws a symbol around the piece of gold. Then he picks it up. The flickering light makes it impossible to see exactly what it is, but it looks like a piece of jewelry. Maybe a watch. The Coachman speaks to the horned creature in the corner. "Darkness, grant my petition. Transfer my soul to this piece of metal so that it may never die. I ask for the ability to nourish my mortal existence with the light of other souls."

The horned man steps forward. "You must keep a piece of the ones whose life force you use to sustain your existence. Bone is recommended. Without it, you'll lose your hold on the mortal world, be trapped forever between worlds. Never harm your mortal body. For although you'll never age, your body will be subject to death. If you lose it, you'll be forced to find another vessel in which to live. Do you agree?"

"Yes, master. I agree." The Coachman trembles, eyes bright and eager.

"Then so it will be. Your petition is granted. I leave behind a symbol. Use it to mark the bone of your victims that you keep." The horned shadow begins to smoke, steam and waves of heat rising off it. "Hide your soul well." Its voice echoes in the chamber. A few seconds later, the goat man bursts into flame and burns.

I wince away from the white light. The fire blazes hot and then dims to nothing. Nothing remains of him but a symbol burned into the stone. I don't recognize the shape. It feels unnatural. Evil in some way. I turn my face from it and watch the Coachman instead.

The gold object begins to glow like afternoon sunlight. It lights the room. The candles and lanterns flare again. The Coachman wraps the piece of gold containing his soul in cloth and disappears down a dark tunnel. Eventually I lose sight of him.

I came to with Cecil leaning over Jadine and shaking her.

Her eyes flew open, and she gripped Cecil's arms. "Papaw?"

"Yes, baby. It's Papaw." He stroked her arms. "I'm sorry to shake you like that, but you were screaming."

"I saw more than I did before. He…" She shook her head and turned to me.

"He sacrificed a baby and made a deal with this goat man for immortality." My mind raced, and more words tumbled out my mouth. "But he's not immortal. He's dead right now. The thing that got inside me earlier today was spirit."

"That goat told him to take care of his body." Jadine pushed Cecil away and walked shakily to the kitchen counter, which she used to lead her to the refrigerator. She took out a can of Texsun grapefruit juice and drank it in three big gulps. She said nothing more until she was seated again. "He must not have taken care of his body, got killed somewhere along the way. Now he's looking for another vessel."

My mind ran over what I knew, but I needed to talk about it. "Earlier today, when Jadine saved my ass, we were expelling a ghost from this kid's house. Right around this area."

Cecil motioned me to go on.

"This kid told us about a serial killer named the Coachman who terrorized these parts some time in the past." Next to me, Cecil jumped at the name. I'd question him about it later. "So combining what this kid told me with what we just saw, this must be the Coachman and he killed people to keep his bargain with the goat man."

"Then somebody killed him along the way." Jadine shook her head. "But no. That doesn't make sense."

"Right, right. Because the goat man warned the Coachman that physical death would trap his spirit in that nasty murder cave." I slumped against the couch. "So how did he get out?"

"My grandmother, Samantha, used to tell a story about —" A knock on the door cut off Cecil's words. Irritation flashed over his face. "Tell you in a minute." He rose to see who was there.

———

FINN CAME into the motor home brushing the black hair he shared with Daddy, Memaw, and me out of his face. Zora shot around him and raced at me like a wild animal at food. I instinctively recoiled, unsure what she wanted. The kid didn't notice.

She climbed onto the sofa, put both hands on my shoulders, and stared into my face. "I remember you."

"I remember you too." I patted my little cousin and tried to ignore the way my chest tightened. My black opal pinged at the magic Zora carried inside her, much stronger than anything I'd felt from Finn, Dillon, Jadine, or Cecil. "Breakfast hasn't been so long ago."

"Before that." Zora drew closer, so near I smelled the chocolate she'd had sometime in the recent past. "Back when I lived in your tummy."

I jerked away from the child and unbalanced her. Her little arms pinwheeled, and I caught her waist with both hands.

Dillon appeared behind her and snatched her off the couch. "Have I not told you to keep your hands to yourself? You don't climb on people like that."

"But I know her." Zora's voice raised dangerously close to a wail.

"It's nothing," I told Dillon. "Jadine and I were having an intense conversation, and I'm on edge. It's not Zora's fault. She didn't bother me."

"See?" Zora yanked away from her mother and climbed back on the couch to sit next to me, legs straight out, hands folded her lap. She gave her mother a look of such solemn innocence I wanted to laugh. But Dillon didn't laugh, so I held it in.

"You gotta mind me, girl." Dillon glared at her daughter for several seconds before turning her attention back on her son, who'd wandered to where Cecil had left the marshmallows and pulled down the package. She took the marshmallows from Zander. The kid shrieked. Dillon silenced his indignation with a stare.

Finn sat on the other side of Zora and smiled at me. "Drama, drama everywhere, and not a drop to drink."

Dillon glared at him but spoke to me. "So you and Jadine have your talk about what she saw in your noggin? That's about the freakiest mess I ever heard. You make any sense of it?"

"I think I know who and what the spirit is." I explained about my experience at Travis's house with the Coachman and then connected it to what I'd seen in Jadine's vision. Dillon swallowed hard and glanced at her son, as though to make sure he was still okay.

Finn twisted to face me. "That Coachman thing sounds like the story Papaw tells us every year when we stay here."

Cecil nodded and opened his mouth to speak.

Dillon interrupted him. "Papaw said you possess the center of our family's power." She leaned against the counter, holding the marshmallows away from her son, who clawed at her leg and made mewling sounds. She had to raise her voice to be heard. "Can't you just send him away?" She glanced at Cecil.

I did too, even though I had a different question. "What's the center of the family's power?"

"The center of our family's power is what you call the mantle," Cecil said. "All the magic practicing women in our family have tried to attain it, but you're the first to hold it since Priscilla Herrera." Cecil gave me a proud pat.

A few months earlier, I'd had to raise the power of the mantle from Priscilla Herrera's corpse and accept it into my body. The reason for that now made sense. She had never passed on her power to anybody else. Reasons for that flooded my mind, but none made sense. Right now, it didn't matter. What mattered was finding out how to remove the spell blocking my power so I could get rid of the Coachman.

Cecil's soft, slow words interrupted my thoughts. "I'm actually curious about the same thing as Dillon. Why weren't you able to use your gifts to send this bad spirit away?"

I hesitated. I had intended to tell him about the spell when we were alone.

"Naw." Finn shook his head. "Tell him now. I'm curious what it is anyway."

I glared at my cousin. "You read my mind?"

Zora pulled herself to a standing position and spoke to me. "You gonna take all his clothes away and make him go naked? Let him see how it feels? That's what Mommy says she'll do if Daddy ever reads her mind again."

Both Finn and Dillon turned the color of strawberry pulp, and Jadine giggled. Finn snatched his daughter, pulled her into his lap, and said with a great deal of dignity, "Go on and tell Papaw about the spell inside you."

"What spell?" Cecil took the marshmallows from Dillon and gave Zander one. The little boy pulped it between his chubby fingers and began rubbing it on his face, totally missing his mouth. *Ewww.* No wonder Dillon took them away.

I gathered my courage, and in as few words as possible, I explained about Mysti's gift and how she'd used it on me. "She said there's a core of magic in everybody like me. She saw a spell wrapped around that core, and it's keeping the mantle from completely absorbing and working with what I've already got."

Cecil's lips parted, and his eyes glazed with shock. I didn't know anything to do but tell the rest.

"Mysti says magic has a signature." I swallowed hard. Moment of truth. "The signature on the spell matched mine very closely. Someone in my family must have put it on me."

Cecil sat so still the only sign of life was his chest moving up and down. The silence sent cold fingers crawling up my back. The cord of tension in the back of my neck pulled even tighter, heating into a headache. I rubbed at it and closed my eyes.

Cecil stood and opened a cabinet over my head. He took out a cracked and battered photo album and stared at Finn until he vacated the couch. Zora maneuvered so she could continue to sit next to me. Cecil sat on the other side of the child and opened the photo album. "I think it's time I give you a little family history."

He turned page after page and stopped at a picture. It showed two young women with an older woman standing between them, her arms around both. I saw a lot of Priscilla Herrera in the older woman's face.

"This is Samantha?" I tapped the older woman's image.

Cecil smiled. "You know of her?"

I nodded. "I saw her in a vision, but she was young, a teenager or thereabouts. She looks like her mother, Priscilla Herrera. And I've seen Priscilla quite a few times."

Cecil paled a bit. "Samantha was my grandmother. Your great-great-grandmother. Samantha used to tell me that *her* mother, Priscilla, was the scariest person she ever met."

Priscilla scared the hell out of me. I could only imagine what kind of mother she was.

Cecil tapped the Samantha's face. "Samantha practiced the old ways her entire life, but she never took on the center of our family's power. She always said the power chose its heir, and she simply wasn't meant for it." Cecil tapped the two young women next to Samantha. "Samantha never married, but she had two daughters, Iris and Fern. Samantha taught both her daughters the old ways." He tapped one of the young women's faces. "Iris was my mother. Your great-grandmother. She had little success with the old ways. Didn't have the patience for it, but she was a good spirit medium."

I leaned close, taking in the shape of Iris's face, the tilt of her head. So this was Memaw's mother. She had Memaw's smile, her dark eyes, and tiny stature.

Cecil tapped the other young woman in the picture. "This is Samantha's other daughter, Fern. She was my aunt, so she'd have been *your* great-great-aunt. Fern had a bit more success with spell making than did Iris."

I shifted in my seat. All this history was great. Just the kind of stuff I wanted to know. But not right now. Right now, getting this spell reversed was top priority.

Ignoring my impatience, Cecil turned another page in the album. It showed Fern sitting at a table with a mess of ingredients and a mortar and pestle in front of her.

He tapped the picture. "Fern had more success with witchcraft than Iris but not quite as much as Samantha. Even so, Fern expected to take on the center of our family's power since Samantha never did." He paused for several long seconds. "Fern is the one who put the spell on you. I suspect Fern did it to keep you from the center of our family's power so she could have it."

I stared at the woman in the picture, at the cold cunning in her dark eyes. I couldn't put all the blame on her. Someone let her put a spell on me, and there were only a few people who could've done it. "Who let her do this to me?"

Cecil bowed his head and spoke to his lap. "My sweet, misguided sister Leticia."

Memaw. The knowledge punched into my chest where it lay coiled tight, ready to strike and inject poison into my emotions. My mouth went dry. I'd loved my grandmother, loved her with all my heart, but she had taught me to hate what I was. The teaching went so deep I didn't think I'd ever let it go. I didn't quite know what to do with the hurt.

The lines on Cecil's face deepened as he watched me process the information. "Leticia believed our family was cursed. She didn't want any of her kids to be the marked one."

"Marked? How?" I touched my black opal pendant for comfort.

"Legend said that the one who'd hold the center of our family's power would be visited by ravens on the day of his or her birth." Cecil watched me.

I put my face in my hands. Memaw had said the ravens showed up as soon as I did. She'd known my destiny, always known, but had denied it when she could have helped me. My head swam with the knowledge. I took deep breaths until I had control of myself and faced Cecil. *Might as well hear the rest of it.*

"Leticia brought you to us when you were just a baby, all upset." He smiled as he told the story, perhaps remembering Memaw in full-on panic mode. "Samantha, my grandmother, was long dead by the time you were born. She'd have told Leticia to suck it up. But Aunt Fern promised to make it so the power would never manifest in you. Leticia agreed before Fern even finished speaking."

The chili in my stomach turned into a ball of flaming acid. I dug for my roll of antacids *Screwed again by Memaw and her panic about what I was.* I ground an antacid between my teeth. Cecil watched with downturned lips.

Cecil closed his eyes and shook his head. "Someone should have stopped Fern. What she wanted to do was impossible. Like trying to take the stripes off a tiger. But everybody feared her, and so it went on."

"Can the spell be undone?" I hated to ask. Cecil might tell me I was stuck with it.

"Maybe." Cecil's crooked hands played over the photo album. "Right before your father died, he contacted me and asked if Fern would be willing to train you in the ways of magic."

"The day he died, he told me we were coming to live with y'all." My voice shook.

Cecil nodded without looking at me. "By that time, Fern had accepted that the center of our family's power, the mantle, wasn't meant for her. She agreed to get you ready for your destiny. But she said an odd thing. She said you wouldn't be the same kid once she removed the spell, that you'd have to be rebuilt from scratch."

The words scrabbled through my brain, mysterious and dangerous. The Coachman had used my memories against me. I could only guess Fern meant that removing the spell would remove my memories of all that I was. The idea scared me almost as bad as the Coachman worming his way into me and taking over. Either way, I'd lose myself.

Cecil's voice bored into my thoughts. "Unfortunately, whatever Fern intended to do to to you is lost. Fern's eldest daughter left Sanctuary after her mother's death and took the family spell book. None of us have seen her since." Cecil paused, eyes narrowed, obviously still irritated at whatever had happened.

Panic expanded in my chest. I might as well have been on a deserted island in the middle of the ocean. There was no help for me. The Coachman would have me.

Cecil gripped my hand, using his thumb to caress the back of it. "There must be another way. You'll find it when the time is right."

I wanted to scream. The problems with the Coachman were happening right now. I didn't have time to figure things out.

Finn's cellphone began ringing. He glanced at the caller ID and spoke to Cecil. "Kenny. Probably calling to ask when we're getting Peri Jean out of here."

Cecil's eyes went flat. I would have bet anything this was how he looked when he taunted Griff over the phone. "You tell Kenny to mind his own business. He ain't the leader of Sanctuary. I am."

Finn walked outside and answered the call, letting in a blast of chilly air.

Cecil put his arm around me. "Don't worry about the spell. If it takes all of us to get the Coachman to leave you alone, we'll do it. Then you can figure out what to do about the spell."

"Papaw's right." Jadine found my arm and squeezed it.

"Yeah. We're the Greggs..." Dillon's mouth quirked into a grin.

"Or the Gregsons. Maybe the Gregorys. Sometimes the Goyos. Occasionally the Griers." Cecil smiled at her.

The two of them said together, "No matter what, we take care of each other."

I had a feeling their help would be like throwing a glass of water on a raging inferno, but my chest tightened in response to their kindness. They'd help me just because we were family. I'd missed that so much during the months since Memaw died.

Finn burst back inside. "Papaw, we've had a change of plans. Those folks from Ohio, the Hollingsworths? They're leaving first thing in the morning."

6

"YOU ARE SHITTING ME." Cecil's voice raised from its paper-thin croon to a nasty shout. "Damn it. It's now or never. You take Peri Jean back to her car." He turned to me. "Sweetheart, I want you to come back real soon. Kenny will just have to—"

"Let her help." Finn stepped into the motor home and closed the door. "We been talking 'bout bringing her in since Livingston."

"You know I like to discuss big decisions with Shelly. I'm sure as hell not calling my wife while she's in New Mexico with her latest grandbaby." Cecil frowned. "Besides, Kenny's just looking for reasons to undermine my authority. If something were to go wrong..." Cecil shook his head and tucked the photo album into the cabinet above the couch.

Dillon crowded next to Cecil, standing on her tiptoes to get into his face. "But we let him bring Danielle the pickpocket in. Look at all the trouble she caused, and none of us said boo."

Cecil took a deep breath and let it out. He pushed her out of his way and headed for the door.

Finn blocked his exit. "You keep saying this community is dying. Peri Jean makes us one more strong, and I want to bring her in. Now. Tonight."

Someone else banged on the door. Cecil motioned at Finn to answer.

A guy with shoulder-length blond hair and an untrimmed beard leaned in. He made a face when he saw me. "This little gal still here? I thought we had an agreement, Cecil. One hour. No more."

This must have been Kenny. He looked like an aging rock star wannabe who was lucky now to get his dick hard once a month.

Cecil stiffened. "My niece is going to help us with the Hollingsworths. We're bringing her in."

Wait a minute, I wanted to say. I hadn't agreed to anything. But I would no more refute Cecil's claim than I would have Memaw's. Doing so would humiliate the old man, probably end his willingness to help me get rid of the Coachman.

"You can't just make decisions like that." Kenny stuck out his jaw.

"Can't I? Are you now the leader of Sanctuary?" Cecil stood up straight, fury crackling off him. He turned from Kenny and spoke to me. "You in?"

Blood pounded in my ears. How did I get into this mess? I glanced at Finn and Dillon. Both gave encouraging smiles. They wanted me here. It was enough. I stared down Kenny. "I'm in."

"We gonna talk about this soon, old man." Kenny slammed the door hard enough to rock the RV.

The relief of making a decision made me lightheaded. Memaw was probably turning over in her grave. Her intentions for me had always been good, but they were skewed by her own prejudices and fears. I had to learn how to live my own life.

"It's settled." Finn's dark eyes gleamed. "You explain to her what her part is, and we'll get set up."

I ended up seated between Jadine and Cecil, Zora's butt planted firmly in my lap. At least she hadn't said anything else weird. After hearing Cecil's explanation of the crime we were about to engage in, I wanted to bolt. My Godzilla pride kept me seated. The plan was for Cecil to keep these folks distracted while Finn and Dillon extracted their personal information from their computer, which they'd then sell in an auction.

Dillon and Finn's son, Zander, hid on the other side of Cecil, stealing peeks at me from around him. A thick, middle-aged woman appeared behind the little boy and tapped his shoulder. He spun around. She gave him a solemn wave, and he threw himself on her legs, laughing. She hoisted him onto her hip and came to stand in front of me. She stuck out one broad hand. "I'm Danielle."

I set Zora on the ground and stood to shake Danielle's hand. Her solid fingers curled around my hand like iron bands. She pumped my arm hard enough to pull on my shoulder. Her energy met mine for a brief second, and the black opal heated in response. *What is she?* In the shadowy firelight, I couldn't tell much about Danielle other than she had a broad face to match her body. Her gaze bored into my skin, direct and unafraid, but I couldn't even see her eye color.

"I look forward to getting to know you." She smiled, revealing blocky, straight teeth. "Maybe sharing some tricks of the trade. I'm a medium as well."

"I'd love to." I returned her smile and sat back down. Zora wandered around the fire, head bowed, eyes on the ground. I let her be. Danielle picked up Zander and toted the little boy to a log sawed flat on top to make a bench. She sat down and rocked him. The little boy leaned his head on her shoulder and gazed into the darkness with droopy eyes. I'd bet he'd be asleep before long.

Jadine leaned over to speak in my ear. "Danielle ain't been with us long. She's the one Kenny insisted on bringing in. She's a pickpocket. Like to've got us in deep shit in Florida. Keep your eyes and ears open."

"And report to us," Cecil muttered out of the corner of his mouth.

Zora wandered over, holding something between her thumb and forefinger. As she came closer, I saw it was a dead bird.

I leapt to my feet. Dillon would kill me. "Baby, let's put that dead thing down."

"But I can help it." Zora's whine set off an alarm in my head. I didn't know a lot about kids, but I knew the sound of a tantrum on the horizon. Zora's age put her smack-dab in screaming, fit-pulling country. I looked to Cecil for help.

Cecil appeared next to me and leaned over Zora. "Don't you dare. Not now."

Does she play with dead animals often? Gross. I wiped my hands on my pants.

Zora stood her ground, the dead bird's leg pinched between her thumb and forefinger. Cecil and the little girl locked eyes. Her lip trembled. The bird slipped from her fingers and fell to the ground. She turned to me and held out her arms.

Hell, no. She's just been playing with dead shit. Cringing, I picked her up and hoisted her onto my hip. Cecil got the dead bird and took it out of the circle. I took Zora back to sit down.

Cecil joined us. "Never when outsiders can see. Understand?"

What does he mean by that?

Zora nodded, lip still stuck out. Feeling sorry for the kid, I rubbed her back and smiled at her. She perked up a little. "Remember when you worked at the dollar store and that man tried to rob it? And you threw a plate at him?"

My mouth fell open, and my brain went on overload. Sure, I remembered that. But it was a long time ago, a time I didn't contemplate much. My ex-husband and I had just gone our separate ways. I worked at a dollar store and shared a seedy apartment with a near stranger. I'd never told anybody about that time in my life. *How does Zora know about this?* I stared into her brown eyes and opened my mouth to say something, I didn't even know what, when Cecil spoke up.

"Here they come." Cecil swatted my leg. "You and

Jadine are my granddaughters. The kids are my great-grandkids." He stared at my face until I nodded my understanding. "Don't give complicated explanations to any questions."

"Here's Papaw." Finn's cheerful voice came from the darkness. "Y'all won't have to leave without hearing his ghost story after all."

I sat up a little straighter and glanced at Jadine. She patted my arm and smiled at the campfire.

The family consisted of a man and woman I guessed to be in their forties and a teenage boy with a peach fuzz mustache. The kid acted bored out of his wits, gaze casting about, wiggling in his lawn chair to make it squeak. If he got up and went back to the family camping vessel, we were in deep doo-doo.

Finn got our guests situated in lawn chairs near Cecil. Cecil stuck out his hand and greeted them in a weaker voice than normal. His hands shook too. Was he getting tired? Or was this part of an act? I suspected the latter and had to bite back a smile, no matter how awful and wrong it was. My family had their act down pat.

Cecil made introductions of our clan, claiming to be related to everyone at the campfire. The mark introduced himself as Chris Hollingsworth. His wife was Jennifer. The son, C.J., or Chris Junior. C.J. stared at Jadine's face, maybe hoping she'd notice him. I had news for him. She'd never see him.

"Is everybody ready to hear a scary story?" Cecil smiled and leaned toward the Hollingsworths. They smiled politely.

"It'll be the perfect end to our stay in Texas." Chris Hollingsworth's Yankee pronunciation of Texas was actually more correct than ours, but it sounded so very wrong. It was short and stiff, while we milked our vowel sounds and drew out the word like saying "takes-us."

Finn leaned down to pat Cecil's back. "Thanks for doing this for the Hollingsworths, Papaw. I'm going to spend some alone time with my wife." He slipped us all a wink and got appreciative chuckles in response. Cecil waved him off, his dark eyes fixed on the Hollingsworths.

"I grew up around these parts." Cecil's lie came out smooth as chocolate pudding. I knew good and well, from the few stories Memaw told me, that Cecil spent his childhood moving town to town, probably learning to perpetrate scams like this before he understood they were illegal. Memaw could have never lied like this. Then I thought about the spell inside me and flinched. But she'd told me nothing but versions of the truth my whole life. She'd lied. Maybe not like Cecil, but lies were lies.

"My grandmother, Samantha, was afraid of nights like this one." Cecil swept one arm out. "Cold nights—"

"This isn't cold." Jennifer Hollingsworth laughed.

"Not to you, no. To us, it is." Cecil smiled at his audience but then glanced away from them. "Like I said, Memaw was scared of nights like this." My great-uncle tipped me a wink and a smile as he stole my pet name for my grandmother. "Cold nights where the sky was clear. Nights where the sounds carried through the trees because all the underbrush was dead and withered away. Those were the nights my grandmother feared. Memaw'd come to our house and spend those nights. I had twin sisters, Ruth and Leticia, and she always insisted on a cot in their room." Cecil faced me for a brief second, a smirk curving his mouth. He enjoyed this. Wrong or not, he loved it.

Where I was and what I was doing ground into my conscience like beach sand on a hot day. The world around me sharpened, the way it does during a moment of clarity. The little girl my memaw raised wanted to get up and leave. The woman I'd grown into was too curious. I stayed where I was.

Next to me, Cecil continued his story. "'What's so bad about winter nights?' I asked her." Cecil changed his voice from an old man's weary brogue to a young boy's excited tone. "See, I thought them pretty. I loved the sparkling stars and the sound of the coyotes howling." Cecil held out his hands to the fire and then rubbed them together, the dry skin rasping. "Here's what she told me.

"In the middle of the eighteen hundreds, there was a huge cotton plantation through those woods right there. The man who owned it was, of course, very wealthy. He had everything he could want, including a beautiful daughter named Vivian.

"Travel being what it was in those days, there weren't many opportunities for this wealthy man and his family to socialize, to meet others of their ilk. This was a problem.

"Vivian was reaching marriageable age, and the cotton planter knew he'd need to find her a proper husband before long. He sent out letters to his friends explaining the situation and asking them to put him into contact with an appropriate young man."

"Why couldn't she just fall in love like a normal person?" The teenage boy spoke for the first time. His voice came out froggy, too low and too high at the same time. "Is it just a Texas thing?"

"In those times and earlier, marriages were often arranged to profit both families. The notion of romantic love is a fairly new one." Cecil didn't miss a beat. I had to admire his ability to tell the story. He glanced at the parents, silently asking if they had questions, but they said nothing, their gazes focused on his face.

"One day a young man showed up asking to court Vivian. He claimed to have been sent by one of the plantation owner's trusted friends. The young man had all the right answers, knew all the right people in proper society. The plantation owner welcomed the young man into his home and introduced him to the beautiful Vivian." Cecil paused and opened a bottled water at his feet. He took several long drinks. "That's when things got weird. The plantation owner, a quiet religious man, began throwing decadent parties. Servants gossiped in town about the kind of debauchery they witnessed at these gatherings."

"Uh, sir?" C.J. raised one pale hand. "What kind of debauchery?"

Cecil gave him a slow smile. "Whatever you can imagine, son." The boy flushed and said no more. Cecil picked back up his story as though he'd never been interrupted. "They also said the young man who'd come to court Vivian was a brute. Other stories about him being some sort of sorcerer began to circulate. The servants, mostly freed slaves, quit their jobs out of fear of the man."

Cecil nudged me and motioned at the pile of dead-wood next to the fire. I got up and put more branches on. He waited until I sat back down to continue his story. "Then, one day, someone in town realized they hadn't heard from the plantation owner for quite some time. They rode out to check on the family. Soon as the carriage came into the yard, they heard the buzzing of flies in the house. They went inside, and blood was everywhere, but they never found any bodies." Cecil paused and took in the shock on his audience's face for several seconds. "The former servants, who lived very near the house, said they heard a carriage leaving late the night before. It was assumed the person leaving was the man who'd been staying with them."

"Did they find the bodies?" Jennifer Hollingsworth rubbed her arms.

"Never did." Cecil took another swallow of water.

"Finn told us this was a ghost story." Chris Hollingsworth made a face.

"That's next." Cecil recapped the water and set it at his feet. "As I've said, the servants were mostly freed slaves. They had a land grant near the plantation house. Members of the settlement claimed to hear hoof beats on cold, clear nights. A few children disappeared. One child claimed that a man with eyes black as coals came to his window and tried to get him to come outside."

"Was it the man who killed the plantation owner and his family?" Chris Hollingsworth leaned forward, his interest rekindled.

So this was the story Cecil had wanted to tell me back

in the RV. I was sorry we'd interrupted him. Now I'd have to wait until the Hollingsworths were gone before he and I could discuss what he knew about my ordeal with the Coachman in Travis's foot-cheese-scented bedroom.

"Nobody knows." Cecil leaned so far forward he had to put his elbows on his bony legs. "But the men and women in the community were scared, and they had no means to move away. They took shifts, waiting to hear the hoof beats. One night, on a clear night just like this one, they heard the carriage coming."

"What did they do?" The teenager, C.J., watched Cecil as though he had the answers to the world.

"They sent one of their strong young men into the darkness to surprise whoever was driving the carriage." Cecil lowered his voice. "But he never came back, and they never found his body." Cecil leaned forward, still speaking in a low voice, his audience hanging on every word. "Time passed, and this area became more populated. People quit talking about a ghostly carriage that might come and carry you off in the night. But every once in a while, people still talk about hearing a carriage in the darkness and about kids who go missing. My grandma sure believed in all of it. She'd say, 'You kids best stop your nonsense. The Coachman'll come for you tonight.' Wait a minute." Cecil cocked his head to the side. "What is that?"

In the distance, barely audible, was the *clop, clop* of horse hoofs on a dirt road. Jennifer Hollingsworth gasped and spun around in her lawn chair, almost capsizing it.

"What on earth?" Cecil stood and peered into the darkness. "Is that a light?"

I stood, Zora tightening her grip around my neck to stay with me, and searched Cecil's face for any sign this was part of his show. Surprise—hell, shock—slackened his features. My heart sped up. My great-uncle could act, but not that well.

Cecil clutched his chest. He'd told me at our first meeting about his heart problems. *Oh, no. Is he going to keel over right here in front of these strangers? Ohshitohshitohshit.*

I gripped Cecil's arm with my free hand and stared into the woods. A dim, flickering light wavered, rocking back and forth the way it might if attached to a moving horse-drawn carriage. Underbrush cracked and snapped as the light drew closer.

The temperature, already chilly, plummeted, and hard wind whipped through the trees, scattering branches and dead leaves in its wake. The black opal's temperature rose in response to supernatural phenomena. For once, the heat, my only source, felt good. The light came closer and, with it, the sound of a horse snorting.

"No. Go away," Cecil muttered under his breath. It hit me that he saw ghosts too, just like I did. Maybe he and I were the only ones seeing the show. I glanced at the Hollingsworths. Mouths open, eyes bugged out, there was no question the Hollingsworths saw exactly what Cecil and I saw. My mouth went dry.

"I see it!" Jadine gripped my arm. "Do you see it?"

I gaped at her. How did a blind woman with precognition see a ghost carriage? But it was obvious, from the wonder on her face, that she saw something.

The carriage entered the glow of the campfire, and I

got my first real glimpse of it. I bit back a scream and clutched Zora closer, more for my comfort than hers.

The horses pulling the carriage were mostly bone with only patches of fur clinging here and there. Boiling red eyes glowed in their empty skulls. Their snorts, which came from lungless chests, came out in white vapor, which curled and danced before spreading and disappearing. A shadowy figure hunched over the reins.

One of the Hollingsworths—I couldn't tell which one —let out a high-edged shriek.

"I see it," Jadine said again from behind me. "Aren't the horses beautiful?"

I stared at the skeletons, then at her. No, I didn't think they were beautiful.

The carriage came closer. Cecil put himself in front of Jadine and me, both arms out. "Spirits leave this place now. Go back wherever you came from. I command it." His voice echoed in the still night, the campfire crackling accompaniment.

The carriage stopped. "Peri Jean Mace. Come now and bring the child." The shadow's hissed words sounded like wind through pine needles, only times one thousand. Behind it, I thought I heard something, voices chanting, but I couldn't concentrate on them. This thing knew my name. How?

"Spirit, leave now. I command you." I yelled the words with as much force as I could. I sounded as weak as nursing home coffee.

Jadine moved past me, faster and more confident than

I thought her capable because of her disability. She walked toward the carriage, hand out.

"No," Cecil shouted, reaching for her.

"Stay out of this, grandson of Samantha." The carriage driver's voice had real force now. It raised a hand and flicked its fingers at Cecil. Cecil flew backward and landed on his butt with a yelp of pain. I set Zora down and gave her a light push toward Danielle the pickpocket. Then I hurried to help Cecil.

"Don't let it take Jadine," he said, his voice tight with pain.

I ran after Jadine and caught her a few feet from the open carriage door. I hooked one arm around her waist and stopped her moving forward. The moon came out from behind a cloud and shone right down on the driver. The Coachman still wore his Victorian garb. He smiled at me and held out one bony arm. Fear beat at my throat and came out of my mouth in a scream so loud it hurt.

"Come now, Peri Jean Mace, and I'll spare this woman." The glow of the campfire flickered over the Coachman's features. Bright, glowing black eyes stared out at me. I never would have thought black eyes could have so much light in them, but these did.

Those glowing black eyes latched onto mine. I stood in thrall, unable to detach myself from the pull of his gaze. I wanted to go with him, even though I knew it meant death. Horror stuttered in my chest. My power, the gift Priscilla Herrera passed on to me, spilled out of my nose. It stretched between the Coachman and me in a thin, glowing stream. My strength went with it. I staggered.

Jadine, sensing my weakening, tried to move forward. I did the only thing I could think to do. I let my legs fold and sat down on the ground, pulling Jadine onto my lap.

Footsteps came from behind me. I thought it was one of the others come to help us. Then Zora, her chubby toddler legs pumping, came around my side. I swung out one arm, but she danced away from me, one clumsy hand reaching for the carriage.

"I make the horsey new again," she babbled.

The Coachman flashed forward, fast as a snake striking, and grabbed her. She wailed and tried to pull away.

"No!" I loosened my grip on Jadine and threw myself at the baby. My hand brushed her ankle, and I clamped my fingers down on the soft skin, ignoring the little girl's pained yelp, and held on for all I was worth.

The Coachman turned his attention to me, malevolent light blazing from his eyes, and tried to push himself into me. The desire to go to him, to let him have his way with me, came back with a vengeance.

I drew on the black opal and the mantle at the same time, feeling that weird, lizardy part of me awake. The world around me sharpened. The caw of Orev and the beat of his wings came from somewhere not too far away. He'd carry this spirit away. I'd seen him do it before.

I pulled harder on the mantle's power, needing all of the energy I could get. It rushed through me, humming as it went. Then the rise of power stopped. My pulse beat a painful rhythm behind my eyes. The feeling of being crammed too full throbbed in my head. *That damn scar tissue. Had to be.*

The rustle of Orev's wings drew closer. I drew deep inside myself and scraped together what magic I could. The effort created an agonizing tattoo of lights behind my eyes. The bridge of my nose ached like it was getting ready to explode in a rush of bone shards and brains.

My knees wobbled. I struggled to hold myself upright. I tried to pull on my magic and got nothing but a blank, rushing sound. Too late, I realized my mistake. The Coachman had tired me out just like a boxer in a ring. He had drained away all my magical energy and used it to power whatever mischief he had planned. Well, he could eat the shit right out of my ass. I would fight him until one of us was dead.

"You might as well be dead, Peri Jean Mace." The Coachman's laughter echoed in my head. He flicked his fingers at me. I blew backward like a piece of paper caught in the wind. He yanked Zora into the carriage.

It took off, rattling and popping again. I pushed myself to my feet and staggered after it. Cecil shouted something at my back, but I didn't have time for him. I chased the carriage, head throbbing so bad I could barely see straight. The carriage reached to the edge of the clearing where we'd had the campfire and vanished.

Orev flapped into the clearing, but it was too late. I dropped to my knees and put my face in my hands.

7

———

A half hour later, the Hollingsworths' RV blasted out of the park. The engine screamed as whoever was driving gunned it, getting as far away from us and our drama as they could.

I watched them go through a fog of guilt. This damn spell, the one Memaw chose to have put on me, kept me from saving Zora. I felt it happen, that sensation of being a suitcase stuffed too full of clothes and having some jerk try to cram more in. And that was when the Coachman had drained me. Memaw would have told me to quit whining about coulda, woulda, and shoulda. She'd have said to get off my ass and do something. And she'd have been right. The spell and what to do about it would have to wait.

I dragged myself to my feet and went to stand a few feet away from Finn and Dillon, still trying to catch my breath. The young woman had her hands covering her face, and her screams echoed in the darkness. Finn stood behind her, mouth half open and eyes glazed, like he didn't know what to do for his wife.

Every muscle in my body ached. The Coachman came for me. He called me by name. Now he had Zora, a little baby who had no chance against a monster like him. The sense of loss went so deep I wanted to wallow in the dirt and yell right along with Dillon. But I didn't deserve to. I had let my family and myself down.

The entire membership of Cecil's Sanctuary watched the show, wide-eyed and silent. There might have been a couple dozen of them, kids included. Both adults and kids glanced my way every once in a while and quickly turned away when I caught them.

Kenny and a middle-aged woman stood apart from everyone, next to the log where Danielle still sat. They whispered among themselves but didn't make an effort to join the rest of the group. Cecil sat apart as well, holding Zander in his lap. The little boy's tear-streaked cheeks glowed in the dim light. He had his thumb in his mouth. A man about my age approached Kenny and motioned at me. They had a short talk.

"Something like this can't go unpunished. Let's call tribunal tonight." This came from the woman standing next to Kenny, probably his wife or girlfriend. She had a curtain of long hair. Her mean, thin-lipped mouth puckered like she'd just sucked on a toilet plunger.

Dillon cut off mid-wail and glared at the woman. "To hell with tribunal and punishments, Anita. I want my baby back. *Now.*" Dillon stood and stalked around the dying campfire, shoulders tight, fists clenched. She whipped her brown hair over one shoulder and glared at me. "Can you get my Zora back?"

"Or die trying." My answer came faster than I intended. Was I willing to go to the ends of the earth for this kid? Zora's face popped into my mind, telling me she remembered me from before, and my heart cramped. Before what? If I wanted to know, I had to find her. But I also had to find her to keep her from whatever fate the Coachman had in store. The vision Jadine showed me kept popping back into my head. The way the Coachman had sacrificed that baby made my stomach spin. No. That couldn't happen to Zora.

"Cecil, I hate to say this, but I told you not to bring your niece in here." Kenny had been first to the campfire after Zora's abduction. He came on the scene and started barking orders like he owned the place and everybody in it. I already wanted to pull his nuts up over his head and staple them to his scalp. Cecil needed to do something about him.

"It isn't her fault." Cecil shivered in his thin coat. The campfire had burned down to nothing but embers and a few stray flickers of light. He had to be cold by now. "She saved Jadine but couldn't get to Zora in time."

Kenny rolled his eyes. I amended my plans for his nuts. I'd transplant them to the back of his neck. With a rusty knife.

My cellphone buzzed with a text message. I took it out of my pocket. The message was from Wade Hill. Relief so deep it hurt rushed through me.

The message said, *You need me?*

I wanted Wade's comforting presence, but it would take him at least four hours to get from Gaslight City to The Woodlands. That was too much to ask of a man who wasn't even my lover. I tapped on my cellphone's screen. *No. You're too far away.*

His message came back before mine finished sending. *I'll be there soon as I can.*

"Look at her. She doesn't give a fuck." Kenny gestured at me. "She's sending a text message." He came over and tried to snatch my cellphone from me. I shot to my feet and stood chest to chest with Kenny. We glared at each other.

"You and your stringy hair and that scraggly beard need to shut it." My power surged back, weak but there. I was ready to see if I had enough juice to scare the fuck out of Kenny. The campfire blew back into existence, roaring as though it was brand new.

"Oh, wow." Dillon's voice came from not far behind me. The crunch of her footsteps neared. She stood next to me. "Better watch out, Kenny. My cousin's a witch. She might decide to turn you into a toad."

Kenny stared into my face. I made myself meet his gaze, even though I felt like overdone pasta.

"I ain't afraid of her." Kenny whipped his long blond hair over his shoulder. He probably thought he looked good with his open shirt exposing too many inches of hairy, over-forty chest.

I wanted to scare him more, but my head still throbbed from the Coachman stealing power from me. I wanted to put my hands around my aching skull to keep it from blowing up. But the power kindled and grew anyway, replenishing itself on my energy the way Mysti said it would.

"She ain't gonna do anything." Anita stepped up next to Kenny. Their bodies leaned together, and they glanced at each other, as though they'd been together a long time, long enough to read each other. "She presents a danger. How many more of us are going to come to harm while she's here?"

"Peri Jean did nothing to call forth the Coachman." Cecil moved to stand on the other side of me. He clutched my arm, and I realized how close he was to collapse.

Kenny shook his head. "Not good enough, old man. I've traveled with Sanctuary lotta years now. You tell that story every time we visit this campground. Nothing like this ever happened before. She's trouble. You made a mistake bringing her here."

Heat flooded through me, followed by an icy chill. I resisted the urge to shiver. This whole scene was close, too close, to something from Gaslight City. The weight of all those angry stares settled over me like an anchor pulling me underwater.

"I'm new here, so maybe I shouldn't speak." Danielle, the psychic medium and pickpocket, said from the log where she'd sat a lifetime ago to hear Cecil's story. She hadn't moved from there since her butt first made contact. She'd used her cellphone to call Finn and Dillon and warned them to get out of the Hollingsworths' RV from that log. She'd cried for Zora from that log. Now she stood up for the first time, smoothing her caftan as she did. "This woman has had a difficult time, no one to teach her. I have faith she'll get Zora back if it's possible."

I made grateful eye contact with Danielle. She gave me a supportive nod in return.

"You just want someone else to run the séances." Anita waved a chicken-skinned arm at Danielle. "You lazy old pickpocket."

"I am your sister-in-law. Why can't you be nice to me?" Danielle glared at the other woman.

"Will all you just shut up?" Finn raised his arms to the sky, and his shout echoed through the trees. Tears streaked his handsome face. "My daughter is gone. Fucking gone. I don't care about punishing anybody—"

"But when somebody wrongs one of our number, the price must be paid." Kenny crossed his arms over his chest.

"Like we did back in Florida?" Finn's face contorted, and his voice trembled. "There wasn't no damn discussion about sending anybody into the fucking darkness. You just beat that poor guy to death, him begging you to stop." He glared at Kenny until the older man dropped his gaze to his feet. Finn approached Kenny, got right in his face. "Now this is my daughter who's missing, and I'm going to find her whether y'all like it or not. If my cousin says she'll get Zora back, she will."

Cecil put his arm around my shoulders and held me tight. I scooted closer to my great-uncle, grateful for his support. The sea of angry faces wavered in front of me and flickered and sharpened. The mantle, sensing a threat, gathered power. It came through the earth, from the fire, and from the wind stirring the trees. The black opal heated. I stiffened. This could get bad. The black opal would magnify whatever the mantle threw out. I focused on clearing my mind, on dismissing my anger. I couldn't lose my temper. I'd already learned the hard way.

"I say part of the problem here is the leadership." Anita spun around the group, making eye contact with each person, trying to get someone to agree with her. Some nodded. Others turned away. Finally, she turned back to my uncle, eyes glowing with hate. "Cecil, the time for your leadership has passed. You know it. Everybody here knows it. You just can't protect us no more."

Kenny crossed his arms over his chest and looked down his nose at Cecil. "Got to say that's the truth, old friend. Your judgment's going."

Next to me, Cecil stiffened.

"It's time for you to step down." Anita grabbed a handful of her thick hair and threw it over her shoulder.

Dillon appeared behind her. My cousin by marriage curled her lips in a snarl and grabbed Anita's hair, winding it around her fist so fast the motion was a blur. She forced the other woman to her knees and stood over her. Kenny hurried toward the scuffle, and Finn stepped in his way, lip curled. The two men stared each other down.

"Never speak against my uncle or anybody in my family." Dillon gave Anita's head a hard yank. She gasped and yelped. "Never interfere with my family. Especially not my children."

"I'm speaking for the good of the group." Anita's voice hitched with sobs. She held trembling hands out to Dillon in supplication.

"This woman can find my daughter. Speaking against her is interfering. Understand?" Dillon gave Anita's hair another hard jerk, putting her whole body into it.

I watched the scene, frozen and fascinated. Suddenly, I knew what Finn loved about this woman, even though I feared her in that moment along with everybody else around me.

"Dillon, honey, no." Cecil's voice was paper thin, an old man's voice, tremulous, ready to break at any second. "Maybe my time has passed, but now's not the time to decide that. If we want a chance of finding Zora, we can't stand around here bickering. We've got to get out there and search."

"I agree." I motioned at Dillon to let Anita go. To my surprise, she did and came to stand by my side. I caught Cecil staring, something brewing in his dark eyes.

"Where do you want to start, niece?" he asked.

"That direction, where I saw the carriage disappear." I pointed. "Let's go in groups. Nobody needs to be alone."

"Who are you to give us orders?" Kenny raised his chin at me. "You're just an outsider. An unwelcome one."

"And you're dangerous," Anita cried. Dillon took a step toward her, fist clenched, and Anita cowered away.

"Don't mess with me, Anita. Understand?" My own anger leapt at its leash. Cecil tugged at my jacket sleeve, but I ignored him. All eyes fixed on me. The effect made me wish I had kept my mouth shut. "Zora is my cousin, my blood. I will stop at nothing to find her. If any of you get in my way, I'll burn you from the inside out." I stared out into darkness, glaring at anybody who dared meet my eyes.

"Whatever internal problems y'all got ain't my problem. But listen to me and listen good. I'm going to look for my baby cousin. Ain't none of you going to stop me."

"What if you fail?" Anita stepped forward until she stood a foot from me. "What if you can't find Zora?"

"In that case, I suppose I'm subject to your laws." I met the woman's crazy stare head on. I saw elation, excitement. Cold fingers danced up my spine.

A murmur went through the crowd, and people began to walk away. Finn and Dillon surrounded me.

"I'll kill you, you don't find my kid." She leaned into my face, hands on her hips.

"I wouldn't blame you." For once, all my righteous indignation was dry as a bone. With the threat of that hateful mob gone, my mind replayed that ghost lifting little Zora up off the ground and pulling her into that carriage. I couldn't live with not finding her. "Why don't the three of us team up?"

Dillon went to get flashlights. Finn turned his back to me and stared out at the starry night. I slumped next to him. Tonight had turned into a shit sandwich with a cup of warm doo-doo on the side.

CECIL WENT to get his golf cart while Dillon talked Jadine into keeping Zander.

"But it doesn't matter that I can't see." Jadine threw her arms around to make her point. "I *know* things. I might be able to see where he took her."

"Somebody's got to keep Zander, and I refuse to not search for my own damn daughter." Dillon's tone could have made paint peel. "Keep your cellphone handy. If you have any insights, get in touch."

Jadine picked up Zander, who'd been using his mother's legs to hold himself upright. The little boy's balance still needed some work. The two of them headed back toward the RV. After a few steps, Jadine withdrew a metal cane and extended it.

"Doesn't somebody need to help her?" I whispered to Dillon.

"Yes, but she'd pull a fit right now if we tried." Dillon stared out at the dark woods and shivered. "Zora's probably cold wherever she is." Her voice broke, and she turned away from me. "You really think you can find her?"

"I won't quit until I do." My family needed my help. It didn't matter if I decided to stay in their lives. Memaw taught me to always help others. No matter the cost.

Besides, I felt responsible. The Coachman came here for me. Didn't he? I thought back over the encounter. Had he engineered it all to get Zora? Maybe. Why did he need both of us?

Cecil approached in the golf cart. "Why'd y'all let Jadine wander off alone?"

Finn shrugged and got into the passenger seat. Cecil turned to him. "Not this time, son. Peri Jean and I need to talk."

Finn frowned but got into the cart's backseat with Dillon. The two of them clasped hands like teenagers. I sat next to Cecil.

"Just pass that bag back to Finn if it's in your way." Cecil gestured at a dark canvas bag on the golf cart's floorboards.

"It's fine." I reached to move the bag, and something clanked inside. "What's in here?"

"It's my ghost fighting stuff. Stuff I ain't used in some thirty years. But I still know what to do." Cecil maneuvered the golf cart onto a wide path going into the woods. It ran alongside the route through which the Coachman had approached. "The woods end at an open field. I've never seen a spirit take a human and can't imagine he could've carried Zora far. That field would be the first logical place for them to stop." He drove a bit without speaking. "The story I told at the campfire was the one I was trying to tell you back in the RV. Seems so unimportant now."

I'd almost forgotten. "I'm sorry we kept interrupting you. Tell me what you know."

Cecil thought for several seconds. "You know Samantha worked most of her adult life for the Lakeworth Brothers Circus?"

I shook my head.

"Well, she did. They called Samantha the Gypsy Woman. She read fortunes, but really she was a witch, just like her mother, Priscilla Herrera." He paused, maybe thinking about Samantha. An orphan most of her life, she must have been a tough lady. "The circus went belly-up in the early nineteen fifties. Samantha and one of the other performers bought an old farmhouse just up the road from this place. Gone now. There's a neighborhood built on top of where it was."

Travis's neighborhood, I'd bet.

"The story I just told those people is one my sisters and I first heard from Samantha. She told it each time my parents passed through here on their lost highway." Cecil spoke so softly I could hear the sound of his lips forming the words. "You know, I'm like you. Seen the dead all my life. But I never saw the Coachman and never gave any thought to the story being real." He stared out into the darkness. A gasp came from him, and it hit me that he was crying. He saw me watching, pulled his cigarettes out of his pocket, stuck one in his mouth, and offered me the pack. I shook my head but lit his cigarette and got my own. He swiped a hand over his face.

"Do you know what parts are true?" Stories like Cecil's were usually about seventy-five percent bullshit.

"No idea." Cecil shook his head. "I can tell you the story was prevalent in this community. It wasn't just Samantha who knew the story. The kids from down the road knew it. The kids from church knew it. They all had different versions. The story I told tonight was made of everything I remember."

I brought up the part still bothering me. "No ideas why the Coachman would want Zora and me specifically?"

Cecil smoked and drove. "Our family's magic is old. When someone has a dose of it, the way you and Zora do, it's strong."

I'd felt Zora's magic but still hadn't identified it. "What is Zora? A medium like you and me?"

"Oh, baby." Cecil laughed. "You're a *medium*. I'm just an old man who sees ghosts. But Zora's something else all together." We came to the field, and Cecil let the golf cart roll to a stop. "She can make dead things live again. Never seen anything like it."

The dead bird. No wonder Zora had wanted to help it. She'd also thought she could help the ghostly horses. If the Coachman wanted to come back to life, Zora might be his chance. But he'd need a body. Maybe that's why he wanted both Zora and me. The idea raised the hair on the back of my neck. I shuddered.

Cecil passed out flashlights. "Just look for signs of magic. Peri Jean and I should be able to feel the presence of a ghost as powerful as that one was, even if he's already gone."

We walked the perimeter of the circle. I opened my senses, feeling for cold spots. Sometimes ghosts left behind the odor of rot. I also looked for signs the carriage had come through, grass pushed down, broken branches.

A white building peeked through the trees. I nudged Cecil. "What's that?"

"There was once an African-American community here. Blessed Union, I think the name was. That was their schoolhouse. A historical group has taken it over, been restoring it." Cecil reached the building. "I'm sure it's locked, but..." He trailed off, staring at the door. It stood half open. I cut around Cecil and went inside.

I shined my flashlight around the empty room. Someone had pushed all the desks to the room's perimeter. Residual magic crashed against my magical core. My head swam, and I grabbed the wall.

Dillon shoved me out of her way. "My kid in here?"

"Nope." I held an arm out to keep from going farther and pointed at a mess surrounded by a bunch of tracks on the floor. "But somebody did some serious magic in here. Recently, by the feel of it."

A familiar creaking and popping drifted into the old building. All of us froze.

"That's it," Dillon whispered. "The carriage is right outside."

She ran back through the door. The rest of us followed. The area around the old schoolhouse was still empty, but the sound of a horse snorting drifted through the trees.

"Mama," came a small, terrified voice.

Dillon crashed off in that direction. I stared into the woods where we heard the sound, trying with all my might to sense the presence of the ghost. Nothing.

I took a few steps running after Dillon. "No! It's a trick."

Dillon screamed. Water splashed. Finn and I charged into the woods, Cecil trudging after us.

Underneath the noise, I heard something else. A very young child crying. *Zora.* This was real. I turned away from my cousins and crashed through the brush and brambles in the direction of the cries. Dead vines clung to my jeans. Branches, stiff and dead with winter, slapped my face and scratched it. The crying was barely audible but seemed to come from the field we'd just left.

I took off that way, making enough noise to alert people all the way on the other side of the county. Sweat dampened the layer of clothes closest to my skin, and the scratches on my face stung. I listened for the Zora's sobs and heard nothing, so I stopped.

The air chilled more. The feeling of being watched crept over me. I wasn't alone. The presence came as a whirl of emotions in my head, words not quite whispered, shadows not quite seen. The hair on the back of my neck stood up, and the black opal heated. I walked faster. Maybe this was it. I'd get my little cousin away from this ghost. Show him how the cow eats cabbage.

Across the moonlit field stood a shadow. The mantle turned over, and the tide of power rushed through me. Moonlight shone down on longish blond hair and a lanky frame. I knew this body, had known it almost as well as my own at one time.

"Chase?" I whispered his name, not quite ready to believe. The day of his funeral, I'd watched him walk into the light and had thought him gone for good.

He raised his head, and I saw the high cheekbones and that dimple.

"Chase." I ran for him, totally forgetting about Zora. It had been so long, and I'd wanted to talk to him so many times, just to know he was okay.

From somewhere far away, I thought I heard Cecil's voice. "Peri Jean, don't. It's not who you think."

I ignored Cecil's voice and kept running. Then Chase and I stood pressed together, his arms around me, his chill spreading through me. He tilted his head toward mine. I stood on my tiptoes, heart jittering, eager for his kiss even if he was just a ghost. Our faces inched closer together until our lips were only centimeters apart. I'd never made out with a ghost, but there was a first time for everything. I parted my lips and stopped.

What was that smell? I sniffed. It reminded me of roasting meat, of barbecue. No. That wasn't right. I took a deeper breath. The smell became more pronounced. Panic ran wild through my chest, and I tried to move away. The arms around me tightened, solid and hard for belonging to a ghost.

The stench intensified, and Chase's face came closer, the skin bubbling and breaking open, blackening and peeling. I tried to break out of his embrace, dug my heels into the dirt, and stiffened my knees to keep him from pulling me closer. Still he came. The foul odor filled my nose. Vomit stung the back of my throat. I thrashed, trying to get away from the smoking corpse. His mouth fell open, and his teeth began to pop out of his mouth. One hit me in the forehead. Warmth streamed down my face, and I knew it had broken skin.

This wasn't Chase. It was the Coachman, back for another round.

I drew in a breath and screamed. It tore at my parched throat. The arms held me tight like a lover. A light smoke came from Chase's open mouth and probed at my lips, trying to find a way inside me. I pressed my lips together, drew on every ounce of power I had to keep it out of me this time.

The mantle responded but without its usual snap. The world brightened a little but not with the ethereal glow I was used to. My power gathered, weak and thready, but better than nothing at all. I aimed at the Chase thing and let go. The thing holding me grew more solid, its arms stronger.

The power flowed from me to the Coachman. I went limp with disappointment. It was no use. The Coachman took another gulp of my power and pulled me closer, opening his mouth for a kiss. Something wriggled in his mouth. My reason fell away, and I howled like an animal.

From far away, too far away, came a raven's caw. Orev's bright, simple presence reached out for me. I held onto it, knowing if I let go, this thing would enter me and eat me from the inside out, the way it tried to do earlier this afternoon. It would get into my thoughts again, turn them on me, and I'd burn alive as I relived the worst moments of my life.

Bit by bit, I wrangled control of my emotions. Again, I pulled on the black opal, hoping for enough juice to send this thing back to hell. This time I found a thread of power and wrapped my consciousness around it. The magic from the earth prickled in my skin. I gave the specter a mental shove, straining so hard it hurt in my sternum.

The facade of Chase melted and rippled away, replaced by the Coachman, wide jaw framing thick lips set in a sneer. His broad forehead and thick brow shadowed his small, mean eyes. Moonlight shone off his Victorian vest and ascot. I recognized the style from the costumes people used to wear to Gaslight City's Heritage and History Week celebrations.

"What do you want?" I used my waning power to keep him from worming his way inside me. My muscles trembled, but I pushed myself to stay strong.

"You." His voice vibrated inside my head and against my chest. He tightened his grip.

I couldn't figure it out. A ghost who kidnapped a human, who took on the forms of other ghosts, needed massive amounts of energy. He needed even more energy to hold me like he was. Where was he getting it? There was no way I could try to see inside him. It took every bit of energy I had to keep him from getting inside me. A second's slip, and he'd have me. This time, there'd be no Mysti to get him out of me.

The caws came closer. I shook with the strain of holding off this ghost.

He leaned close and tried to kiss me. I turned my head away, nearly losing my grip and allowing him inside. I shook with my struggle. Then Orev hit him, claws digging in.

The ghost fought, arms pinwheeling. Earlier in the day, Orev had pulled the ghost away from me with no problem. Now the raven struggled, wings flapping uselessly. The ghost spindled energy from somewhere, his form growing more solid by the second.

The sound of running footsteps came from behind me. Finn and Dillon. I couldn't have them here. I yelled without turning, "Go away."

"Throw the salt now," Cecil yelled from farther away. Granules peppered my arms and the back of my neck, but the salt hit the ghost too. It broke his hold enough for the bird to gain control and lift him off the ground.

An angry howl filled my head. My head popped the way it did when the altitude changed, and my eardrums rattled with the noise. I sank to my knees, hands over my ears.

"I'll get you. You can't escape from me." The ghost's shouts vibrated in my teeth.

The ghost didn't so much disappear as it broke into at least a dozen little pieces. They floated off in different directions. I focused on one of them and tried to engage it. It shoved me away. Too weak to fight, I had to let go. Before I did, I realized the spirit belonged to a woman, not a man. That confused me. The Coachman was male. I was sure of it.

Finn and Dillon surrounded me, both shouting questions. I couldn't hear them over my ringing ears but had enough sense to know they weren't asking about me. They wanted to know if I was able to get information about Zora. I shook my head. Their shoulders fell, and they stared at each other, looking for all the world like two kids who'd just realized they were grownups and didn't want to be.

"You all right?" Cecil joined us, breathing hard, one hand on his chest.

I nodded and leaned over to put my hands on my knees. The exhaustion was worse this time, and a headache burned at the back of my neck.

"Lucky you bought your ghost hunting kit." I tried to smile at my great-uncle.

"And lucky I watch a lot of TV. That's where I got the idea for the salt." Cecil took my arm and led me back toward the golf cart. He had to help me inside it. We headed back for camp.

"What are you going to do next?" Dillon didn't so much ask a question as she demanded an answer.

I only knew one place to turn. "My bosses are an investigator and a witch. They'll have some ideas."

Before long, they had me at my car. The crippling fatigue had ebbed enough for me to get myself inside it. I drove back to The Woodlands, this time too distracted to enjoy the tall trees and cloudless night.

8

I ATTEMPTED the drive through the spider's web of asphalt roads to The Woodlands without GPS and got lost a couple of times. An hour later, I pulled into Mysti and Griff's driveway.

The porch light glowed like a lighthouse across a turbulent sea. I needed to thank Mysti for leaving it on for me. She did every time I was out after dark. It reminded me of the way Memaw cared about me.

Mixed with my gratitude lurked emotions that disturbed me. Here I was, past thirty, needing, *wanting,* another adult to watch out for me. Did I trust my own judgment so little? Maybe so. I did some pretty stupid things from time to time.

Mysti met me at the door. "Oh good. Griff and I were just about to go to bed, but we wanted to hear what you found out."

We sat in the living room on Griff's cold leather furniture. Mysti heated up some milk and served it in mugs. I didn't realize how cold I was until my lips touched the warm liquid. Between sips, trying to ignore the growing need to sleep, I filled Mysti in on what little Cecil told me about the spell. Then I told them about the Coachman's kidnapping of Zora and his appearing as Chase.

"The worst part?" I directed the question to the shocked faces of my friends, not really expecting an answer. Griff tried to nod but only managed a tip of his chin. "I could feel the mantle trying to help me, but it was like when you try to cram too much stuff into a too small container. It hurt. Bad."

Mysti glanced at her mug of milk and set it aside, a sick expression on her face. "Because that's almost exactly what's happening. That crack was small, tiny. If more of the mantle tried to go through it, it would be like pouring too much liquid into a small funnel."

"Does that make it easier for the Coachman to steal her power?" Griff gulped down the rest of his milk, his eyes bright and awake. He thrived on fixing problems and would probably lie awake the rest of the night working on this one.

Mysti groaned. "Probably. And now that he's fed off Peri Jean three times, he's gained a taste for her." She curled her legs around her and draped one arm over them, hugging them to her. "This is so terrible."

"It gets worse." I explained, in halting words, about Jadine's vision of the Coachman sacrificing an infant and bargaining with a goat man for immortality. "But when he died, he should have been confined to wherever he stowed his soul."

Griff leaned forward, eyes crackling with energy. "Then it's our job to find how he got out. Somewhere in *that* story is the way to get rid of him again."

The memory of what I saw in the old schoolhouse flooded back. I'd gotten so focused on the horror of the Coachman tricking and attacking me, I'd nearly forgotten. "I found where someone did a spell, right near where the Coachman posed as Chase and attacked me."

Mysti rose and began collecting the empty mugs. "If we combine our gifts, we might be able to see what kind of spell it was, maybe even who was involved." She waved off my offer of help and disappeared into the kitchen. Water ran in the sink, and the dishwasher door squealed open.

Griff stood and paced the living room, hand over his mouth. He muttered to himself behind his hand. "There's something else, right on the edge of my mind." He paced some more.

Mysti came back into the room, sat down on the couch, and watched. She fisted one hand and leaned her cheek on it. Her eyelids drooped and slid shut. Her elbow slid off the spot where she'd anchored it on the armrest. She yelped into surprise and sat up straight.

Griff stopped mid-stride. "Maybe it'll come to me if I lie down." He went into their bedroom and shut the door without so much as a goodnight to either of us.

Mysti leapt off the couch. "Goodnight."

I headed for the stairs. "Same to you."

It wasn't until I lay down in bed and began drifting off to sleep that I remembered the way the Coachman broke apart into little pieces, how the one piece I connected with didn't seem like him at all. No answers came, and I fell asleep thinking it over.

I woke after only an hour to the sound of Zora crying. The crying got louder and closer until it vibrated my teeth. It was coming from inside my head. Some part of me recognized it as Zora. It went on and on until I wanted to scream.

"It's going to be all right," I whispered. "I'll come get you." But I didn't know if I'd ever find Zora. All I could do was listen to her cry and worry.

———

LOUD 80S MUSIC blasting from next door woke me again after dawn. I groaned and checked the time. Barely past eight. Unreal. I flipped off the covers, slid my feet into my house shoes, and went to the window to glare out.

The view of the next-door neighbor's poolside bar greeted me. He sat in a lounge chair wearing sweats with the hood pulled over his head, a beer bottle pinched between his first and second fingers. The idiot raised one hand in a wave. He knew we could hear the music, knew it was annoying, and didn't care.

I turned away, fantasies of using my magic to short out his stereo dancing in my head. Mysti would never approve. She'd talk about karma and tolerance. She'd tell me the irritation was the price of all the good stuff the city had to offer. Maybe so, but the idea of living here long term made my heart hurt.

Much as I loved her and Griff, it was past time for me

to figure out my next living arrangements. I'd sacrificed so much to find the Mace Treasure. Might as well use some of the money on making my life pleasant. The problem? Finding a place where I could commit to staying more than a month or two.

I wandered downstairs and found Mysti, Griff, and a bleary-eyed Brad sitting at the wrought iron and glass breakfast table. They all turned to watch my approach but said nothing until I sat down at the table with a cup of coffee and one of the doughnuts Griff always bought on Saturday mornings.

"I was right." Griff took a bite of his bear claw. "It hit me in the middle of the night."

Mysti yawned. "So he got up, turned on all the lights, and rummaged around for a place to write it down. Then he woke me to send an email."

"Are you going to let me tell this my way?" Griff waved one hand at Mysti for her to shut up. She shook her fist at him. He pretended not to see. "Today, you and Mysti are going to research the Coachman. It's obviously a regional piece of folklore, maybe an urban legend. There's bound to be documentation."

"This is where I come in." Mysti held up her hand to Griff. "One of my Tarot clients studies local folklore. Last night, Griff had me send her an email to see if she can meet with us." Mysti smoothed her napkin out. "She sent a reply early this morning offering to meet us on her lunch break. She's a little out there, but she's sincere."

I nodded my thanks and forced down a bite of dough-nut, too nervous to enjoy it the way I usually did. "You aren't going?" I asked Griff. He always asked the best questions and had a talent for getting information out of people.

"I got a call from a client this morning. Could mean big bucks. I just can't join the two of you." Griff took a sip of his coffee. "Let's talk about what we hope to get out of this information."

Mysti pulled her robe tighter around her. The house, elegant with its high-ceilings and stone floors, was cold as a hooker the day before payday. "The Coachman has called you by name, your full name, has he not?" She waited for me to nod, and I did. "See if we can find out his real name. I think we can use it against him."

Griff gave Mysti his nod of approval. "Look for ideas on where he may have taken Zora. A ghost can't hide a corporeal being."

Was Zora still alive? I didn't see how a ghost could take care of a little girl, especially one Zora's age. "Have you ever heard of a ghost kidnapping a person?"

"Not a ghost. Other entities, yes." Mysti watched my face as though she knew there was more to my question.

"I'm worried about her having something to eat, staying warm." Zora's face appeared behind my eyes. *I remember you from before.* Way in the back of my mind, terrified wails started up. My teeth snapped together. The sound cut off.

"You okay?" Mysti squinted at me from across the table. I nodded.

Brad drained his coffee, eyes clearer than when I first sat down, and spoke for the first time. "Peri Jean's got a good point. A ghost'll just let the little girl starve or die of exposure." He propped his elbows on the table. Mysti swatted him, and he removed them.

"Tell me something." Griff turned to Brad. "Do you make it a goal each day to be so encouraging? Or does it just naturally flow from you?"

"Don't be mean to my brother." Mysti's voice rose. No matter how awful Brad acted, she'd defend him to her last breath.

Brad gave Griff a triumphant smile and put his elbows back on the table. "If the folklore expert is that Tyler chick, I want to go with you and Peri Jean."

I tuned out their banter so I could fully focus on worrying about Zora. Mysti rose from the table. I reached for her sleeve. "Wait."

She took one look at my face and plopped back into the chair, nearly leaning over the table. "Tell me."

I did. I went through the way the Coachman broke into little pieces but stopped as I tried to describe the female entity. I was still missing something big. It wouldn't come out. Finally I waved my hand in frustration.

Brad rubbed the stubble on his chin. "That makes sense. If a bunch of ghosts band together, you get a super-charged ghost like the Coachman. I still think if we find out his name, we can break up their little party."

"But the spell in the old schoolhouse. Zora's kidnapping." Who was I kidding? I couldn't even articulate it. How did I expect to put it together? Then it clicked, at least partially. "He has humans helping him." I struggled with all the threads again but still couldn't tie anything together.

"Either way, there's a trail leading back to him. Ghosts, humans, whatever." Griff checked his watch and stood. "I'm sorry, but I have to go."

Mysti gathered the dishes from the table. "We do too. Bradley, if you're going, be ready in an hour. No excuses." She crossed the room and stared out the window, glaring at the source of the loud music. "I can't believe this guy. We ought to make his stereo short out."

"Really?" I hurried to stand next to her at the window.

"Don't you dare." She continued to stare into the gray day. "You know something?" Her tone of voice indicated she didn't expect an answer, so I didn't bother to give her one. "The Coachman wants to be resurrected. He needs Zora because she can raise the dead. I get that. But he needs you too. I wonder why that is."

"Do you think his history is going to help us figure that out?" I didn't see how.

Griff joined us, also staring at the source of the noise coming from next door. "Know your enemy like you know yourself. Sun Tzu." He stepped out into the backyard, walked across the cobblestone courtyard, and shouted something through the fence. The music shut off.

———

AN HOUR LATER, we left for the library, Mysti driving. We were to meet Mysti's contact at The Woodlands Waterway, a place neither Mysti nor I had ever visited. Brad said he took dates there occasionally. He sat in the passenger seat to navigate. Mysti coasted down the right hand lane that emptied onto a larger, four-lane road.

"You gotta speed up, Sis." Brad put his hand on his sister's knee and pushed down. Mysti would have smote me, and righteously, for pulling such a stunt. But from Baby Brother? She ignored it and went along.

I buckled my seatbelt and held tight to the oh-shit bar as Mysti swung into traffic, speeding up to sixty miles per hour to merge onto the busy road. I said a silent prayer we wouldn't have to get onto the freeway. My asshole might chew a hole in my panties if we did.

Shopping centers and entrances to subdivisions flashed past. I paid close attention to what I saw but knew there was no way I'd remember if we passed anything I'd want to explore. With a population fifty times bigger than Gaslight City's, The Woodlands was my first dose of living somewhere other than a small town. I'd thought Nacog-doches was a large town when I lived there. It had been Hicksville compared to this place.

A suburb of Houston, thirty-some-odd miles away, The Woodlands was home to warrens of housing subdivisions full of identical, mostly fancy, abodes. The first month I lived with Griff and Mysti, I went to the wrong house on three separate occasions. One lady called the rent-a-cop hired to patrol the neighborhood. The off-duty deputy escorted me to Griff's house and then made sure I belonged there.

And the neighborhood rules. Sheesh. The deed restric-tions for Griff and Mysti's subdivision could have taken up a law library. I knew because Mysti and I printed a copy after the Christmas light fiasco.

Mysti and I decorated the house for Christmas, which she called Yule, and thought it very pretty. A certified letter came a few days later informing us we had three too many items standing on the front lawn and we couldn't string lights on the shrubbery. The letter made vague threats about removing our indiscretions and billing the home-owner for the service.

Mysti screamed and ranted about neighborhood busy-bodies calling themselves homeowners' associations. We took down the whole shebang and left the house's exterior undecorated, Mysti muttering to herself the whole time. It had been a sight to behold.

Outside the endless subdivisions lay acres after acres of shopping centers full of stuff I couldn't imagine paying for even though I had a little money. And the restaurants. The variety boggled my mind. I had delighted in trying Italian ice and gelato for the first time and could eat Indian and Thai food anytime I wanted.

But the longer I lived in The Woodlands, the less I went out. The maze of streets, businesses hidden by scrub brush—which the locals considered woods—turned me into a nervous wreck. It was nothing to spend thirty minutes driving somewhere four miles away. And everybody ran around in such a hurry, powered by some manic urge I neither under-stood nor had the desire to imitate. People even talked fast. I had to ask them to repeat themselves. Most gladly did so because people here were friendly. At least there was that.

Mysti's tight voice pulled me out of my musings. "No, no, no. Please don't run the red light."

"Just keep going." Brad reached for Mysti's knee again, but she slapped his hand away and took her foot off the gas pedal. A Cadillac Escalade hurtled toward the intersection.

"They're not slowing down." My throat strained with the volume of my voice.

"Hold on," Mysti yelled and jammed on the brakes. Mysti and I both screamed as her Toyota sedan—the same model as mine—slid toward the luxury SUV. Tires squealed, horns blared, but the Escalade kept right on trucking, through the red light and beyond, probably to cause more havoc somewhere else. Just before they got out of sight, the driver's window lowered, and a closed fist popped out. Slowly, the person raised their middle finger. The Escalade disappeared around a bend.

"Go after him," Brad shouted.

Mysti ignored him and blew out a relieved breath. We finished crossing the intersection, took a right, and drove a few blocks on a smaller road with a perfectly landscaped median. The posted speed limit was thirty-five, but Mysti did fifty miles per hour.

Other cars whizzed past us. A dude wearing a golf visor pulled alongside, slowed, and yelled something. I made a face at him. He slammed his fist down on his horn and screamed at me until his face turned red.

"Peri Jean, stop the trailer trash routine." Mysti glanced into the rearview mirror.

"But he started it," I whined, bored with all the minutes spent in the car. Brad laughed.

Mysti sighed. "Be that as it may, we can't stop to whup the world right now." She turned onto yet another road.

"Here, Sis." Brad shook his finger at a driveway. "Park in there."

We climbed out of the car and followed Brad across the parking lot. At the end of the lot was a small, asphalt-paved opening obviously not intended for cars. We walked through.

The asphalt path ended facing a canal, which sparkled despite the gloomy sky. Native plants and young trees banked the stretch of water for as far as I could see. Of all the things I expected to find back here, this never hit the list. I stopped in my tracks.

A woman jogger approached, panting, her feet slapping the pavement. A guy on a bicycle rode over a concrete and iron bridge that led across the canal and ended near a shack advertising kayak rentals. He turned and continued his ride down the wide sidewalk.

"This way." Brad led us down another branch of sidewalk past a wide, grassy field where people sat on blankets watching their kids play.

"Mysti!" A girl with shoe-polish black hair and a silver studded face jogged toward us, waving. She grabbed Mysti in a hug, which my friend returned. They broke apart, and the girl turned to Brad and gave him a shy smile. He had the humility, or good sense, to keep his big mouth shut. Then she stared at me, bright-eyed and expectant.

"Tyler, I want you to meet Peri Jean Mace, my business associate." Mysti put her arm around me.

"Wow, that's a country name." Tyler laughed and held out her hand. She had crosses tattooed on the backs of each finger. On her thumb was a pentagram. Hadn't Mysti said this girl worked in a library? In Gaslight City, the only job she'd be able to get would be cashier at a convenience store or bartending work. Maybe. The differences in the two places danced around in my head until I felt dizzy. I shook her hand. "Nice to meet you."

"I know you only have an hour, so I'll get right down to business," Mysti began.

"I'm ready for action." Tyler showed us a manila folder.

We sat on graduating steps overlooking the canal. Another jogger, this one a well-built man, sweat damp shirt clinging to his muscular back and his leg muscles bunching, ran past.

My head turned as I watched his progress. I hadn't bothered with a man since Wade Hill turned me down flat a few months earlier. Did I want to get back into the dating game? Not really. But looking never hurt.

"I can't thank you enough for your hard work. Your next tarot reading is on the house." Mysti nudged me with her elbow. Brad chuckled and snapped his fingers in front of my face. I dragged my gaze off the pretty boy and nodded my thanks.

"Not a problem. I already had a lot of this stuff in my personal file. I'm thinking about doing my thesis on the Coachman."

Male scenery forgotten, I turned my full attention on

Tyler. Some of the piercings on her face made me want to flinch.

"That caught your interest, didn't it?" She smiled wider. "I'm guessing you know the story then?"

I nodded and told her the two versions I'd heard so far.

"Those sound about right. I'll tell you what I know. Then we can play Q and A. The cotton plantation referred to in the legend was Camilla Plantation. It was built in the late 1840s and operated as a full plantation up through the early 1870s." Tyler took out a photocopied picture and handed it to Mysti.

She held it where I could see too. The place wasn't as impressive as my ex-boyfriend's family home, but it was right on up there with its Georgian columns and circular drive. I passed the picture to Brad who barely gave it a glance. Why had he come again? Oh, to flirt with Tyler. Good gravy.

"Camilla was built and owned by a man named Rodney James. They farmed cotton and a few other things." Tyler passed us another photocopy of a picture. This one was of the same plantation gone to ruin, one wall fallen into rubble on the lawn and half the house open to the elements. One of the huge columns had started to crumble around its base, and the roof sagged.

"What about the actual Coachman? What do you know about him?" I handed the photo back to Tyler.

"There's several different tales about the Coachman floatin' around, Peri Jean." She tried to imitate my accent, grin widening. One glance at my face, and she dropped the grin. "Sorry. I really do find your accent and your name adorable." I wasn't sure what to say to that. Tyler squirmed at the silence. When she spoke again, her voice was tight and her cheeks red. "I've been studying this bit of folklore, urban legend, whatever you want to call it for six months now. Urban legends like this are a reflection of our fears as a society. One this old, it's hard to find the truth. I've heard versions where the mysterious stranger mentioned in the story is a sort of vampire, other versions where he's a were-wolf, and a really interesting version where he is a Bloody Mary-like character."

"Bloody Mary?" I almost hated to ask because I had the feeling she could go on and on about any topic that might come up and never really talk about the Coachman.

"You stand in a darkened room in front of a mirror and say the name "Bloody Mary" a set number of times. She appears in the mirror next to you. Whether or not she's malevolent depends on the version of the story you're told."

What did this have to do with the Coachman? I hoped this didn't turn out to be a waste of time.

Tyler broke off staring at my raven tattoo and laughed. "Listen to me. You asked what I know about the Coach-man, and we're talking about vampires and Bloody Mary. Very little is actually known about the Coachman." She thumbed through her file and took out a photocopied arti-cle. "The first information I found documented comes from the nineteen-fifties." She handed me the page. I scanned over it, but she began talking again. "Camilla Plantation sat empty after the murder scene in your version of the story. It fell into ruin. In the years just before the Great Depression, a young man showed up claiming to be the last remaining heir of the original plantation owner. He went by the name of Elijah James."

"But I thought the whole family went missing and all anybody found was a bunch of blood." Mysti's face creased as she tried to understand.

"That's true, and I actually found a newspaper article about the missing family. The plantation owner originally came to Texas from Ohio. During that period of history, there were a lot of incentives to attract settlers. Including free land." Tyler withdrew a sheet with formal handwriting on it. "Elijah James claimed to be Rodney James's last living relative from Ohio. Apparently, he was pretty convincing because local authorities cleared him to live in the old place and start farming it again."

This was all very interesting, but Tyler hadn't told me anything helpful so far. A cold wind found its way under my leather jacket. I hunched my shoulders against the discomfort and hoped she'd get to the good stuff soon.

"An African-American community named Blessed Union had built up around the old plantation grounds, and the residents weren't too happy to see this stranger move in on them." Tyler tapped the photocopied page she'd handed me. "The author of this article talked to a man who was born and grew up in Blessed Union."

That caught my attention. Cecil had mentioned the name Blessed Union. And the community's old school house was where I found the spent spell.

Tyler smiled at my interest and continued. "The man interviewed for the article was just a boy when Elijah

James took over Camilla. But he remembered a man named Israel Beard, one of the elders of the settlement, said Elijah James was evil."

Mysti stiffened. "What kind of evil?"

Tyler raised her eyebrows. "Israel Beard swore the man claiming to be Elijah James looked exactly like the mysterious stranger who murdered the original James family." She leaned forward. "But here's the kicker. Nobody believed it because if this Elijah James, fake name or not, was the murderer, he hadn't aged a day since the original incident some forty years earlier."

Mysti and I both sat up straight and exchanged meaningful glances. The Coachman's deal with the goat man probably kept him from aging.

"The freaky part?" Tyler grinned ear to ear, barely able to sit still. "This mysterious stranger drove a carriage. Israel Beard claimed it was the same one driven by the man thought to have murdered Rodney James and his family." She leafed through her file some more. "The man interviewed for the article said he awoke one night to find Elijah James standing outside his window, beckoning him to come outside. The interviewee said Elijah's eyes were glowing black, even though it was a moonless night."

Cold seeped into me and found places to hide. It had been the Coachman. I knew it in my bones.

"People, mainly kids, started going missing from Blessed Union. The residents made as much of a stink as they could, but things were different then. Because of their race, they were largely ignored." Tyler removed a photocopied picture of a bunch of burned-out shacks. "Then, one day, Blessed Union burned to the ground. Israel Beard, the man who'd made all the claims of this stranger being some sort of ghost or demon, was found tied in a barn. He'd died a pretty gruesome death."

Someone had wanted to shut him up, to shut the whole community up.

"Once Blessed Union was gone, the disappearances spread to the white community. People claimed to see Elijah James's carriage coming through town late at night, driving really slowly." Tyler took another photocopied article out of her folder and showed it to me. "Rumors started about Camilla Plantation, about Elijah James. A group of men went out to confront him, but none were ever seen again."

"What happened? How did it stop?" Mysti's voice was barely above a whisper.

"Nobody knows. People reported hearing an explosion. A group went out there, only to find the house laying in pieces all over the ground." Tyler showed us another photocopied picture of the wreckage. The lower part of brick chimney jutted out of the ground, the upper part scattered all over the ground. Pieces of the Georgian Columns lay among the bricks. Broken bits of wood littered the mess.

"The last odd thing I'll share is that no bodies or remains were ever found." Tyler packed her papers away and checked her watch, a gaudy, tarnished silver affair. "Any other questions?"

"I'm guessing the Elijah James name was a fake, right?" All that, and we didn't even get the Coachman's name.

"I've never found records of an Elijah James who was related to Rodney James. Was that the Coachman's real name?" She shrugged. "Could be. Maybe the surnames being the same was a coincidence. I can see someone using that as an opening to introduce himself to Rodney James in order to court his daughter." She held both hands up. "There's just no way to know for sure. The identity of Vivian James's suitor—probably the man who murdered the original James family—seems to be lost to history."

I slumped. Finding out the Coachman's name was against the odds. We'd have to refocus. An idea hit me. All this information about the plantation might give us an idea where Zora was taken. The way she disappeared had me baffled. She had to have been hidden. "What about a map of the area where Camilla Plantation was?"

She opened her file again and rifled through the papers but stopped. "That's right. I never replaced those." She raised her head. "You three aren't the first to approach me about this. A guy about Brad's age, but not as cute"— she winked at Brad—"contacted me about the Coachman. He wanted copies of my maps, but the copy machine won't do sheets that big. I had to send off special for those. Then he said he wanted copies of my documentation. While I was making them, he walked off with the maps of Camilla's grounds. And they were good maps too. They showed where a storm cellar had been, the location of a grain silo, all sorts of things."

The remnants of the spell in the Blessed Union Schoolhouse appeared in my mind. The humans helping the Coachman. The map thief may have been one of them. "What'd he look like?"

Tyler, head down scrolling through her phone, only muttered, "One step ahead of ya, cowgirl." She held up the cellphone. A picture of an unfamiliar male filled the screen. "There was just something off about him. He was intense, sort of scary. I took this picture without him knowing and sent it to my mother in case I went missing."

"Mind emailing it to me?" Brad rattled off his email, probably more to get a contact on Tyler than to help. She sent the picture, and his phone dinged. He opened the file and held the phone close to his face. "Hey, what's this thing in his hand?"

"Oh, that! I almost forgot." Tyler stuffed her cellphone back in her pocket. "He had this tile, like mahjongg tiles..." She trailed off and snapped her fingers. "No. Now that I think about it, the tile was more like Elder Futhark runes. The symbol on it looked similar to those." She grinned at the expression on my face. "Elder Futhark is the oldest known runic alphabet."

I grabbed a stick and drew the symbol I saw in Jadine's vision in the dirt. "Like this?"

Her mouth fell open, and she rubbed her arms. "Exactly." Tyler checked her watch again. "I hate to run, but my lunch hour is past over." She turned to me and held out one hand. We shook. "Guys, seriously, anything else you need, give me a call." She gave Brad a meaningful smile and walked away.

9

———

BRAD WATCHED HER GO, also meaningfully. He caught Mysti and me staring at him and tried to play it off. "What's this symbol?"

"I saw it in Jadine's vision of how the Coachman became immortal." Just looking at the thing made me shiver.

"If I were religious, I'd call it blasphemous." Brad swiped his foot over my stick drawing until nothing was left. Then he shook his hands, a gesture I recognized from the spells we did together. He used it to let go of negative energy.

"That was the symbol the goat man left behind, wasn't it?" Mysti leaned forward, taking shallow breaths. I nodded.

The pieces clicked together in my mind. The goat man commanded the Coachman to keep a souvenir of his murder victims, to put that symbol on the part he kept. Those objects were to be the Coachman's link to the living plane. I'd kiss a wild hog if the rune Tyler's map thief held hadn't once belonged to the Coachman. Where'd the stupid idiot find it? And how did he know to call the Coachman? No matter now.

Mysti tapped me. "Don't shut us out."

I gestured at Brad's cellphone. "That map thief must have used the rune to get the Coachman out of the place where he hid his soul."

"The Coachman killed his mortal body." Mysti's face paled. "And now he's looking for a new vessel."

If the Coachman needed my body for a new vessel, why did he need Zora to raise the dead? I was missing an important link. Worse, it hovered just out of reach, jumping out of my grasp every time I closed in.

Brad pulled out his cellphone. "We need to find this guy and now." He used his thumb and forefinger to enlarge the picture Tyler sent him. All three of us stared at the image of a nondescript nerd with a wispy mustache. He wore some kind of uniform and had an eyebrow ring. Brad tapped the screen. "Dude has a name tag. The light's got his name blurred, but I can almost see the place where he works."

We spent several minutes squinting at the tiny square on the guy's shirt. Finally, Brad snapped his fingers. "I know. I recognize the shape. It's from a little pub right near here. Maybe he's at work."

"I don't know." Mysti glanced back toward where we'd parked the car. "Griff likes to be the one to question people. And he is better at it."

Brad slipped his arm over his sister's shoulders. "We

made it just fine before you decided your happiness hinged on him. What'd he do? Steal your brass?"

Mysti stiffened. "Of course not. It's just good to know your skills."

"Well, I want to get Tyler's maps back. See if she'll go out with me." Brad took off walking without waiting for his sister's consent, his expensive leather shoes tapping on the concrete sidewalk.

Mysti and I trailed behind Brad, both of us quiet. For my part, I thought about how Brad would be lost without Mysti. From his fancy clothes down to his orthodontically straightened teeth—the man still wore a retainer at night—Mysti always let her baby brother have his way, even when it was foolish. I didn't dare challenge her because she showed me the same unflinching loyalty. Maybe I was just jealous I didn't have anybody to love me unconditionally anymore. The wind whipped down the canal, icy and unforgiving.

Mysti picked up the pace. "We didn't get a damn thing we came for." She tightened her hand-crocheted shawl around her and raised her eyebrows. "Or did you hear something I didn't?"

"No. I'm trying to pound all these bits of information into something that makes sense." I shoved my hands in the pockets of my leather jacket, silently berating myself for deciding the jacket and a tank top would be warm enough.

"Spill it." Mysti shivered.

"When my cousin and his wife threw salt on the Coachman, his ghost broke into a bunch of pieces. I latched onto one of the pieces, and it seemed female, not like the entity of the Coachman at all." I couldn't get the image out of my head. "Now this map thief is involved, and there's some connection I'm not making."

Mysti walked along beside me, face lined with concentration. "So this map thief has a rune with that symbol on it. You think he's somehow providing the Coachman with power?"

"Maybe. I've encountered all kinds of ghosts. The Coachman is by far the most powerful. I've never seen a ghost do what he does." My stomach rolled into a hard ball as I thought about Zora. "I don't see where a ghost could access that kind of energy and control by himself."

"But the Coachman had made himself into an immortal being. No telling what points that garnered him in the ghost world." Mysti's words might have refuted my point, but she wasn't trying to shut me down. She never did that. This was her way of pushing the thought process further.

We stopped under a bridge to watch the shadows of the water moving over a stunning fish mosaic. Footsteps scraped on the concrete. Mysti and I no longer had the pretty space to ourselves. Best to discuss this elsewhere. We turned to catch up with Brad.

"You Peri Jean Mace?" The voice came from behind us and was not one I knew. Sometimes people recognized me as the girl who found the Mace Treasure. *Great. Just what I need today.* I gritted my teeth and turned.

"Help you?" My gaze settled on the person who'd

called my name, and I had to use all my self-control not to gasp.

The man or woman—I couldn't tell which—had a blanket covering head and shoulders. Overly bright eyes glowed out from the shadow the blanket cast. My heart rattled harder as panic seeped into my bloodstream. Fear squeezed my bladder.

"I'll bust your nose, you don't tell me what you want," I squeaked.

Run. The whisper came from all around me. I recognized Priscilla Herrera's voice. I grabbed Mysti's hand and tensed my body to escape.

The shrouded figure shot forward, closing the distance between us before I could move even a step. It brought a hand out of its pocket, opened it, and blew some kind of powder in my face. I gasped before I thought about it and sucked heaven only knows how much of the crud into my lungs. Some of the dust hit my face and burned like pinpoints of fire on my skin. I clapped my hands over my face. Mysti screamed and threw her arms around me.

"Are you okay?" Panic raised Mysti's voice several octaves. It echoed off the water and concrete and reverberated round my brain until it became so much nonsense.

"What's going on down there?" Brad's shout echoed all around us.

My attacker's retreating footsteps slapped against the concrete sidewalk. Brad ran past us, already gasping like a locomotive. He wouldn't last long. Didn't matter, though. They'd already gotten me good. A metallic taste filled my mouth. My heart felt as though it was filling up, stretching, getting ready burst at any minute. I gasped for air, and my chest moved, but no oxygen went into my lungs.

"You two need help?" asked a deep voice. I smelled his sweat, sour and reeking of last night's beer. "Is she okay?"

"I don't know." Mysti sobbed, her voice hitching between the words.

"Let's get her some air." Sweaty hands gripped my arms and lifted me. I dragged my eyes open and stared into the face of the runner I'd seen earlier. His features stretched and undulated like a funhouse mirror come to life. He pulled me from under the bridge and dumped me on the lawn of a fancy hotel. I whooped deep breaths, my lungs still screaming for oxygen.

The runty trees undulated, more sensuous than any exotic dancer. Their clattering branches drummed together, and the wind crashed their evergreen leaves like cymbals. The dim sun burned like a muted ball of molten lava behind the clouds.

Mysti squatted next to me and said words I couldn't hear, tears rolling down her face. I held out my hand to her. She took it and lowered her head. Her shoulders hitched, jerky in my fragmented vision.

My consciousness quivered as something pulled at it. I drunkenly called on the power of the black opal to ground myself, using all the strength I had to keep my focus, to keep control of the situation. My mind, my magic, all of me began to roll, and I drifted away like a leaf caught in the wind.

Something inside me pulled away and rose above my body and hovered over myself. Horror raced through my mind. I lay on my back, one foot tucked behind my knee. A thin line of drool snaked out of my mouth. Another raw wind blew through, sending leaves to tangle in my hair. My eyes stared straight ahead, blank and empty.

Am I dead? The thought sent a current of fear through whatever I was, so intense my vision turned bright yellow and green. I stared hard at my chest and finally saw the slight rise and fall of my breathing.

"She didn't take anything," Mysti yelled at the runner. "This person blew something in her face."

"Powder?" The guy held open my eyes. "White powder? Brown powder?"

Mysti shook her head and put her face in her hands. People surrounded us. A few assholes took out their phones and began recording the spectacle.

The tugging on my consciousness came again, pulling me higher into the sky, where I could no longer see the people huddled around me. Brad sat hunched on a bench, sides heaving, head between his knees. The person who'd blown the powder into my face stood right around the next bend from him, across the canal from where my body lay, watching. The brown blanket hung over one arm. She took out her cellphone, punched a few buttons, and spoke into it. Then she turned away and walked down the sidewalk as though she hadn't a care in the world.

From my vantage point, I watched the crowd surrounding my body. I needed to get back inside myself so I could tell Mysti what I'd seen. Instead, something drew me farther away into the cloudy sky. The air rippled as something big parted it and rushed toward me. The Coachman's face appeared, mouth fixed in a mean grin.

I didn't know how to fight him, if there was even a way, so I tried to dart away. He flew at me and hit me hard. He found my weaknesses and parted them, rending and tearing as he went. My bad memories opened and spewed hurt everywhere. They settled over my awareness like a dark veil between the present moment and me.

———

I WAS BACK in that dingy, roach-infested apartment with my ex-husband, him screaming about me stealing his money. His fist hurtled toward me and slammed into my lips. Pain flashed bright, and salty blood filled my mouth. He slammed another fist into my ribs. "Give me the money, you stupid bitch." I hit the floor chin first and bit my tongue. He kicked me in the stomach once, twice, three times, and I felt something inside me let go.

Terror exploded in my chest. I brought my knees up to protect myself from his blows, trying to remember how this went. Then it hit me. This wasn't real. It had once been real, but it wasn't anymore. It was a piece of scar tissue, of armor, that my mind created to protect me. And now it was preventing me from using my gifts to protect myself.

I rolled over just as my ex-husband reared one Doc Marten boot back to give me another kick.

"Stop it," I yelled at the memory.

He let the kick fly. Air burst from my lungs. Sobs crawled up my throat and twisted my mouth. My throbbing chest hitched once, twice. I cried, trying to ignore the sticky wetness between my legs, trying not to think what it meant.

The front door to the rat hole I'd rented on my dollar store salary banged open. My daddy slammed into the room, grabbed my ex-husband by his shoulders, and spun him around.

Tim's face slackened with surprise. My father's fist pistoned into Tim's face over and over again, until the other man crumpled to the floor, hands out to ward off more blows. Daddy grabbed him by one arm and hauled him out the door. The sound of him falling down the metal stairs shook the apartment.

Daddy came back into the apartment and helped me stand. I held my stomach. It felt like I was about to shit out all my insides. He wrapped his arms around me and held me.

The door to my bedroom opened, and Priscilla Herrera stepped out. Sometimes she appeared as a young woman. Not today. Today she was a frumpy woman sliding out of late middle age, the way she'd been the day she died.

My throat tightened. Things never got more fun when she came on the scene. I turned to my daddy for reassurance. Priscilla waved one hand at Paul, and he evaporated.

I gasped. "Daddy?"

"He was never here. Your mind conjured him to help you. It knew no other way to save you." She sat down on the tattered couch and motioned me to sit with her. I limped toward her. She held up one hand for me to stop. "Look at yourself. You're not injured."

I glanced down to see my modern-day body, even raised my shirt to see if bruises were forming on my chest. She was right. I wasn't hurt. Not physically anyway.

"Don't let these memories trick you into living in the past. It won't serve you." Her brisk, iron-plated voice hit the deepest, rawest nerve in me.

"You think you could do better?" My body went cold. I didn't fear her as I once had, but she was a formidable woman, even dead.

"It doesn't matter. This is your affliction, not mine." She gripped my arm, her hand hard and strong, and pulled me to face her.

I gaped at her.

"You'll get no sympathy from me." She raised her eyebrows, daring me to get angry. "This Coachman of yours is an old creature, as old as me, and powerful. He knows the perfect way to exploit others. You were too easy."

Her chiding sunk deep and settled with all the other hurts. I hung my head.

She grabbed my hair and yanked my head back up. I yowled and struggled against her. "Right now, he's out there eating my gift to you." She let go of me and made a disgusted face. "Disgraceful."

"But I don't know how to..." I heard the whine in my voice. If it pissed me off, and it did, it would infuriate Priscilla.

Sure enough her lips ground together, and her dark eyes blazed sparks of fury. "Then you figure it out." She spoke through clenched teeth. Then her face softened.

"He's eating my gift to you. Take a bite of him. Turn his power on him." Her arm tightened around me, holding me in place. "Then go back to Tyler. Ask to look at *all* her pictures. You'll know the right one when you see it. Take it to Cecil. He'll know what needs to be done." A hole opened up in the threadbare and stained apartment-grade carpet. Priscilla shoved me off the couch and into it.

I rocketed along through the blackness, suffering the worst case of rollercoaster stomach I'd ever had. Images flashed as I flew past. The greatest hits of my worst memories.

Felicia and another girl shoved my head into an open toilet. My body flailed while filthy water splashed out of the commode. Time jumped forward. Wade rejected me, telling me we'd never be together because of a future he feared. Time flashed backward. Memaw's funeral. I sat between Rainey and Hannah, the three of us holding hands and bawling. Time tripped backward even further. I knelt next to Eddie Kennedy, the only man who'd been a father to me after mine died, and watched his life slip away. Somewhere in there, my sanity slipped, and I began to wail.

I dropped to the surface of a rocky plane covered in white mist, shivering and gasping, pardoned from the worst hell imaginable.

The Coachman knelt, sucking up as much of the white mist as he could through his nostrils and mouth. Priscilla was right. He was eating up my power. The mist around the Coachman thinned and swirled toward me like a dog coming to its owner.

Get him out. Priscilla Herrera's voice came from somewhere near, but I couldn't see her. *Get him out now.*

The power she'd given me, that of the mantle, crawled up my spine and cloaked my shoulders, hot and electric. I took several running steps and leapt onto the Coachman's back. Priscilla said to bite him, and so I did.

His power flowed into me, stronger but with a scattered feeling, as though one good kick could break it apart. I heard chanting somewhere. Beyond that, I heard a child crying. Not just crying, screaming in terror and pain.

Zora. I have to go get her. Now. I pushed myself into the Coachman, the same way he'd done to me. I'd get into his mind. Find where he hid Zora. Something slammed into my chest, paralyzing me.

Get out, girl, get out! The howl of fury came from inside my head, inside my body, shaking my whole world.

Some force larger and greater than I ever would be slung me from the vision and threw me across the floor of my consciousness. I rolled to my feet, ready to fight the Coachman, but he'd already gone.

The frantic desire for oxygen beat in my lungs like a bird trapped.

"Breathe, Peri Jean," Mysti's voice screamed.

I had to go back. It was time.

10

———

I SUCKED IN ONE BREATH, then another. My eyes flew open. Mysti and the runner leaned over me, desperation pinching their faces. A sea of curious faces hovered behind them. The runner had his hands clasped on my chest. Had he been giving me compressions? I didn't want another one, so I grabbed his wrist. He let out a thin scream and leapt away from me.

Mysti rose and put her cellphone to her ear. She said the name of the hotel we were in front of to whoever was on the other end. Somewhere in the distance, a siren wailed. Had she called emergency services? I wanted to ride in an ambulance and be tended by paramedics almost as much as I wanted a do-over with Dean Turgeau.

"Let me up." My words ground out of my throat, clotted and strained.

Mysti shoved the cellphone in her fringed bag. She and Brad pulled me to my feet. I staggered against her, and she slipped one arm around my waist and held me upright.

"I don't want the hospital," I muttered. Brad pulled my other arm over his shoulders.

"I know. Hurry." She hurried toward a set of steps next to the bridge where we'd been attacked. She and Brad yanked me along much faster than I could walk.

"Wait a minute," the runner yelled from behind us.

Mysti waved him off with one hand and spoke to Brad. "Where the hell were you when we needed you?"

Brad let out an exasperated grunt. "I got there just in time to see what happened. I ran after the poisoner."

Mysti let out an angry hiss but said no more. The two of them hoisted me up a steep set of concrete stairs, yelling at people, "Emergency! Get out of the way."

We reached the street level, and a familiar SUV swung to the curb. Griff leaned over and popped open the door. "Get in. The ambulance is right behind me." He reached for me, and I took his hand and crawled into the passenger seat. Mysti climbed into the backseat. We slammed our doors, and Griff peeled away from the curb.

"Let's go home now. We can pick up my car later." Mysti's seatbelt clicked. Griff sped into traffic.

I sat in a daze. Whatever drug I'd been dosed with still clouded my head, leaving pockets of dizziness. It mixed with the mantle and lent an edge of unreality to my vision. Normal things took on a life I never wanted to see.

A human-ish face stared out of a tree, eyes following the SUV as we passed. On the curb stood an elderly man dressed in a suit. He raised his head as we passed, sensing us, and another face moved behind his, distorting it for just a second. A black dog as large as a pony trotted down the sidewalk. Shivers ripped through my body. I fought for clarity. There was no time for this nonsense.

Priscilla said to get Tyler's research. Though she wasn't nice to me, she always helped. I needed to do what she said.

"Griff, I need to talk to Tyler again." I slapped at his arm. He took his foot off the accelerator.

Mysti leaned between the seats and looked me over. She shook her head. "No. You need home and rest, plus something to cleanse the toxins from your body." Her voice took on the determined edge that reminded me she was technically my boss.

"Priscilla Herrera talked to me while I was out of my body." I turned in the seat to face her and almost enjoyed the way her face got waxy with shock. Mysti feared Priscilla Herrera just as much as I did. "She said we need to see all of Tyler's pictures. There's one we need to take to Cecil."

"I'll go to the library parking lot." Griff eased the SUV into the line for the next turnaround. He glanced at Mysti in the rearview mirror. "It's not like the sheriff's deputies will be doing a car to car search. And we can pick up your car. I don't like leaving it."

Mysti huffed in irritation but took out her cellphone and tapped on the screen. She put it to her ear. "Tyler, hon. I need to ask one more favor." Whatever Tyler said made her smile. "Of course Peri Jean will do a séance for you." She winked at me. I turned around and stared out at the road and listened as Mysti arranged for Tyler to make copies of her notes, especially the pictures, and meet us in the library parking lot. Mysti put her cellphone away and turned to Brad.

"While Griff drives, tell me why you ran off while I was trying to help Peri Jean." She turned to face him. "Now."

"But—but—but I ran after the poisoner. You were screaming and crying. Somebody had to do it." Brad held up both hands and shrugged his shoulders.

"She was right around the corner from where you stopped." I grinned at Brad.

His cheeks reddened, his eyes bugged out, and his lips puckered. This was his mad face. "After I lost her, I went back to that pub. Talked to a guy who was friends with the map thief." Brad stopped his story to explain about the map thief to Griff. "The map thief's name is Jeremy. Hasn't shown up for work in three weeks. His friend is worried about him. Seems Jeremy found that rune out in Coachman Country." He smiled at his witty name for the area where Camilla Plantation had been. "Jeremy got all weird and secretive after that. Obsessed with the Coachman. Made a bunch of new friends."

"Surely you asked where to find this Jeremy, where he lives." Griff didn't sound happy about Brad's mini investigation.

"Hasn't been home in three weeks." Brad smirked at Griff. "Anywho...Jeremy had been going out to an old school building near where Camilla was."

I held up one hand to stop Brad. "I've been there. That's the place I found where someone had been doing magic."

Brad shook his head. "Wait. That's not all. Guy I talked

to said he saw Jeremy with his new friends. Said the way they looked at him, he was afraid of them."

"Did he give you any useful descriptions?" Griff's tone implied he'd have gotten way more information.

Brad sighed. "Not really. Just a bunch of kids with an older woman. He thinks they killed Jeremy. Maybe for that rune."

Griff whipped into the library parking lot. He drove under the portico as though we belonged there. Tyler rushed out of the building with her coat clutched tight around her. I rolled down my window. She stopped in her tracks, mouth open, and stared at me.

"Were you able to get the copies?" I went for meek and grateful, but I probably sounded like a loan shark.

Tyler's shoulders dropped. "I wasn't. All the copiers are in use right now, and I couldn't very well kick library patrons off to do personal stuff. But I'll scan them into PDFs and email them to Mysti within the hour. Would that do?"

There was no other option than to say that was fine. I managed a hollow version of the words.

"What happened?" She came closer and leaned into the car to look for Mysti. "Were those sirens for the two of you?"

"I just had a little trouble." I heard the slur in my words and winced. I sounded just like my old boyfriend, Chase Fischer, at the end of one of his alcohol and drug binges.

"You look like my sister did the day she ODed on sleeping pills." She shoved her hands deep in the pockets of her jacket. Another car pulled up behind us. Rather than coming to a stop, they edged forward in tiny increments, as though doing so would make us go for fear of them rear-ending us. Griff glared into the rearview mirror.

"That's pretty close to the truth." I knew I ought to lie to her, but the truth came rolling out almost on its own. "Someone blew some powder into my face down on the Waterway. Made me..." I trailed off and shrugged. Tyler didn't need to know too many details. Her curiosity might kill her. "Sick."

Tyler blinked twice. "What do you remember?"

"Where it hit my skin burned like fire." I rubbed at my still tender cheeks.

"Did it taste like metal?" Tyler focused on me so intently my heart ramped back into gear. I nodded my answer. She said, "Mysti?"

Mysti scooted forward until Tyler could see her face.

"Have you ever heard of Bengalo Dust?" Tyler stood on her tiptoes and leaned into the SUV.

"I've heard it's a mild hallucinogenic made of dried and ground branches from a Devil's Bone bush and a little magic." Mysti studied me, probably speculating on whether that's what I'd been given. "But Devil's Bones is a hard bush to get hold of. And the spell requires the shifting of more energy than most are willing to risk. It's rare. I've never even seen it."

"Maybe you did today." Tyler lowered her voice. "Someone approached a member of my coven trying to buy some Devil's Bones. They wanted to make a batch of Bengalo Dust." Tyler took in the expression on my face.

"Maybe you should talk to the woman they approached. She has a shop in Old Town Spring."

The car behind us honked. Tyler shot them a glare. The driver noisily shifted into reverse and zoomed backward out of the portico. He shot around the side of us, leaning across his seat and scowling. Had I not felt so bad, I'd have laughed.

"Where is your friend's shop?" The likelihood the shop owner would have any useful information was low, but I had gotten a good look at the woman who blew the powder in my face once she took the blanket off. I thought I could describe her well enough to get a confirmation on whether it was the same person who visited the shop.

Tyler took out her cellphone and tapped a few buttons. Mysti's phone dinged. Tyler said, "She closes early on Saturday, but I'll call and tell her to expect you."

"Thanks for your help." This time, my words had a little less slur. At least Bengalo Dust wore off fast.

"I'll scan the pages and send the email as fast as I can." Tyler knocked on the door and walked away.

"So much for that," I muttered.

"It's not a total loss." Griff drove Mysti to her car. After a side trip back home to drop it off, we were on the road again.

Mysti enabled the map feature on her cellphone, and a robotic voice began spitting out directions to Old Town Spring. The traffic rushed from one red light to the next. The fast starts and stops had my head swimming. I couldn't take much more without puking.

"Mysti, is there any chance you have a magic potion to help me feel better?" I turned in my seat and tried to smile.

"Barf, and you're walking." Brad curled his lip in disgust.

Mysti swatted him. "She is not." She obediently dug in her purse and handed me one of the remedies she made out of tamarind and magic. I licked the goop off the wax paper and leaned my head back on the headrest and closed my eyes. I must have dozed, dreamless, for the short drive to Old Town Spring. I awoke when Griff bumped into a public parking lot and shut off the SUV's engine.

"Looks like we walk up this street here and then take the first right." Mysti opened her door and climbed out. "The name of the shop is Morrigan's Attic."

Mysti and Griff locked hands and walked ahead of me. Brad and I tagged behind them. He walked as though nothing was amiss, but I felt acutely aware of being the third wheel. The idea I was intruding poked every tender spot in my emotions. Soon as we got this mess straightened out, I'd move out of Griff and Mysti's, even if it was to a short lease apartment. The idea of taking action brightened my disposition. The potion and my short nap had done me a world of good. The phantom tinges of intoxication had passed out of my system. I hurried after my friends.

This was my first visit to Old Town Spring, and I took in the many shops and eateries the historic area offered. I could buy anything from wine tastings to hats to financial advice. Unlike The Woodlands, where everything was made to look shiny and new, the buildings of Old Town Spring seemed proud of looking old.

Tourists jammed the streets, passing in and out of the shops, many red-cheeked with booze and good cheer. The place reminded me of all the things I liked to remember about Gaslight City, even though so close to Houston, Old Town Spring had a more of a big city feel than my hometown.

"Here it is." Mysti stopped at the walkway of a quaint wooden house with wood siding painted a soft grape color. We walked up the unfinished two-by-four walkway and past an elaborate bottle tree made with indigo and green bottles. A wind chime made of metal bent into shapes that I recognized from Mysti's grimoire rattled at its top. The porch floor, carefully painted the same color as the house, creaked beneath our feet.

A strong memory of the porch on Memaw's house, now nothing but charred wood and ashes, popped into my memory. I swallowed the lump in my throat and blinked back tears. To distract myself, I raised my head and stared at the porch's ceiling. It was painted the aqua color old timers called "haint blue" because folklore claimed it would keep away ghosts. Memaw had always kept the ceiling of our porch painted the same color. I was still smiling, almost crying at the same time, when the door opened.

I pegged the woman in her late forties or early fifties because of her skin, which had absorbed more sun than any skin needed and looked the way chicken skin looks after a stint in a high temperature oven. Her bleached, almost white, blonde hair rustled dry and stiff in the cool wind. But her smile, tobacco-stained teeth and all, was genuine, her dark eyes full of kindness. "Tyler send y'all?"

"Sure did." Mysti strode forward, her hand out. The woman shook it. "I'm Mysti Whitebyrd." Griff, Brad, and I introduced ourselves in turn.

The lady shook with each of us. "I'm Yvonne Miller. Come on in."

The shop smelled like patchouli and love. Yvonne had a wide selection of mundane items in the front room, but I saw a few more specialized goods in the second, smaller room. We quickly explained what had been done to me at the Waterway. Yvonne's crinkled skin paled, but she listened without interrupting. I described the woman who'd poisoned me, realizing she'd been young, very young, and Yvonne's head bobbed up and down. She knew exactly who I meant but said nothing.

I prodded her gently. "If you've spoken to this woman, any information you have would help."

Mysti smiled at her and fingered a display of necklaces, cheap glass balls set into faux silver pendants shaped like bird claws. I fingered my own black opal pendant and took comfort from the singe of magic it sent through my fingertips. Yvonne's nostrils flared at the surge of magic. She seemed to decide something.

"I've got no problem telling you what I know." Yvonne reached under the counter and took out a small white notepad with writing all over the first page. "That woman scared the life out of me. I remembered her as soon as Tyler called." Yvonne glanced around, as though afraid of being overheard, even though we were alone in her little shop. "You see, not many people know about Devil's Bones or Bengalo Dust. But even fewer know of Lazarus Root."

Mysti drew in a sharp breath. "I wasn't aware there was any in existence."

"If someone has enough money and enough stupidity to look for it, it's out there." Yvonne straightened. "Not from me, of course. I don't deal in that kind of stuff."

"What else can you tell us about your customer?" Griff's voice still had that lighthearted, glad-to-know-you brightness, but he'd fixed his gaze on Yvonne, and I knew from experience it was intimidating.

"She parked in my side lot." Yvonne raised her eyebrows at us.

Mysti and I exchanged puzzled looks. I sure didn't get the significance, so I shook my head.

"I've got video surveillance," Yvonne stage whispered. She tore the top page off the notepad and held it out. Griff took it from her and began to smile. I leaned into his personal space and read the string of seven numbers and letters. Her license plate.

"Right after I spoke with Tyler, I called up the surveillance videos for that day. She was my only customer, so it was pretty easy." Yvonne gave us a short laugh.

"Thank you for your help." I smiled at Yvonne. "I'll definitely be back to look around."

Yvonne walked us to the door and turned the Open sign to Closed. The deadbolt slid home behind us.

Griff led the way back to the SUV. "I have a contact

who can run the plate, but probably not on a Saturday." I gave him a vague nod.

Mysti's phone dinged, and she checked it. "It's the files from Tyler."

We huddled together to scroll through the images. I dismissed the ones that only had text because Priscilla mentioned a picture.

Finally, I found it. I used my fingers to enlarge the image and stared into the face of my great-great-grandmother, Samantha. I had no trouble recognizing her from the photos Cecil showed me, even though she was at least twenty years younger in this picture.

"Why is there a picture of her in this stuff?" I pored over the tiny text until I found the passage that concerned me. "Lakeworth Carnival, in town at the time Camilla Plantation was destroyed, reported hearing a loud explosion that day."

Cecil told me his grandmother had no firsthand knowledge of the Coachman. She'd either kept it from him, or he was lying. I had no trouble believing the second one. Cecil hit me as a man who hoarded information the way squirrels hoard acorns.

I looked up from my reading. "Let's go see Cecil."

———

GRIFF GOT us back onto the freeway, and we sped north to the RV park. I sat with my head down, still trying to put everything together. "The lady blew Bengalo Dust into my face to immobilize me, right?" I spoke to everyone and no one.

Griff glanced at me. "Bengalo Dust doesn't just immobilize. It opens your consciousness."

Mysti rubbed at her forehead, thumb massaging her temple. "The users want to allow entities into their bodies. Bengalo Dust was blown into your face to make it easier for the Coachman to get into you."

"What about Lazarus Root?"

Mysti shook her head. "It allows a dead person's spirit to be reborn into another person."

My stomach twisted, and cold spread over my body. "So that thing, whoever it is, wants to be reborn in me or Zora?"

Griff shook his head. "We're going to take care of it. It's not going to go that far. Besides, I doubt they were able to find any Lazarus Root. The last mention I saw of it dated back to the nineteen-seventies, and the person claimed they went to South America to get the ingredients."

"What's not going to get that far? Griffin, you talk to me." My chest tightened. I had a feeling this was about to get so, so bad.

"It's likely the Coachman plans to resurrect in Zora—not you. The Lazarus Root will allow him to transform her body into his likeness, basically be reborn through her. She's a child, so more malleable, and she's got your family's magical blood to help the spell along."

Zora didn't just have my family's magical blood. She could raise the dead. Terror took root and spread through my body. My throat tightened, and I choked, whooping for air. Griff took the next exit and whipped into a gas station. I leaned my head between my knees and coughed. *Zora, poor Zora. That's what he wants with her.* Mysti pushed a bottle of water into my face and yelled for me to drink.

"He's got another reason for wanting Zora." I whooped for breath, but my heart wouldn't slow down. "She can raise the dead."

Griff stared at the road, his hands clenched on the steering wheel. "If he has the Lazarus Root and Zora, he only needs one more thing. You. Your blood specifically, for the human sacrifice required. The more powerful the human, the more chance the resurrection succeeds."

Something still bothered me. "You keep saying resurrection. How is that different from possessing Zora?"

"He'll be reborn of her body," Brad muttered. Mysti swatted at him, but he shoved her off and yelled, "She needs to know what's at stake." He spoke to me. "Have you ever seen those time-lapse films? How it'll speed through a day?"

A picture started to form in my head, an ugly one, and all I could do was nod.

"The Coachman'll implant himself in Zora, incubate, and be born really fast—like over the space of a few minutes." Brad swallowed hard. "That little girl's magic will resurrect the Coachman. He'll grow to adulthood in a matter of a few more minutes. Then Zora'll be sucked dry and torn apart. The Coachman gets both her life force and her ability to raise the dead. He'll be a god." Brad looked sick.

My ears began to ring, and sweat broke out on my

head. The images in my head made me want to scream. "What are we going to do?" My gaze darted between my friends.

Brad wouldn't look at me. Griff and Mysti stared back, faces tight with fear. Neither gave me an answer. Their silence was worse than them pulling a fit. I hadn't realized until just then how much I depended on them having all the answers I needed. Dread teased at me and begged me to panic some more.

"There's a way to outsmart this spirit." Griff's nostrils flared, and his chest heaved with each breath. "There is. We will fight until we can't anymore."

"Tell us everything you saw when you were out." Mysti glanced at Griff, and he nodded. "Let's try to find this thing's weakness."

Leaving out the details of my final meeting with my ex-husband, even though Mysti already knew, I told Griff about my hellish visit with Priscilla Herrera. "Then I was on top of the scar tissue caused by the mantle-blocking spell." I closed my eyes and ransacked my memory for the clearest way to explain what I saw. "The Coachman was on his hands and knees sucking up the mantle. It looked like a white mist. I had to stop him, so I bit him."

Both Griff and Mysti stared at me, mouths open. Brad started laughing, and Mysti pinched him. He yowled and shoved her away.

"Priscilla told me to do it." I raised my voice. "She said to turn his power back on him."

"And did you?" Mysti leaned forward, mind working behind her brown eyes.

I let out a breath. "I was going to, but I heard Zora crying. I forgot about using his power against him. I tried to get in him and go looking for her, maybe in his memories or something?" I glanced at Griff for approval, and he nodded. "But the Coachman kicked me out, and then he left."

Griff's head snapped back as though someone had slapped him. "You have to get back in him. There's some secret you can use against him, and he knows it."

"But I don't know how to get back in him." Impatience bubbled like a pot of spaghetti sauce about to explode. "I don't even know how to find him."

Griff slowed the SUV and turned onto the road toward the RV park.

Brad held one hand up. "Patience. Just have patience. We'll figure it out."

I directed Griff through the RV park to Cecil's motor home. Griff stopped in front and let out a long whistle.

"How much you wanna bet old Cecil has the only nice rig in the bunch?" The nastiness I'd heard when Griff first mentioned Cecil the night before came back.

Griff had told me the history between him and Cecil was none of my business. That was all fine and dandy before the Coachman took Zora. Now we all had to work together. "Tell me what happened between you and Cecil and if you're going to be able to work together."

Griff jutted out his jaw and frowned.

"Tell her or I will." Mysti glared at Griff. "And while you tell it, let go of it enough so you can work with him."

He grunted. She leaned into his space. "I'm serious. Get to it."

Griff hung on to the SUV's steering wheel for dear life. "My father had a taste for gambling. It got him into all kinds of trouble. Before I was born, he did some federal time. He met Cecil in prison." He smiled and raised his eyebrows at me. "Every time Daddy ran out of money, Cecil would help him get loans from the wrong people. It just got him deeper in the hole." He stopped speaking, and I thought he'd finished. He stared at the RV, eyes narrowed, then spoke again. "Mom and I would have no groceries in the house, and Daddy would be out rolling dice, like it was a paying living. He'd come home broke a few days later. Cecil'd call him up, offer him little illegal jobs to get him going again. When Daddy died—"

Mysti interrupted. "Was beaten to death over a gambling debt."

Griff swallowed. "Cecil came by the house with one bag of groceries and a suit for me to wear to Daddy's funeral. Told me I was the man of the house now." His shoulders tightened, and he snorted.

"How old were you?" Also not my business, but might as well put both feet in the pool of shit.

"Twelve. Me and Mom were probably better off without Daddy. She remarried a real nice guy. Our lights never got turned off again, and we always had groceries after that." Griff bit his lip, eyes dark in thought. "My path has crossed with Cecil's a few times over the years. He always mentions that sack of food and that cheap fucking suit he brought over. He's right proud of it." Griff turned to me. "The part that stays with me, though? I think Cecil could have saved Daddy from those people and chose not to. He just cut his ties and let them kill him. I think that's what Cecil does. So watch yourself."

My great-uncle picked that moment to come out of his motor home, Jadine right behind him.

"Who is *that*?" Brad came to life in the backseat. "She is smoking hot."

"Jadine," I said. "But she's not looking for a slobbery hound dog like you. She's out of your league. So don't even try it."

"That's the blonde from the picture. The one with no paper trail." Griff stared at Jadine like she was a rare bird.

"Cecil and his wife adopted her. She's family." My toes curled as the words left my mouth. I'd known this last night when Griff showed me her picture, and I'd chosen not to tell him. Now it was obvious I'd held back information.

He turned to me, aghast. "You knew when you saw her picture and never said anything. Why?" I didn't know, so I shrugged. Griff grabbed my arm. "Don't you see how they're pulling you in? Don't you understand—"

Mysti spoke up. "Griffin. No."

He let go of me, and I climbed out of the SUV. Griff scrambled out and practically ran around the vehicle. Mysti followed at a safe distance. Brad got out, grinning like a used car salesman. He made a beeline for Jadine.

Cecil walked across his small yard, Jadine at his elbow. "Park's owner doesn't like people just coming in here, barreling through. You're supposed to sign in at the front."

Cecil's eyes were red-rimmed. Had he been crying for Zora? Worrying about her? I had even more bad news for him, for all of them.

Griff stomped into Cecil's space. "Anything to get me out of here, right? So you can turn on the charm, pretend to be a kind old uncle? Get my friend involved in your craziness?"

"Can the two of you not—" I didn't even know what I wanted to ask them not to do. Didn't matter. Both of them held out their hands to shut me up. It was between them. None of my business.

Cecil stood his ground. "Griffin, never fear leaving my niece with me." His smile had all the warmth of a snake's eyes. "She's my family. My blood. I always keep my *family* safe."

Understanding flashed through me, followed by an ugly guilt. Cecil had not protected Griff's father because he hadn't been family.

Griff's face darkened as Cecil's meaning soaked in. He turned to me, mouth silently opening and closing. Finally he shook himself and said, "Watch yourself with these people. I'll go sign in."

Griff walked stiffly back to the SUV, got inside, started it, and sat staring straight ahead. Mysti tugged on Brad's arm. He tried to shake her off, but she gave him a harder yank than I'd ever seen. The two of them got back into the SUV, and Griff drove them away, leaving me there with Cecil and Jadine.

Finn and Dillon came out of the RV, both with wet, bloodshot eyes. Dillon hiked Zander up on one hip. The little boy kicked to be let down, but she held him tight.

"We gotta have a serious talk." I spoke to Cecil, but Finn and Dillon were the ones who really needed to know what the Coachman wanted with Zora.

Cecil took one look at my face and jerked as though he'd seen a booger or a haint. He had a lifetime reading people and must have seen the bad news on my face.

"It's about Zora, ain't it?" Dillon's voice broke. Finn tried to take Zander from her. She slapped him away and turned her blue eyes on me, so terrified they'd gone cold and lifeless as stone. Her words came out guttural. "Tell me. Now."

So I did. I told her Griff's theory about Zora being the one the Coachman planned to be reborn through and how he planned to use me and Lazarus Root to do it. I couldn't quite bring myself to tell them what would happen to Zora, but I think they saw the horror on my face. It was enough.

Dillon let out an animal howl, shoved Zander at Finn, and ran over to Cecil's gas grill. She reared back and kicked the thing. The grill, mostly metal, fell over with a massive clatter. It had to hurt, but Dillon just reared back for another kick. Finn passed Zander, who'd started to whimper, to Jadine. The poor kid popped his thumb in his mouth and watched his mother's tantrum with wide eyes.

Finn pulled Dillon off the grill. She threw her head back and screamed, her whole body tensing with effort.

A couple approached holding hands, and as they came closer, I saw it was Kenny and Anita. They stopped to watch Dillon's grief.

Cecil stepped forward. "This is a family matter. Leave us alone."

"We got a right to observe." Kenny planted his feet in a wide stance. "We's a part of this community too."

Dillon let out another howl, and Cecil glanced between our unwelcome guests and his mourning kinfolk. I motioned at Cecil to go help Dillon and stood between our intruders and the awful scene.

Anita let out an ugly snort that sounded like a baboon trying to pass a dry turd. "Oh, you Miss Badass now?"

I stepped toward them, each step deliberate and slow. I gathered the mantle as I came. The energy coming off the trees seeped into me, and the wind picked up, ruffling my hair.

I stopped a foot from Kenny and Anita. "Do you want to find out what I am?" I pulled hard on the mantle. Thunder grumbled in the sky, and lightning flashed.

Kenny and Anita backed away. They didn't turn their backs until they were a good ten feet from me. I didn't blame them. I scared me sometimes too. I had to wonder just what I was capable of if I ever integrated the mantle completely. The thought left goose bumps on my arms.

Cecil turned away from Dillon long enough to give me a respectful nod.

Dillon ran at me, tears rolling down her face one after the other. "You can't fix it?"

I backed away from her. Those fists looked like they'd hurt. "If the Coachman doesn't get me, he can't be reborn in Zora's body."

"But why does he need you, specifically?" The question

came from Jadine. I thought it was a damn good one. Other than the weird connect I felt every time I got around Zora, I saw no reason for the Coachman not to get another psychic medium to help him. I sure wasn't the only one in the world and not even close to the most skilled one.

Cecil sat hunched over the table, shaking his head. "Peri Jean holds the center of our family's power. She and Zora share blood." His gaze snapped to mine, and for just a second, I could almost read his command for secrecy about the connection I felt to Zora. Strange. I never even discussed it with him. "She's the perfect conduit for the Coachman to use to get into Zora."

"So all we have to do is keep Peri Jean away from the Coachman." Finn led Dillon to a picnic table, forced her to sit down, and got Zander for her.

"I don't know that it'll be so easy." I told them the rest, about the effort to poison me and presented the idea the Coachman had people helping him.

"He won't quit." Cecil went to sit at the picnic table with the others. Jadine followed and motioned me to join them.

"So this whole thing's a done deal?" Dillon's voice rose to a scream. "Bullshit!"

"Maybe not." I took out my cellphone and showed Cecil the picture of Samantha. "She knew more about the Coachman than she told you." Still suspicious that Cecil had omitted part of the story, I watched him carefully.

Cecil slumped. He dropped his head and heaved out a deep sigh. "We're going to have to contact Samantha to find out what she knew."

His show of disappointment could have been an act or not. I didn't have the skill to pick up anything other than disappointment and dread. I didn't understand. Didn't Cecil share the same connection to the dead? What was his problem? "Let's do it. What are we waiting for? The way to kill the Coachman might be with her."

Cecil wagged his head. "After I had my big heart attack, I lost most of my ability to call spirits." He closed his eyes and shook his head. "Besides that, Samantha's never allowed contact before now. I've tried many times."

I bet she'd do it for me. A smile spread over my face, and a feeling I wasn't too familiar with made me sit up a little straighter. "Let me show you what I can do, *Papaw*." This was the first time I'd used the nickname Cecil had requested.

His eyes widened, and he slung an arm over my shoulders. "Show me."

Griff's SUV eased to a stop in front of the RV. He got out and stood with his arms crossed over his chest. Mysti and Brad flanked him. Together they approached us.

Before Griff could speak, I stood. "Papaw, I'd like you to meet my friends and roommates. This is Mysti Whitebyrd and Brad Whitebyrd. And you know Griffin Reed. They've saved my ass more times than I can count." I hoped my meaning came through. These people meant something to me. They were my family, maybe not by blood but by chance and choice. I wanted them in my life. Griff shot me a grateful smile.

Cecil stepped toward Mysti, smiling. "I know of Mysti Whitebyrd. Her reputation as a powerful witch precedes her." He stuck out his hand. Mysti shook it, a flush darkening her cheekbones. Cecil let go of Mysti and frowned at the RV. "That's not going to be big enough for all of us. Let's go use the rec room." He led the way across the park, Jadine on his arm.

11

A GLOOMY TWILIGHT, the kind where the dark deepened until the shadows swallowed any natural light, hung in the sky. Lights on tall creosote-coated poles blinked on and glowed weakly. The humid chill worked its way through my thin clothes. My toes felt like frozen fish sticks in my boots.

Brad maneuvered his way through the group until he walked next to Jadine. He leaned close and spoke to her. She giggled.

I glanced at Mysti. She watched the exchange with a vague smile on her face. No matter. I'd tell Brad to leave Jadine alone later. She didn't need his bullshit. Brad considered himself a lady-killer. He went out with a lot of women, but I'd bet it was because he made such a nuisance of himself, they only agreed so he'd go away.

"We don't need to be at a séance, do we?" Dillon marched alongside me, Zander riding her hip. The kid looked at me and popped his thumb in his mouth. Dillon reached over and took it out without missing a beat. "The dead don't communicate with us."

Cecil shook his head. "What did I tell you after we met Peri Jean? The day we met her for breakfast. What did I tell you that day?" Cecil's voice took on the cadence of a parent speaking to a not particularly bright child. "Do you remember?"

"That she's the center of our family's power." Dillon recited the words, no meaning behind them. She was in good company. The term puzzled and sort of scared me.

"Center of our family's power." I said the words slowly. "You've said that about me several times now, and all I know is that it's Priscilla Herrera's mantle. I have no idea why it's so important. Why should it mean anything to Dillon?" The sound of my voice shocked me. I hadn't intended to speak aloud, and I certainly hadn't meant to say as much as I did.

Why not? asked a querulous inner voice. *They're talking about me. If they're mad because I ask, they can kick me out. Get Zora back themselves.* The force behind the force startled me. It sounded like Memaw on those days nobody messed with her.

Cecil slowed to walk beside me. "Well, I only know what Aunt Fern said when I asked her why she was willing to teach you witchcraft. She said you hold the power to bring us together..."

Something heavy crashed to the ground. A woman screamed, loud and long. The sound of metal rending drowned her out. The crashes came closer and closer, shaking the ground.

"What is that?" My voice trembled right along with the rest of my body.

"I—I don't know." Cecil's voice trembled too. "Finn, get your family into the rec room. Lock the door and stay there." He gave Jadine a light push. "Go with them." Cecil hurried in the direction of the noise.

Something groaned. A loud snap cut the night, and the lights fluttered and went dark. Cecil disappeared into the darkness.

"Wait," I hissed. I hurried along behind him until I clipped my thigh on a picnic table. "Damn it all to hell." I changed course and ran over a lawn chair. I sprawled on the ground, hitting my elbow on a patch of concrete.

"Peri Jean?" Griff called from nearby.

"Griff?" I yelled. "Where are you?" He'd know what to do.

"Just stay where you are." He had to shout to be heard over the din. "We're coming."

A stiff, icy wind picked up. Aluminum cans and other light items rattled as they took flight.

"What is happening?" a woman cried.

Another crash came out of the darkness. I stumbled toward the noise. A hard, familiar hand gripped my arm, and a huge hand covered my mouth.

"Stay still," Wade Hill whispered in my ear. He yanked me against his chest and clamped an unyielding arm over my middle. I relaxed into his bulk, and he took his hand off my mouth.

"How did you find me?" His ability to locate me, no matter where I was both unnerved and flattered me.

"Same way I always do." His chest rose and fell against my back. "I'd have been here last night, but King was unhappy about me cutting out of town. Then, once I got down here, my signals got all crossed. I went to Griff and Mysti's, and nobody was home."

"How'd you find their house?" Talking to Wade made it easier to ignore the chaos around me. People ran past crying and screaming. Wade backed us up until he leaned against a tree.

"You sent me directions in one of your emails." I heard the smile in his voice.

"Which you never answered." I wiggled in Wade's arms, wanting to face him, and he locked his arm where I couldn't move.

"You need to move on. Emailing me isn't going to help." The finality hung heavy in Wade's voice. Arguing the point would only piss him off. He didn't want me. That was that. It was foolish for me to keep hanging on.

"Cecil Paul Gregson, son of Iris, grandson of Samantha." A gravelly voice echoed through the camp. "Come speak to me at the campfire."

I tried to pull away from Wade to go help Cecil. He might not be perfect, but I thought he needed me.

"Cecil Paul Gregson," the voice grated again, ringing through the trees and around the RVs like it was on a loud-speaker system, making me jump. "Come talk to me, or I'll kill everyone here."

Several screams met the demand.

"It's the Coachman." I struggled with Wade.

"That the booger you got yourself in trouble with?" His arm felt heavy as concrete over me.

I pulled at it. "I want to hear what it says to him. I need to."

He heaved a sigh but put one arm around me and walked me in the same direction everyone seemed to be going. We passed a pickup truck bent neatly in half and a golf cart torn to pieces. The roof had been ripped off one of the pavilions, the aluminum siding curled like the lid of a sardine can.

We ended up at the fire pit where the ghostly carriage took Zora. The fire roared again, flames licking so high they seemed to go into the heavens. Wade held me back at the edge of the clearing.

"Watch from here," he whispered.

Cecil stepped into the clearing, the flickering light of the fire creating shadows on his face, giving it a skeletal, spectral appearance. He glanced around and said, "I'm Cecil Paul Gregson, leader of Sanctuary. To whom am I speaking?"

"Your grandmother knew me," the awful voice chuckled. "Are you ready to deal for the little girl?"

"State your terms." Cecil sat down heavily on one of the logs.

Something rustled in the bushes on the other side of the campfire. The fire's light fell on a dimly outlined form. It stepped out of the woods, features coming into focus as it approached. I recognized the ascot first. Then the blazing fire lit the Coachman's almost handsome, but too mean, face. "Your grandmother stole something from me,

Cecil Paul Gregson. If you want the little girl back, you'll give me both what was stolen and Peri Jean Mace." The ground vibrated with the thunder of his voice.

"Tell me where she is, and I'll bring her to you," someone, I thought Kenny, called out.

The fire grew bigger, spitting and roaring. The Coachman stepped out from behind it, all shadows in the flickering light. "She stands by the far tree, a healer at her back."

Wide-eyed faces turned to regard me, many filling with contempt. Feeling more like I was back in Gaslight City than I had for months, I pressed my back against Wade's chest. He clasped one arm over my waist. He wouldn't let go, I knew, but he also couldn't win a fight against the Coachman. Matter can't kick spirit's ass.

"And if I refuse?" Cecil held his voice steadier than I'd have been able to manage. He sat calmly on the log, his ankles crossed, as though this was a board meeting or a civil negotiation.

"See what I've already done?" The Coachman belched out a grinding glass chuckle. "If you don't give me what I want, I'll destroy all of you, take what I want anyway, and keep the child."

A trio of three shadows approached the pit, Dillon in the lead, Finn plucking at her shirt. She slapped him away. Jadine stopped several feet back, Zander in her arms. Dillon turned to stare at me, her face lost in undulating shadow.

"And if I give you what you want?" Cecil still sat calmly, frowning at the fire.

"You can forget this ever happened." The Coachman stuck one hand in the fire, pulled out a ball of it, and tossed it into the crowd. People screamed and leapt out of the way.

Cecil sat on the log, still except for the slight rise and fall of his thin shoulders. His face, reflected in the firelight, wore a sheen of sweat despite the cool night.

"I say we do it." Kenny walked to the edge of the campfire. "That woman is trouble."

A murmur of agreement rippled through the assembled group. My stomach dropped, and sweat prickled on my scalp. These people, the ones I spent months chasing down, really would give me over to a monster. And, in doing so, they'd doom Zora. Had they not believed what I told them about the Coachman needing me to complete his rebirth into Zora?

Dillon approached the Coachman and stared at him the same way she'd stared at the waitress in that breakfast joint. "Give my Zora back. Now."

Wade drew in a deep breath at Dillon's show of bravery, stupidity, and impulsiveness.

The Coachman laughed. He grabbed handful of fire and lobbed it at Dillon. She stumbled out of the way, but it caught her jeans somehow. They began to smoke. Finn wrestled her to the ground and rolled her.

She scrambled away from him and went right back to the edge of the fire, glancing at me every so often. So she did remember. She knew the Coachman wouldn't trade her child for me, that he was lying as bad guys are apt to do.

Danielle walked to the edge of the blaze, smoothing down her caftan. She touched Dillon's arm. "Sugar, he's not going to give Zora back unless we trade the other girl for her. Now I know she's your cousin, but don't you want your child more?"

Dillon whipped her head back and forth, her anger burning almost as bright as the fire.

"You're all being stupid. We're talking about the safety of the group." Kenny walked to the edge of the fire to stand next to Danielle.

Dillon exploded. She grabbed Kenny by the shoulders and pushed him at the Coachman. "He's lying, you stupid sack of shit." The words tore out of her, each one punctuated by a hysterical breath. "We give him Peri Jean, and it's all done. He has to sacrifice Peri Jean, to take her last blood, so he can be born again. And he's going to kill my sweet Zora in the process. Papaw, you know this." She ran to stand beside Cecil.

He sighed and stood, putting one arm around Dillon. "I do, honey, but I'd hoped we could get through this without him knowing we know." Cecil faced the Coachman. "No deal. You'll never have Peri Jean. You'll never complete your resurrection. Now give the child back, and we won't retaliate."

The Coachman shook. At first, I thought it was anger. But then he reared back and faced the sky. "Make me the fire, Darkness."

The Coachman grew more and more transparent until nothing was left of him. He stepped into the fire and disappeared into the orange and blue flames. A roar came from within the flames, and the fire exploded outward, throwing burning logs and flaming debris everywhere.

Shrill cries of pain and fear filled the night. The Coachman, now a thing made of coals, stepped out of the fire, a halo of heat wavering around him.

"There is no refusal." The rough voice echoed throughout the camp. "I'll simply kill you all and take her anyway."

"We're not giving in to you," Dillon shouted, spittle arcing from her lips. "I won't help you kill my baby. You give Zora back. Now." She ran at the Coachman, but Finn grabbed her around the waist. She doubled over, weeping.

"You don't have a choice, little mind controller." The Coachman's voice thundered through the camp. "It's either that woman and your child or everyone here."

Dillon's sobs competed with the roaring fire. Nobody else made a peep.

Kenny stepped forward again, eyes wide and nostrils flaring. He raised one shaking hand. "All right, folks. We've got a choice to make here. We give up two to save the rest of Sanctuary."

His wife, Anita, came to stand next to him. "You all know the right thing to do."

Dillon wrenched out of Finn's grasp, leapt on Anita and began to pound her, arms swinging wildly.

I tried to move forward. Wade held me against his chest. I pulled at one thick arm. His strength far outmatched mine. I wouldn't go anywhere unless he allowed it.

"I think I know something to do." Wade's whisper was hot on my ear.

I turned to face him, too aware of the way his body felt against mine. I gasped. His face bore the marks of a fight. He had a deep cut under one eye.

"W-w-what?" I gestured at his face, unable to get the words out.

"I told you King was pissed at me for cutting out." His gaze cut away from mine, and he reached into his jacket. I stared stupidly at the vial in his hand. He held it closer to my face. "Holy water. It'll get rid of him."

"Forever?" I stared into Wade's face, hoping.

He shook his head. "Maybe long enough to make a plan. It'll take him a while to work up the juice to come back."

I grabbed the vial and took off. Five feet from the monster, heat rolled off it, ruffling my hair and fluttering my eyelashes. The skin on my face tightened and dried. I could go no closer.

The Coachman held out one shapeless, firey hand. "You know this is the best thing."

"Maybe." I struggled to get the vial's cap off using only my thumb.

"No," Dillon wailed. "Don't go. He's gonna kill my Zora. Please don't." Her shout dissolved into grunts and squeals as she tried to get away from whoever held her back.

Cecil appeared next to me and gripped my wrist. "Absolutely not."

"Uncle Cecil, there's no other way." I called on the memory of every soap opera I'd ever seen for just the right amount of drama and martyrdom. My thumb finally got the vial's cap rolling. It came off and fell to the ground. I prayed to the goddess of luck that the Coachman hadn't seen it.

Running footsteps came from behind me. I knew without looking it was Wade. It was time. I flung the contents of my vial of holy water on the Coachman.

He screamed, the sound of two trains colliding, shaking the earth and trees. My ears hurt, and I clapped my hands over them. Cecil grabbed my arm and began dragging me away. Wade slung the contents of his vial on the Coachman. The smell of burning garlic gagged me. The Coachman flickered. One piece of him broke off and floated away. He flashed back into existence, again wearing his old fashioned clothes. His face was set in a snarl.

"This is not over." He pointed one finger at me. It turned to mist. The fog worked its way up his arm, disappearing him a little at a time. "You decide what's more important—one woman and one little girl or the lives of all these people." Piece by piece, the Coachman broke up, each pinpoint of light going a different direction. "You cannot run or hide. I will find you." The Coachman had faded down to one point of light. It shot away from us and went into the sky, glowing until it faded from sight.

Kenny rushed over to us. "What is wrong with you? The safety of Sanctuary as a whole is your priority. Not your special favorites." He gave Cecil a hard shove.

Cecil staggered backward. I caught him by the arm and spun on Kenny. "Try it with me. I'll shove ten pounds of shit down your throat faster than you can say 'gimme more.'"

Kenny's mouth fell open, and he doubled up his fist. "Don't you talk to me that way, you anemic little whore."

I let go of Cecil and closed the space between Kenny and me. "Save it for pillow talk with your sister." I tipped my head at Danielle. So what if the words made an enemy out of her. She'd been willing to give Zora and me to the Coachman.

Kenny grabbed a handful of my shirt and reared back his fist. Wade pushed himself between us and leaned into Kenny's face.

"You wanna fight?" He grabbed both of Kenny's arms where the other man couldn't back away from him. "Or do you just save it for women who weigh a hundred pounds less than you?" Wade shoved Kenny. The other man sprawled on the ground. He lay there, lip curled, glaring first at Wade, then at me. Wade shoved me at Cecil, who gripped my arm and pulled me next to him.

"My niece and I will fix this." Cecil fell into a coughing fit at the last word. I held onto his arm and stared out at the crowd.

"My uncle's right. We are going to keep all of you safe." The words came out before I had time to think them over.

One man lingered as though he might want to say something, but someone smarter dragged him away. Nearby, a generator began blatting, and the camp lights came back on.

"What are we going to do?" I spoke into Cecil's ear. "He's coming back."

"We're going with our original plan. We're having a séance." Cecil coughed into his hand. "Samantha killed it before. She'll tell us how to do it again."

"Good grief," Wade muttered. He slung his arm over my shoulders. We followed Cecil to the rec room we'd set out for a lifetime ago.

12

THE REC ROOM turned out to be several rooms in a huge metal building. A small room with wall plugs and tables where people could plug in laptops or charge cellphones sat to the right of the entry hall. Across from it, a room with long benches and a podium up front might have served as a meeting room or a makeshift chapel.

Cecil led us right into the main room. Vending machines selling soft drinks and calorie-laden snacks lined the walls. Cheap tables were scattered around the room. Old board games, their worn cardboard boxes leaning precariously, were stacked on a long, narrow table in the corner.

Dillon went straight over there, sat down, and stared into space, rocking. Zander struggled until she let him down. He baby-walked to a wooden trunk, pushed it open, and pulled out several threadbare toys.

"Finn, move some of these tables out of the way." Cecil went to sit in a metal folding chair.

Finn began working. After a second, Griff, Brad, and Wade helped him. Jadine led us to a closet where we found emergency candles and a black tablecloth. Jadine gave us specific instructions for setting up for the séance. Once we had the candles set up, she removed a lighter from her pocket and lit each one, her slim hand going right to the candle as though she could see it.

I watched, feeling a combination of shame and awe. Jadine mastered her disability admirably. My ability was a gift, not something like what Jadine dealt with every day. I had a lesson to learn from her. She must have felt me watching her because she smiled at me. "We call what I do a séance too, even though I'm really just dream-walking into possible futures and distant pasts."

"She's a big money-maker." Finn pushed chairs around the table, seeming to need the movement, the busy work, the same way I did. "Part of it's because she's so pretty, I think."

Cecil sat down at the table. "Are we ready to begin, people?"

"So how are we doing this?" Griff approached the table, arms crossed over his chest, staying as far from Cecil as possible.

Cecil thought things over. "Let's just try this with Mysti, Peri Jean, Jadine, and me."

"Why only you four?" Griff put his hand on the back of one of the chairs.

Cecil nodded, as though he'd expected the challenge. "None of the rest of you are gifted with sight beyond the veil."

Griff made a face but moved away from the table. Brad took a chair near the séance table and clasped his hands between his knees. Wade moved off to a corner of the room, sat underneath a No Smoking sign, and lit a cigarette.

"Mr. Hill, please turn off the lights. They're to your right." Cecil ignored the cigarette and the sign. Wade stood and did what he asked.

Darkness swallowed the room for several seconds until my eyes adjusted to the candlelight.

My uncle opened his mouth and took a breath to speak but then closed it again. A lifetime of knowledge moved behind his dark eyes. "My grandmother ended her life angry at all of us. Her judgment wasn't what it once had been, and we sold the house she owned near here. Samantha was forced to live in Mama and Daddy's caravan. That's what we called them back then, caravans not RVs. Samantha went downhill fast after that." He took Jadine's hand on top of the table and gave it a squeeze. "After Samantha's death, some of her things were missing. Fern and Mama both wanted them. Mama ordered me to contact Samantha's spirit for information. It went bad. Samantha made it clear she wanted nothing to do with any of us." Cecil spoke directly to me. "I have no idea how this is going to go."

I nodded my understanding.

"I want to call a circle." Mysti looked to Cecil for permission. He nodded.

I began gathering the extra emergency candles to make the four compass points to represent the four elements.

Mysti put her hand on my arm to stop me. "Just a basic circle. Samantha's your ancestor, and this is what you're made to do. I just want to discourage interference." I nodded and set the candles back down.

She got up and dug through her bag until she found a container of sea salt. She walked slowly around our séance table until she closed the circle. With a nod, she indicated I should join her. We stood with our arms out, palms facing the ceiling. I imagined a hole in the crown of my head and the brightest of light streaming from the heavens into me, lighting me all over. A hum worked its way through my body and warmed my cold toes. Mysti nodded at me, and we spoke together.

"To the god and the goddess, we ask for blessings within this space. We ask for protection in crossing the veil between this world and the next." The hum of Mysti's and my energy grew within. The circle went up like a sheet of invisible lightning. The hair on the back of my neck stood straight with its static pull. Mysti nodded. "So mote it be," we said together.

We sat back down at the table. Cecil stared at me as though seeing me for the first time. Jadine had a half smile on her face. She had liked the ritual.

"And so we begin," I said and called the spirit world through my black opal. The mantle whipped inside me like a torn sail. Now that I knew it hadn't absorbed properly, I worried every time I felt the power moving on its own. But right now I needed it and would just have to make the best of it.

"Uncle Cecil? Papaw? Do you want to call your grandmother?" Maybe she'd forgiven him by now. Their connection in life was more likely to entice her to visit than the call of a stranger. I could force her, but I'd save that for a last resort.

"I flat-lined during surgery for my heart. I haven't been able to call a spirit since." He watched me across the table, something dangerously close to excitement, dancing behind his dark eyes.

"Why don't I lend you the power?" I held my hand across the table, fingers splayed.

Cecil watched my hand, curiosity, then worry, moving across his face. He took my hand and nodded. I closed my eyes and found the thread of magic deep inside me. It vibrated, hot with promise. I closed my will on it and pushed it through the black opal. The stone heated in response, burning my chest. The power arced down my arm and into Cecil's hand. He jerked and sat up straight.

My uncle took several deep breaths and then spoke, his soft voice raised to a baritone thunder. "Samantha Jeanette Herrera, I call to your spirit. I beg forgiveness for the indignity of your final days and request the honor of your presence this night."

We waited. The candles flickered, the guttering flame hissing. The coldness of spirit spread throughout the room and seeped into my skin. Whispers filled my head. Mysti's grip tightened on mine, signaling she heard them, too. I waited for Samantha to make herself known. Instead the room faded. Samantha wouldn't grace us with her presence after all. She was going to show us a vision.

The four of us fade into being, still holding hands, in an overgrown field overlooking Camilla Plantation. The house, heyday come and gone, is now a leaning wreck. A heavy, ugly pall hangs over the house. In another situation, I'd have gone a hundred miles out of my way to avoid it. And nobody could pay me enough money to go inside.

The noise of a horse's hoofs filters through the trees. A huge mule with two riders, a male and a female on its back, climbs the rutted and potholed driveway and stops in front of the house.

The woman, petite with short, black, finger-waved hair climbs down. I recognize the young version of Samantha from Tyler's research. She hitches up her high-waisted black pants, obviously not cut for a woman's figure, and tightens the belt. I almost ooh over her boots. The boots are cream colored with a dark brown toe cap and heel cap and have a chunky high heel. Samantha brushes some dirt off her white button-down shirt.

"See there? You've already gotten my shirt dirty." The man, his round moon of a face set in distaste, climbs off the mule. He pushes back his black hair and shoves a Humphrey Bogart hat over it. He adjusts his high-waisted pants. "I told you not to wear my clothes."

I've only seen Samuel in a couple of visions, and he'd been a boy in both, but I know him anyway.

Samantha bitch-faces him until he glances away from her. In only a few seconds, he faces her again.

"This is not our fight." He smooths down his tie. The contrasting color on the geometric pattern matches his shirt. "Lakeworth said we'd cut out before tonight's show. Just leave this craziness behind."

"You listen to me, Sam." Samantha points her index finger

at her brother the way Memaw used to do when she'd had about enough. It must be a family tic. "I saw little Billy get into that carriage in the middle of the night and knew I should have stopped him. His ghost showed me what that thing inside that house did to him. Little Billy was one of us. It's our fight now too."

"Do you want your baby girl growing up motherless?" Samuel purses his lips at his sister. "You got no husband to raise her. She'd be stuck with me."

"Don't you understand? What happened to Billy could have happened to my Iris." Samantha whirls away from her brother and marches toward the crumbling steps. Samuel hurries to catch up to her.

"See her courage? And she wasn't even as powerful as you are." The voice comes from behind us. Jadine lets out a little scream, and I nearly leap out of my skin, shoulders ratcheting up to my earlobes. I turn. Priscilla Herrera has her hands on the hips of her old-fashioned dress. "Go on. Follow them."

Samuel and Samantha climb the steps of the crumbling mansion and push open the door. Both recoil. Cecil, Mysti, Jadine, and I, hands locked to avoid losing each other, float along behind them, there and not there.

"You see? He's making sacrifices to the dark ones." Samuel's face wrinkles in distaste. "We can't interfere."

"We can if we have more power." Samantha gives her brother a hard shove into the house. "And today, I do."

Brother and sister walk through a house strewn with bones and the rotting corpses of animals. From somewhere upstairs comes the sound of a woman's hysterical laughter. It ends with a loud crash. After a few seconds of silence, the laughter starts *again. Samuel and Samantha ignored it all, eyes straight ahead, and walk until they reach a closed door.*

"This is the one," Samuel says. "I feel his magic in there. Now, Sister, are you sure?"

"I have to do something. Momma would have." Samantha takes a fabric-wrapped object, tied with a black ribbon, out of her pocket. Samuel kicks open the door.

"We've come to end you," he yells into the gloom.

"In here," comes the Coachman's horrible voice.

Samuel and Samantha creep into the room. It had once been a study, but all the books are gone, the bookshelves filled with skulls, some animal, some human.

"You've chosen foolishly, little witch." The voice emanates from a dark corner of the room, and a match flares to light up a handsome face alight with the deepest evil. The Coachman's lips curl into an ugly, perverse smile. "You could have ridden out of town. I'd have let you go, Samantha Jeanette Herrera."

Samuel's head whips to stare at his sister. His mouth drops open, and he tries to pull his hand from hers. She holds him fast. "Let me go. He's already got you. Had I known, I'd have never come." He tries again to yank his hand away from his sister. But she's the boss. He doesn't stand a chance. Samantha turns away from her brother and back to confront the Coachman.

"And how long before you followed? You're nothing but a disease." Samantha's voice sounds calmer than mine would have. My fear would have awoken my temper, made me shout.

The Coachman laughs, his baritone so rich and pretty it seems it should have been in a fancy ballroom somewhere and not in this stinking old wreck of a house.

Samuel gives up trying to get away from his sister and

closes his eyes, his lips moving. Samantha does the same. The candles lighting the room flare bright and then die back down.

"Is that all the two of you can do?" The Coachman rises from the corner and tosses away a gnawed bone still half covered in bloody meat. His long fingernails curl into jagged hooks, filthy and bloodstained around the cuticles. "At least it'll be quick. Come closer, pretty ones." His voice echoes, and his eyes go black and brighten with otherworldly light. Samantha and Samuel stare glassy-eyed at the Coachman, mesmerized by his voice "Come on," the Coachman croons. "I won't bite." He chuckles.

Now his voice isn't so scary. It's like music, the most hypnotic sound I've ever heard. Samantha rises a few feet off the floor and begins to float toward the Coachman. He smiles and holds out his arms.

She's hypnotized. My mind races for a solution. Samantha gets closer each second I waste thinking. I run forward and grab at the back of her shirt. Cold spreads through my body at our contact. I gasp at the intensity of it. Samantha's head whips around, eyes wide with surprise. She takes a deep breath, as one just awaking, and blinks. Samuel jerks into awareness and pulls his sister away from danger.

"Let's just go," he says, his voice tight with panic. "We can still leave."

The Coachman's laugh thunders through the house. The door to the study slams shut. Samuel runs to one of the windows, lifts a foot, and kicks at it. The impact sends him sprawling backward but makes nary a mark on the window.

Breathless panic beats at my chest, as though I stand in this disgusting lair, just as real as Samantha and Samuel. And maybe I do. I stopped her from going to the Coachman. How did I do that?

Samantha takes the fabric-wrapped object out of her pocket, unties the bow, and lets the cloth fall to the grime-caked floor. Gold flashes in the dim candlelight.

I strain to see what she has but can only make out that it's flat and round.

"Give that to me." The man's voice throbs, persuasive and seductive.

Samantha shakes her head and throws the disk to the floor. She takes a straight razor from her other pocket and cuts her hand. Blood drips onto the disk.

"I call to the power of the dark outposts. I call to the one who walks between worlds." Samantha's elbow shoots out and jabs her brother. He winces.

Samuel reaches in his pocket and withdraws a folding knife. He opens the blade and slashes his palm. He makes a fist so blood drips to the floor. Together, they chant, "We call to the one who walks between worlds."

The disk begins to glow. Soon, its light shines brighter than the candles. I go closer. I need to see the disk. My instincts tell me this disk was how Samantha got rid of the Coachman.

The disk is about the size of a dessert saucer, with etchings on it. Before I can identify what they depict, they hump together, roll around each other, and swirl in a circle. A black dot appears at the center of the circle and widens.

A pruney, waterlogged finger hooks over the edge of the black dot and pulls it wider until the disk disappears, and a black hole opens up in the floor. Hands clasp the sides of the hole, and a white, bald head emerges.

Fear jumps inside me, once twice. I know this guy, remember him from the day I found the Mace Treasure hidden away in the dark outposts. This man isn't human, probably never has been. He's powerful and dangerous.

"Stop this now." The Coachman drops the dime store hypnotist voice. His voice squeaks like a bully facing his worst nightmare.

A man wearing a wet, black suit climbs out of the black hole where the disk used to be. He stands perched on the blackness, suit dripping. The water rolls over his waterlogged, pruney hands and patters on the floor.

The sound needles at me, drilling into my brain. I remember my last encounter with this man. Nausea burns at the back of my throat as the image of him eviscerating a man in front of me and forcing me to read his guts like tea leaves plays on loop in my head.

As if he feels my thoughts, the man in the black suit turns and bares his needle teeth at me in a smile. He sees me. Oh, holy goddess, ghost of Elvis, and unicorn king, he sees me. No, no, no. My throat closes. He takes his awful gaze off me and turns back to Samantha and Samuel.

"Samantha Jeanette Herrera and Samuel Cristobal Herrera, I have come at your request. Do you have my offering?"

Samantha holds out one hand, and the not-man approaches her. He crouches underneath her hand, awful mouth open. She squeezes and blood droplets patter around his mouth. He turns to Samuel. He closes his eyes and sways. Samantha pops him one on the arm. He straightens up and does what his sister did.

"What will you have me do?" the prune-skinned thing asks.

"This one must end. He is full of the flesh of others, ripe with power." Samantha gestures at the Coachman.

The wrinkledy-skinned monster nods. "Then it's done." The monster turns to the Coachman and licks his lips.

"You can't take me. We have a deal."

"Your body wasn't part of your immortality bargain. Only your soul." The prune-skinned thing takes squishy steps toward the desk.

"But you can't," the man behind the desk gibbers. "I only get this one body, and I was told as long as I took care of it, I could continue to use it."

"Allowing yourself to be recognized as a monster by an entire town is lazy and risky. You're not worthy of the gift bestowed on you." Pruney leans over the Coachman.

The Coachman shoots to his feet and grabs a handful of ivory tiles, each emblazoned with the mark given to him by the goat man. "Accept these. They're the souls of those I've consumed. They hold power, great power."

Pruney takes one of the runes, turning it over between his wrinkled fingers. He tosses it to Samantha. "Gather every last one of these and hide them well."

"We'll destroy them," Samantha says.

"Don't do that." The creature is fierce for the first time. "They're your only power over him. You need them to..."

"Please don't end me." The Coachman cuts Pruney off, voice trembles with sobs. "I'll do anything—"

Pruney doesn't let the Coachman finish. He leaps on the Coachman, lighting on his shoulders like an oversized, featherless buzzard.

The Coachman screams, high and hysterical. He could be a star male soprano in an out-of-tune opera. "I made a deal—"

Pruney hovers on the Coachman's shoulders, hunched and horrible. "Your bargain is forfeit. You chose to separate your soul from your body. You agreed to steal life force to continue a mortal existence in a soulless body. You lived a careless existence, and your final victim, the boy Billy, doomed you because he was under the protection of this witch."

The Coachman clawed at Pruney with both arms, yelling pleas, protests, and curses.

"Hush now. I know your true name." Pruney whispers in the man's ear. The Coachman's eyes widen, and acceptance of his fate passes over his face." Pruney's mouth opens, saliva dripping from his sharp teeth. He strikes like a snake. His teeth crunch down, cracking the skull. He makes slurping sounds as he sucks the brain out of the Coachman's skull.

My stomach tosses and heaves. Beside me, Cecil clutches his chest and sucks in air. Jadine opens her mouth to scream, but only emits a hiss. The hysteria in her eyes says she won't last much longer. Mysti, eyes wild and mouth twisting, pulls us back from the spectacle. I can't look away. Pruney lifts the headless corpse as though it weighs nothing, holds it over his head with his arms outstretched, and begins to eat the corpse from the head down. The sounds he makes are nothing I want to hear again.

Samantha races to the desk and gathers the runes into her hands. Some spill onto the floor. She turns to her brother. "Help me. We must get them all."

Samuel, lips the color of spoiled liver, helps his sister for a few minutes, the slurping and crunching sounds continuing as Pruney eats his meal. Samuel stops gathering tiles. He stares at something on the floor and picks up a diamond ring.

"Good god, brother, don't worry about something you can use in a card game. Take the tiles." Samantha barely turns from her task.

Samuel scoops the ring into his pocket. He grabs a few more handfuls of runes and staggers away.

Pruney finishes his meal and walks back to the black circle. "Samantha Jeanette Herrera, our business is concluded. Thank you for honoring your end of our bargain. I am sorry to say I cannot bestow the power of Priscilla Alafare Herrera upon you as you asked. It would kill you. Instead I offer you wisdom. Listen and heed..."

The room fades around us.

I came back to myself still lying on the rec room floor, Wade looming over me, wild eyed and yelling, "Are you okay?"

I shoved at him. "Vomit," was the only word I managed. He helped me up and hauled me to the bathroom. By the time I finished emptying my stomach, my skin flashed hot and cold, sweating pouring down my face. Wade approached me holding a damp paper towel. He pressed it to my lips and stroked my back.

———

Mysti, whose pale cheeks were the only hint of what she'd just seen, was telling the others about our ordeal when

Wade and I walked back into the larger room. I wobbled back to the séance table and fell into a chair.

"Okay?" He stooped over me. "Want a Coke?"

In Texas, all soft drinks are called Coke. Wade was offering me my choice of anything the vending machine had. I dug in my pocket for a dollar. "Something clear."

"They've got canned seltzer water." Jadine leapt from her chair and led the way to the drink machine. Wade followed. The two of them had an overly long conversation by the drink machine. Brad watched, cheeks reddening.

My cheeks got hot too. Much as I hadn't wanted Brad coming onto Jadine, I wanted Wade flirting with her even less. My panties still burned mighty hot for Wade Hill. Didn't matter he'd told me no way ever. I silently willed Bradley to get his narrow ass up and go over there. He didn't, and Wade brought me back a can of lime-flavored seltzer water. I nodded my thanks and opened it.

Cecil put one shaking hand over mine. "I've never seen anything like that. Never want to again." He removed his hand and used it to massage his chest. Was he getting ready to keel over from a heart attack? This whole thing was taking so much out of all of us.

Cecil took his hand off his chest. His shoulders straightened, and he cleared his throat. "Do we agree the tiles Samantha and her brother took are the stolen items the Coachman demanded?"

We all nodded. Brad took out his phone and approached the table. Cecil turned and raised his eyebrows. Brad showed him the picture of Jeremy, the jerk who'd stolen Tyler's map.

"This must be how the Coachman managed to come back," Cecil muttered.

"But how did that little punk know to call the Coachman?" This part kept hanging me up. None of the legends Tyler talked about mentioned the tiles.

Griff pulled out his phone and began tapping the screen. "I've been thinking about this tile since I saw the one in that picture. It seemed so familiar. Then I remembered I ran into a similar object years ago." He turned to Mysti. "Do you remember the first time you consulted with me?"

Her eyes widened. "I sure do. The Ingermann case. That camera." She spoke to the rest of us. "These people had bought an old property out in the Hill Country, the site of two separate mass killings. Their son found a camera in the attic. It had a similar mark carved on its case. Soon after, he began disappearing for hours with an invisible playmate. One day, the mother got a glimpse of him walking out the door holding the hand of this...how did she describe her?" She nodded at Griff.

"Murder fairy," Griff supplied immediately. "She hired me to investigate. The whole thing was beyond my skill set. I hired Mysti. We discovered this evil young woman—she'd been a cannibal in her human life—had somehow attached her essence to the camera. Anybody who found it was toast."

Jadine spoke up. "Would destroying the tiles destroy the Coachman?"

Mysti shrugged. "That nasty creature in the vision implied they could be used to send the Coachman away.

But I suspect the only way to destroy him would be to destroy the metal where he hid his soul." She glanced at me. "Did you say it was a watch?"

"Might've been. What did you think, Jadine?" She could, after all, see in visions. Maybe she'd noticed something I hadn't.

"Maybe. Or a pendant. It was so far away." She turned toward Wade again, smiling. My green-eyed monster growled.

Across the room, Dillon stood and brushed off her jeans. She squatted next to her son and asked him a question. Finn joined them. He and Dillon talked with their heads together for several minutes. They approached us holding hands.

Finn cleared his throat. "We'd like to know what y'all actually plan to do to get Zora back."

"So far I ain't heard nothing about saving my Zora." Dillon took her cigarettes out of her pocket and lit one. I stared until she handed me one and lit it for me.

I blew out a jet of smoke, and a sheet of nicotine comfort cloaked my emotions. "I got inside the Coachman's head after his people poisoned me. I could hear Zora."

"Poisoned?" Wade nearly yelled. I told him about my fun afternoon. His face turned gray. "That was when I nearly ran off the road."

Dillon grabbed my arm and squeezed too hard, trying to take my attention off Wade. Her hand was like ice. "You see where he had her?"

"He kicked me out too quick." I put my hand over hers. "But if I can get back in there, just for a little more time, I could maybe see where he has her." I watched her face for signs of understanding. All I saw was dull grief. "All this stuff we're talking about are ways to immobilize him."

She slowly nodded. "Y'all mentioned the disk that water monster crawled out of." She slumped in a chair next to me. "Is it just lost?"

Cecil shook his head. "I don't know. This was one of items Mama and Fern argued over after Samantha died. It never turned up."

"Maybe it's for the best." I dragged hard on my cigarette. "I'm not negotiating favors with that *thing* from the dark outposts." My one dealing with him had been quite enough for one lifetime. I couldn't fathom why Priscilla and Samantha sought him out and made bargains with him. I'd never be that desperate.

"No. Don't ask for his help." Wade pulled up a chair next to Jadine and sat in it. Brad watched, lower lip stuck out. "One of those things killed my Aunt DeeDee." Wade's aunt taught him the old ways. His stories painted her as more of a mother than his birth mother.

"For once, I agree with Wade." Mysti pulled her purse onto the table, took out a scrap of paper, and began drawing the disk we'd seen on it. She saw me watching her and shrugged. "I wanted to document it before I forgot it. It'll go in our files."

Cecil leaned across the table. "I could hardly see the thing. Mind if I look?"

Mysti handed him her drawing, and he held it close to his face, studying it.

"The family has a storage unit not far from here." Cecil pushed the drawing back at Mysti. "We'll head over there tomorrow. Might be right there in Mama's or Aunt Fern's things. Both were capable of lying about having it." Cecil yawned so hard his jaw cracked.

"Before we go home, there's one more thing I'd like to do." Griff had never sounded so unsure.

"What's that?" Cecil managed to keep his expression neutral.

"Peri Jean said she found the remnants of a spell in an old schoolhouse. We'd like to examine it." Griff crossed his arms over his chest again and gripped his sides as though he had to hold on for dear life just to confer with Cecil.

"Of course." Cecil hid another yawn behind his hand. "What is it you're looking for?"

"I'd like to scan the spell." Mysti gave Cecil a sweet smile. She didn't even look like someone who could make an abusive man impotent with a few herbs and a powerful incantation. But she could.

"Ahh, yes. Peri Jean mentioned your talent for detecting magical signatures." Cecil yawned again and shook his head in apology. He reached for a bottle of unopened water on the table and knocked it over. Mysti grabbed it before it rolled off the table, twisted the top off, and handed it to him.

Dillon watched us talking, a blank look on her face. "What's the use in that? What if they turn you all into toads?"

Griff laughed when she said toads. "I have a theory the Coachman needs those people to summon him, at least right now when he's weak and without another source of power. Without those peoples' power…" He trailed off with a shrug. "Now if he could gain control of Peri Jean, he'd have his own power source. We couldn't stop him then."

Cecil stood, hiding another yawn behind his hand. "Kids, I just can't go any more. I'm going to bed. Do whatever you need to get Zora back to us. You have the use of the entire property. Jadine, honey?"

She stood and took Cecil's arm. Wade got out of his chair so hurriedly he had to grab it to keep it from turning over. "Mr. Gregg? Cecil? Could I escort you and Jadine back to your RV?"

Cecil motioned with his free arm for Wade to come along. My entire body flamed as I watched Wade hurry ahead to hold the door open for them.

Brad leapt out of his chair, features set in more determination than I'd ever seen from him. "I'm going too," he announced to Mysti.

Finn gathered our empty cans and bottles. When he got to me, he leaned and whispered in my ear, "Don't worry. The big guy's heart belongs to you. He just can't admit it yet."

My face heated, and I turned away from my well-meaning but nosy cousin. No wonder Dillon threatened to make him go naked. Nobody had any privacy around him.

Dillon began corralling Zander. His eyelids drooped, but he kicked and screamed when she pulled him away from the toys. She stared into his face. "Stop crying." To my amazement, he did and lay his head on his mother's shoulder.

Griff smiled at Mysti and me. "Guess it's just us, huh?"

I could have punched Wade right in the gonads. He'd climbed to the highest ranking of douchecanoe in my estimation.

13

WE TROMPED through the park holding flashlights. At the trailhead, I shone my flashlight on the sign, looking for the one marked Blessed Union Schoolhouse.

Wade buzzed up to us in the golf cart. "Cecil suggested we use this."

I glared at Wade. He stared back, mouth open in puzzlement. I wanted to tell him not to bother with giving me a ride, that I'd just walk to the damn schoolhouse. Even if it broke both my feet and pulled out all my hair. Then I remembered what Finn said about Wade not being able to admit his feelings for me. What if he never did?

"You want a ride or not?" Indignation, which would blossom into anger soon, laced Wade's voice.

I climbed into the back of the golf cart without speaking. Griff, eyebrows raised, climbed in next to Wade.

"Take the trail to the left," I said without turning around.

"Jadine gave me a map," Wade returned.

I fumed all the way to the Blessed Union schoolhouse. We all climbed out of the golf cart. Wade stopped at the historical marker to read it. "'The schoolhouse was the only building to survive when arson destroyed the African-American settlement of Blessed Union.'" Another, smaller sign read, *Upkeep provided by Crossroads Full Gospel Church.*

Mysti tried the door. It swung open with a tired groan.

"Wait a minute. I'll go first." Wade pushed around me, but Mysti ignored him and went inside.

"Damn hippy witch," he grumbled.

We shone our flashlights around the empty room. The desks were pushed to the room's perimeter, as they had been when I found the place. We took a few more steps inside. Mysti stopped again. She held an arm out to keep me from going farther and pointed at a mess surrounded by a bunch of tracks on the floor.

"Yeah, that's what I saw last night." I felt like a silly kid with her arm across my chest.

"No. This is fresh." Mysti sniffed. "Smell it?"

I sniffed once, twice. "No."

Wade inhaled noisily and shook his head. Griff shrugged.

"If the three of you didn't smoke like some weird breed of tobacco dragon, you'd be able to smell incense." Oh, boy. Mysti the teacher had come out to play. School was in session.

She led us over to what looked like melted licorice and burned mushrooms.

Mysti put her hands on her knees and bent at the waist. "The black stuff is candle wax. Here's the incense."

She tapped at one of the things I thought were mushrooms, and it fell apart. Ash. She lifted her finger and sniffed it. "High quality incense too." She took her seer crystal out of her purse. "Just had a feeling I might need this." She winked at me. I held my light on it. The smoke inside had started to swirl. I definitely wanted one of these. She glanced around. "Looking for the circle. If we can get inside it, we can see more."

I shined my flashlight on the floor.

Wade rubbed his hands on his arms. "This ain't no good. At all. Something bad was done here." He walked around looking for the circle. Finally he turned to Mysti. "I've heard of people who summon without a circle. Usually it's people summoning things they ought to leave alone. They think summoning with a circle is a sign of mistrust to whatever they're calling. They don't realize it leaves them wide open for the entity to control them, terrorize them..." He caught Mysti and I watching him with interest and stopped. "Like I said, something bad got my Aunt Deedee. She summoned it without a circle. Thought she had the power to control it. It rode her to death." Wade leaned over and ran one finger over the unfinished floor. "This is blood. These people are in way over their heads."

I made a face at the black candle wax. "Why I am I not feeling the residual magic?"

"Maybe whoever did this magic took whatever they used to do the calling, a sigil or maybe a mojo bag, with them." Wade knelt on the ground and ran his fingers over the candle wax.

"Why take it with them?" My newness to magic meant I never quit running up on stuff I didn't know.

"They probably use the same one every time they call the Coachman. I would." Wade shrugged. "Make a good one, and you can use it several times."

"It'll only take me a few minutes to scan this." Mysti glanced at Wade. "But I need you not to react to what you see here. In Peri Jean's parlance, I don't need your shit."

"Is there a way I can help?" Wade might have enjoyed ribbing Mysti, but he knew when to keep his mouth shut.

"Actually, yes. Peri Jean told me about viewing Jadine's dream-walking vision of the Coachman making himself immortal. I'd like to see if she can view this spell with me." She glanced at me. "You up for it?"

Fear clenched my guts, a sure sign I needed to at least try. I managed one word. "Y-yes."

"If something goes wrong..." She shrugged at Wade.

"I'll do what I can to break y'all out." He gave me a hard pat on the back. "You can do it."

I considered wiping a booger in his thick, black beard but didn't quite have the brass.

Mysti took my hand and made me kneel with her in the remnants of the spell. She put the seer crystal right on top of the pile of black wax, leaned her head back, and went into her trance. She got bright, and her fingers lengthened again.

My black opal heated. Her magic seeped through her hand and into mine. My vision blacked out. Chanting echoed, too garbled to understand. I sank deeper and deeper until I again smelled wet stone.

Please, please, let it work. The voice trembles, but I still recognize it as the Coachman's. His thoughts are mine. He's been trapped in this dank hell for almost a century, isolated and cold with no form or body. The day the boy, Jeremy, found the bone rune changed everything. Now he might actually escape this place.

Chanting reverberates in the small enclosure, all through the Coachman's spirit. The garbled words, if they work, mean freedom from this prison. His hope soars.

The words increase in volume. Magic, heavy and powerful, creeps into the darkness and lends it a tiny glimmer of light. It is working. All the effort will finally pay off.

The Coachman rises from the depths and passes through a fire, which feels no hotter than warmth radiating from a heater, and stares upon a circle of blurred faces. All young, all but one, and she'll be disposed of when her purpose is served.

They drop to their knees. "Lord of Babylon," they chant.

"Only one thing left," says an almost familiar voice. I strain to place it, but the Coachman's thoughts in mine are too much.

"No, no. Please. I thought y'all said the dog would be enough." The male voice, a young one, rises in hysteria. His blurred form is forced to his knees. Silver flashes and blood arcs over the fire. The figure slumps.

Someone holds up the tile with the symbol on it, and the Coachman moves into it, happy for the first time in many years.

The vision faded. I glanced at Wade to see his reaction. His eyes showed white around the almost black irises but he let nothing else show. Mysti slumped forward, breathing hard, the glow around her fading. I waited for her to tell me how to help.

"Just give me a second," she said between gasps. Griff dug in her bag and handed her one of her tamarind remedies. She ate it and regained some of her composure. She spoke first to me. "That voice. Could you place it?"

I shook my head. "His thoughts, the Coachman's, overpowered everything else." She nodded and tucked the seer crystal back into her bag.

I tried to stand and nearly fell down. Two visions in one night had sapped my energy. I needed sleep and maybe a leftover doughnut. Wade caught my arm with one hand and helped Mysti stand with the other.

"You think the guy they killed was Jeremy?" I stepped away from Wade. The silly way he'd acted around Jadine still chapped my ass.

"Wait a minute." Griff held up both hands. "Nobody but the two of you knows what you're talking about." When we said nothing, his jaw tightened. "It's not fair. I want to know what happened."

We filled Griff in on everything we saw. He led the way out of the schoolhouse when we got to the part where they'd murdered someone. He started talking as soon as we got back out into the cold. "I'm sure the murder victim was Jeremy. The Coachman probably promised them all their wildest dreams. Getting rid of one heir to the throne makes the pot even bigger."

"You heard a familiar voice?" Wade walked back to the golf cart, zipping his jacket.

Mysti and I both nodded. She spoke. "And I sensed the magical signature. It's something I've felt in camp."

"So there's a rat in Cecil's cellar." Wade's brow

furrowed. He glanced at Griff. Usually Griff couldn't wait to hear details. But now he stood at the tree line staring into the field where the Coachman had pretended to be Chase.

He turned to us. "I've got a gut feeling about that field."

"That's where the Coachman attacked me last night." I walked to stand at the tree line with him.

"I've just got a feeling about it." Without another word, Griff plunged through the thick stand of trees and stepped into the field. He turned back to us, brow creased into a frown, and he rubbed one temple. He shook his head. "The fillings in my teeth hurt." He tugged at his shirt collar. "I'm hot, burning up." Griff tried to laugh, but he gagged. The retch turned into a volley of coughs that doubled Griff over.

Mysti ran to him, holding both hands out. I followed and stood at his other side. She held on tight to Griff's arm. "Did you stop at one of those roadside taco stands again?"

Griff didn't answer and sat down hard on the ground. Sweat rolled down his face, and he shivered. He coughed into his hand and ended up dry heaving. "Do either of you smell smoke?"

Mysti and I exchanged a glance. Her normally placid brown eyes had gone hard with fear.

"I don't smell smoke, honey." Mysti's gentle voice trembled. She glanced at Wade. He grunted but came forward willingly enough.

"Gonna touch you," he said to Griff. "See if I can figure out what's wrong."

Griff didn't answer and continued shivering. Wade put

his hand on Griff's back, frowned, and put it on the top of his head.

"You're not sick, bro." Wade squatted down beside Griff and stared into his face. He put his hand on Griff's stomach and shook his head. "This never happened to you before? Like in the presence of a ghost? Or maybe something else you saw?"

Griff shook his head, and a bead of sweat rolled down his face. "I c-c-c-can't stay here." He doubled over coughing again. This time I did smell smoke, but it came from the Griff's direction and nowhere else. I opened my second sight and could see smoke rising from his body.

"We need to get him out of here," I said to nobody in particular.

Wade grabbed Griff and pulled the other man's arm over his shoulder. He stood, and Griff rose with him. He dragged Griff out of the clearing. Five steps out of the clearing, Griff straightened and took a deep breath. He let go of Wade and stood on his own.

"What the hell was that? Felt like an elephant sitting on my lungs." He took another deep breath as though to make sure he could. A giggle bubbled out of him. "I can breathe," he yelled. He ran back into the clearing.

"Griffin, no!" Mysti hurried after him.

I rolled my eyes and followed without much hope for a good ending.

As soon as Griff crossed into the clearing, he doubled over coughing again. This time, he shook with the effort. His face darkened and spittle flew from his lips. Mysti went to stand beside him and pointed the way we'd come. Wade hurried to his side.

"Don't help him this time," she snapped at Wade.

Griff staggered out of the clearing. Again, his symptoms disappeared as soon as we left it. We rode the golf cart back to the RV park. The lights were out in most of the RVs, including Cecil's motor home. Jadine and Brad sat at a picnic table in front of Cecil's motor home talking. Brad saw us, said something to Jadine and rose. She held out one hand. He grabbed it and kissed it. *Ick. Ick. Ick.* Wade glared at Brad as he approached us.

"Ready to go home?" Brad grinned ear to ear.

I got out of the cart and approached him. "I need to talk to Cecil about...a new development." I kept my voice low in case the traitor was listening.

"He went straight to bed. Can't you hear him snoring?" Brad pointed at the motor home's metal side. Sure enough, the sound of Cecil's exhausted snores filtered through.

"You're seeing him tomorrow." Wade climbed out of the golf cart. "Tell him then."

We staggered toward the SUV, Griff leaning heavily on Mysti. I felt like I'd fought a million wars and lost them all.

"Staying in a motel?" Griff spoke to Wade.

Wade shook his head, still glaring at Brad.

"Come back to the house." Griff opened the SUV's door.

Wade stared at Brad a few more seconds. "'Preciate it, man."

Brad scooted in the SUV and shut the door. I thought I heard him lock it.

Wade gestured toward his bike and grinned. "Want a ride?"

"And freeze to death? Pass." I got into the SUV and left him standing there. Then I saw Jadine still sitting at the picnic table and immediately regretted it. I leaned my head on the window. When would I ever learn?

———

I DIDN'T REALIZE how tired I was until we walked into Mysti and Griff's nice home, and the hot blast of central heat warmed my cold skin. I stood underneath the vent soaking up the dry heat. Mysti stopped next to me, probably wanting to talk.

Brad pushed around us and raced up the stairs, already tapping on his cellphone. Griff brushed past without speaking, went into his office, and shut the door. Mysti and I raised our eyebrows at each other.

"Is he okay?" Griff's coughing fit had me worried. The way it disappeared as soon as he got out of the clearing made me think he was the victim of more than seasonal allergies.

The roar of Wade's motorcycle carried through the walls as he piloted it down Griff's short street, soft at first but then loud enough to rattle the pictures on the wall as he pulled into the garage. The sound cut off abruptly. Mysti walked to the garage door and opened it a crack.

"You know Griff doesn't like to lose control. He'll go in there and research until he has an idea what happened to him." Mysti stopped speaking when Wade came to the garage door and waited to be invited inside. She smiled and motioned him to come in. We walked from the kitchen into the living room.

Wade immediately stripped off his coat and many shirts and draped them over the back of the couch until he wore nothing but a black ribbed sleeveless T-shirt. I watched in a languid haze. Feeling someone's gaze on me, I gave up my eye candy to find Mysti staring at me.

"Wade, you can stay in Peri Jean's room with her if you like. We're all adults here." She picked up his two denim shirts off the back of the sofa and rolled them into a ball. "I can wash these tonight. We'll dry them in the morning."

Wade folded his coat over his arm and studied me. He shook his head. "No. I'll take the couch."

The rejection sank into my bones. It wasn't like it came out of the blue. But that didn't make it hurt less. For no good reason, the memory of the way Wade's hands felt on my body, the way his lips felt on mine the one time we almost made love, came back to me. My shoulders slumped.

"You'll be cramped on the couch. We have an air mattress." Mysti tugged my arm. "We'll set it up for you."

"Mind if I get a quick shower?" Wade plucked the tight T-shirt away from his chest. "Get the road grime off?"

Mysti got Wade a towel and showed him to the upstairs guest bath Brad and I shared. We left him to his business and went out to the three-car garage. I climbed into the attic and found the box containing the air mattress and a couple of sleeping bags to zip together. We went back upstairs to the den. The sounds of Wade splashing in the shower came through the walls.

Brad opened his bedroom door and tapped to get our attention. "You think Wade's mad at me about Jadine?" He directed the question at me, so I answered.

"Fuck him if he is." I jerked the air mattress out of its carrying case. Brad's mouth fell open. Mysti came to stand next to me. She shook her head at Brad.

"But I…" His voice raised in a nails-on-chalkboard whine.

"Bradley, be a grownup for once. Please?" Mysti stood with her hands on her hips.

Brad slammed his door and turned on his TV.

I plugged in the air mattress and started inflating it while Mysti unrolled the sleeping bags. She did so with her eyes firmly fixed on the dark fabric, the poster child for discreet politeness.

"I'm sorry I suggested Wade sleeping in your room." She raised her head from her task, and her cheekbones wore slashes of deep red. Mysti liked being wrong almost as much as folks liked a sunburn on the ass. "I thought the two of you had an occasional thing. The chemistry between the two of you is almost tangible." Her lips curved into a lewd smile.

"I'd like to. He wouldn't." I rested my hand on the on/off switch for the air mattress. It was almost full but needed just a little more air. "I take that back. I think he would like to, but…" I trailed off and rolled my eyes at Mysti. "His sister read his cards in the matter of our relationship. The reading said getting involved with me would have dire consequences."

Mysti, never one to brush off a card reading, nodded, a thoughtful expression on her face. "Seems kind of silly in this day and age, doesn't it?"

I snorted and turned off the air mattress.

"I don't always agree with Wade, but I admire his determination to stick to a decision once he's made it." She must have seen something on my face for she came to stand near me, always ready to comfort and show love. "But that doesn't make it easy when you feel a certain way about somebody. I know."

"Some sick, twisted part of me thinks this is another chance for me to—you know—change his mind." My body flushed. When the only long-term boyfriend I'd had since my failed marriage dumped me, my love life had flatlined. Mostly by my own choice. A few stray pickups showed me that alley-catting no longer filled the void. The almost-sex with Wade was like a taste of real sugar after a lifetime of artificial sweetener. Nobody else could measure up.

"I understand. When I knew Griff was the one, I wouldn't let him walk away." She unrolled the sleeping bags, and I began zipping them together. We spread the now huge sleeping bag over the air mattress. "At least not without letting him know what he'd be missing."

"So, if you were me, you'd keep after him?" The idea of sneaking into the den after lights out appealed to me more than it should have.

"Maybe not so overtly." She tipped one eye into a wink. "Right now, he knows he can have you any time he wants you. If he thinks you've moved on, he'll have to rethink the situation."

This idea went against my nature. But then, chasing after Wade like an awestruck teenager went against my nature too. A smile tugged at my lips.

"Just understand one thing. That card reading wasn't a joke." She shook her finger at me. "If the two of you get together, there'll be consequences, both good ones and bad ones. Maybe more bad than good."

The shower shut off, and a board creaked on the staircase. We both jumped and spun around. Seeing nothing there, we shared a giggle. Mysti motioned me to follow her into her witch room.

"Let me show you the reason you shouldn't let that reading keep you from being with The One." She stood on her tiptoes and pulled a wide and flat plastic storage box off the highest shelf, undid the catches, and opened it.

I leaned close, eagerness beating at my chest. These boxes contained Mysti's personal items from her early life. She kept this period of her life closed off. This was the first time she'd invited me to share any of it.

"Things happen every day to change the road we're on." She took out a picture of toddler with wild light brown hair down to her waist. She wore a plaid jumper and held a ball in one chubby hand. Her smile was bright as sunlight. "I was born Melissa Jane White, but my parents got involved with a cult. That changed the path of my life." She handed me another picture.

The same little girl, now a couple of years older, wore a faded shift. Dirt smudged her arms and face. She stared at the camera the way animals in the zoo watch the people who come to see them. My emotions stung as I studied it, but I forced my face to stay neutral. Mysti was showing me the wounds that made her the woman I cherished as a friend. She was showing me her scars. When I told people about awful stuff I'd experienced, I didn't want their horror, their outrage, or even their sympathy. I just wanted understanding and acceptance.

"Then my parents tried to escape the cult. That changed the direction of my life again because I was killed in that escape." She stared at my face, searching for something I didn't know how to give her. "But someone I never knew, maybe a healer like Wade Hill, brought me back. That changed things again. I spent the rest of my childhood in foster care." She showed me another picture of herself.

This time Mysti was in her early teens, a skinny woman-child with her thick brown hair pulled back. Haunted, too-old eyes took up most of her face. An awkward buck-toothed boy slouched next to Mysti. It took me several seconds to identify him as Brad. They stood in the hallway of some industrial building.

"This picture was for my social worker's file. Brad and I had just been kicked out of another foster home. You could have said my fate was sealed then. I'd maybe finish high school, do some vocational training, hopefully marry someone who didn't abuse me." Mysti handed me one last picture. "But here's the thing. It's never over until you're dead. Before then, you always have a chance for something better."

I couldn't help smiling at the change in Mysti. This time in her late teens and already transforming into the beautiful woman I knew, she grinned ear to ear, silver bracelets stacked on each arm. Next to her stood a dark-skinned woman with a gap between her two front teeth and long, dark hair slowly fading to gray. They had their arms around each other. Brad, now a teenager stood off to the side, his face bright, more like the man I knew.

"The very next foster family we were placed with lived next door to Petunia LeBlanc. My fate changed again." She stared at the picture of herself and her magical mentor for several long moments. Tears brimmed in her eyes. She placed the picture carefully back in the box and closed it again. "You never know what life will bring your way. Keep an open mind and always be ready. Only stuff like your ability to see ghosts, Wade's ability to heal, maybe Griff's ability to grave dowse are destinies you can't escape. The rest of it is shaped by chance and circumstance."

I thought it over. My life had changed directions dozens of times, but I had never seen it as a changing of my fate. I had always seen the web of my life as a set of events, mostly negative, determined at my birth. No matter what road I took, they all ended at the same place. Had I been wrong all this time?

The last big change in my life was finding the Mace Treasure. It forced me to become something I never intended. It closed some doors of my life but opened a few new ones. My bank account was fatter than it had ever been in my life. I had shed the skin of Gaslight City, gotten out alive. Nobody knew me in this huge place of teeming activity. I really could start all over, if not here in The Woodlands, then in one of the smaller towns near here and still work for Griff.

Mysti watched me think, ever patient, ever calm. She waited until I glanced at her face again to speak. "I'll give you one warning. You and Wade may live happily ever after. If that's the end you want, I encourage you to seek it." She paused, and I nodded. "But I also encourage you to pay attention. Don't walk a lost highway. Look for the signs life throws at you. Be ready to walk a new road if life shows you that there's something, or someone, different in store."

She was right. But I had invested so much time and emotional energy into wanting Wade, into falling for him. Right then, I couldn't imagine having feelings for someone else.

Someone, probably Wade, began to rustle around in the den.

"I'm not saying make a change right now." She pulled me into a hug and led me out of her witch room. "But keep your mind open."

Wade stood next to the air mattress, shirtless and wearing his dirty jeans. His hair, unbraided, hung down his back. He winked at me.

Little gestures, like the wink, kept me guessing and drove me crazy. If he'd given up on us together, why did he bother with the little touches, the casual flirtations? Did he want me or not?

"You want to brush my hair?" He rubbed his towel over it, watching me and my reactions.

His stare burned down to the soles of my feet. I opened

my mouth to say yes. Mysti put one hand on my back. Everything she said was right, and I knew it. I had to put Wade on the spot and be willing to move on when I had the truth. That confrontation could wait for another day, a day when I felt stronger. Still didn't mean I had to let him flirt with me.

"Not tonight. It's been a rough day." I glanced at Mysti. Her tight face suggested either an intense need to fart or a herculean effort not to laugh.

Wade's shoulders dropped, and his flirty confidence fell right along with his jaw. "But I thought we could talk over what happened. Maybe get some ideas."

"Actually, Griff'll want to do that downstairs." Mysti frowned at Wade's jeans, which had a mystery stain all the way down one leg. "I can also loan you some of Griffin's sweatpants. They'll be too short and too small, but I could wash your jeans with your shirts."

"Yeah," Wade muttered and gave his hair an angry flip. "I'd appreciate that."

A few minutes later, we sat in the living room holding steaming cups of what Mysti called drinking chocolate. It wasn't as sweet as the regular stuff and a lot richer. I took cautious sips of mine, though my impulse was to greedily gulp it.

Wade came in from the backyard, tucking his cigarettes and lighter into the pocket of a pair of black sweats that came up to the middle of his calves. I patted the spot next to me on the sofa. Obviously still insulted over my rejection, he gave me a derisive snort and went to stand in front of Brad who sat in the room's one recliner. Brad held his ground almost a minute, but his tapping on his cellphone increased in urgency. Finally he bolted out of the chair and scurried to sit on a throw rug.

Wade continued to glare at the poor man. "Bradley, you try to cock block me again with a woman, and I'll beat your ass."

"Save the drama. It's time to work." Griff had his yellow legal pad in his lap and his pen poised over it to check off each item as he covered it. "I had an email from my license plate contact. We have an address on the woman who poisoned Peri Jean."

"She sure was easy to find." I wanted to beat the IQ points out of her.

"Maybe too easy. We'll check out the address tomorrow. Wade? You up for it?" Griff glanced at Wade. The larger man nodded, and Griff's pen scratched on the paper as he checked off that item. He moved his pen to another spot on the page. "Cecil mentioned going to that storage building for the disk and the runes. Are we really at a standstill without those items?"

I winced and nodded. "The only power we have over the Coachman is in those runes. The disk is…"

Griff held up his hand. "So if we destroy the runes, we destroy the Coachman?"

The impossibility of what needed to be done solidified into a headache. "Not really. We'd only destroy his connection to the living plane. Pruney—that's the monster from the séance—implied we could use the runes to send the Coachman *back where he came from*. Not destroy him. He'll still be wherever he hid his soul."

Wade shrugged. "So what? Find the runes and destroy them. The Coachman will be trapped."

A slow smile spread over Brad's face. "Not necessarily."

Wade narrowed his eyes at Brad, a silent threat to beat him senseless. Brad found enough courage to glare back. I knew I'd better stop the pissing match before it got started good, throbbing headache or not.

"Wade just got into town. Give him a chance to catch up," I squinted against the pain in my head, rubbing at the tension in the back of my neck.

Brad, grinning ear to ear, couldn't wait to deliver the right answer. "To trap the Coachman wherever he hid his soul, every single rune would have to be destroyed. He was summoned this time because Samantha and Samuel missed a rune and the wrong person found it." He smiled, eyes cutting shyly at Wade as though he'd bested the bigger, stronger man by knowing the right answer.

"Brad's right." I hated to say it. He'd float on air for days. "There's bound to be more runes, maybe scattered all over Texas. Even the entire United States."

Wade shot Brad one more mean look, then nodded at me. "I see the point. How do we use the runes to send the Coachman away?"

He had me there. I shrugged and looked at Mysti for the answer.

"If the runes serve as the Coachman's earthly essence..." Mysti's eyes moved as she thought it over. "We'll take the object of connection—the runes—and use them in the banishment ritual. We can cleanse them to break his connection then bind them to keep him from using those particular runes to return."

I knew all these techniques and felt comfortable using them. But one problem remained. "We won't get to do any of this unless we find the runes."

Mysti shrugged. "Now about the disk…" She stared at me.

"The only way I know to use it is to call that being from the dark outposts and make a deal with him." I shuddered at the thought.

"You're not doing that." Wade spoke as though he had the final say in all things Peri Jean Mace. I wanted to let him know he didn't, but I agreed. No calling Pruney.

Griff nodded and wrote on his pad. "I guess that's it. Anybody have something to add?"

"What about your coughing fit?" I asked him. Mysti whipped her head side to side, but I ignored her. "You get any ideas what caused it?"

Griff stood. "No, and it's my business." He marched into the master bedroom and slammed the door. Mysti leapt up and went after him.

I started Wade's laundry before I got ready for bed. Sleep came only sporadically. The sound of a very young child wailing—my heart knew it was Zora—cut into any peace I might have had. Right before dawn, I fell into a fitful doze. Griff's shriek of pain and fear snapped me awake.

14

I SHOVED my feet into my house shoes and charged out of my bedroom. Wade met me at my door, a pistol in one hand.

"Stay behind me." He turned his back on me.

"Get out of my way." I pushed past him and darted down the stairs.

"Dammit. What's got into you?" His footsteps thundered after me. I beat him to Griff and Mysti's door and stopped.

It was closed. I couldn't just open it. What if the scream hadn't been a bad one? I tapped on the door. Wade rolled his eyes and opened the door. Griff sat on the bed with his hands over his face, sides heaving.

Mysti came out of the attached bath with a glass of water. She pushed it at Griff. "Drink this. Might help your throat."

Griff raised his head. "I was tied up and burning in a barn or something. My lungs..." He barked out a cough, and the smell of smoke came with it, this time pungent enough for my cigarette-smutted nostrils to catch it.

"You think it's a ghost?" Mysti peered at me from Griff's side. "The spot where this started happening is where that Blessed Union community was. The one Tyler said the Coachman burned to the ground."

"Maybe, but I don't sense a ghost." I crept into the room and approached Griff. I hovered over him with my hand out. I wanted to touch his back to see if a ghost had somehow attached itself to him. With a ghost already trying to possess me, why wouldn't one try to possess Griff?

"Go ahead." He made a sour face.

I pressed my hand to his sweat damp T-shirt. Nothing came to me but the smell of fire and frying flesh. I jerked my hand away. "I don't know." Just as I spoke the words, Zora's wailing started up inside my head. I ached to go to her for reasons that made no sense. Her little voice saying, *I remember you from before,* echoed in my mind.

I grabbed Griff's ever-present pack of cigarillos off his nightstand and let myself out the French door leading from the master bedroom into the backyard. I stomped across the field stones and parked myself in a metal chair. My hand shook too bad to light one of Griff's cigarillos.

Inside my head, the wailing continued, relentless, maddening. I tried again and this time got the cigarette lit but dropped the lighter. I got on my knees, wincing at the cold ground on my bare knees, and felt around for it, incessant wailing my constant companion.

Don't you remember me? the whisper came from nowhere and everywhere. It came from inside me.

I jerked and hit my head on the underside of the chair. The lighter was right in front of me. I snatched and slammed it down on the little metal table. Too agitated to sit, I paced across the field stones, jetting smoke like a locomotive on a mission.

Do you remember? The whisper came again. My black opal sent a shock through me. I clapped my hands over my ears, even though it came from inside me, tugging at my heartstrings, bringing back memories I'd locked away in the most secure vault in my mind. It was no use. The Coachman's tampering had broken them loose.

I remembered the lines on the home pregnancy test, the feeling of fear laced with excitement. The promises I'd be a better mother than mine had. The ideas for building a better life. And, then, the day it all ended at the hands of an abusive asshole who'd tricked me until it was too late.

Were spirits reborn? My gut said yes. What's more, it said Zora and I had known each other before.

The door opened, and Griff appeared in it. He hacked several times. "I think I'd feel better if I smoked."

Mysti appeared behind him. "That's stupid."

Wade came out the main set of double French doors off the living room holding a pack of his own cigarettes. Griff hurried toward us. I handed over his cigarillos.

I waited until he lit one of his death sticks and inhaled before I spoke. "Do you know anything about reincarnation?" My breath came out in vapor.

"Just that I'm not sure if it exists." Griff sat in his metal chair with his head leaned back.

"Oh, I believe in it." Mysti joined us, belting her robe around her. She handed me mine. "Are you saying Griff's issues are because he's the reincarnation of someone who died in that fire at Blessed Union?"

"It's all I can figure." I ignored the incredulous face Griff made. "Look, I've been having some odd shit happen ever since I met Zora." I glanced at Wade. I didn't want him to hear this. Saying it hurt every inch of my heart. "I think maybe she's the reincarnation of a baby I, uh, lost when I was married to my first husband." The details were too much. I couldn't even verbalize them. Tears stung the back of my sinuses. I sniffled.

Wade hurried to my side, reached out one hand to touch me, drew it back, and backed away from me. Was that the signal I'd been looking for? The one that said never ever ever? Or was it the signal that maybe?

"So whatever psychic connection you have with Zora means I'm the reincarnation of some poor person murdered in that fire?" Griff pulled hard on his cigarillo, eyes averted from me.

I shrugged. "Maybe not." I stubbed out what was left of the stolen cigarillo in the ashtray, stood, gathering my robe around me, and went inside.

The kitchen, lit only by the pre-dawn gloom and the ambient glow of the streetlights, fit my mood. I made coffee in the dark and pulled myself onto the counter to sit while it brewed. Wade came back in the house first. I heard Mysti's fierce voice before he shut the door.

He came into the kitchen and stood in the dark. "I didn't, uh, know."

I shook my head. "I can't. Okay?"

Telling Griff about Zora and about my secret had cost me too much. The idea of discussing it with Wade, after everything between us, hurt in a way I couldn't handle right now. Neither Wade nor I spoke until Griff and Mysti came into the house. One of them snapped on the kitchen light. I winced and squinted against it.

Griff came to stand next to me. "I'm sorry for talking to you that way." He glanced at Mysti and reddened. "I'm sorry for discounting your opinion." He stood over me, for once not my boss but just a guy as scared as I was.

The coffee finished brewing. I poured Griff a cup and handed it to him. He sipped from it but wouldn't look at me.

I got my own cup of coffee and stepped away from the machine to stand nearer to Griff. "You don't have to apologize to me. I understand. This thing with Zora is both great and horrifying."

"Horrifying." He nodded. "Burning to death is a bad way to go. But I wonder if that man knew something we could use now against the Coachman."

Mysti set down her coffee. "Nothing is ever random. The universe has a design. Most of the time we wander unaware. But sometimes..." She shrugged.

"Maybe I should do a past life regression." Griff put both hands around his coffee mug, cradling it.

"That's outside my wheelhouse." Mysti glanced at Wade.

He shook his head. "Where's Bradley? Maybe he can do a past life regression." The expression on Wade's face suggested he believed no such thing.

Mysti gave him a wry smile. "Sleeping. Baby brother likes the easy life. As for past life regressions, he's never done one that I know of."

Griff rolled his eyes. "Then let's get to work on something we do know how to do." He drained his coffee cup and poured another. "We've got about an hour before full light. Let's surprise this poisoner in her home. Show her what happens when she jeopardizes my star employee."

———

THE COMING DAWN silvered the sky, and nobody except the GPS robot talked as Griff drove north on the freeway until he found the right exit. The subdivision, built sometime in the *Saturday Night Fever* era, had started its decline a few decades before we found it. The streetlights, still glowing in the morning haze, cast a grim pallor over the run down houses. We passed a house someone had started painting a too bright blue only to stop halfway up the first wall. Griff turned onto the street next to it. He drove only a few yards, stopped the SUV, and turned off the engine.

"Continue onto the route," the GPS robot narrated.

Griff tapped the screen of his cellphone to stop the directions. He started to speak but stopped and stared out the window. We all tensed for trouble. A barefoot man walked past the SUV, holding a joint to his lips as though marijuana use had already been legalized in Texas. His squinted eyes saw only the sidewalk ahead of him. We weren't on his radar. He turned the corner and kept walking. Mysti let out a nervous giggle.

"Best I can tell, our poisoner's house is right over there." Griff pointed at a house across the street we'd just left. The cockeyed green shutters needed a new coat of paint. Untrimmed shrubs covered the front window, making the place look deserted. But a newish economy sedan sat in the driveway. "The license plate matches the one on Yvonne Miller's security video."

"So we just go over there and beat on the door?" My fists itched for revenge, but the closer we got to confronting the woman, the more anxiety tightened my body. What else did she have ready to blow into my face? The next dose of poison might kill me.

"We'll go through the backyard. Give her a good shock." Wade had scooted forward on his seat and leaned between Griff and Mysti's bucket seats. "See the gate? It's not really closed."

We climbed out of the car and walked down the sidewalk, casual as clowns wearing rainbow Afro wigs, and crossed the poisoner's lawn. The winter grass crunched under my feet, and a dog next door began to bark. I quickened my steps and wrestled the backyard gate open all by myself.

The shaggy grass humped in furry, crisp bluffs of brown death that crackled as we crossed. Wade pulled black leather gloves onto his hands and pushed around us. He gripped the patio door's handle, probably getting ready to yank it off track, and froze.

"Aw, shit. Somebody done beat us here." He glanced at Griff and tipped his head at the door, open a tiny crack.

Griff joined him and slumped. "Go on in. Might as well look around." He raised one finger to Mysti and me. "Touch nothing."

Wade slid open the patio door. He led the way inside.

The patio opened into a dining room dominated by a cheap wood and glass table. Makings of a witch altar, not unlike Mysti's, crowded the table. The living room lay directly behind it, a green cloth recliner positioned so whoever sat in it could enjoy the fabulous view of the tiny backyard with its rotting privacy fence.

At first glance, the woman in the recliner appeared to be watching us, but the blood running from the corners of her squeezed shut eyes, and the bib of blood on the front of her clothes told a different story. She had died hard and ugly. Duct tape, blood covered and barely visible, bound her to the chair. We crept across the carpet as though making too much noise would disturb her eternal rest and came to stand around her.

My black opal pulsed against my chest. The Coachman's presence lingered the same way a stinky fart does in a closed-up car. My throat closed, and I took several steps backward.

Caw. Caw. Caw.

I glanced back at the patio door, and saw Orev perched on the fence.

Caw. Caw. Caw. He leaned forward with each one.

The black opal heated until I had to pull it away from my skin. Priscilla Herrera's mantle, my power now, stirred.

I had called neither the power nor the bird. They had come on their own to help. What was wrong? It hit me that we might not be alone in this house. I whispered to Orev. "Is the Coachman still here?"

Mysti jerked to attention. She closed her eyes, and I could almost see her turning herself inward, searching. Her chest rose and fell with quick, panicked breaths.

"You see him? Feel him?" She reached into her bag, probably clutching some potion to repel ghosts.

"I feel him." My voice trembled. "I can tell he killed this woman by sucking out her power, but I can't tell if he's gone."

Something moved behind the corpse's still, pallid skin. A set of ghostly eyes opened. Bright light flashed in my brain and shocked its way through the rest of my body. My knees buckled, and I went down, the rough, stale carpet scraping against my cheek.

The sunset pours through the patio door, glowing off the items assembled on the table. A group of people stand with their backs to me, blocking my view of the chair.

"Don't. Please don't. Nobody knows me. Nobody saw me." The poisoner's voice is guttural and ugly.

"A sacrifice must be made." The Coachman's voice comes from everywhere and nowhere.

"And it's going to be you." This voice of an older female, the same one I'd heard when the Coachman was summoned, pings against my memory. I stumble after the memory, but can't catch it. She continues speaking, her voice dull and emotionless. She is just stating the facts. "You're the weakest link. The only one who can lead back to the rest of us. And you've already

served your purpose." Duct tape rips, and someone slaps it into place.

Dark energy, sharp and ruthless, rumbles at the edges of the room. The Coachman forms out of the dust motes and shadows and saunters toward the woman, eyes gleaming and a sneer curving his lips. A mumble goes through the witches surrounding the recliner. The ghost passes through them. The woman bound to the chair begins to scream through her nose.

The Coachman leans over her, mouth opening and elongating. Her life force leaks from her nostrils. The Coachman sucks it up like it's an extra-rich chocolate malt. She screams through her nose, body straining in agony. The screaming goes on for a long time.

I came to with Wade slapping my cheeks, his brow pinched. He pulled me to my feet. My knees buckled again. The floor rushed up to meet me. Wade clamped one arm around my waist and pulled me upright.

"What's wrong with you?" he muttered under his breath.

"The Coachman drained my energy again. I don't know how, but he did." A cold sweat broke out on my face, and the coffee I drank on the way over gurgled in my stomach. My teeth began to chatter. "I ache all over. Like I've got the flu."

"It's like he has you wire-tapped." Mysti came closer. "Every time you interact with the spirit world, all your energy flows to him. There might be a way to block him, but we won't find it here."

The poisoner's ghost appeared in the hallway, presumably leading to the small house's bedrooms. She beckoned with one transparent arm.

"The ghost wants to show me something." Forming words took great effort, and black dots appeared at the corners of my vision. I gestured at the hallway where the ghost waited.

"The Coachman?" Mysti rapid-fired the words at me. I had to think for a second to interpret them.

"No. The poisoner." My head swam.

"If you harm Peri Jean, I'll banish you into darkness forever." Mysti spoke in a loud, clear voice. She took a vial of holy water out of her purse to back up her claim.

The ghost made no response other than to lead us deeper into the house. We walked through a master bedroom furnished with a black, metal futon bed and a thrift store chest of drawers. On top of the chest of drawers lay a keychain with *Neecie* spelled out in baby blocks. I groaned. We'd been set up from the start.

"What is it?" Mysti whispered from behind me.

"Travis's girlfriend." I pointed at the keychain. "Remember his older woman? He was impressed because she had a house?"

Mysti closed her eyes.

Neecie's ghost beckoned me from the tiny master bath. I stepped inside and tripped over the peeling linoleum. Wade grabbed my arm and stopped me from cracking my skull on the sink. The ghost gestured at a book lying on the floor next to the toilet.

"Reading material for the thinking throne." Griff reached past me and picked up the book.

The ghost's face morphed from normal, if plain, to wider eyes than any living human ever had and a mouth set into a howl of rage. She lashed out at Griff, growing bigger as she came, and knocked the book from his hand. Griff yelped and danced backward into Mysti. The two of them tangled and fell back into the master bedroom. The book bounced off the toilet. The ghost gestured for me to pick it up.

"You're lucky it didn't fall in the toilet." I bent to pick up the book. Wade reached for it. "No. Don't. She only wants me to pick it up." I reached for the book, the idea that it could be poisoned twisting around in my brain. I closed fingers around it, and the black opal heated.

His secret is in here. The whispered words snaked through my thoughts, sinuous and creepy. I held the book up to the brightening light streaming through the window. *Nineteenth Century Spiritualists of America.*

The doorbell rang. We all froze. I held my breath. It rang again, and someone pounded on the door. We crept into the living room. The doorbell rang and the door rattled as the person banged on it.

"Neecie? You in there? Coco ran away again. She was barking a few minutes ago, and now she's just gone." *Pound pound pound* on the door. "You hear me?" The sound of footsteps on concrete came through the door as she walked away. We all relaxed. Then the gate creaked open. Griff and Mysti raced for the hallway, Wade dragging me behind them. Coco's owner tapped on the patio door. We leaned against the hallway wall, all of us breathing hard. I peeked around the edge of the wall.

The woman cupped two skinny hands to the glass. "Neecie? I see you in the living room. You just asleep?"

Wade dragged me back to the master bedroom, motioning Griff and Mysti to follow with his free arm. He pointed to the room's one window. It opened onto the narrow alley between this house and the next one. Griff worked the lock, pushed the window up, and knocked the screen out. From the living room came the sound of the moronic neighbor still trying to wake up Neecie's corpse. Mysti climbed out the window and dropped onto the ground. Griff went next and reached back inside to help me out. The last thing I heard from inside the house was the sound of the patio door sliding open.

Then the screams started. "Oh my God! Neecie! You all right?"

Of course she isn't all right, you nitwit.

Wade bailed out the window and scooped me into his arms before I could resist. Griff, Mysti, and Wade high-tailed it back to the SUV, me bouncing along for the ride like a big dummy. We got into the car, and Griff sped away from the curb just as the neighbor ran out the front door, hand over her mouth. She must have finally realized Neecie would not be able to help her look for Coco.

15

———

MYSTI GAVE me one of her herbal pick-me-ups. I ate it, expecting the usual fast recovery. The overpowering sluggishness lifted. I leaned against the door and closed my eyes.

"Better?" Mysti turned in her seat to watch me.

I nodded, eyes still closed.

"This whole thing is taking its toll on you. The weaker you get, the more vulnerable you are." She glanced at Wade.

He glared at her. "That a hint for me to heal her, hippie witch?" His voice raised to a near holler. "I can't. If that spirit had taken a bite out of her, I could fix that. But not this." He took off his coat and spread it over my lap.

"Y'all cut it. I'm better now. Let's get back on the clock." I held up *Nineteenth Century Spiritualists of America*. "Neecie's ghost said the Coachman's secret is in this book."

"Good idea." Griff pulled over in the next gas station and turned off the SUV's engine. I leafed through the book, not sure what I was looking for, until I saw a familiar face. It was a picture of the Coachman. I held up the book for my friends to see.

"This is him." I turned the book back where I could see it and read aloud. "'A more interesting case of obsession is that of Oscar E. Rivera, a native of Houston, Texas. Rivera enjoyed success leading séances for the Houston rich but became obsessed with an ancient immortality rite he discovered. Rivera took on the name Lord of Babylon and left Houston in 1870 seeking an underground river he believed would connect him to the underworld. He never returned.'"

My cellphone picked that moment to blare out my stupid ringtone. Fear charged though my body and made two or three laps before I realized what the noise was and took the offending instrument out of my pocket. I answered.

"Papaw?" If Cecil liked being called Papaw, I'd do it. Having him like me felt good. "What's going on?" I felt too funky to make small talk.

"What's wrong, child? You sick?" Highway sounds drifted through Cecil's end of the call.

"Nothing a little rest won't fix." Would it? Might not. Every time this dude got into my magical dance space, he put a bigger hurt on me. Next time, I probably wouldn't have the strength to fight.

"Tell me what's going on when we meet up." Cecil paused as though I should know exactly what he meant.

I frowned. Had I agreed to meet Cecil today? I couldn't remember. My brain limped along in last place.

"The family storage unit." He said the words slowly, as though he needed to make extra sure I understood. "To find the runes Samantha stole? And maybe that disk?"

Ah, yes. Those. "Hold on just a second." I took my phone away from my ear, muted it where Cecil couldn't hear our conversation, and told Griff the gist of the call.

"I'll give you a ride." Griff barely glanced at me in the rearview.

I un-muted the conversation. "I'll be there."

Cecil rattled off an address and told me he'd be waiting on me.

The storage units sat on a busy highway one mile off I-45. As promised, Cecil waited in the parking lot next to the office. When he saw us, he started up his truck and led us through the complex. He stopped in front of a row of larger units.

I got out of the SUV and met him where he was already fumbling with a rusted padlock. Cecil stopped what he was doing and hugged me. I surprised myself by hugging him back.

"I've got another matter I want to discuss with you today. It's about Sanctuary. Don't let me forget." He stared at me, something brewing in the dark depths of his eyes. I bet I didn't want to know what he had to say.

"Then we're even. I've got a matter to discuss with you. You were already in bed by the time we finished scanning the spell."

He closed his eyes and shook his head. "I am sorry about that. If I were even twenty years younger, I think it would help. What's up?"

I told him about the familiar voice in the vision where I saw the Coachman summoned and the way Mysti recognized the magical signature as something she felt in the camp. "So you've got a traitor in your midst." I expected shock followed by outrage.

Instead, Cecil squinted and nodded, dark eyes moving back and forth. "Let's keep this between us for now. If Finn and Dillon get wind of it, they'll go on a skull-cracking crusade. The rat'll go underground."

"How are Finn and Dillon?" I took the keys from him and worked the lock.

"Devastated. Hysterical." Cecil shook his head. "They've given up hope, I think." He glanced at the SUV. His mouth thinned into an angry slash when he spotted Griff.

Somewhere, very distant, Zora began to cry. It kicked a little of the fog out of my head. "Well, I haven't given up." Wade joined us and helped me roll up the sliding door.

"Holy shit." Wade surveyed the stacks of boxes in front of us, a sick expression on his face. I felt the same way. We'd never be able to find the right box. Many of them had no more label than a year or a single name. There was no way Cecil knew what was in each one. I groaned. This would be almost as easy as slipping a haystack through the eye of a needle.

Cecil spoke to Wade. "Son, can you make a path to the back?"

Wade made a face but obeyed, moving the boxes as though they weighed nothing.

Cecil surveyed the boxes with an almost wistful

expression on his face. He caught me watching and huffed a short laugh. "My whole life's in here. Everything that has ever been important to me is packed up in this depressing little room."

I nodded. Everything I'd once had was ash. All the pictures, the mementos, even Memaw's beautiful furniture. Burned down by people who hated me for being what I was. Maybe the boxes weren't so bad.

"As you get older, your life gets smaller instead of bigger." Cecil stood very close and spoke into my ear. "You see things you love and believe in change, and you're too old to stop it happening."

Was Cecil talking about Kenny, about maybe handing over leadership of his community to him? There was no way I'd ask. Despite the time I'd spent with Cecil over the past few days, he still felt like a stranger. He probably always would. We met too late.

"Family is priority. Protect them above all else. That's the way my momma and daddy taught me." He put his arm around me. "We can't allow an outsider to lead Sanctuary."

So he was talking about Kenny. I shifted in his embrace to stare into his face but still said nothing. Whatever he saw made a smile spread on his face.

"What would you do about Kenny, Leticia's granddaughter?" he whispered. "I see something in you, something neither Finn nor Dillon have, something Jadine's too young and inexperienced to understand."

Still I said nothing. I thought I'd fight Kenny to the last breath in my body, not just to save my family's legacy but to show him I don't eat anybody's shit. Cecil's smile grew. He patted my arm and let me go. "I think you'll do."

Do for what? I opened my mouth to ask, but Wade called to us from across the room.

"Mr. Gregg? Gregson?" He shrugged. "What do you think of this?" Wade had made a narrow trail through the boxes, piling the ones he took out in front of the unit.

"I think you should call me Cecil, for one thing." Cecil headed into the forest of boxes and motioned me to follow.

I clicked on my flashlight and shined it on boxes. As the boxes grew deeper, the writing got more faded. The quality of the cardboard changed. It went from thin and flimsy to thick and sometimes waxy. At the back, Wade had widened the walkway to go to both sides of the room. He'd left behind a row of a wooden boxes.

"Let's see what's in here." Cecil pointed at the first one.

I knelt and wrestled off the top. Footsteps gritted behind me. Griff and Mysti approached, curious expressions on their faces. Inside the box lay a folded military uniform. A tarnished silver lighter, engraved with flowers, lay on top of that.

"Those are from my time in the Army." Cecil picked up the lighter and turned it over in his hand, pensiveness darkening his eyes. "I bought this in Japan." He handed it to me. "I want you to have it." Cecil took my arm again. He leaned close to speak into my ear. "I could let you turn Kenny into a toad."

I shrugged. His insistence on pulling me into Sanctuary puzzled me. I didn't think I had what it took to help him.

"What do you think?" He put his arm around me again. "Talk to me."

I searched my mind. Cecil's idea could result in a civil war of sorts if Kenny and his group decided to take over using force. My knee-jerk solution was to scare Kenny to the point he was afraid to retaliate. It sounded harsh, even in my thoughts. I didn't want to speak it aloud and fixed my gaze on the military uniform.

The black opal warmed on my chest, and the flapping of wings came from behind me. I turned but did not see Orev. The sound of flapping wings came again. This time, I recognized it as being inside my head. My hand moved on its own, plunging into the crate and rummaging around.

I drew out a single black feather. The beating of wings grew louder inside my head, and I pushed the military uniform aside to find a bag made out of an old quilt lying underneath it.

"How did Samantha's special bag get in here?" Cecil leaned on me. He was getting tired. I remembered Memaw like this after she got sick.

Just how sick was my uncle? Was he pressing me to be his right hand, and presumably assume a leadership position of Sanctuary, just because he couldn't find anybody better? My jumbled thoughts wound up for another pitch, but I cut them off. I couldn't give in to brain melt. I had to focus on the contents of this bag and worry about Cecil's intentions later.

I took one deep breath to center myself and pulled on my mantle for strength. "What was Samantha's special bag?"

"I never rightly knew. She wouldn't let any of us touch it. I just know that bag wasn't here the last time I found my Army uniform. Which was around the time Finn and Dillon got married a few years ago. Dillon wanted to wear my first wife's wedding dress." Cecil tugged at a box near his legs and finally motioned to Wade. "Son, will you get this where I can sit on it? This concrete and my wore out old feet are having a pissing match." Wade did as asked, and Cecil sat down with a grunt.

Griff watched from a safe distance, his arms crossed over his chest, the usual scowl he reserved for Cecil set on his face.

"Mr. Reed, we don't have to be enemies, you know." Cecil raised his eyebrows at Griff, who shrugged. "We both care for Peri Jean, albeit in different ways. I know you believe I did your daddy wrong, and maybe I did, but perhaps you'll give me another chance since we're stuck working together anyway."

Griff took in Cecil's speech with a frown. Mysti spoke his name, and he jumped as though startled. He turned to her. She gave him a pointed glare. He nodded at Cecil and came closer.

"I last saw the bag Peri Jean holds the day before Samantha died." Cecil reached out to finger the bag. "She was packing to go see a friend of hers in Nacogdoches. Of course, she was so senile by then she couldn't go anywhere. The next day, she died, and the bag was gone. Mama and Fern both thought the other had taken it. If Samantha had the runes and the disk at the time of her death, they would have been in here."

From the outside, the bag looked empty, but I felt many items rattling around inside it. The first one I pulled out was a black, fabric book. Written in a spidery hand were spells, not unlike the ones in the grimoire I inherited from Priscilla Herrera.

I read a few. Most were simple and light. Love spells. Good health spells. A potion to clear a sore throat and another to make chicken pox go away. A little zing worked its way into my fingertips reading the last one. It would work for me, I bet.

I held out the book for Mysti to examine. She tentatively touched it with one finger to see if it had the same spell on it as my book of shadows, which didn't like anyone other than me trying to use it. It did nothing, and she took it from me and began turning pages.

I dipped my hand into the bag and rooted around. This time, it closed on a hard object wrapped in fabric. I had a pretty durn good idea what it was before I drew it out. "It's the disk."

As I'd seen in the vision where Samantha got the Coachman killed, the disk was about the size of a tea saucer. I tried cupping it in one hand and unwrapping it with the other, but almost dropped it. Cecil leaned over and pulled the ribbon holding the fabric together. The fabric fell away. He grunted and made a face.

"It's not the same one we saw in the vision." He was right. The disk, a tarnished brass, was smooth and blank as it could be. The one Samantha used in the vision had shapes etched in the metal.

Mysti reached out for it, and Cecil handed it over. She

rolled it around in her hands. A frown creased her brow. "But it's magic." She held it out to me.

I took the disk, and my black opal jumped against my chest and heated faster than usual. I yelped. "Maybe she was getting ready to make a new one?"

Mysti shook her head. I could see the answer on her face. She didn't know how to do that and wouldn't be able to direct me.

I set the disk aside and rooted around in the bag again until I came up with a black pouch with a drawstring tie. I opened it, expecting to see the tiles Samantha and Samuel took from the Coachman's house of horrors. I recoiled. "Ugh. A bone."

Wade leaned forward and made a face, but Cecil smiled. "That's a black cat bone. Belonged to my great-uncle Samuel. He carried it gambling."

"Did it help?" The bone transferred a slight hum of magic into my fingers.

Cecil laughed. "I think not. He lost more than he won."

I reached into the bag again and came up empty. Wherever the tiles ended up, they weren't here. "That's it."

"We'll figure out something else," Mysti said. She glanced at Griff, but he was staring into the crate.

"What is that?" Griff leaned around me.

I turned to see what he meant. Just looked like some old metal junk to me.

Cecil spoke up. "It's antique spurs. As a boy, I found them near the old schoolhouse. Samantha lived nearby, and us kids explored everything. There was part of a barn, half of it had burned—" Cecil's face darkened as he realized the implications of what he'd just said. As a boy, he'd played on the ruins of Blessed Union, the African-American community who'd known the Coachman for what he was.

Griff reached past me, grabbed one of the spurs, held it upright. Now I saw where the leather strap would have gone. Griff's hand began to shake, and the shiver spread through his whole body. One tear streaked down his cheek.

"These were mine," he muttered. His eyes rolled back in his head, and he slumped to the floor. Wade rushed forward and kept him from cracking his skull.

———

I LEANED over Griff and drew in a sharp breath. His eyes had rolled up to show only whites. I grabbed his shoulders and shook him hard. "Griff! Come on. Wake up." The smell of smoke wreathed us, its stench parching my throat.

Mysti pushed me away. She went through a similar routine. She ran her hands over Griff's face. "He's burning up. Like a fever." Eyes bugged out and full of fear, she stared at me. "What do I do?" Her mouth trembled.

"I don't know," I muttered and glanced at Wade for help.

"There's nothing wrong with his body." Wade shrugged. *I can't fix it*, the shrug said.

Griff's clothes began to smoke. I had to do something. Griff always went out of his way to help me. I couldn't let him or Mysti down.

I put both hands on his chest and closed my eyes. The black opal wouldn't even give me a ping, but I forced my mind into the place where all my bad memories hid and saw the white mist of the mantle floating on top of the scar tissue. I pushed myself into the mist, down into the depths of Priscilla Herrera's mantle, now mine. The power rushed on me like liquid fire. It bathed me with light and power. I opened myself and sought Griff's mind.

Everything faded to black, and I shot down a tunnel with a light at the end. In those stories about people dying, they always talked about going into the light. What if I was killing myself and maybe Griff too? I didn't have a choice. I had to risk myself for him. What kind of friend was I if I didn't? I pushed myself toward the light, fear filling my throat, and passed into the light.

Acrid smoke shot down into my lungs. I gagged on the sour taste of it and forced open my eyes. Smoke stung them, and a tear tracked down my face. Horror at what I saw threatened my hold on sanity.

I stood in the middle of a burning village of ramshackle wood buildings. People ran every which way, wide-eyed and yelling in fear, sweat running down their dark skin. I searched for Griff. A hand curled around my upper arm. I spun to face whoever had a grip on me. A scream erupted out of my mouth before I thought better of it.

The Coachman stood in front of me, stinking of kerosene, and grinning like a madman. "You'll die here with them. Only thing is, your body won't die, and I'll have you. That way I can bleed you out, use those precious last drops to be reborn in that little girl."

A fist flew over my shoulder and slammed into the Coachman. He disappeared into dozens of tiny pieces. Wade Hill, red-faced and gasping for air winked at me. "Fuck him. Know what I mean?"

"How did you get here?" I gingerly sipped the caustic air, careful not to send myself into a coughing fit. If I started coughing, I didn't think I'd be able to stop.

"You think you're the only one who can learn new tricks?" Wade's grin closed the conversation. He wasn't going to tell me more, not even if I begged.

Flames roared around us, punctuated by the screams of people trying to escape. A familiar voice rose above them, screaming in fear.

Griff. Where is he? I took off walking toward the sound of Griff's terror, Wade following me. He pointed at a barn with boards nailed over the doors. Fire blazed from the roof.

I ran to the structure and tried pulling the boards off the door. The heat burned my hands, and I had to jerk them away. Wade tried but found he couldn't stand the pain any better than I could. We stared at each other, panting.

If what the monster said was true, Griff's spirit could die here. Mine and Wade's spirits could die here. We had to get out. Urgency beat at me, but my mind was going the speed of a ball rolling uphill. I clapped my sore hands over my face. It couldn't end like this. I dropped my hands and glanced around. An axe leaned against the wall of the shack next door. I ran over to get it.

I grabbed the axe and slammed it into the door, expecting to break it down. The axe bounded back and nearly whopped me in the face. Probably would have if Wade hadn't grabbed it.

Then it hit me. "We're spirit here."

Wade cocked his head and squinted his eyes at me. Slowly he began to nod. "We are."

I leaned my head back and focused on the thread of my raven familiar, Orev. His blood ran through my veins and mine through his. We were born of each other. I focused in on his thoughts, which were really more like impulses, and called him. It was possible he couldn't come over here, but mythology and folklore named members of the Corvidae bird family as psychopomps—guides to help souls reach the land of the dead.

Orev's familiar caw filled my mind, along with his struggle to get to me. I searched deep within my spirit for the power of the mantle and pushed it at him. The effort drained me of my energy, and I rocked on my feet, sick and dazed.

Caw. Caw. Caw. I heard his call and the rustle of his magnificent wings before I saw his blue-black plumage. He landed next to me and cocked his head to one side and then the other.

"Griff's spirit is trapped in there. If we don't get it out, he'll die here. What can I do?" It felt funny to talk to a bird as though I expected him to understand, but Orev often did.

He took a few hops toward the cabin.

"Wait, I need to go with you." I staggered after him, fatigue and heat waves wavering my vision.

The bird hopped back to me. His mind reached out to mine, and we connected. Orev and I floated inside the cabin.

A bound and gagged African-American man lay on his side. His sides hitched, struggling for oxygen, and his eyes rolled up to stare at me.

I gathered my strength. The Coachman had called me by my full name. It must have more power than a nickname. I called out with my mind. "Griffin Dewayne Reed. Come out now." I searched for and found Griff's spirit. I concentrated on it until it was so real he could have been standing right there in the flesh. "Griff. Come on. We've got to go."

"I can't leave. I can't get out." He broke off sobbing. "I'm stuck."

I had no idea what to do, so I searched Orev's mind. We hovered over the dying man's chest and pulled with all my strength. I shook with effort. My energy stores, already seriously depleted, began to dry out. I didn't have much juice left in me, and I needed enough to get home. Just when I thought I could pull no more, a wavering cloud wiggled from the man's chest.

Halfway out, it turned into Griff. He put both hands on the floor and clawed his way out of the trussed-up man. His gaze swung around the room. "You came for me."

"I had to." Orev and I said together. The sound of it was garbled and shrieky.

Griff jerked in surprise and leaned forward. "Are you dead?"

"Not yet. Come on." I moved toward the window.

"No. We can't leave him." Griff gestured at the man on the floor. Without waiting for my answer, he sank to his knees and began trying to pull off the ropes binding him. His hands passed through them.

Above us, the roof creaked, getting ready to collapse.

"Griff, this man died a lot of years ago. We have to leave him." There wasn't much time left to get out of here.

Griff turned, his face twisted in sorrow, and climbed out the window with me and Orev. By the time I got out, I couldn't do anything but crawl.

Wade hitched me up and grabbed Griff's arm. "I'll take us back." He bowed his head and clenched his fists. It looked like he was trying to fart.

Orev perched on my shoulder and cawed softly. The power building in him passed through his feet and into me, but I was too tired to help the bird. I couldn't do anything other than lean on Wade and hope for the best.

"It's the past." Wade said to me. "Just concentrate on the present."

I closed my eyes. A rush of wind pulled, sucking me down a tunnel with a light at the end, and we were back in the storage unit.

Mysti sat with her back to me, shoulders hitching with sobs, both hands on Griff's chest. He twitched under her touch and gripped one of her hands. She bowed her head and moaned.

The fatigue swept through my body like a relentless

tide, washing away my will to do anything. I slumped over on my side. Someone put their hand on my back. I didn't know who.

Thirty minutes later, we sat around Mysti and Griff's dining room table again, and I had no memory of how I got there. Music from the next-door loudmouth's stereo blasted through the glass as he threw his usual noise fest. I wanted so very badly to go over there and rub his nose in the mud. I didn't have the energy.

Griff and I had both taken Mysti's homemade herbal treatment for shock and fatigue, but the deep, dark half-moons under his eyes made him look like he'd gone a month without sleep. I suspected the potion had more than a little magic mixed in its ingredients. It didn't help much. My energy stores were too depleted.

Wade had a glass of milky looking stuff in front of him. Mysti said it would restore his psychic energy. He took occasional sips and traded insults with Mysti as though it was a wonderful day in the neighborhood. Cecil sipped at a dark drink Mysti said would be good for his heart. He hadn't said much since the storage building, but his dark eyes were pensive.

"I'm sorry for what happened today." Griff's words came out scratchy and broken, as though his body, instead of his spirit, had almost died of smoke inhalation.

"You couldn't help it." I gripped his forearm. "At least we got you back."

Griff pressed his lips together and shook his head. "The night we came back from the campground I had a nightmare, and I wouldn't tell any of you about it." He pulled his gaze off mine and stared at his hands. "I watched the Coachman dragging a dead woman into the ground. He saw me watching him and smiled. He had blood on his teeth." He bit his lip and took a few deep breaths. "Then I dreamed the Coachman sat outside this house in a carriage, waiting for someone to come out."

"The night you woke the house screaming?" Wade drank more of Mysti's elixir.

"Yes." Griff paused and seemed to gather his words. "In the second part of the dream, I could see the Coachman sitting inside the carriage, and he had changed. He was more monster than man." Griff slumped and leaned his elbows on the table.

"In your past life, you were Israel Beard, the man who tried to warn the Blessed Union community about the man in the carriage, weren't you?" I paused, and Griff nodded. "And the Coachman killed Israel and burned down Blessed Union to keep his secret. Because if Israel had been able to get anybody to listen, they'd have known the Coachman wasn't human."

Griff nodded and blew out a long breath. "When I was in that shack, I saw Israel's whole life. I know where the Coachman hid the bodies of the original family who lived in Camilla Plantation." He shivered. "And I think it's where he's keeping Zora now."

"Then we've gotta move fast," Wade said. "He saw us in that other place. I hit him, made him break up into little bits."

"A-a-are you saying you know where Finn's daughter is?" Cecil blinked rapidly.

"I hope so." Griff's gaze bored into Cecil's. The anger was still there, but he didn't seem to be as focused on it. "Because we're going to get her right now."

"I'm going too." Brad stood in the doorway, rubbing sleep out of his eyes.

16

I FOLLOWED Griff and Mysti out to the garage, prepared to get into the SUV, but Cecil tapped my shoulder. "Ride with me. Please?"

I turned to go with him, but Wade grabbed my arm and leaned to whisper in my ear. "Want me to go too?"

Cecil spoke up before I had a chance to think on it. "I'd like to speak to my niece alone."

I patted Wade's arm and followed Cecil to his truck. We climbed in and rode in silence for so long I thought maybe he'd just wanted my presence. Traffic slowed until we had to stop. Back home, something like this meant a wreck. Here? It could be as simple as a traffic stop. One person stomped his brakes, and the whole freeway could grind to a halt.

Cecil cleared his throat. "I know you have enough sense to notice I've been talking to you about Sanctuary's problems, involving you."

I nodded. It scared me, though maybe not as much as it

should have. The members of Sanctuary lived so differently than Memaw raised me. My family welcomed me with open arms, but did I really fit in? Probably not.

"I don't share Finn's talent for mind reading, but I sense your uncertainty." He turned to me. "This is where you belong. With your family. You're the center of our power. We need you, especially if we want to continue to hold the leadership of Sanctuary."

I broke in. "You keep saying that. 'Center of our family's power.' I still don't know exactly what it means."

Cecil didn't answer. Had my insistence made him angry? Too bad. I had no intention of pledging allegiance to Sanctuary without knowing every detail I could. Traffic began moving again. Cecil crept along as people on all sides of us wanted to change lanes. A few miles later, he sped up to the speed limit and drove without speaking until we were almost to Woodsy Haven RV Park. I kept my silence as well, waiting for his answer.

"I'm not completely sure what the phrase means." Cecil glanced at me out of the corner of his eye.

Great. He didn't know, but he still wanted me to make decisions based on it. I pressed my lips together.

"Samantha mentioned it a few times. Especially after she got older." He squinted at the road in front of him. "She claimed her mother, Priscilla Herrera, was the center of their family's power. Samantha said, 'Momma, Samuel, and I could do more when put our power together.'"

I tried to reason out the concept. "Bigger spells? Or more accurate results?"

"She never said." Cecil spotted Griff's SUV parked on

the roadside and began to slow. "But that's not the only reason I want you involved." He pulled the car to a stop but put his hand on my arm to keep me from jumping out. "The first thing is you have something special, a presence about you. That's what we need. But the second thing's a bit more personal." He smiled. "We like you. Jadine can't quit talking about you. And me? You remind me of Leticia when she wasn't acting like the Princess and the Pea. Finn and Dillon already liked you, but they'll owe you for life once you get Zora back. You're one of us."

"Finn and Dillon will owe me for life *if* I get Zora back," I muttered. Somewhere, way in the back of my mind, Zora started crying.

Cecil laughed. "Never, ever underestimate yourself. I see great potential in you. I just hope you'll choose to use it on us."

Griff came to stand at the back of the SUV. He didn't glare at Cecil, but he didn't smile either.

"Get on out." Cecil unlocked the doors. "I'll go back to camp. Once Finn and Dillon know what's going on, we'll probably join you." He pulled me into a hug, and I returned it. "Be careful," he whispered into my hair.

I got out of the car, and Cecil drove off.

"He's not going to help?" Griff's voice had a mean edge to it.

"He's too old, and you know it," I snapped.

Griff jumped at my rebuke and walked into the woods next to the campground with his shoulders hunched. I exchanged a glance with Mysti.

She moved close to me. "It's just going to take him

some time with Cecil. You know how childhood villains are." She clutched her coat around her and stepped into the thick trees.

I followed. "What do we do if the Coachman is in there with her?" I had to speak to her back. "He's bound to be guarding her."

"Run?" Wade grinned at me. Since I stopped acting like an infatuated puppy, he had dropped his aloof act. He smiled at me. Teased me. Tried to touch me. I ignored it all. Games like this were stupid. Why not just get down to business if you wanted each other?

We came to the field where Blessed Union used to be and stopped. Griff stood overlooking the empty field where his soul, in another incarnation, died a gruesome death.

I shrugged and moved closer to Mysti. "You hear me?"

"Griff is concentrating." She gestured at Griff, who paced the perimeter of the clearing, his hands on his hips.

"The Coachman put his victims in a root cellar." Griff spoke almost to himself. "The house was over there." He pointed. "The Blessed Union settlement was right in front of us. The root cellar was built into a hill, but where was it? I don't see a hill here."

Griff held up a finger and walked away from us, skirting the perimeter of the clearing. Wade, giving me a confused frown, followed Griff. Brad tagged behind them like a little boy trying to learn to be a man.

"Don't worry about the Coachman being there. I have a surprise for him." Mysti took quick steps through the brush, leaving me behind.

"What is it?" I called to her back. She kept walking. I stopped to stare at a pile of limbs and other debris. It looked as though someone had piled it here on purpose. Didn't make sense. Nothing else in these woods looked as though anyone was working to clear the undergrowth. Had someone, one of the Coachman's helpers, done this when they uncovered the root cellar to hide Zora? If so, the entrance to the root cellar might be hidden somewhere near here.

"Mysti?" I called. My friend turned around. "Tell Wade and Griff to come here. I think I've found something."

The two men came back, and I pointed at the trash pile. "Either somebody cleared this to get to something, or they're using it to hide something. Like maybe the root cellar?"

"But there's not a hill here." Griff squinted at the terrain.

"Not a big one, but we've been walking at a slight incline for the last several yards." I grabbed a handful of brush. Might as well see what was under it before we got too excited. Wade helped me, purposely brushing his arm against mine. I moved to the side a little to give him more room. He grunted like an angry boar.

"What's your problem?" He leaned close to my face, black gaze boring into mine.

"What's yours?" I widened my eyes and hoped it looked more innocent than smartassed.

He ground his teeth and picked up a double handful of branches and vines, tossing them away from us. We got to the bottom of the pile but found nothing. Wade kicked at the mess he'd made and turned his back to me.

"I don't think this is a steep enough hill." Griff chewed on his thumbnail.

"It wouldn't have to be steep." I walked a few feet, realized I was no longer going uphill, and changed direction. "They might have built the root cellar like a cistern, lined with bricks. It may have started out more of a safekeeping place for valuables during the Civil War than a root cellar."

Griff nodded slowly and walked in the same direction as I was. Without warning, he stopped in his tracks and sank to his knees. He dug away the leaves and pine needles and began to excavate the dirt. I squatted next to him, cold moisture soaking through the knees of my jeans, and joined Griff in digging. The smell of damp earth drifted up as a pile of dirt grew next to us. Griff stopped digging and swept dirt off something hard. I leaned in for a look.

The flat stone probably sat on the surface of the earth once, but time had covered it layer by layer. An X had been etched on the surface of the stone. Griff, without speaking, scooted about ten feet away and began the exercise again. This time Wade helped him. The two men unearthed another stone. Griff took five steps into the space between them and stopped. Then, he walked ten paces up the incline and brushed at the ground. The rest of us followed him.

Griff bent and hooked his fingers into the dirt. He dug down and nodded at Wade. "Help me pull this up." The two men grunted with effort and lifted a piece of plywood off the forest floor. Someone had glued a very convincing tapestry of leaves, branches, and pine needles to it. That was why they'd cleared the branches I found. To make this ugly thing.

For no reason, I thought again about the way the Coachman's manifestation broke into a bunch of pieces when he started to lose the fight. The idea wormed around in my brain. I tried to connect it to some other idea and couldn't. I hurried to help Wade and Griff flip over the camouflaged spot. Underneath was a very new steel door with a padlock on it. I let out a groan.

"You think that thing'll stop me?" Wade took a set of lock picks from his jacket and went to work. He sprung the lock in seconds, waved his arm at it, and smiled. "What's behind door number six-six-six?"

Mysti snickered but sobered quickly. "Peri Jean asked me earlier what we'd do if the Coachman confronted us." She withdrew her hand from her pocket and opened it to expose a bunch of nickels.

I made a face. "Even if we tried to pay him, that wouldn't be enough."

Wade took a nickel and squinted at it. "Silver repels evil spirits, ninny. Year's right. Good job, hippie witch."

Mysti somehow managed to roll her eyes and preen at Wade's compliment at the same time. "Throw the coins at him. That should break up the manifestation long enough to get Zora out of there."

"But what then?" I thought about the tantrum the Coachman pulled at the RV park, how powerful he'd been. "I mean, how do we keep him from killing us after that?"

A raven cawed from somewhere near. More of them took up the call until the forest sounded full of them.

"Orev has an idea." I tried to latch onto the animal's thoughts but got nothing more than a set of blurry images. I hoped he knew what he was doing.

"Then we're ready?" Wade put one hand on the door.

"Ready as I'll ever be." My muscles tensed, and I waited for the worst.

Wade swung open the door. I expected a haunted house squeal to come from them, but they whispered open, their silence somehow more eerie than a loud screech would have been. Blackness and the smell of damp stone greeted us. I sucked in a deep breath and took the first step inside. And nearly fell ass over shoulders down a set of steps. Wade grabbed my arm.

"Steady now." He crowded behind me, the muscles of his chest brushing against my shoulder. Raunchy thoughts warring with any good sense I had left, I ascended the short staircase, one hand out to balance myself. The wall fell away at the last step. I pulled out my cigarette lighter and thumbed the wheel. The flickering light showed me something I never wanted to see again as long as I lived.

We were in an open, brick walled room. At its center was a long table with seven corpses seated around it. The remains of rotting clothes hung from the skeletons. Four were adult sized, but the other three were clearly children. Rotting ropes bound the bodies to the chairs. Each one had a place setting before it, complete with a tarnished wine goblet.

"What did he do with them here?" Brad stepped into

the room and crept over to the table, holding his flashlight aloft. He leaned close to one of the corpses.

"Stay away from that." Mysti shone her own flashlight on Brad.

He reared away from the table, one hand over his mouth. "There's bite marks on the bone. He set them up at this table and ate their corpses."

The table had an eighth chair, pulled out and empty. Who was supposed to sit there? Zora? My chest tightened. After all this, had I failed her again? No. I couldn't deal with that.

A child's crying drilled into my consciousness. I tried to take hope but knew it could well be her ghost, lost and scared, forever looking for her mommy. The crying increased in volume. I couldn't stand it. "Zora? Sweet pea, you in here?"

Wade took my cue. "Zora, honey? I'm here to take you back to your mommy and daddy." He stepped deeper into the chamber, using his own cigarette lighter to see. "I got a niece just about your age. She loves her mommy and daddy. I bet you do too. Call out to me. I'll get you out of here."

Wade walked the perimeter of the room, fingers climbing over the brick walls, probably searching for an antechamber. He stopped and slumped. He shivered head to toe, head jittering with the force of it, and stood up straight again.

"Wade? You all right?" Griff came forward.

Wade turned back to us, eyes glowing black, full of electric, murderous midnight. That scared me more than his little dance. Wade's eyes usually glowed gentle with good humor. He moved toward us, muscles bunched, like he might grab any one of us and break us like twigs. "Thank you for bringing Peri Jean Mace right to me. I'd hoped you'd be this stupid, but there are never guarantees."

My chest tightened. I told my feet to move backward, to get away from Wade. But I couldn't do it.

Griff clambered in front of Mysti and me. "You're never going to be able to carry off this silly plan. Hand over Zora. We might consider not banishing you from this world."

Wade threw back his head and laughed. "You don't have anything to bargain with, Griffin Dewayne Reed. You'll be lucky if I wait until after you're dead to eat the flesh from your bones."

A mist I recognized as the magic the Coachman stole from me slithered along the edges of the room. It gathered at Wade's feet and rose in bands over his legs. His hands glowed.

The black opal pinged me, warning me, but I couldn't cut and run. Wouldn't. I'd come here to get Zora, and I wouldn't leave without her. I reached for my own magic. It boiled out of my center and into the black opal.

Wade's face faded, and the Coachman's smirking likeness rippled underneath his skin. The scream built in my throat. I fought against it, swallowing it down like bad medicine.

The Wade thing, teeth bared in a vicious parody of a grin, grabbed Griff's arm. Griff's back arced. His body jittered, hair standing on end.

"He's shocking him." Brad jammed his hand in his pocket, came up with a closed fist and threw it on Wade. He shook off the shower of sea salt.

Mysti and I launched ourselves at the fight. I went for Wade, slamming both hands into his chest. I channeled the mantle through my arms and pushed a jolt of magic at Wade. But I forgot something important. The Coachman knew how to steal my magic. My energy drained away as my magic flowed from me to Wade. I jerked my hands away and crumpled to a heap on the floor, head swimming.

Mysti, nickels cupped the palm of her hand, slapped her open palm on Wade's forehead, standing on tiptoe to do so. She yelled, "In the name of the Goddess, get out of him, right now."

Wade's legs went loose. He crumpled to the floor and lay still. Griff fell to one side and crab walked away from us, one arm held to his chest. Mysti went after him.

"Wade?" I crawled over to him and touched him. His chest rose and fell steadily. His eyes fluttered.

"I knew you still cared." He tried to pull me to him. I wrenched away and bolted to my feet, ignoring a wave of dizziness. Wade crawled to his feet.

"I'm sorry, y'all." He leaned against the cold bricks and wiped his hands over his face. "Griff, man, I...you know I'd never..."

Griff got to his feet, also breathing hard. "Forget it. Let's just get Zora and go." He walked around the room, knocking on walls. I listened for the sound of Zora crying. It was gone. Had the Coachman just used it to confuse and weaken me? It might have never been there at all. The Coachman was probably storing up power for his next tantrum. We needed to get out.

"Zora's not here." Frustration rolled in, high tide and ready to drown me. "Let's get out before someone really gets hurt."

Wade leaned so close to the mildewy brick wall his nose nearly touched it. His nostrils flared. "She is too here. Otherwise the Coachman would have never put on that show."

No, no, no. He's smelling for her corpse. What am I going to say to Finn and Dillon? I probably wouldn't have to worry about it for long. Dillon would tear my head off my shoulders and eat it like some weird mythological creature. The crying came back, this time closer than ever. I perked up and tried to latch onto Zora's presence.

The wall. He put me in the wall. The high, sweet voice came from inside my head. A memory whispered behind it. *I remember you from before.*

"She's in the wall." A gout of puke almost came out with the words. Zora couldn't have survived being put in the wall. If the Coachman had killed her, I'd destroy him. I'd never stop until I ground him to nothing. My throat tightened as I walked the room, waiting for Zora to make contact again.

Right here. Her whisper made my heart ache, and the tears started. I knew she wasn't mine, but in a way, she was and I had to save her. I had to, since I wasn't able to save her the last time. I clawed at the old bricks. "Hang on, baby. We're going to get you out of there."

Wade joined me. He took out his pocketknife and scraped mortar from between the bricks. He held out the knife to me. "Fresh."

Griff and Mysti stampeded to the wall. Together, we knocked the first brick loose. After that, it went pretty fast. The little girl lay curled on her side in a dugout in the wall. I backed away, dread cutting a cold path through me.

"Is she…" I couldn't make myself say it because I couldn't imagine telling Dillon and Finn that I hadn't been able to save their child, their only daughter, after all. I couldn't face the fact I'd failed this beautiful soul once again.

"No. I feel her chest moving." Wade scooped up the little girl and held her against him with one arm.

I held out one shaking hand to touch her for myself. My fingers made contact with the warm skin, and I nearly swooned with relief. "Come on. Let's go."

Something sharp pricked the skin at the back of my neck. I clapped my hand to the wound, spinning around. Nothing was there. I held up my hand to the flashlight Mysti still held. Blood stained the fingers. The Coachman had bitten me. Maybe payback for biting him.

"She'll stay like this until her body wastes away." The Coachman's voice vibrated all around us. "Peri Jean Mace, your power will be the death of her. I'll have you both. There's nothing you can do to stop me." His words ended on a shout, and a brick popped out of the wall. The little chamber where Zora had lain collapsed on itself. Another brick fell from the wall, and several more followed it.

"It's falling in." Wade grabbed me with his free hand

and dragged me toward the door, forcing me along behind his mile-long footsteps. Mysti, Griff, and Brad crowded close behind us. From my peripheral vision, I saw one entire wall collapse. Dirt salted the brick floor in a dry patter. Wade yanked me up the steps and handed me Zora. My nerves ground together at the limp way she flopped into my arms. I backed away as Wade jerked Mysti up and out. Griff came next. A rumble shook the ground and Brad began to shriek.

I ran to the opening, not sure what I thought I'd do with an unconscious child in my arms, but determined to help. Brad lay on his stomach. He'd been last, and the brick stairwell wall had collapsed and knocked him down. A combination of bricks and dirt scattered over the backs of his legs. Wade nodded to Griff, and the two men each grabbed one of Brad's outstretched arms and pulled.

"My ankle, my ankle," he screamed.

"It's either your ankle or stay down here," Wade snapped. "You're about to be under a thousand pounds of dirt. I won't be able to help you then."

Tears streaked down Brad's cheeks. My stomach did a slow flip. He was hurt. Really hurt. And it was because he'd tried to help me.

The old guilt and horror came back. Would whatever became of Brad make a new layer around my magical center, keeping me from accessing my true power? Probably. That was the problem with this spell. There was no way to stop it growing. Wade and Griff set their heels and pulled Brad out of the chamber just as it collapsed around him.

He clutched his ankle, gasping and sobbing. Wade knelt next to him and spoke in a low voice. Brad nodded and said something back. Wade motioned me over. I handed Zora's still form to Mysti, walked over, knelt next to him. We locked hands.

I let my eyes slide closed and pulled on my power. It was there, weaker from the Coachman feeding off me a few minutes earlier, but there.

Wade began to whisper his words, in that old, old cadence. He sounded like he should have been in a church, but he was in the woods trying to heal a guy he didn't even like very much right now.

"When thou wast in need, I found thee. I knew thee by thy real name, Bradley Jamison White, and I laid the hands of heaven above upon thee. By faith, I healed thy wounds. The old gods have blessed me and will bless thee. My blessing is yours." Wade's voice rose as he spoke, and he elbowed me. We repeated the verse together.

Wade's skin glowed. There was no other way to describe the bright, warm light within him. I lent my power and kept repeating the words until they were nonsense to me. Wade's body heated next to mine, and a drop of his sweat hit my arm.

The light passed into Bradley, all the way through his body, and down to his ankle. Heat emanated from him. He gripped his calf and ground his teeth together, tears squeezing from his eyes.

Wade let go of him. "It's done." He leaned closer to Brad, still shaking with the effort he'd just made. "And I'll still beat you to a pulp if you cock block me again."

I got away from them. Nausea rolled across my stomach like a coming storm. Wade's magic always did this to me. Wade jumped to his feet, staggered away and vomited in the bushes, holding onto a tree to keep him out of his own mess. My chest hitched, and the nausea passed without me having to empty my stomach. Brad got up, tentatively tested his ankle, and snorted a disbelieving laugh. I tried to smile back but couldn't quite make it.

I went to Zora and touched her still face. Mysti offered her to me. I reached to take her, and the first crack of thunder shook the sky. Lightning sizzled into the ground somewhere near.

17

THUNDER RUMBLED AGAIN, this time hard enough to shake the ground. Freezing wind cut through the trees, kicking up dead leaves. They chattered together like dry bones. A bolt of lightning hit the tree next to me, its flash so brilliant, black motes swam in my vision. I reared away from the tree and took several stumbling steps in the opposite direction. Maybe I didn't need to carry Zora.

Wade caught me before I got too far and wrapped one arm around my shoulders. I leaned into his side. No matter our relationship, I still looked to him for protection. When would I ever let him go? We stared at each other several long moments, and I turned away.

"Let's take Zora back to her parents." What had happened to Dillon and Finn anyway? I figured they'd have joined us by now. Were they lost? I took off for the trail that would lead us straight through the woods and to the RV park. The others followed.

"What are we going to do about the Coachman?" I

paced myself to walk next to Mysti. It wasn't that I didn't trust her carrying Zora. But if something happened, maybe I could help.

"That book you found at the poisoner's house. It had his name—" Another clap of thunder cut off Mysti's words.

Wind blasted through the dead trees, and rain hissed right along behind it. It hit us hard, ice cold and stinging. Wade took off his jacket and put it over Zora. We couldn't do any better for her other than walk faster, which we did. Thunder came at regular intervals now. Lightning flashed all around us. The air crackled with electricity.

Icy rain needled at my face, each drop an assault. I lowered my head and let it drum into my scalp. It didn't hurt much less. Wade stopped, and I ran into his back. Wind whipped harder than ever. Leaves rose from the ground and blew around us, sticking to our wet clothes.

"Aw shit," Wade yelled. "What *is* that?"

Wade rarely sounded scared. My fear awoke and curled into sharp hooks. Griff's scream sunk them as deep as they'd go into my nerves. I peeked out from behind Wade. My skin went even colder than it already was, and my ears began to ring. Terror wound its way through me. I'm not sure if I screamed. I couldn't think.

The first thing I saw was its eyes. Glowing black holes of madness. The rest of the monster, made of leaves and branches, stood several feet taller than Wade. The bits and pieces of the monster writhed as though they had their own life.

"Peri Jean Mace." Its voice was like ground-up leaves and mulched branches rolling together.

I forced my gaze off the thing and spoke to Mysti. "Take Zora back to her parents."

"I can't leave you." She glared at me, her hair plastered her cheeks. Her teeth began to chatter.

I tried to think of an argument, but then the leaf monster took a step. The impact shook the ground and knocked me off balance. "Run!" I yelled at Mysti.

She shoved Zora at Brad. He ran without being asked. Mysti dug in her pockets, probably looking for more silver coins. She came out with a few and threw them at the monster. A few patches of leaves fell off it, but more took their place.

Wade drew his pistol and started pulling the trigger. Mysti's coins had done more than the bullets did. The leaf monster somehow channeled the sound of the falling rain and the rumble of thunder into a roar. I clapped my hands over my ears. Wade loaded another magazine into his pistol and kept right on firing, eyes bugged out, mouth open in a scream.

The leaves moved faster, swirling in the shape of a tornado. The chittering mess came right for me. Good buddy of cowardice that I was, I ran. My shoulder clipped a tree. I hit the ground and rolled. I lay there gasping, knowing full well the cyclone of leaves waited at my back, but not sure what to do. Then the roar came again, the pain of it incredible in my ears, and it fell on me, blocking out the meager gray light.

I tumbled backward into my own psyche, past the pristine white mist of the mantle and right into the layers of scar tissue I'd built up to protect myself. The force of my screams tore my throat raw and made my eyes feel like popping out of my head. I landed in the wilds of my own bad memories, trapped and alone with the demons I'd fed and nurtured without meaning to.

I stood at the backs of dozens of people. They faced a stage festooned with red, white, and blue streamers. Dean Turgeau and I stood on the stage, holding hands and smiling, blissfully ignorant of the way the next few seconds would change both our lives.

No. I didn't want to see this again. Living through it once had cost so much. I had to get out of here. The black opal pulsed heat on my chest, almost as though it had its own heartbeat. I tried to grab onto the magic, but it skittered out of my reach.

"Thank you all for coming out tonight, and thank you for your votes," Dean drawled. "I only hope I can prove myself worthy of your confidence—" The crowd cheered.

My heart banged inside my chest. Dread of what came next made me shuffle backward. From the back of the crowd, I had a perfect view of the entire courthouse square. A lone figure skirted around the edge of the crowd, hand held stiffly to one side.

"No," I whimpered, and my voice came like it did in a dream, all soft and weak. *Please. I don't want to see this.*

The figure crept through the crowd, working through to the middle where there'd be a perfect, clear shot at me on the stage. I stood next to Dean, my grin stupid and innocent.

"Stop it," I tried to scream, but the word only echoed in my head, blunted and useless.

A murmur ran through the crowd. The shooter must have made herself known. A wide circle formed around some people in the middle. The chrome of a wheelchair, Memaw's wheelchair, winked in the bright lights.

"Stop right there." Memaw's words ended in a cough. This time, I heard her gag at the end of her coughing fit. This time, I saw her stand from her wheelchair and grab the shooter's arm. The gun went off, a blast of fire coming from the barrel, right in Memaw's face. She fell against King Tolliver, President of the Six Gun Revolutionaries, like a marionette with its strings cut. He put one hand to the back of her head, maybe trying to hold in her brains. My chest ached and the salt of unshed tears stung my eyes.

The shooter stepped away from them and pointed the gun at the stage, screamed "Die, witch!" and shot again. The dark figure ran from the scene of the crime and down the street.

King struggled out of the crowd and lurched past me, Memaw draped over his arms. I got a good look at her face, eyes wide, and a dark hole right in the middle of her forehead. Her mouth hung open.

My chest throbbed as a tide of grief bigger than I could handle surged through me. I sank to my knees and watched King carry Memaw toward the hospital. Unshed tears built a lump in my throat. I clutched at it like someone choking to death. King, his back to me, shouted for someone to help him, but nobody did. They were too busy running for their lives. A shadow fell next to mine. I turned to find my grandfather, George Mace, standing next me, his ghost solid as a real person.

"Might shoulda listened to your Memaw, hon." He lit a Kool cigarette and watched the outlaw biker carry his dead wife to the hospital. "This right here was why my wife wanted you to just ignore what you was, to pretend to be normal. She always said it would do nothing but hurt you, said her family would do nothing but corrupt you. Look how it's all turned out." He waved one muscled arm at the mayhem in front of us—me trying to save Dean on the stage, yelling at Wade to help us, him obeying, his head hung in grief. "You think all this ugliness is what she wanted for you?"

I stared at the ground and shook my head. Why did this, the only time I'd ever spoken to George Mace, have to be him rightfully chewing me out?

"Its too late for you, little darlin'." George's voice took on a familiar cadence, but I didn't understand why I recognized it. The grief took up most of my attention. "You got yourself in a mess. You could save a lot of people if you'd just give up."

My head popped up. I stared at my grandfather. Something about him had changed since he first came over to me and started talking. I stared hard at him, trying to see what it was.

"My Leticia loved you, child. Gave her life so you could live." He thumped his cigarette away. It bounced on the asphalt, a shower of red sparks rising from it. "But you did all you were supposed to do, which was find the family treasure, put that mystery to rest. Your purpose is served. Don't you want to honor your Memaw by knowing when it's time to quit?"

It hit me what was different about George. His shoes. When he first came over to me, he had on roach stomper cowboy boots. But they'd changed to a pair of lace up ankle boots. It was the Coachman in the guise of my grandfather. *Cheater.* I'd show him. I called on the mantle and got only a ping of power.

The George Mace thing took another step toward me, its creased jeans and pearl-snap cowboy shirt melting into its skin and Victorian era garb appearing in its place.

"You're nothing, Peri Jean Mace," the Coachman chanted. "Nothing but a loser and a failure. You're alone now, truly alone, and you'll die alone. But not until after I eat your power and your soul." His mouth opened wide.

I wanted to scream, but all I could do was moan in pain and fear. Then I remembered my special trick. The one the Coachman didn't like me doing. I sent my consciousness into his nasty mouth and pushed myself toward his secrets, praying I'd find the one that would rid me of him forever.

I run down the narrow, haunted corridors of the Coachman's mind, his heavy footsteps pounding behind me. The sound of Zora crying comes from somewhere near. I take a sharp turn toward it. A wooden door held shut with a padlock too ornate and pretty to be of my time blocks in my way. I grab the lock and yank on it.

"Zora in here. Come get Zora now." The little girl's high-pitched voice comes through the heavy wood, traveling along our connection.

I reach for the mantle but remember I am mired in scar tissue. What now? I am trapped. Aren't I? Zora begins to cry again. The hell I'm stuck. I gather my energy and push through the scar tissue, reaching for the mantle with all my effort. Its power meets me like an overeager puppy. It will snap the padlock. It will—

A force far stronger than anything I knew how to fight hurled me out of the Coachman's memories. I came to on the forest floor, freezing cold and unable to move. My eyes flashed open, and I sucked in a deep breath.

I had failed again, except for one thing. I knew now where the Coachman had Zora's life force. All I had to do was figure out a way to get it. Easy as learning Latin.

Wade elbowed Mysti out of the way and gathered me into his arms, squeezing so hard I thought my ribs would crack.

"I found where he's got Zora," I said into his ear.

"What's she saying?" Mysti shrieked from behind Wade. "Put her down so I can hear."

Wade put me back on the ground, and I panted for a few seconds before I spoke.

"He's got Zora's spirit behind a padlocked door in his mind. That's why she's limp. He's taken her spirit and stored it away." Each word felt like razors in my throat, and I didn't feel my magic at all. Had the Coachman taken it for good?

"Thank goodness for small favors. Maybe this little girl's parents won't kill us." Mysti held her hands up to the sky.

Then it hit me. We'd given Zora to Brad and told him to run. Camp wasn't that far away. Someone should have come to check on us by now. We ran down the trail, all of us hurting too bad to go really fast. I text messaged Dillon, still unable to understand why she and Finn hadn't come. I got no answer.

Griff, who'd been walking in front of me with his head hung, suddenly stopped. I ran into his back. We both grunted. I peeked around him and groaned.

Kenny had a long gun trained on Brad, who still held Zora in his arms. Brad trembled from head to toe, his eyes rolling wildly.

———

"You ain't coming into camp." Kenny put his finger over his rifle's trigger guard.

Wade drew his pistol and let it hang by his side. I'd watched him use up all his ammunition. All he had was a couple of empty magazines. I guess Wade figured Kenny didn't know that.

"Can't your bullshit wait?" I gestured at Zora's unconscious form. "We've got Finn and Dillon's little daughter."

"She's dead," Kenny crowed. Gladness and triumph rolled off him in waves. It pissed me off. I wanted to knock him down and jump up and down on his chest.

"She is not dead. Look at her." Mysti shook her head for emphasis. Her sane delivery contrasted so sharply with Kenny's that the situation took on a blurry sense of unreality. I rubbed my temple and shook my head, trying to rub some sense back into myself. I didn't feel any better.

"Don't matter anyway." Kenny crossed his arms and stuck out his chin. A slight tic in his eye was the only indication he might be scared of us. "The ones of us whose last name ain't some form of Gregg took a vote. The Greggs, Gregsons, whatever you want to call 'em, is done in Sanctuary. It's mine now. We throwing them out tonight."

My mouth fell open, and a zillion arguments ran through my head. "You can't—"

"You got five seconds to put down the gun." Wade interrupted me. The tone of his voice kicked my heart into overdrive. He may have sounded bored to anybody else, but I knew this tone of voice. It was the one he used before he got wild-eyed and went on a rampage. If he did that, Kenny might shoot him. Kill him. I took careful steps toward Wade. There was no way I could stop him if he lost control. He was too big for that. But I might be able to talk him out of whatever he thought he wanted to do.

"Wade, look at me." I stared at his broad back, for once scared enough not to think about his body pressed against mine, his mouth on mine. "Get away from Kenny."

Kenny raised the gun to his shoulder. Nausea gurgled in my stomach, and sour spit rolled into my mouth.

"Wade?" My voice shook.

Wade glanced back at me and winked. I shook my head at him. He grinned, and the hair stood up on the back of my neck. Wade took three fast steps, grabbed the gun, and yanked it away from Kenny. The smaller man's eyes widened until they took up most of his face. He shuffled several steps backward, hand out behind him, reaching for help that wasn't coming.

I came around Wade, adrenaline churning, and kicked Kenny in the chest. He fell on his ass in a rustle of leaves and the pops of branches breaking.

"Hey!" Kenny grabbed for me.

"Better be sure, Kenny. I'll whup your ass righteously." I had both fists up but didn't think I could win a fight against a grown man. Someone came to stand next to me, but I didn't dare take my stare off my opponent.

"You better be more sure than you've ever been in your life." Brad spoke loudly, still clutching the too-still toddler. "My brother-in-law and I will beat you until there's nothing left."

Wade advanced on Kenny. He held the rifle loose in his hands. "Get up. Start walking. Or I will kill you now."

Wade's quiet voice sent chill bumps racing up my back. When super pissed, Wade talked like this, like he was saving his energy to do maximum damage. I stared at Kenny, hoping he knew the kind of madman standing in front of him.

Kenny curled his lip. "Fuck you."

Wade's brows and mouth drew inward, his eyes expanding. He shoved the gun at me, knocking me several steps backward. I'd have gone down had Griff not righted me. Wade grabbed Kenny by the scruff of his neck and slung him. The man pitched forward several steps, tripped, and sprawled to his knees. He caught most of the fall with his hands and grunted in pain. Wade straddled him, grabbed both ears, and twisted them. The man howled.

"I will pull your ears off your head if you ever disrespect me again." The low, dangerous growl held no more reason than an animal's. I took my eyes off Wade and nudged Griff.

"We've got to get him out of here," I whispered. "Or he's going to kill Kenny."

Griff nodded, marched over to Kenny, and kicked him.

"Griffin!" Mysti screamed.

Griff ignored her. He leaned down to speak to the top of Kenny's head. "Get up and walk with us into camp. You're going to talk to Cecil about what happened here and the vote you've taken."

Wade gave Kenny's ears another good twist. "I don't know what he'd do, but I'd kill you as a traitor."

"Sanctuary ain't a safe place anymore because Cecil's too old to keep things in check, and I ain't got nowhere else to go." Kenny's voice came out all wobbly and snotty. He was crying, actually crying, after he'd pulled a gun on us. Griff kicked Kenny again, teeth bared with effort. I wanted to turn my gaze away from the ugly scene but knew I couldn't. I took a deep breath, went to the other side of Kenny, and crouched down.

"Kenny? You can't just banish people because you feel like it. You have to be civil, willing to compromise." I tried to pretend I was Mysti, to keep my voice calm and non-confrontational. "Maybe it's time for you and the Gregg family to part ways. But you gotta talk to Cecil."

Kenny turned to me and spat in my face. It stunned me so much I just sat there, the glob of saliva sliding down my cheek. All hell broke loose. Wade lifted the man by his ears. Kenny kicked and flailed, and one kick caught me in the chest. Griff yanked me out of the way and tried to pull the man away from Wade.

"Wade, look at me," Griff yelled. "Look at me now."

Wade didn't drop the man but turned his dark eyes on Griff.

"Do you want to kill this man? Do you think what he's done is punishable by death?" Griff stared unflinchingly into Wade's face, several inches shorter and many pounds lighter, but not afraid. "Is this who you are?"

Wade dropped the man on the ground in a heap. Kenny's hands went straight to his ears, moaning and feeling them for damage. I imagined they'd be big as Mickey Mouse's ears by the next day, but they were still intact. Wade stood over Griff, his face set and hard. The two men glared at each other for several seconds.

"Thanks," Wade muttered to Griff. "You're right. He's not worth it."

Griff relaxed and patted Wade's arm. Then he squatted next to the injured man, who cowered away. "Get up now and walk with us, or I'm going to turn that giant loose on you."

We started walking. The white paint on the RVs peeked through the trees as we neared the park. Someone stood at the end of the path waiting.

A woman I'd seen but not spoken to sprinted toward us. She took in the sight of Wade hauling Kenny along by one arm and seemed to relax. She spoke to me. "You Peri Jean, ain't you?"

I nodded but kept my distance. After the show with Kenny, I wasn't sure what to expect from these people.

"You gotta do something. Anita and a couple of other nut-cases is trying to kick the rest of the Greggs out of camp."

I rushed forward, worry knotting inside me. Kenny'd had a gun for us. Anita was crazier than him by a mile. What if she'd hurt Cecil? Or someone else in my family? I broke out in a run, hand clutching my aching gut and ignoring Wade's shout to wait for him.

A small crowd stood in front of Cecil's motor home, all of them shouting. I shoved my way to the front.

A man about my age held out one thick arm to block my way. "This ain't your fight, witch. You need to just leave camp."

Still fighting exhaustion from the Coachman's most recent attempt at draining me, I reached deep inside myself. The small effort rocked me. I dug deeper until I latched onto to Orev's thread. *Trouble. Danger.* The man and I had a glaring match while I waited.

The sound of wings flapping came from all around us. The caws grew louder until they surrounded us, drowning out the shouting and name-calling. The ravens landed, one by one, on the ground until their black-feathered bodies hid the fallen, drying pine needles littering the ground.

The first human scream cut through the bird noises. "It pecked me. One of these devil birds pecked me."

Wade leapt up on the picnic table, fierceness boiling in his dark eyes. "Go back to your campers. Go home now. Leave here." He shouted his words over and over.

More screams answered him as more birds took a bite of human flesh.

People left one by one, sometimes in couples, all with wide eyes, many rubbing wounds, until only Anita was left.

She held a pistol in each hand and had backed my family against Cecil's motor home. They stood in a row, Cecil, Jadine, Finn, and Dillon. Zander stood on the ground, shoved behind his parents, clinging to their legs. Tear stains streaked his chubby cheeks. The ravens stood silent now, waiting to see what had to happen next. It was my call.

Cecil's and my talk about Sanctuary rang in my ears, as did all the hints he'd dropped, all the ways he'd tried to pull me in. My family wanted me. They wanted me to help them run Sanctuary. Did I want them? I stared at their faces, stared down the fear in their eyes. No decision came.

"You can't make me leave, you damn thug," Anita screamed. "Cecil is gonna listen to our demands. Me and Kenny have tried to do this the nice way."

Something awoke inside me, something outside anger. This part of me viewed all this clinically. It didn't matter how Anita and Kenny had done things. They were outsiders, not family, and I knew what Cecil wanted done. I spun slowly until my gaze locked on Orev's. I nodded toward Anita. The birds converged on her.

She screamed, spinning around and around, trying to slap them off. Soon all I could see was flapping black wings. She dropped both pistols in her frenzy. Wade rushed in to snatch them but got right back out of the way.

Birds bit chunks out of Anita's skin. One hovered over her face, clawing at it. Anita screamed, hysterical and in pain. I watched the scene, my emotions like still water. This had to be done. Anita had to be shown what I'd tolerate. I counted to ten, my serenity horrifying me. I shouted,

"Enough." The birds flew off Anita and away. Their forms darkened the sky for a few seconds, and then they were gone.

Anita sat on her ass between the campers, sobbing and shaking, face and arms bleeding. Dillon stepped around her as though she didn't exist. "You get my baby?"

I nodded. "Bradley?" I yelled, never taking my eyes off Dillon's face, still scary calm.

Brad rushed forward with poor little Zora. He held her out to her mother.

Dillon let out a primal howl of rage and grief. She clutched her child to her chest and sobbed, falling to her knees. I wanted to help her but was too scared of her fists to do it. She'd have to get over the shock, and then we'd talk.

Jadine, using her cane, picked her way to Dillon's side. She put one hand on her shoulder and bowed her head. Dillon cried herself out in the same frank way she conducted the rest of her business. Finn and Zander ran to join her, both of them trying to get a look at Zora. Dillon hunched over her protectively. Finished, she turned to me, eyes blazing.

"What's wrong with her?" Dillon's shriek echoed over the park.

"I can fix it. I promise." I kept a safe distance from all of them. Getting hit or spit on again didn't much appeal to me.

"The Coachman's got her little spirit, doesn't he?" Cecil's voice came from several feet away. He trudged to us, his shoulders rounded, and his head down. "Got whatever makes Zora herself locked away."

I nodded. "She's in his consciousness. I saw her. She communicated with me."

Dillon stared at me through her tears, question on her face.

"It's true." The weird calm finally let go of me enough to give her an encouraging smile. "She's alive. I couldn't get her this time, but I think I can with one more chance."

Cecil came to stand next to me and hugged me to his side. "Proud of you for getting her back."

Anita, over her shock, slowly got to her feet and crept away from us. Griff met her and pointed at the picnic table where they'd sat Kenny, who still held his sore ears. Anita opened her mouth to argue but Wade came over, fist already doubled up. She sat.

"How are y'all going to get back into the Coachman and get my daughter back?" Dillon glared at first me, then Mysti.

"If we can find those runes, I've got an idea." Mysti stepped forward. "If it fails, I'll come up with another plan."

Cecil put his arm around Dillon. "I have an idea for getting the runes. We will get it settled. Now wouldn't you like to take Zora home? Get her cleaned up?"

I didn't think this would work, but Dillon clutched Zora to her and grabbed Zander's hand. "Come on, Finn." The four of them left us without a backward glance.

It hurt to watch them take her. I wanted to run after them, insinuate myself into their family, just to stay near

Zora. But feeling that was wrong. A previous incarnation of her might have been mine, but I failed her. Now she belonged to another family. She had a different life ahead of her. My job now was to make sure she got a chance at this life. No matter what it took, no matter what it cost me.

Cecil approached the picnic table. "Ms. Whitebyrd? Will you scan Kenny and Anita for the traitor's magical signature?"

The memory of Mysti's white-eyed face and long, silver-tipped fingers came back. I gulped, not eager to see it again.

Her chipper voice broke into my thoughts. "I'd be happy to. Just let me get back to the SUV and get my witch bag."

"Take the golf cart." Cecil never took his eyes off Kenny and Anita.

"What's she gonna do to us?" Kenny's eyes rolled from one member of our group to the next.

"Shut up now," Cecil whispered to Kenny.

18

WE MARCHED Anita and Kenny to their camper, a relatively new fifth-wheel. They'd set up a little patio with a roll of artificial grass and had a folding table with two chairs. The couple stopped in front of the door to their home and turned to us, faces set in pleading expressions. Anita was crying.

"What if we was to hook up our camper and drive off?" Kenny tried hard to sell his escape plan. I'd have been willing to give him a gold star for effort.

"It's too late," Cecil muttered. "Just go inside." He motioned to Wade. "Stand guard, son?"

Wade nodded and held open the door for Kenny and Anita. She went on inside, but Kenny stopped to size up Wade. Wade ignored the smaller man, shoulders back, eyes straight ahead. Kenny's chest deflated, and his shoulders curved inward. Head down, he went inside.

Mysti stopped in front of Cecil. "What you see inside this camper must stay there."

"You have my word." Cecil gave her a small bow. "And Kenny and Anita's too."

Anita began to sob. She put her hands over her face to do it, but it annoyed me. She and Kenny had caused this whole, ugly scene. We desperately needed to work on our plan to rescue Zora. Instead we were farting around with these dingleberries.

The three of us went inside. Mysti took a quick look around. "Kenny and Anita, lie on your bed, please."

Anita cried harder. Kenny, white-faced and shaking, said nothing.

"Do it now." Cecil's voice was casual. The gun in his hand wasn't.

Mysti didn't pay either of them any mind. Already standing next to the bed, she took the seer crystal out of her bag and handed me the bundle of sage. I pointed at the fire alarm. She made a face but nodded. "Ready?"

I nodded. We bowed our heads and took deep breaths. Mysti began her chant. I concentrated on the ring of her voice more than the words and focused my intent. The seer crystal awoke. Though my eyes were closed, the movement of the smoke inside stirred my magic. I concentrated on joining with the crystal's power and opened my eyes.

Mysti's eyes had gone that all-white quartz color, and her fingers elongated and went silver and sharp on the tips. Those weird orbs focused on Kenny and Anita. They both went bug-eyed with fear.

Mysti held out her hands to Anita. She raised a hand to fend Mysti off. Cecil pointed the pistol at Anita and laid the hammer down. She put her hands by her sides and squeezed her eyes shut. Mysti's freaky hands settled on her chest.

Mysti's shoulders rose and fell as a hum grew in her throat. Fear of the thing standing in front of me, worry it wasn't really Mysti but some changeling, gnawed at my concentration, begging me to get the hell out of there. But doing so would be unforgivable, a slap in the face to Mysti.

My mentor pushed me to the point of discomfort. If I complained, she ordered me to try some more. She made me think about the things I didn't want to and wouldn't let me take the easy way out. Mysti made me a better person. She demanded it and fostered it. I was sorry we hadn't met sooner. But right now, she scared me.

Mysti took her hands off Anita and put them on Kenny. His body trembled head to toe as the magic surged through him. The hum in Mysti's throat stopped, and the glow around her faded. She went back to normal. "We're done. Good news and bad news. Kenny and Anita don't have enough magic between them to even see a ghost. Neither of them is the traitor."

Cecil pressed his lips together and exhaled through his nose. "All right then." He held a hand out to Mysti and tried to smile. "Ms. Whitebyrd, you've greatly impressed me. Please send your bill through Peri Jean and know you have a place among us if you ever want it. Mr. Reed does too, although he'll never take it."

Mysti took Cecil's hand. "Thank you, Mr. Gregg. Peri Jean?" She motioned to the door.

Cecil gripped my arm. "I need my niece's help right now."

Mysti gave me one last glance and disappeared out the door.

Cecil sat down at the dining table and motioned me to sit across from him. He set the pistol on the table between us.

"You gonna kill us now?" Kenny rose from the bed. "After everything we been through together?"

Cecil stared at me several long seconds. I didn't want to watch him kill Kenny and Anita, no matter how much I hated what they'd done, so I shook my head. Sadness filled his dark eyes. He dropped them to the table. "Kenny, you've left me with few choices. I can no longer trust you after today, not to be here with me or to leave Sanctuary."

Anita sat up on the bed. "What if we can tell you who the real traitor is?"

"No." Kenny reached for Anita.

"How can you let that awful, greedy pickpocket get us killed?" Anita screamed. Her shrill voice rang in the tiny home.

"Well?" Cecil put his hand over the gun. "What would you do?"

I glanced at the door, wanting my friends so badly my insides ached. They'd know what to do. If only I could ask one of them.

"No." Cecil seemed to read my thoughts. "Only you can decide, and you must."

My heart sped up. Nausea rumbled in my stomach. "Depends on whether the information pans out, I guess."

Cecil shook his head. "You can't guess. Make a decision."

I took a deep breath and tried to clear my mind. The clutter flooding my thoughts stayed in place. "They tell us the name of the traitor. If they're telling the truth, and if I get Zora back, they get another chance." Some of the tension let go, and I slumped.

"You'll have to announce this to the group at tribunal. It'll be your responsibility to keep them in line. What's more, people will have to believe you can keep Kenny and Anita in line." Cecil watched me carefully. "Sure you wouldn't rather kill them?"

I climbed out the booth, unable to bear Cecil watching me any longer, and walked into the little bedroom. Anita and Kenny huddled together. I fixed them both with my hardest stare. "Tell me the name of the traitor."

"It's my s-s-s-s-sister." Kenny could barely get the words out. "Danielle."

My knees wobbled. Behind me, I heard Cecil get up, open the door, and mumble something to Wade. Cecil came to stand next to me at the bedside, the pistol held in his hand. Was he going to go against my decision? A bolt of anger flashed in my head.

Cecil's spoke so softly that I could barely hear him. "How long have the three of you planned to do this to my family?"

"No, no, no, you got it all wrong, m-man." Kenny waved his hands.

The door opened, and Finn walked in stony-faced. He held a pistol too. I tried to back away from the bed, but Cecil put one hand on my back to keep me in place. He turned to Finn. "Is Kenny telling the truth?"

Finn walked over and put his free hand on Kenny's head. He closed his eyes and cocked his head as though he was listening. Nothing happened. He gave Kenny a hard slap. "Remember what she said so I can see it, moron." He closed his eyes again and began to nod. "Yeah. Danielle told Kenny she'd help him take over leadership of Sanctuary. He hasn't trusted you since your last heart attack." Finn took his hand off Kenny and wiped it on his pants. "But Kenny had no idea what Danielle had planned. He's horrified and embarrassed."

Kenny scooted toward Cecil. My great-uncle's gun hand twitched, and Kenny stopped moving and put his hands up. "That was when that little gal who painted face tattoos got raped and killed by those local boys. You's in the hospital. Nobody knew what to do. I had to take charge then, and—"

Cecil interrupted with a short laugh. "And you decided you liked it?"

Kenny stared at Cecil's gun but squared his shoulders. "I saw I could do it." *And that you couldn't anymore.* Kenny didn't say the words, but they hung in the air like a ripe fart.

I glanced at Cecil. He'd stiffened, his face gone red. The gun jittered against his leg.

Sweat broke out all over my body. *Oh, no. He's pissed, and he's going to kill them right now, and I'm going to have to watch and probably help clean their brains off the wall and dispose of their bodies.*

Cecil sat on the bed, his back to Kenny and Anita. He put one shaking hand to his face. "You're right." He let out a sob, and it was the saddest, forlorn sound I think I've ever heard. "I've gotten too sick to fulfill the duties I promised I'd carry out." He turned to me, tears flooding down his cheeks. "I might have a plan to make things right. If it doesn't work out, I'll name Kenny as the new leader of Sanctuary."

Kenny's mouth fell open with a pop. His dream was within his grasp.

Finn backed toward the camper's door. "You can't do that. This is all I know. This is where I want to raise my family."

Cecil put out a hand to him. "Life goes on. No matter how broken we think we are, we keep going until we're dead. And we make it work." The old man glanced at me again, his meaning clear. I could agree to help. We could keep Sanctuary going together.

Finn, reading Cecil's mind, rushed to hover over me. "My grandmother taught me everything I know." Finn knew who he had to convince. "She was so proud of this community, of us being able to travel around and..." He trailed off.

I considered ways he might have completed his sentence. *Steal? Murder? Con people out of their worldly belongings?* My grandmother taught me everything I knew too, and it had been nothing like the lessons Finn learned.

Finn's grandmother and mine had been sisters. Twins. The two of them must have been dual opposites. Memaw would never have encouraged me to swindle people. Her abandoning these people finally made sense. *But now I'm in, and I don't know what to do.* Both Finn and Cecil watched me. Nothing like a little pressure. Someone knocked on the door, saving me from answering.

"Who is it?" Cecil called.

"Wade Hill." He didn't open the door.

"Come in." Cecil got off the bed.

Wade had to duck to cross the threshold. He leaned against the counter so his head wouldn't brush the roof. "Danielle's not in her trailer. All her stuff's there, and her truck's parked beside it."

"She told me not to call a vote." Kenny stood from the bed, but Wade motioned him to sit back down. "Said me and her was done if I did."

It all made sense to me. Danielle'd come back for her stuff when the Coachman's rebirth through Zora was done, when I was dead. "The Coachman's coven is going to do something soon. We need to table this whole issue and get ready. Otherwise, I've got no chance of getting Zora back." I turned to Cecil. "Or do you want to keep at this?"

He waved me off and spoke to Wade. "Set up guards. If either Kenny or Anita comes out, shoot them."

"But we did what you said." Anita threw her pillow at Cecil.

"I don't give a shit." He took my arm and marched me out the door, already speaking to Wade. "Set up another guard near Danielle's camper. If she comes back, detain her. Wait until I speak with her to finish it."

"Who do I use for guards?" Wade leaned down to speak quietly to Cecil.

Cecil glanced around the crowd that had gathered. He pointed at a man about Finn's and my age and at another man probably in his fifties. Then he led me away, already speaking in my ear. "As I told Dillon, I have an idea on how to get the runes. But we need privacy."

———

CECIL and I walked to his motor home in silence, me reeling from the scene I'd just witnessed. They would have killed Anita and Kenny. I was sure of it. The worst part? I understood why.

Sanctuary probably relied more on homemade law than the law of the outside world. Kenny and Anita represented a threat. If they were allowed to walk away, others might rise in their place. Or they might come back for revenge. Eliminating them made sense.

I jumped away from the direction of my thoughts, scared sweat dampening my clothes. A stiff wind whipped through the park. I began to shiver.

Memaw had hated Sanctuary, even though she never called it by name to me, had hated her family. I saw now her reasons were valid. The problem? It wasn't as simple as turning my back. I saw the need for a community like Sanctuary.

Could it be saved? I glanced around me at the grouping of campers, set aside from the rest of the RV park. People stood around talking. Some of them glanced in Cecil's and my direction.

Finn stood outside his and Dillon's camper. He raised a hand to wave at me and gave me a thumbs-up. A mix of feelings—guilt, anger, sadness—fought for master of my emotions.

Sanctuary had been in its death throes for a long time before I cast a shadow over them. I didn't know where things went wrong, only that they had. Maybe the only fix was to let it go. I was scared to take on a leadership role within it. My magic wasn't strong enough to save lost causes.

We reached Cecil's big, fancy motor home. It was the nicest one in all of Sanctuary. Griff had been right about that. Cecil unlocked the door and gestured for me to go in first. "Sit down."

I took the couch, and Cecil sat in the recliner. Age creased his face like a roadmap of hardship. "I know you came over here to find out what I know about the tiles, and I am going to tell where I think they are. But first I wanted to..." His voice faltered. "No matter what you decide about helping me run Sanctuary, I wanted to say I love you. These last few days have been awful. Just awful. But I can't think of anybody I'd have wanted by my side more than you." He held out one hand, and I took it.

The desire to tell him not to worry, that I'd help, rose up in me like a fire-breathing monster ready to take out a village. I couldn't do this. My own problems were about to bury me.

This layer of scar tissue keeping the mantle from properly manifesting made me a target to any powerful magic practitioner who wanted to take advantage of me. And I had no way to fix myself. Saving a rag-tag group of two-bit criminals went beyond my pay grade. Didn't it?

Learning with Mysti and working in Griff's business were my life. My new business cards said so. No, it wasn't the white picket fence of normalcy I'd always pined for, the one where I didn't see ghosts or do witchcraft and nobody knew me as a freak. I'd accepted that kind of normal was beyond me.

But with Griff and Mysti, I had a chance at another normal, one that sounded pretty good. In this normal, I'd be an average woman who went to work every day—albeit doing supernatural things—but came home to a nice husband, a cute dog, or maybe both. Taking on Cecil's battle to save Sanctuary would kill that dream of normal. I couldn't do it. I needed this last chance at normal.

Once I got Zora back safe in her parents' arms, I'd break the news. Then stepping away wouldn't seem like such a blow. If I failed, I'd be dead. Out of the race by default. I caught Cecil watching me worry.

"You look so much like Leticia right now." He dropped my hand and let his drift to hover around his mouth, a nervous gesture he must have learned to control over the years but couldn't help when things got out of control. "Those eyes of hers would get darker and deeper until they were like twin black holes. Yours almost smolder. I'm going to throw out one more thing."

I wanted to say it didn't matter, but I couldn't quite get those words to come out.

"That spell my Aunt Fern cast on you, the one keeping your powers from fully manifesting?" He dropped his hand from his mouth and leaned forward. My uncle obviously thought we were negotiating, and he had experience with that. "I know a lot of people. There has to be some-body who can help us figure this out. If you stand with me, I'll turn over every resource I have to you." He smiled and winked. "Don't answer now. Think about it."

I already was. The spell had to be stopped before the scar tissue got any bigger. If Cecil could help me do just that one thing, how much difference would it make in my life? *Memaw wouldn't have wanted this*, my mind whispered. I let the thought drift away. "I promise to think about it. So what about the runes, the tiles, or whatever they're called?"

Cecil stood and took his photo album from the cabinet above the couch. "I hadn't thought of this in years. I think I had convinced myself it was a dream." He sat down next to me on the couch and opened the photo album to a place he'd marked. "But I been feeling sorry for myself, hashing over old times. I saw this picture. Nearly gave me a heart attack." He pushed the photo album at me.

Cecil, his facial features rendered sharp and his hair a colorless dark shade by the black and white picture, cuddled a pure white cat. The cat looked ready to claw him, but Cecil had the sappy grin of a kid in love with an animal. "This was Snowball. Samantha had her waiting for me when we visited that summer." Cecil shut the photo album and set it aside. "A neighbor's mean dog got a hold of Snowball and killed her. I cried until my daddy whipped me for ruining our visit with grandma." The old man smiled sadly at the memory. "Samantha got me aside and said we could make it live again, only it couldn't live in our world."

I pointed at the photo album. Cecil nodded and

gestured for me to pick it up. I turned a few pages and found a picture of Samantha. Legs encased in baggy pants, suspenders over her shoulders, she stood in front of a sign with the words Lakeworth Brothers Circus.

Cecil began his story again. "I thought Samantha was just telling me a story to stop me crying. But she picked up the kitten's broken little body and told me to come with her. We walked into her house, and she held open the door to her kitchen. I walked in, and all of a sudden, it wasn't her kitchen." Cecil waved his hand in front of his face like a magician. "It was a beautiful, sunny meadow. Full of flowers and butterflies. My kitty came back to life and bounded off." The old man's voice rose like an awestruck kid's. "Samantha took me to a little cottage at the edge of the meadow. She served me hot tea and warm cookies, and we spent all afternoon watching my pet kitty chase lizards in the yard of this little place. When we got back to her kitchen only a few minutes had passed." He put his hand on my arm and stared into my eyes, maybe wanting me to tell him I believed. But I was too freaked out. Cecil let go of me and stared at the ceiling.

"She ever take you back?" I thought I already understood Cecil's point. Samantha had taken the runes to this place and hidden them there, where she thought the Coachman would never find them. Now I needed a way to get to this place.

"I asked a couple of years later, almost to make sure I hadn't just dreamed the whole episode." Cecil smiled at me, and I smiled back. I'd have done the same thing.

"Samantha told me I could never go back. I didn't have enough magic in me."

"Do you remember anything special she did to take y'all there?" Frustration got a foothold and started climbing. What the hell was I supposed to do with this information?

"Not really. Samantha saw the dead just like you and me." Cecil pointed one crooked finger at himself, then at me. "She said reality was just a bunch of layers. She claimed the ghosts showed her how to walk between realities."

Cold fingers crept up my spine. I knew a bit about these different realities, had even visited one of them. My mind balked at the idea of going back. Cecil kept talking, oblivious.

"She never took me back, but sometimes my grandmother'd go into a room and disappear for hours. You'd go in there, and she'd be gone." Cecil smiled. "But the thing is, she couldn't have left. There was no way for her leave without someone seeing her."

"And you suspect the runes are in this place you've been telling me about?" I knew the answer, had known it all along. Some naïve part me hoped I'd misunderstood. But life didn't work that way for me. If it was difficult, I got a double scoop of it.

"It's all I can guess since we didn't find them with her grimoire and other belongings." He pressed his lips together. "That water monster or whatever it was we saw in the vision..." He frowned at whatever pictures his memory showed him.

"I call him Pruney." I didn't tell Cecil that Pruney and I already knew each other. Saying it aloud felt like a silly kid's jinx.

"Horrible, ugly thing." I nodded my agreement. Pruney scared me worse than any horror movie boogieman. "But I know those tiles are important. The monster told Samantha the tiles couldn't be lost because they'd be her only power against the Coachman if he were to return."

Mysti said she had a plan for the runes, one we'd use to banish the Coachman back to the prison where his soul was stored. But I didn't know how to get to this perfect meadow Cecil described. Didn't have one single clue. The tension inside me wound tighter and tighter. I looked down at the picture of Samantha. The lights on the sign behind her had begun to move. She winked and put her finger to her lips. I couldn't speak. Seeing a person in a picture move did that to me.

The raven tattoo on my arm started to itch. I scratched at it, still staring horrified at the picture. The silhouette of a bird passed over Samantha's smiling face. A few seconds later, Orev cawed. His presence pushed at mine. I opened myself to him and saw in my mind the place Cecil had described. Orev knew where to go. I stood.

"You won't stop thinking about helping me run Sanctuary?" Cecil half stood.

"You mean in addition to saving Zora and getting rid of the Coachman?" I faced my great uncle without blinking.

He shrugged, not the least bit guilty. "All of that too."

"No. I won't forget." I let myself outside.

19

I OPENED the motor home's door to the deepening gloom of evening and looked for my familiar.

Caw. Caw. Cawwwww.

Orev perched on a wooden post with an electric meter attached to it. The bond between us awoke. Power thrummed through me, stronger than it had been since this waking nightmare started. The electric meter ran faster as I neared it.

Orev cocked his head to one side, tilting it to and fro. Then he took off. His black form almost disappeared in the darkening sky, but I felt him and had no trouble following.

The raven tattoo on my arm stung the way it had when I got it inked more than a dozen years earlier. I absently rubbed at it as I walked.

"Peri Jean?" Mysti's voice came from behind me. I waved her off and kept walking. She quit calling me, but I heard her quick footsteps. She wouldn't let me out of her sight. Something about that kind of devotion opened the wellspring of guilt I carried. I pushed the thoughts away and concentrated on Orev.

He led me into the woods, as I'd expected, but instead of the barren field where Blessed Union had stood, he flew in the opposite direction. We came upon a deep ravine with a scum of black water flowing down its center. Orev flew to the other side and waited on the bank.

Caw. Caw. Caw.

"You're kidding. That's deeper than I am tall." I knew the bird wasn't kidding and set about finding a way across. A branch snapped behind me. *Must be Mysti.* Somehow I knew she couldn't join me on this journey, but I felt better just knowing she had my back.

I backed up a few feet and took a running leap across the ravine. Being five-foot-nothing, I didn't make it. I grabbed for a skinny tree and wrapped my arms around it, heart slam-dancing. Little by little, I pulled myself onto the bank. Orev waited on an old wooden fence post.

"You thought that was funny, didn't you?" I didn't expect Orev to answer, and he didn't. He cocked his head in the direction what lay on the other side of the fence.

Only a little ambient light was left of the day, and I gingerly felt for the barbed wire fence I suspected was attached to the fencepost. But my fingers found nothing other than a soft buzz of magic.

This was the place. I took a deep breath and passed the barrier. I felt the warmth of the sun on my face before my eyes adjusted. A mockingbird called somewhere near, and a peacock answered him. Another bird, one whose call I didn't recognize, joined the chatter.

The meadow Cecil described came into focus bit by bit. The lush green grass waved in a soft breeze, and the sky above was the deep, perfect blue of spring, the sun a white-hot ember. A peacock strutted across the meadow, his tail fanned out. His mating call echoed across the meadow. A monarch butterfly as big as my hand floated past my face.

The sound of two women talking and laughing came from somewhere near. I walked across the meadow, the thick grass like carpet under my feet. Soon I saw the cottage Cecil mentioned tucked into a copse of thick, old growth trees.

I had expected a log cabin, but this was straight out of a fairy tale, a stone house with a thatched roof, rounded over the circular windows. A rough stone walkway led to a small courtyard where two women sat at an iron table, parasols hooked onto the backs of their chairs. A fat white cat, more ancient than any cat I'd ever seen, raised its head, regarded me briefly, then rolled its eyes shut.

"See? I told you she'd find us. Peri Jean is smart. Not brave, but smart." Priscilla Herrera said to her daughter. Samantha gave me a wink.

"If I'm not brave enough, why'd you choose me?" An extra chair appeared at the table, and I sat without waiting to be invited.

"Because you'll learn." Priscilla offered me a plate of tea cakes with pink icing. I shook my head.

"Please eat one." Samantha smiled, reminding me so

much of Memaw that tears stung my eyes. "You won't be able to stay here if you don't."

I took the cookie and bit into it, expecting the worst of all medicines, but it was sweet, light, and crisp, the way tea cakes should be. My stomach reminded me how long it had been since my last meal. I ate the cookie in three bites and took another.

"You've made quite a mess of things." Priscilla Herrera sipped from a dainty cream-colored teacup with a jade rim. "Your ineptitude has forced me to retreat here, where your Coachman can't reach me."

I realized the tea cake had parched my mouth. My own cup appeared in front of me, brimming with smoking liquid. I sipped from it and felt immediately better. "What did you expect? You had to know that spell was in me when you chose me to receive your power."

"No task I've put on you is impossible." Priscilla sat down her cup with a hard click.

"Mother, don't break the china." Samantha patted Priscilla's arm. "I won't be able to find more like this, much less get it over here."

"You and your dumb games." Priscilla turned on her daughter. "This is why you couldn't receive my power. You wasted your gifts on stupid pursuits like this." She waved her hand and took another sugar cookie. Samantha shrugged at her mother and smiled at me.

"I'm pleased you've come to visit me, Peri Jean." Her eyes crinkled when she smiled. Just like Memaw. Even the way she held her teacup to her mouth, barely tilting it to sip, was like Memaw. She set down her cup and pulled something from her lap.

Unlike the dainty and pristine setup on the table, the bundle of white cloth Samantha pushed across the table was stained and grimy. Something inside moved. The runes?

"This is what I stole from the Coachman." Samantha grinned. All of a sudden, she didn't look like a sweet little lady. Her teeth seemed sharp, feral and dangerous. "But I didn't know him as the Coachman. The name told to me was Lord of Babylon. You'll need his true name to destroy his hold on your reality."

"I think I know his name. Oscar Rivera. But I don't want to call the dark being like you did." My mouth felt full of cotton, so I took another sip of the tea and found it almost too sweet to swallow. "I don't want to owe him."

The two women exchanged glances. Priscilla shook her head at Samantha.

"There's a banishment you can try. First, you'll need to destroy a few of these." Priscilla tapped the bag of runes and drew back her finger as though afraid of getting it bitten off.

Samantha held up one hand. "Do not destroy all of them. Understand?" Lips set in a severe slash, she waited for me to acknowledge her order. I nodded. She said, "Tell me."

Feelings of inadequacy crowded my mind, assuring me I wouldn't know the right answer. "The dark being told you these runes hold the only power over the Coachman. They're the only way to send him back where he came from." I swallowed hard. That was the end of my knowledge.

"Tell her the rest." Priscilla toyed with her teacup, hooded eyes on her daughter. "You had to die to figure it out. Peri Jean needs the information now."

"You'll never be fully rid of the Coachman until you banish his soul from your plane." Samantha watched me digest the information. I sat there several seconds before understanding washed over me. The knowledge sat on my stomach like boiling poison.

"I'll have to find the place where he hid his soul." No telling what it would take to kill the Coachman for good. I put my hand over my aching gut, wishing for my antacids.

Both women smiled at me. Samantha spoke. "The tiles will lead you to that place. Use my wheel to make them talk to you."

Wheel? Then it hit me. "The disk?"

"It is the wheel of all seasons, places, and things." Samantha made the shape of a circle with her hands. "Learn to call forth what you need, and it will serve you well."

Priscilla held out a hand for Samantha to stop. "She can't stay long. We must concentrate on stopping the current danger."

Samantha nodded and made a hand motion that said we'd take it up later.

Priscilla shook her head, muttered something about silliness, and focused her sharp gaze on me. "Choose a few of the runes. Grind them and use the powder in a wax likeness of the Coachman. The method is in the book of recipes I left for you. Melissa Jane White can help. She'll argue, but tell her there is no such thing as dark magic, only the magic you need at any given time, and consequence is simply a fact of life."

Waves rippled through my vision, rolling the way heat rolls out of a hot oven. The peacock came close to the paved courtyard and let out his call again. The cat let out a scratchy meow. Somewhere distant, a horse whinnied. Samantha stood, smiling her gracious, yet savage, smile again.

"My dear, you must now leave. Inside you I see where the man you call the Coachman seeks you." She took my arm and pulled me from the chair. "I'm afraid if you stay too long, he'll come looking for you here."

"What is this place?" I glanced back at the table, looking for Priscilla. As much as she frightened me, she was still a known quantity, and the known was much more comforting than the unknown. I got only a glimpse of her back as she bent to scratch the cat's head.

Samantha smiled again, all savageness gone. "It's my hiding place, darling. I'll call you back again. We'll talk about building one for you. I think you're going to need it." She took my arm and walked me to the edge of the meadow. Though a hazy membrane, I saw the fencepost. Orev called to me. Samantha gave me a light push, and I took a big step. The meadow was gone as neatly as it had appeared.

———

MYSTI TURNED white when I told her what Priscilla said for us to do. We sat in the darkened SUV with the heater running. Way in the back of my mind, I heard Zora crying. It made me want to scream, to beat my fists against the windows because I couldn't fix everything this second. I did my best to ignore it. "Are you in?"

"It's a banishment spell. I've only seen it performed once." Mysti's normally bright eyes clouded with insecurity. "The person being banished ended up actually vanishing from the face of the earth."

"Who cares what happens to the Coachman?" I made a face at Mysti.

"Not me, certainly. But the earth, and therefore magic, is about balance. The evil we conjure will be balanced in some way." She waited for me to answer.

I didn't know how to answer her, so I pulled Priscilla Herrera's grimoire, her recipe book, out of my backpack. The book flipped open to a page I'd never noticed before. The words, written in a language I doubted anybody on earth could read, squiggled into something I did understand. "Here it is. The name of the spell is 'Banish a Threat.'"

Mysti put her hand on my shoulder and accessed my power to make the spell readable to her. "This is dark, so very dark."

"There's no such thing as dark magic." I found myself quoting Priscilla Herrera. "There is only the magic you need."

Mysti stared at me, face slack. Several seconds passed.

She straightened, regaining her composure. "My student has chosen her path."

"Will you help me?" I waited for her no.

She nodded. "Of course. But understand that every witch comes to a crossroad. Magic like this shapes your path forever."

"Do you have a better suggestion?" Part of me hoped she did. Priscilla Herrera's suggestions scared me. She wouldn't try to protect me. She'd drop me in a vat of boiling oil and expect me to find my way out. Mysti would try to protect me, to make things as easy and safe for me as she could.

"At this point, no. The Coachman will likely come for you tonight. Otherwise, he'll have to wait another month." Mysti stared out at the darkness.

I opened my mouth to ask why, but then it hit me. Moon magic. Mysti conducted important rituals at specific times during the moon phase. "Because tonight's the new moon. The new moon is for new beginnings."

Mysti nodded. "I'll need to check my supplies, see if I have what we need." She carefully went through her traveling witch kit, stealing glances at me every few seconds. Finally she closed the case and turned to me.

"Is it all there?" I was tired of the weighted glances, of the long pauses that ended with her shaking her head.

She nodded and bit her lip.

"Why don't you just say whatever you're thinking in English plain enough for me to understand?" I'd feel better with it out there.

"The kind of consequence you're looking at is letting

darkness dwell within you, letting it become a part of you."
She raised her eyebrows. "You have to be vigilant not to let
it take you over."

Her words seeped into me, cold and hard like a stone
in winter. I knew them for truth. "I have to do this. Zora
deserves a chance to turn her life into a living hell on her
own terms."

Mysti smiled at that. She put her arms around me and
held me tight. We began preparing.

Finn and Dillon cleared out of their camper to let us
use it to build the spell. Wade gave up flirting with Jadine
long enough to talk one of the camp's more adventurous
cooks out of a meat grinder. "Those are just bone, right?
It'll work." He plugged the thing in and got to work. I
thought of the people those pieces of tile had once been
and shuddered.

"Don't grind them all up." I had to shout to be heard
over the machine's whine. Wade gave me a solemn stare
and shoved some of the runes aside.

I returned them to the bag I got from Samantha. Using
the runes to find the Coachman's soul was a worry for
another day. But I had to be ready when it came. My luck,
it would be sooner rather than later. Problems followed me
like stink on shit.

Mysti dug a disposable storage dish, the kind we
usually kept lasagna leftovers in, out of her bag. Inside lay
a blob of clear whitish stuff. She popped the lid off. "This
is special candle wax I buy from another witch. It's made
with the rendered tallow of animals she slaughters on
her farm."

I wrinkled my nose. I saw my future, and it was gross.

I read from the spell. "We also need grave dust and black salt." Then I read further and groaned. "But it says you have to create an upper and lower circle of power, like the life tree, and you need amber to protect yourself."

Mysti clasped her hands in front of her face and frowned. Finally she nodded. "We can handle all those things."

Mysti and I started the unpleasant task of mixing ground-up bone and grave dust into the stinkingest wax I'd ever smelled. We then had to use our bare hands—just as I suspected— to fashion the wax into the shape of a man. We coated it with more of the powder from the ground-up runes. I picked up a container of coarse black powder.

"We forgot something." I inwardly groaned at the idea of starting over in any form or fashion. As it was, I figured I'd never get the stench of the tallow wax off my hands.

"No. That's black salt. We're going to use it as part of the banishing ritual." Mysti packed up the rest of her things. She opened the door, and seven wary faces turned our way. "We're going to the site where Camilla stood because that's where the Coachman died."

We walked out of Finn and Dillon's camper. My family crowded around us.

"Peri Jean has mentioned to me that you can combine your power as a family as long as she's the hub." Mysti settled her gaze first on one face, then on the next.

Cecil nodded. "But I don't know how to do it."

"There's no special procedure. You've given your raven tattoos the power to bind you together." She smiled at me, and I could almost hear her voice in my head over the crying. *Magic is mostly about intent.*

Jadine turned her back on Brad, who'd been talking a mile a minute while Wade was gone, and approached us. "If the tattoo and not the blood make the difference, I'm in."

Finn and Dillon had a hushed conversation a few feet away. Dillon had wrapped Zora in a heavy blanket and pulled the toddler across her lap. She held Zander's chubby arm in the other hand. The little boy did everything he could to pry his mother's fingers off him so he could waddle off. She wasn't having it.

"But I need to help," Finn raised his voice.

"Well, I want to help too, but we need to stay here with our kids." Dillon went ahead and yelled her answer so we could all hear.

"What if me being there is the difference between getting Zora back and not?" Finn gestured at his still little girl.

"Tell them they can stay here." I spoke into Cecil's ear.

"We need all the power we can get to make it work," Cecil whispered back. He approached the arguing couple. "The Coachman's coven will make an effort to get Zora. His rebirth can't be completed without her. Dillon, why don't you keep the kids in the rec room? It locks from the inside."

Dillon slouched. "Why can't I bring my kids with me?"

"There'll be nobody to watch them." Cecil's words had an edge of impatience. "We'll have plenty of power with Peri Jean and the three of us. It is no place for the kids, and you certainly don't want to put them in danger."

Dillon eyes hardened. "But if I don't go, and I never get Zora back, then I'll always have to wonder if things could have been different." Her voice wobbled on the last word.

A gray-haired woman approached. "Eric and I would be happy to watch over them, either at the spelling place or in the rec room. Sanctuary used to be about family."

Griff stepped forward and turned to the older gentleman, presumably Eric. "Know how to use a shotgun?"

Eric smiled. "I duck hunted until my arthritis got too bad."

Ten more minutes of arguments ensued about where the couple would watch the kids. Wade finally took the batteries out of the keypad lock on the rec room door so only the lock on the inside worked.

"They can't get in here from the outside," he told Dillon.

She crossed her arms over her chest and danced around. If she insisted on bringing the kids with us, it would put them in a lot more danger. Finally she nodded.

We packed up our supplies and took two golf carts and a four-wheeler down the trail in the dark. It ended at the field where Griff had died in a past life. I wondered if, now that he knew the secret of the place, the horror of its past would still affect him.

Cecil cut across the field without stopping. I watched Griff with concern, but he showed none of his earlier symptoms. Maybe his former incarnation had just wanted his story told. Another, smaller clearing lay beyond the first one. Nothing marked it as the former site of a palatial home.

Only a brick-lined hole on one edge of the property hinted people had once lived there. Another neighborhood, built pretty much on top of Camilla's grounds, peeked through the thin screen of skinny pine trees and overgrown vines.

We climbed out of the golf carts, and Mysti and I began setting up. Once we had our pentagram drawn in the dirt with her candles set in their usual places, she directed my family, both blood and chosen, to their places around the circle. She turned to me. "Once we get the Coachman into the wax effigy, you'll have to enter him and rescue Zora's spirit. Move as quickly as possible. Every second we delay completing the spell is another chance to lose him." She held my gaze. "You can do this. Are you ready?"

I nodded.

Mysti raised her athame over her head and began to speak.

I call upon the east and the element of fire
I call upon the west and the element of earth
I call upon the north and the element of air
I call upon the south and the element of water.

She stopped speaking and signaled I should start. I took a deep breath, cleared my mind, and tapped into my power. I expected nothing but a weak ping, but being in Samantha's hideout had somehow given me a second wind. That too-full sensation of the power backing up as it tried to make its way into my magical center throbbed at the center of my chest. But some must have gotten through. My limbs and fingertips prickled with the force of it. The movement of the trees under the wind became a dance, and the wind a language of its own.

I call upon the living world

I call upon the dead world

The ground moved underneath my feet, and I steeled myself to keep from gasping and ruining the moment.

Surround us above and below

Protect us on high and on low

Bless our work, bless us this hour

Let evil be banished into the darkest tower.

The hum of power surrounded us, electric, pure, and terrifying. A charged wind blew around our circle. It flowed over me, testing me and moved on to Finn who stood next to me. He clenched his jaw, and it moved on to the next person. Jadine gasped when it hit her.

But then my power and that of my family connected with an almost audible click. The voices Finn dealt with crowded my head. Dillon's power to persuade fluttered through me, confident and proud. Cecil's ability to see ghosts opened my mind to another, darker world, so different than my connection to the spirits. Then Jadine's light hold on the waking world inched into me. Somewhere I saw a circle of people chanting. The Coachman's coven. They were getting ready for their own strike.

Mysti laid the wax figure at the center of the circle. She and I stood facing on opposite sides of it.

"Everyone, it's time to focus your energy on the wax doll. Imagine it as a vortex, pulling the Coachman into it. When he gets in there, focus on keeping him there."

We got a few sets of wide eyes and nods in response. Only Wade stood calmly throughout it all.

Mysti handed me the long-stemmed utility lighter.

By the power of earth, air, fire, and water

Let this wax doll represent Oscar Rivera.

She gestured at me, and I burned a hole in the wax figurine's chest. I rolled up the slip of paper on which Mysti had written the name and stuck it in the soft wax. I stood and raised my athame over my head.

I call upon the power of earth, air, fire and water,

Draw this spirit into the hell of his making and stay him.

The ground moved again under my feet. The Coachman was coming. I braced for whatever lay in store. Dirt blew up from the center of our circle, and the Coachman took shape. His translucent form wavered toward the wax figure, but he fought his way away from it. His rage and frustration bounced around the circle. Someone moaned, and I hoped they didn't lose it. Jadine chanted, "Go in. Go in. Go in."

The Coachman wavered again. His struggle filled my mind and body, drawing energy from me. His intent and its results spurred me into action. "I banish thee," I shouted. "You will reside here." I pointed my athame at the wax form.

Mysti's eyes snapped open.

"I banish thee as well." She pointed her athame at the figurine as well, hand shaking with effort. "Reside here." Each person in the circle pronounced the Coachman's banishment.

A wispy tendril of the Coachman inched toward the

figure. I kept up my concentration, ignoring the exhaustion aching inside me. I willed the Coachman into the wax figure. A little more of him went inside. His presence brushed my mind. His coven chanted inside my head. We had to hurry. I focused my power and poured all my strength into pushing the Coachman into the wax figure. My body shook with the effort.

He shot into the wax figure. It jittered on the ground, turning black with the taint of the Coachman's evil, negative spirit. Using Jadine's ability to walk in dreams, I propelled myself into the Coachman's being. The door to Zora's prison loomed big in front of me. I rushed toward it.

The chanting of his coven splintered at my hold on the Coachman. Then it began to push at me. I fought my way toward the huge door, each step its own battle. I fell to my knees and slid backward. I clawed at the wood floor, splinters wedging themselves under my fingernails, but still I slid backward. Then I was back in my body. "I couldn't get her. They pushed me out."

"You what?" Dillon's furious voice came from a few feet away.

"It's okay. Let's just get him bound to the wax figure." Mysti, out of breath, had to gasp the words.

As one, we spoke the words Mysti and I had made up.

Oscar Rivera, we bind your soul

We bind you from harming the living

We bind you from theft of souls

We bind you from contacting the living.

Mysti signaled to me, and I picked up the wax figure in both hands. The cold coming off it burned my skin.

The Coachman's voice surrounded us. "Not good enough. You lose."

The chanting came again, this time all around us. The candles on the outer edges of our circle flickered. Behind them, something moved. I focused my vision into the darkness and saw the shapes of other people, transparent, but here all the same.

"Oh Mysti. Do you see them?" The memory of the Coachman's many pieces, made up of those who summoned him, came back, and the truth slammed into me. As long as these people were able to provide the Coachman energy to exist, they bound his spirit to our plane of reality. It didn't matter what we bound him to or how we tried to destroy his spirit.

"What is it? See who?" Mysti's voice trembled.

"They've got us surrounded. They're countering everything we do." Bile stung the back of my throat. "Don't you feel it?"

"I see them." Jadine's chest heaved. She clung to Wade's hand. I didn't blame her. I wished I could run over there and do the same.

The wax figure grew so cold it burned my fingers. I yelped and dropped it. It hit the ground and shattered into a dozen pieces. The Coachman rose from the trap we'd built for him, his spirit emanating more power than any of us had after we exhausted ourselves trying to send him away. He slammed into me and knocked me backward into Cecil.

"Catch her Papaw," Finn screamed. "Don't let her break the circle."

But it was too late. Cecil stumbled away from me, and both of us fell out of the circle. The Coachman's face appeared in my vision, and the chants of his followers filled my head. His tainted, sickening presence violated every inch of my psyche, pushed me to my feet, and made me run from my friends. I was too weak to stop him.

20

Losing control of my own body was like falling off a cliff and having only a sea of black waiting at the end. I came to rest somewhere in my mind, vaguely aware of the blood whooshing through my veins and the thunder of my own heart. Voices rose somewhere at my back, Wade's among them, and I forced my eyes open but found the Coachman was already using them.

I hurtled through the night, arms pumping, feet painfully striking the earth. Branches, stiff and winter-dead, slapped at my face and gouged my skin. I ran faster than I'd ever pushed myself. The Coachman was at the wheel, and he didn't care how much he hurt me. He planned to kill me and use my blood to be reborn in Zora.

Got to get control back. Got to get him out of me. I pushed against the heavy presence glommed onto my mind. It felt like hitting a wall of bubble gum. It stretched but went nowhere. I pushed again. My body's movements slowed and then stopped.

This is it. The Coachman's voice rumbled in my head. *You're defeated. Give up.*

I will never stop fighting until I am dead. I tried to make my words roar like the Coachman's, but I just sounded like a redneck whore after a three-week drug binge.

The Coachman herded my body deeper into the woods and made me huddle behind a curtain of dead vines. His presence widened and lengthened until my brain swelled with it. My head pounded as though it would burst open, spraying bone and brain all around me.

I tried to run, but I couldn't move.

The Coachman gave my mind a push, and the image of all my calloused and rotten layers of memory rose up before me, the mantle resting white and shining on top like a layer of angel clouds. I slammed into the scar tissue at full speed. It swallowed me whole.

I ran down a wide, brightly lit corridor, the smell of hospital strong in my nose. *Oh no. Not this again.* Footsteps pounded the linoleum behind me. I jerked myself out of my thoughts and started running again.

Strident, annoyed voices yelled, "Peri Jean? Come on back here, sweetie. It won't help to run."

Anxiety whipped around inside me, erasing all reason. Hadn't I escaped the mental hospital and grown up with Memaw? I couldn't remember. All I knew was that I had to get out of that place. I didn't want to grow up there. But I didn't know where to go.

A row of numbered doors came up in front of me. I grabbed the handle of the first one, ran inside, slammed it behind me. I leaned against it and breathed so hard my chest ached. The room, half-dark with the shutters drawn, looked empty. Maybe I could rest here.

"Who is it?" a nervous voice whispered from inside the room.

"It's okay," I whispered back and tiptoed further into the room.

Hannah Kessler lay on the bed, hair greasy and wild, a crop of acne on her oily cheeks. Her eyes widened when she saw me. "What are you doing here?"

"Somebody's after me. I need to hide here." The truth was, I couldn't remember who'd been chasing me. It seemed whatever I'd been running from already had me, and it was too late to change things.

"But I told them not to let anybody in here. You especially, Peri Jean." Her voice rose, and by the end of the sentence she was screaming at me.

Tears stung my eyes, and my stomach did a dizzy flip.

"I don't want to even look at you." She crumpled a piece of paper that had been sitting on her tray, and I recognized the stationery. It was a letter from me. I sent it before Rainey told me the private hospital for trauma victims where Hannah was recovering had stopped accepting mail for Hannah. Had I been the reason she had her mail stopped?

I took another step backward. My throat ached with unshed tears, unspoken apologies, and wishes it would have been me instead of her. The horror she lived through happened because of me.

"Every time I look at you, I see those fucking fucks climbing all over me, over and over again." She reared her fist back and slung my wadded-up letter at me. It hit me in the chest and bounced off. "It should have been you." Her hateful glare burned me to my core.

I took a step backward and bumped into her dresser. The items on its top jingled and rattled. Something slid off and broke. I jumped, cheeks burning.

"Now see what you've done?" Her freckled face reddened, and her mouth contorted with rage. She picked up her water glass and chunked it at me. It hit the floor a few feet from me and sprayed glass fragments and water all over my bare feet and legs. In the very back of my mind, the last of my sanity whispered *plastic.* But I was too freaked out to make sense of it.

The cold water ran between my tiny little girl's toes. My skinny legs sticking out of the hospital nightgown began to tremble.

"Get out." She spoke with her teeth clenched. Before I had time to react, she picked up a doodad and pressed a button on it. An alarm blared in the hallway.

"It's okay." I held out my hands. "I'm not here to hurt you. I'm just hiding from..." What was I hiding from? It had been so important. I'd been so scared. Now I couldn't remember.

"You already hurt me." Hannah's mouth twisted, distorting her words, but I understood just fine. They stabbed right through the center of my chest and leaked stinging poison all over my body. "Wade was right, you know? It would have been better if they'd killed me. Because now I don't have anything to live for."

Arms closed around my middle, and my father spoke

into my ear. "You bothering normal people again, Peri Jean?" He dragged me out of Hannah's hospital room and down the wide hallway.

"Daddy, please help me," I whispered. "Please. I don't know what to do any more."

"Oh, we're gonna help you, all right. Make it where you won't hurt anybody else, long as you live." He dragged me into a room with a stretcher and lifted me onto its black rubber cushion.

"Daddy, wait. What's going on?" He pushed me down on the stretcher and buckled the straps across my chest.

"It was too late for you the day I was murdered." He fastened the last strap across my legs. "Mama shoulda left you at the mental hospital."

The door swung open, and heels clacked across the linoleum. My mother's face appeared over me, dirt sifting from her hair. "Your grandmother never could listen to reason."

"That's all right," came a familiar voice from my other side. Eddie Kennedy leaned over me and fastened something to my forehead. "We'll fix it all up right now."

"No, no. I'll be good." My words came fast, so fast they barely had syllables. "I'll do better. Don't. Whatever this is, don't." I knew what it was, deep in my mind. I remembered hearing Memaw hollering about it when she came to get me from the hospital. *You quacks sure ain't giving my granddaughter electroshock therapy.*

Fear burned in my stomach and sizzled the rest of the way through me. No. They couldn't do this to me. Wasn't there some form I had to sign? *Wait a minute. That's all wrong.* What was I forgetting? I saw myself standing in a circle with my friends and family. Before I could remember what it was all about, Eddie leaned over and shoved a piece of rubber between my teeth.

"You got me killed, Peri Jean." He stared into my face, eyes blazing. "I hope this hurts like hell."

I wanted to tell him I was sorry, but my mouth was full of rubber. My mother turned the dial on the white machine, and I heard the hum as the electricity came to life. It jolted through my body like liquid fire. I stiffened and strained against it, thinking it was going to kill me, and then it stopped. I opened my eyes and remembered what my panic and fear had erased. My tormenters leaned over me, faces expectant.

I pushed the rubber out of my mouth with my tongue. "You aren't real. None of you."

The faces of my loved ones faded and disappeared, leaving me to stare up at the cracks in the ceiling.

"This isn't real. It didn't happen. Memaw got me out of the hospital and took me home." I waited for the restraints holding me down to melt away, for the hospital around me to turn into the scarred landscape of my magical core. The door creaked open. Footsteps approached.

The Coachman leaned over me. "It's real to you, and that's all that matters." He turned the dial on the machine. The electricity hit my body. The Coachman turned off the current, waited a few seconds, and did it again. Over and over. "Tell me when you give up."

The current of pain arced through me. I didn't know how many more times I could stand it. My body begged me to give up. I'd be dead, and I'd never have to worry again about anybody or anything. Normal wouldn't matter. Neither would the loneliness that plagued me even when people surrounded me. The thoughts lost coherence and turned into a mindless chant, *give up, give up, give up.*

Priscilla Herrera's voice spoke from somewhere just out of reach. "Call the man from the dark outposts now. Monster or not, he is your only hope."

I didn't want her to be right, but I knew she was. Against my better judgment, I closed my eyes and pictured the thing I'd last seen eating the Coachman's earthly body from the head down. Darkness awoke in my blood, because that's where he'd been all along, and whispered through me.

Please help me. I thought the words as hard as I could. The intermittent shocks and the hospital room went somewhere far away, but this time I didn't fall. I just shifted to another reality.

————

I CAME to in a dark place. Somewhere nearby, water lapped against rocks or a beach. The smell hit my nose, and I knew where I was. My eyes adjusted to a sliver of moon hovering over an endless expanse of water. A beach of sugar white sand stretched before it. Something splashed in the dark water, coming closer and closer.

A white pig rose out of the tide and shook like a dog. Droplets of water sprayed. The pig trotted toward me. Bones rippled under its skin as it came. Its back legs lengthened, and it began to walk upright. Its face narrowed. The snout shrank into a regular nose. Bit by bit, the pig became a man, his hairless skin wrinkled and waterlogged. A black suit formed over the man's nakedness. Water began to drip from the hems. Pruney stopped a few feet from me.

"Peri Jean Mace." His words ended in a squelching oink. "It has been a time since our last face-to-face chat. Did the treasure fulfill all your dreams?"

The Coachman was electrocuting my consciousness to death, and Pruney wanted to hash over old times? What a freak. I didn't have the nerve to disrespect him. "Some, I guess."

"And now we are reunited at your request." He showed me his needle tipped teeth, the same ones I'd seen crunch into the Coachman's skull. My skin tightened and flinched at the sight of those teeth.

I had no answer for him. If there were any other way, or if I had time to brainstorm with Mysti, I wouldn't do this. Wade Hill's fear of this thing told me all I needed to know.

"I see you are still undecided in accepting my help." Pruney came toward me, and I shrank away. Undeterred, he slapped one pulpy hand to my forehead. "See what the Coachman plans."

Zora and I lay unconscious at the middle of a circle, surrounded by people chanting. My head was turned to one side, my eyes open and glazed, not a shred of sanity in them. My chest rose and fell ever so slightly.

Metal clinked together and squalled, and my feet began to rise, hoisted by a pulley system somewhere out of sight. They raised me until my limp body hung upside down with my arms extended over my head.

The chanting increased in volume. *"Now we offer the sacrifice of this powerful blood."*

A woman, face hidden in the shadows cast by the undulating firelight, came forward, an athame held aloft. Danielle knelt beside me. Fucking traitor. She flicked the knife under my throat in one smooth, experienced motion.

My skin opened, and blood flowed thick and heavy, pattering onto the old wood floor. It spread in a wide puddle, extending to flow over Zora's chubby little hand.

The last drops of blood dripped from my neck, and the blood swelled, taking an almost human shape. It hovered over Zora several seconds. The chanting picked up again, and the candlelight hissed and fluttered. The blood covered Zora's face and drained into her nose, eyes, and ears.

The chanters droned on. *"With this blood shall he live. With this blood shall he live."*

Zora's little body jittered like a bag of snakes. The skin on her arms dried and withered as though being sucked from within. The deterioration continued until she was nothing but bones with dried eyes wide and staring and her lips pulled back from her baby teeth, which had turned black.

"Now the final sacrifices," Danielle boomed.

A murmur went through the chanters, and a man wearing a dark hood was dragged into the circle. Danielle whipped the hood off the man's head, revealing Cecil's horrified face. He took one look at me, then Zora, and began to tremble.

"No," he moaned. Danielle used the same practiced motion to open his throat. A twenty-something woman rushed forward to catch the blood.

Two twenty-something men dragged Finn into the circle, bound at the arms and ankles. They tossed him on the ground next to his daughter's shaking form. "What did you people do to my daughter?" he screamed. Nobody answered. Danielle cut his throat. Another idiot with another bucket collected the arterial spray.

One by one, my friends were dragged into the circle. The knowledge of their impending deaths shone bright in their wild eyes. One by one, they died. My mind melted down at the sight of Wade. He'd been drugged or knocked out. His head flopped as four grunting people threw him in the dirt. Some broken, agonized part of my mind began to scream.

Danielle crept over to Zora's dried up body and stuffed a handful of sickly green, spongy stuff into her mouth. Nobody had to tell me what it was. The Lazarus Root. So they had managed to get some.

Zora's body cracked open, and an adult sized head rose from her abdomen. His neck and shoulders formed from nothing. The Coachman raised his head, and the brutal smile I'd come to hate quirked his lips. "Wash me in their blood so that I may live."

The Coachman's coven came forward and splashed the blood of my friends over the Coachman and what was left of Zora. He climbed out of her body, naked like a newborn, and raised his arms over his head.

"Please, no," I whimpered.

"If you give up, this will happen." Pruney's voice whispered through my mind, squealing like unoiled gears. "Don't you want to see the fruit of your decision?"

"No," I sobbed. "I don't want to see anything else."

"Then you're ready to deal with me?" His damp hand rested on my shoulder.

I wasn't. He scared me. Making a deal with him, letting him help, terrified me.

"Oh, don't be afraid. Your family has dealt with me for centuries." He came closer, and his fishy smell enveloped me. "It was I who bound the raven to them. We made a deal."

"I need to know what you want up front." Chills wracked my body, clacked my teeth together. "And what you're going to do to me."

Pruney snapped his fingers, and we were back on the beach in front of the moonlit water. "I'll widen the hole in the scar tissue caused by the spell Fern Wilhelmina Gregg placed upon you. This will let enough of your power through to beat the Coachman." He raised one still dripping finger. "But beware. You'll not have the full measure of your power. This is just a—what do you mortals call it? A quick fix. You must stop the spell from continuing to grow and remove it."

"What do you want in return?" The smell of him was making me sick.

"Two things. The first is simple and immediate. You

must deliver the twelve souls helping the Coachman to me." He rested his shining black eyes on me until I nodded. "The second will be a task that will cause neither you nor your loved ones any harm. But you must do it when I ask, regardless of your feelings about it."

The second thing was the killer. I couldn't agree to do an unknown service for this thing. Could I? *Zora. I have to save her.*

He bared his teeth at me in a smile as he waited for his answer.

I tried to think it over, to analyze what it might entail, but I had no choice. This was the only way to save Zora and to save my own sorry skin. "I agree to both."

In front of me appeared the disk I'd taken from Samantha's things. Pruney handed me a jeweled dagger.

"Your blood," he said.

I slashed my finger and let the drops splatter on the disk. They sizzled when they hit, and Pruney hissed, a snake tongue flickering from his mouth. When the third drop hit, he turned and embraced me. I wanted to scream at the dead, damp smell of him and at the feel of his wetness seeping into me.

"Everything will be fine." His cold whisper made my ear go numb.

———

THIS CLOSE, I couldn't help focusing on my new ally's ugliness. His skin had the crosshatch pattern of pork skin. In the corners of his eyes was the same black gunk of animals.

"You must let me into your body so I can widen the crack in your scar tissue." His breath, humid, rotten sewer mixed with burning garbage, turned my stomach. If we were inside my head, why couldn't I be spared his olfactory essence? "This is the only way you'll have enough power to beat the Coachman."

My heart stuttered. I'd felt okay when I thought the deal was done. Realizing I had one more barrier to drop, one more thing to give up, spooked me. I had one last chance to run from this awful thing, and I couldn't afford to take it. My deal with him was my last chance to save Zora.

I couldn't invite a thing I called Pruney into my body to perform psychic surgery on me. Memaw taught me better than that. "I don't know your name," I whispered, voice quaking.

The thing chuckled. "My name is—" He spoke a word that sounded more like grunts and squeals than words. Then he said, "But Priscilla Alafare Herrera called me Sol, and you can too."

"Sol..." I trailed off and screwed up my courage. "Will you come into my body and break open the scar tissue keeping me from the power of Priscilla Herrera's mantle?"

"Understand this might kill you." His lips looked like slabs of liver in the moonlight.

Of course there was a catch. I nodded my assent. Why the hell not? The Coachman's followers would kill me anyway. Why not do this and maybe live to fight another day?

Sol's back bowed, and his body rippled. His face flattened and elongated. His clothes puddled onto the ground. I inched closer. Something underneath the clothes moved. *Don't let that be what I think it is.* A dark colored snake, thick as my arm and as long as one of my legs, slithered out of the pile of clothes and watched me with its cold eyes.

"Sol?" I peered into the snake's eyes, trying to find anything I could of the monster I already knew. I'd only seen his pig to quasi-human trick. This quasi-human to snake trick was new.

The snake drew back its triangular shaped head. That and the shape of its body made me think this was a water moccasin, one of East Texas's venomous snakes. These things scared the taco meat right out of me. Sweat popped out all over my scalp. *Please no. Don't bite.*

I scooted away from the snake. The inside of my mouth dry as a prude at a porn movie, nerves trying to crawl out of my skin, I forced myself to stay still. Maybe it wouldn't bite if I quit moving.

"Please don't," I whispered. Few animals scared me. Snakes managed to make the cut. I could imagine nothing worse than that long sinewy body unfolding and flying at me, those fangs piercing my skin and forcing poison into me. The idea made me do a full body shiver. It was enough.

The snake struck. Time slowed for me. The snake's pure white mouth opened impossibly wide. Its fangs looked like huge curved needles. My thoughts sparred and tripped over each other, all trying to tell me to move, to run, but I knew it was too late. The snake hit my neck hard and closed its jaws.

Its venom burned my skin and forged through my bloodstream like lava in my veins. I fell back on the sandy shore and watched the ripples on the water and the moonlight dancing over them. Sol, or whatever his name was, had fooled me. He'd killed me here in the dark outposts and would probably take over my body himself.

The center of my chest throbbed. The venom had found my heart. It wouldn't be long now. Facing psychic death, conflicting emotions ran through me. Anger at my own stupidity prevailed. Nobody would be able to help Zora. The Coachman would kill my family and friends and win the day. A seizure ripped through me. Spit flooded my mouth and leaked out. My vision began to cloud.

I drifted back through the layers of my consciousness and came to a stop in front of the festering blob covering my magical core. The mantle glowed on top of it, the crown jewel I couldn't access. I became aware of a chilly hand gripping mine.

"What a mess," Sol said from next to me, his suit dripping brackish water on the floor of my soul. "You'll have a battle getting rid of this. Take it a little at a time."

"But how? You said devour it. How?"

Sol chuckled. "I don't do two-fer-ones. If you want my advice, negotiate for it." He rubbed his stomach, which emitted a sick gurgle. "I'm hungry. Brace yourself. This won't feel good." Without giving me a chance to change my mind, his hand slipped from mine, and he hurtled into the accumulated scar tissue from the horror of my life. His mouth opened wide, like the snake's had, and he bit down.

Blinding pain shot through my skull and radiated to the roots of my teeth. It hurt the same way my dream electroconvulsive therapy had. I pitched to my knees and screamed. The pain spread through my jaw and into my sinuses, packing them with hot sauce and salt. Moisture leaked from my eyes and nose. It could have been tears. It could have been blood. Either one would have made sense.

Sol's head moved as he ate through the membrane. The mantle came to investigate, nudging at Sol like a hungry pet. It curved around him. Did the part of it that was still Priscilla Herrera remember him? Was she glad to see him? Probably. She wasn't like me. Nothing scared her.

The pain multiplied in intensity as it moved through the rest of my body. My joints throbbed. Cold chills consumed me. Only Sol's wiggling feet were still visible. The pain spread to my stomach, lancing through my body and pushing out the last of my self-control. I curled into a ball and sucked breaths through my clenched teeth. My calves and feet cramped, but my stomach hurt too bad to straighten out and relieve them.

I screamed, tearing my throat raw, and not caring. I did it until I ran out of breath. Then I drew another breath and did it again. I don't know how long I lay there yelling, but I became aware the pain was gone. I let out a ragged breath. A hand appeared in front of my face.

"Come. Your Coachman realizes what has happened

and has gone deep into the protective webbing." Sol pulled my hand off my stomach. "Come now if you want your last chance to beat him."

I climbed to my feet and followed Sol to the hole on shaky legs, the pain receding to a deep throb. The mantle, now a silver white with threads of gold running through it, flowed into the hole. I hesitated before the hole, not sure if it was okay to touch it. Sol gave a frustrated grunt and shoved me into it.

I fell through my worst memories. Felicia, my lifelong nemesis grabbed at me from an open toilet stall. I slapped her hand away. My mother snuck up behind my father, ready to cut his throat. I passed right through her. My ex-husband reared back his fist. I ducked and ran around him, focused instead on the Coachman, thinking of his runes, of the way he looked as Samantha bested him. Far away, I heard running footsteps. Sol was right. The Coachman knew I was coming for him. If he thought he could get away, he was wrong. I was about to rise up on him. Beat his ass righteously.

I followed the sound of the footfalls through dark hall-ways and moonless nights, through screams and crying. Our chase ended at the center of me, in front of a big, locked door.

"If I open this door, you'll die." The Coachman held up a key.

"Do it then." I walked slowly toward him, savoring the fear on his face. When I got close enough, I snatched the key and unlocked the door myself, praying I hadn't over-played my hand.

My father's ghost floated out of a darkened room, the death wound on his neck gaping open. He smiled at the Coachman. "Time to go." To me, he said, "Get him out of you, baby. And shove him down his followers' throats."

My father floated away before I had a chance to ask what he meant.

"I have a question for you." I put one finger to the corner of my mouth. "You were going to eat my soul and absorb my power. What if I were to eat your soul?" I had no intention of taking his evil into me. I'd only wanted to distract him long enough to give him a taste of his own medicine. The horror on his face almost threw my concentration off to the point where I couldn't do what I wanted. I focused again and jumped into the Coachman.

His soul was a maze of torture devices manned by black robed beings. His victims' faces contorted in agony. The ones that weren't human howled in dumb pain. Rage, my old friend and sparring partner, glimmered in the recesses of my consciousness. If I had been unsure of the Coachman's evil, this little slice of hell let me in on what he was. He had none of the decency most people had, none of the compassion. And he deserved none in return.

I rooted around, cruelly tearing up his playground and letting his victims go free to torture his conscience. They gave me a reward in return for their freedom. All of the Coachman's victims called his true name. My recitation of his name had been wrong when I tried to banish him with the wax figure. The Coachman had a middle name, and now I knew it. The tortured victims floated away.

The Coachman jumped on my back like a girl who

didn't know how to fight. He tried to claw at my eyes. I shrugged him off like a bag of trash. It was time to find Zora, set her free so she could do the things she was meant to do. I ran down hallway after hallway, searching for that old wooden door.

Call her. Priscilla's voice filled my head. *The two of you know each other from before.*

Zora? My voice sounded tinny and fragile, but I felt her pull and ran down a dark hallway. The door appeared. I kicked it open. Inside was nothing but a jar of blue glass with a gold top, the kind Memaw called a Mason jar, regardless of whatever brand we bought.

Pinpricks of light danced around inside the glass. It reminded me of the way older people talked about gathering what they called "lightning bugs" into a jar, which most people no longer did because it killed the poor creatures. But these were no bugs. This was a human soul, a very young one, untainted by the indignities of living life.

"Zora?" I whispered.

The pinpricks of light whirled around the jar faster, bouncing off the sides. I reached for the jar, intending to grab it and break it on the floor, to let Zora free. I figured between Mysti and me, we could direct her back to her body.

Something hit me from behind. The Mason jar danced out of my sight as I flew backward through a brick wall. The Coachman and I faced each other, circling with our hands curled. He was bigger, twice as thick, his fists twice as large. I didn't care.

I called to the mantle and felt it pour into me stronger

than ever. My eyes felt too big for their sockets, and my heart beat too hard. The black opal sizzled on my chest, and the smell of burning flesh drifted up to me. The Coachman struck. I fell to the ground, him on top of me. He crouched over me, slamming punches into my face, one after the other.

I brought my elbows up to guard but thought better of it. I could never beat him here. As long as his followers sent their power, he'd never run out of energy. All I needed to do was get him out of me. Rescuing Zora would have to wait. There had to be a way to surprise him, a way to throw him out fast, or he'd wear me down and overpower me.

The Coachman stopped hitting me. His gaze probed mine, and he tried to work his way back into my scar tissue. I unleashed the power of the mantle on him and blew him backward. It drained me to the point my bones ached. I rushed at him and hit him hard. I wrapped my arms around him, opened my jaw the same way the snake had, and bit his neck.

I ground my jaws down and shook my head, worrying the wound.

The Coachman howled and tried to push me off. I gnawed at him and felt the tough skin break. A light, sweet taste flooded my mouth. It was his soul, his power. So rich and full of promise. For the first time, greed for more power awoke inside me and stretched. Before I had time to think about it, the Coachman wrenched me away from him and tore out of my body. I remembered my father's words. *Shove him down his followers' throats.*

I repelled the Coachman's retreating form with the last

of my power and hoped it was enough. I awoke lying on the forest floor, mouth open, sucking gulps of cold, dry night air into my lungs. Sol, more monstrous in my reality than he'd been in my head, leaned over me.

"Good job. You managed to burn his followers." Sol tapped the side of his head to show me where it burned them. His pale, puckered skin gleamed in the moonlight. The water dripping off his suit pattered a tiny drumbeat on the cold ground. "Listen to me, and I'll tell you how to end this threat. Are you ready?"

"Yeah," I whispered and pulled myself to a sitting position. My head swam drunkenly, and I lurched to the side. Sol pulled me close, his wild, fecund smell nearly overpowering me, and spoke in my ear.

21

"Hurry. Once your enemy's followers realize they're about to lose, they'll pull back and regroup for another try." Sol shook one black-tipped finger at me.

I crawled to my feet, reaching into my pocket for my cellphone. Gone. Shock twisted inside me. How would I ever find the others in time?

Sol put one cold hand on my shoulder and pushed me back down. "Save your energy. I've sent help." The monster walked into the woods and became one with the darkness a few feet in.

With Sol gone, the unreality of the situation set in. The shakes overtook me. I clutched my arms to my chest, hunched over my legs, and took hitching breaths. Images and thoughts tossed in my mind, too wild and overblown for me to latch onto any of them.

The increased power of the mantle surged behind it all, a wild horse on a frayed lead. According to Sol, this was still only a fraction of the mantle's full power. How would I handle all of it without exploding? My heart beat too hard, and my fingertips hadn't stopped prickling. The unusual sharpness in my vision had returned with a vengeance. A shiver so strong it was nearly a convulsion ripped through my body.

"No, no, no, no." The moan came from a few feet away. Wade Hill took careful steps toward me, pistol pointed at me. He took a deep breath and put his finger on the trigger guard.

I held up both quavering hands. "I got him out for now."

"How do I know?" He took a few more steps toward me, mouth twisting with grief. "Make me believe it."

"I had to make a deal with that thing from the dark outposts to do it. Remember him? The pig guy? He widened the crack in my scar tissue to make me strong enough to get the Coachman out." I laid my head on my knees and let myself shake. There was no way I had enough power to do what Sol told me, let alone overpower twelve other people who knew far more magic than I did.

"What'd you give him?" Wade squatted a few feet from me. He stayed far enough away so I couldn't touch him.

"He said he'd tell me when it was time. He's also taking the souls of the twelve who summoned the Coachman." Freezing sweat ran down my back in rivulets.

"You can't make open ended deals with those—" He pressed his lips together and shook his head. "We'll figure it out when the time comes."

"He said he sent you to help me." Another shudder ripped through me.

Wade nodded, eyes downcast. "Yeah. I was headed the other way. All of a sudden, I knew I had to come this way. Had to tromp through a fucking creek to get here." He shoved his gun into the back of his pants. "Got my damn boots wet." He raised his head, teeth flashing in the moonlight, eyes crinkled into a grin.

"Can you fix me? And then go back to camp and get the stuff I need?" Part of me wanted him to say no, to get up and run out of these woods, his wet boots sloshing, and get as far away from me as he could. My deal with Sol was something I never intended. It scared me, made me question who I'd be from now on. First the mantle and now Sol. Before long, there'd be nothing of the old me left. Normal slipped further from my grasp with each step.

I shook off the negative thoughts. They were a luxury I could no longer afford. I had a little girl to save and some people to hurt. Wasn't that always the way it ended up?

"I'll never turn my back on you." Wade came close and put both arms around me. I laid my head on his chest and breathed in his smell—sunshine, gasoline, and the open road. He spoke his magic words, and the power hummed from him to me. It woke me and pushed some of my long lost psychic energy back into place. A few stray shivers bucked through me, and my nerves went calm again. The whole thing took less than a minute. He let me go and stared into my face.

"Better?" he whispered. I nodded. He leaned forward until his lips brushed mine. My arms tightened around him, and we kissed hard.

A branch popped behind me. I jerked in Wade's

embrace. He lurched away from me, pistol already out. Mysti came close enough for us to see her, her hands out. Wade put his pistol away and let out an irritated snort.

"Sorry." She raised her eyebrows at me.

I told Mysti what I'd had to do to get the Coachman out of me. She moaned and closed her eyes but motioned with one hand for me to continue. Then I told her what I needed from camp and where I needed her to meet me.

"Hell, no. We're not leaving you here alone." Wade's voice raised and echoed through the still night.

"It's better this way. We can meet at the schoolhouse."

"Ten minutes." She motioned Wade to follow her. He hesitated, but I nodded at him to go. I needed to gather myself if I wanted to pull this off. Wade would do nothing but distract me. My lips still thrilled from his touch.

Mysti drew out her cellphone and put it to her ear. I heard her voice raised in agitated tones. I got up and started walking to the old schoolhouse. I had farther to go than Mysti and Wade, but if I kept a good pace, we'd reach it about the same time.

At first, I tried gathering my energy, concentrating it on the task at hand. But I couldn't quit thinking about Wade's lips on mine. What had it meant? Likely, nothing more than the heat of the moment. If I was going to let go of the trauma surrounding my battle scars, I ought to let go of Wade Hill while I was at it. Something was wrong, some reason we couldn't be together. Either it was him or me. Didn't matter. Maybe it was for the best.

I neared the old schoolhouse and stopped in the woods to watch the lights flickering inside. Sol had been vague in his instructions, maybe purposely so. I wished he hadn't. This whole witching thing was new to me, and I might screw it up.

"There you are." Danielle's voice came from behind me.

I stared to turn around.

"No. Not so fast. I've got a gun pointed at you." The hammer clicked as she pulled it back. "Just start walking toward the schoolhouse."

I stood still, ideas flashing behind my eyes. None of them would work. I needed what I told Mysti and Wade to bring me. The barrel of the gun jammed into the area between my shoulder blades. If she shot me, the bullet would go through my heart. I'd be dead in a couple of minutes. Might as well buy myself some time. I started walking.

When we got close to the building, Danielle yelled, "It's me, and I've got both the vessel and the source. Help me."

She had Zora? I tried to twist around to see the child, but Danielle dug the pistol's barrel into my skin. I froze. No way to save the little girl if I was dead.

A woman barely out of her teens came out of the building. She reached for Zora.

"No." I stuck out one hand, and she batted it away.

My fist curled, and I cocked it back. I'd knock this hussy into tomorrow if she touched Zora. The impact of the pistol's butt hitting the back of my head knocked my teeth together. I pitched to the ground and hit my forehead on the side of the building. My fight left me, and the world turned a hazy gray. Danielle's hand closed around my upper arm, stronger than I'd expected, and she dragged me inside. A young man appeared and helped Danielle drag me to the center of their circle. The two of them zip-tied my hands and ankles and hooked me up to their pulley system so I'd be ready when they slit my throat.

They'd hung me right over a black, burned spot on the floor. The odor of charred wood still rose off it. I turned my face away to find a young male nerd, the wizards and warlocks type, leaning over me.

"You almost burned this place down without even touching anything." His breath smelled like tuna and onions. "No wonder the Lord of Babylon wants your blood."

"The Coachman's not a lord." The movement of my cheek scratched against the dirty floor. "He's just a power hungry asshole. You know how he got his power?"

Nobody answered. I took that to mean they wanted me to tell them.

"He devoured people's souls and ate their flesh. My ancestor got rid of him once. Stop this silliness and help me get rid of him again." I searched for a face with reason still left in it.

They all just stared at me, eyes shining with irritation and impatience.

"Do you not understand what he can promise us?" Danielle laid Zora out beside me, hand behind her head to keep it from knocking on the floor. "If we help him be reborn, we'll be his chosen ones. No more telling fortunes, picking pockets, or working in convenience stores. We'll live in mansions with dominion over all."

"Nah." I rolled onto my back to face her. "He'll string you along until you're no use to him. Then he'll kill you and eat your power too."

Danielle's face darkened with rage. She stepped over Zora and delivered a kick to my ribcage. I yelped. Maybe I'd be better off saving my energy. I needed to call up my power and wasn't sure what it would be like now that I was getting more of the mantle's magic. I didn't think I could do it.

"You can control it," said a familiar voice. Priscilla Herrera stepped out of the shadows. "I gave my mantle to you, not to my daughter Samantha, because you're stubborn and resourceful, capable. Give yourself up to the power. Work with it instead of against it."

But I needed the items Sol spoke of. Otherwise, I didn't think his plan would work.

"Prepare anyway." Priscilla faded.

"Wait." But I was alone. I squeezed my eyes shut and took a shuddering breath. Nothing left to do but fight. Time to win or die trying.

I looked inside myself for a white mist shot with gold threads, the image I associated with the mantle. The black opal came to life on my chest, pulsing with the beats of my power. I let it flow through me, fingers, toes, until even my lips crawled with it. Ripples of magic worked their way through me. They strained at my skin, making it feel too tight to hold it all.

"It's time to begin." Danielle took a position at the top of the circle. She seemed ignorant of all I'd seen. Good. She held up both hands. "I call to the power of the Lord of

Babylon. Join us, your highness. Your vessel awaits. Join us." She repeated herself, and the others chorused, "Join us," when she got to that part.

Wind, one carrying a high, rotten stench, came from nowhere and caressed my face. It moved my hair and circled around my ears. With this new, increased power of the mantle, I saw the Coachman's presence as a slithering shadow, creeping along the corners of the room. Where were my friends? I was running out of time.

"Lord of Babylon, join the blood of Peri Jean Mace as it flows from her. Let yourself be carried into the vessel by her power and by the psychic bond connecting the two." Danielle moved toward me, athame clutched in one hand.

Fear broke out over my body and closed my throat. My mouth went dry. I was out of time. Everything I'd endured, everything I'd given up was for nothing. We'd failed. I squeezed my eyes shut and waited to feel myself being hoisted feet first to hang upside down from the ceiling.

"Here it is, Peri Jean," Wade screamed from outside. The window nearest me broke, and something golden caught the candlelight. Samantha's disk skidded across the floor. It clattered to a stop in front of me. I turned my intent on it.

"Snake and rat king," I yelled. These were the words Sol told me to say.

Danielle dropped her raised arms and rolled her eyes. She glared at the disk. "What the hell is this?"

The Coachman's presence swirled hysterically around the room. "Stop it." His voice shook the room.

Danielle grabbed at the disk. I directed my power at

her mind and squeezed. She fell on her back, convulsing. The others kept their distance, eyes eating up their fool heads.

The disk jittered and rippled. On it appeared diagonals, the same way you'd cut a pie if you wanted to make twelve pieces of it. In the center of the disk a coiled snake etched itself into the metal. In each of the twelve diagonals appeared the image of a rat also etched into the metal. The Coachman's spirit shot out of the circle. I didn't see where it went, but I doubted it left. This was too much opportunity to run away from. I might still shit the bed.

"I call on the power of the dark outposts." I barely recognized my own voice. It rang with a depth I'd never heard before. "The sacrifice is ready."

The snake etched into the disk rose and glided off the metal. It wasn't the same one Sol disguised himself as earlier. This snake was decoratively patterned and twice as big. It had two rattles on its tail and the oblong head of a python. It slithered to me and rested its black eyes on me. The message came into my mind, clearer than I wanted. *If this doesn't work, I'll take you.*

I focused my power on the disk and imagined the magical essences of each member of the coven. Just like Mysti, I saw them now. I committed the essences to the disk and imagined them being reborn as rats. The disk rippled again.

"Rat king," I whispered, pouring my power into it. "Rat king."

The rats rose out of nothing, brown bodies writhing,

the noise of their squeaks maddening. Their tails twined together.

"I order the souls of these twelve inside the rat king to be crushed, suffocated, and devoured. The power of three is three. You have caused harm and now must pay." These were also the words Sol told me to speak. I concentrated on moving the souls from the human bodies into the rats. My body stiffened and shook with the effort. The first one, belonging to the weakest member of the group, pulled free from its body and fell into a rat.

"Let it flow through you," Priscilla's voice whispered in my ear.

I did as she said, giving myself up to it, forgetting there was a Peri Jean Mace. I focused every piece of my being on the task at hand. Sickness and fatigue beckoned somewhere deep in my mind. I ignored it. The power rolled through me, arching my back, making my hair stand on end. My vision grayed out.

The souls rushed over me, one after the other. The rats squealed louder as each soul found its home. My body relaxed, bathed in sweat. I lay on the floor panting. The snake slithered toward the joined rats, its tongue flicking out to test the scent of their fear. My own fear threatened to swallow my sanity. I turned my head away. Priscilla Herrera leaned into my face.

"No. Watch." Her dark eyes glowed with something that scared me worse than the snake about to eat its gruesome meal.

I turned back in time to watch the snake strike. Its thick body whipped and bulged over the mass of rats.

Their squeals became unbearable and then just stopped. The snake's jaw unhinged, and it began swallowing the dead rats one by one. As each rat went down, the human body it coincided to slumped to the floor, skin pale and waxy in the dying candlelight. When the last one went into the snake's gullet, the candles all flickered out.

I'd thought I had control of my fear, but it jumped back to the surface, screaming hysterically. I didn't want to be in the dark with that snake. Something cold and long nestled against me.

"Send him away." The snake's head bumped against my neck, and its rattles chittered in the darkness. "Say his true name."

"Not yet." I pushed my consciousness out of my body and into the Coachman.

His shriek of fear and rage shook my entire being. He whipped at me, trying to enter, but it was too late. His followers were dead. There was no one to sustain his presence. I blew a little puff of air at him, and he flew away, light as a piece of ash.

I went straight to the blue Mason jar and broke it on the brick floor of the little room. Zora's tiny spirit raced around the room, ready to go back to her own body. I pulled her little soul against me and sheltered her from what I was about to do. I gathered my power again, noting how little was left but still awed at its magnitude. Then I screamed his true name. "Oscar Elias Rivera."

The Coachman, who'd at some point re-christened himself as Lord of Babylon, howled at the sound of his true name. He wouldn't be able to resist me, not with his followers being digested in the snake's belly.

I yelled his name again, just because it felt good to hear him cry out. "Oscar Elias Rivera, leave this place. Go back to your soul's home immediately without going anywhere else." It wouldn't help for me to tell him not to come out. I couldn't stop him if another group of idiots summoned him.

The old schoolhouse shook. Something cracked deep inside it. The sweet, rotting odor came back. I gagged and retched. The rest of the windows burst outward. The Coachman disappeared, roaring his displeasure to the world. A few dogs and coyotes returned the sentiment.

Then it was just me and Zora's spirit. I marveled at the brilliant ball of light and saw the blue thread connecting us. That must have been where her memories of me came from. Gently as I could, I snapped the thread and pushed the little girl back into her body. Her eyes flew open. She sucked in a breath and began to wail.

The clattering of the snake's rattles came near, and Sol's whisper filled my head. "Job well done, exactly what I expected from you." Then he was gone. I let out a sigh of relief and began to worry how I'd get up to help Zora with my wrists and ankles bound. Where were her parents anyway? And Wade?

"Let me go." Wade's shouts came from right outside the building.

I expected him to kick down the door, but Dillon and Finn did that, shining their flashlights around the room.

"Over here." I gasped out the words, all traces of power

gone from my voice. It was just the voice of a woman who'd smoked two packs of cigarettes every day for way too long.

"The fuck?" Dillon breathed. "This room's full of rotting corpses."

A flashlight beam flickered over me. I winced, squinting my eyes at the glare. "I did it. He's gone." I felt like a million bucks in spite of my aches and pains and my numb hands and feet. Pride may have been one of the seven deadlies, but I sure felt it right then.

Wade charged around her and knelt over me.

"I did it," I whispered to him, a smile cracking my dry lips.

He smiled back and stroked my cheek. "You did." He cut the zip tie holding my wrists together and raised me to a sitting position. His rough hands began to massage feeling back into my numb hands and feet.

I glanced at the disk laying on the floor a couple of feet away. It had gone blank again. No snakes. No rat king. Just a blank metal disk. Griff and Mysti surrounded me, their concerned questions fading into one long, hysterical sentence.

Dillon grabbed her daughter up off the floor. The kid continued to scream, shrill, hysterical screams. Was something wrong with her? Finn joined them, putting his arms around both of them. Neither of them seemed alarmed by her condition. Dillon planted a loud kiss on Zora's check and whispered in her ear. The sobs decreased in volume.

I opened and closed my hands against the pain of

circulation returning to them. Wade grabbed me under one arm and pulled me to my feet.

Dillon stopped kissing her child's face and turned to me. "You saved my baby."

I nodded, face still split in what I knew had to be a stupid grin.

Finn turned to me and threw his arms around me, pressing his wet cheek to mine. "Thank you." He whispered the words over and over.

Dillon joined us. She spoke into my ear. "There will never be anything too big for you to ask me. I will stand by your side." She drew away from me. "Understand?" I nodded and returned her hug.

Turned out I couldn't get up by myself. I held up my arms for Wade to pick me up, but he shook his head. "You'll have to walk."

I stared at him, confused.

"They're waiting for you." Mysti pulled one arm over her shoulders, and Wade took the other. They helped me hobble to the old schoolhouse's door. Griff opened it, and I gasped.

The entire membership of Sanctuary, including Kenny and Anita, stood scattered in front of the schoolhouse. They held bats, axes, and not a few guns. Cecil stood in front of all of them.

"What's next, niece? What needs to be done?" Even in the soft glow of a dozen flashlights, craftiness glowed in his dark eyes. He'd won. I'd help him run Sanctuary now, and he knew it.

"We're ready to help," someone yelled.

"Tell us what to do," said someone else.

I turned to Griff. He nodded, giving me the only blessing I'd get from him.

"Dead bodies inside," I croaked. "We gotta get rid of 'em."

My knees buckled, but Wade and Mysti held me upright.

———

ONE WEEK LATER

The smell of barbecue brisket and the shrieks of kids playing filtered through the aluminum walls of Danielle's trailer. I glanced around the place, still shell-shocked it was mine. The community of Sanctuary had given both it and Danielle's heavy duty Ford pickup truck to me in exchange for ridding them of the Coachman and rescuing Zora. I hadn't wanted to take it, but Dillon told me it would be an insult for me to refuse.

The camper was nearly brand-new. Still had the new smell even. The cushion in the table bench had a butt indention marking where Danielle had liked to watch TV, and the mattress had a hollowed-out spot where she'd laid her large body each night, but those were small things. I was proud to have a home on wheels. Thanks to Dillon's skill as a forger, I was the legal, registered owner of the camper and the truck. For all the State of Texas knew, Danielle had sold it to me. I paid the taxes from the supposed sale. It was mine, and I'd earned it the hard way.

"What are you going to do with this thing?" Mysti said

from her perch on the bed. "Griff's subdivision won't allow you to park it out front." She smirked. "They'd probably call out the League of Decency." We giggled.

"I found storage for both it and the truck. Not far from Griff's house either." Cigarette clenched between my teeth, I straightened my jeans over the tops of my brand-new cowboy boots.

Look tough, but feminine, Cecil had said.

I stared at myself in the mirror and stubbed out my cigarette in the glass hotel ashtray someone had stolen sometime or another. Maybe I didn't fit the bill, but it would have to do. I faced Mysti. "Unless y'all want me to move out of your house right now."

"Hell no." She said it too quickly. I couldn't begin to imagine what having both Brad and me as permanent houseguests must be doing to her relationship with Griff. It was time for me to go, had been for a few months. "I just don't want you to go gallivanting off with this bunch. Griff and I might be bailing you out of jail before it's all over."

"I'm not leaving for another month, and I'll see you every time we come through the area." I threaded the black belt, also bought for the occasion, through my jeans and began tucking in my Johnny Cash giving-the-finger T-shirt, keeping my head down so Mysti couldn't see the excitement on my face. This new adventure was a mixed bag. Most things in life worked out that way. But I had the feeling it was going to be a hell of a ride.

"You're not wearing that T-shirt, are you?" Mysti squinted at me.

"Cecil said look tough. This was the tough part." I held out my arms.

Someone banged on the door. It rattled the whole dwelling.

"We're going to sit down now," Dillon yelled.

A lighter rap drummed on the door. "Sit down now," a childish voice echoed.

I smiled, and so did Mysti. Zora acted as though she'd forgotten the whole ordeal with the Coachman. She hadn't mentioned remembering me from before again either. Other than bringing dead birds back to life on occasion, she was a normal little girl with too much energy and a wide stubborn streak. Each day I spent with her made me more and more proud of who and what I was. This kid wouldn't have lived without me.

"Let's go." I held out my hand and pulled Mysti off the bed. She'd fallen in the mattress's dimple, and we both struggled to get her off the bed. I'd have to buy a new mattress if I wanted to sleep in here.

We walked out into bright winter sunlight glaring against a turquoise sky. The aroma of sizzling hot dogs joined the barbecue brisket smell. A queasy rumble came from my stomach. I put my hand over it and munched an antacid tablet.

"It's not too late to tell Cecil you don't want to do this." Mysti gripped my arm. Griff appeared on my other side and put his arm around me.

"Mysti's right," he whispered in my ear. "It's not too late."

But it was too late, had been since I stepped out of that

old schoolhouse and started planning what do with all those dead bodies. Maybe it had been too late even before that. But Griff and Mysti weren't the right people to tell that to.

"This is the right thing to do." I drew myself up as straight as I could. "The scar tissue surrounding my magic almost got me killed. The only way I'm ever getting it off me is to seek the real me. To accept the real me. Cecil says he'll find help for me. I need to help him too."

"You don't have to do this to seek the real you." Griff's arm tightened around me.

"She can make her own decisions." Mysti's voice trembled. "We can't protect her forever."

Zora rushed at me, hair flying back from her face, eyes wild with excitement. She held out her arms a few seconds before she reached me, and I scooped her up and perched her on my hip. She tugged my hair. Hard. "Mama say you come now."

I walked toward the pavilion and saw the empty lawn chair right next to Cecil's. People had started gathering, and all of them gave me curious glances. Some of them whispered to each other. I hugged Mysti and Griff.

"Passing a crossroads isn't the end. It's a new beginning. I've got to see where this takes me." I stared into both their faces. My heart ached at the idea of hurting them. They'd been so good to me. "I can still work for you. Griff only needs me some of the time anyway."

Mysti threw her arms around me. "We're not angry at you, and we don't feel betrayed. We want great things for you."

"May this be one of those great things." Griff gently drew Mysti away from me.

I took the final steps into the pavilion, boot heels ringing on the concrete floors. Cecil patted the seat next to him and smiled. I handed Zora to Finn. She struggled, but her daddy gave her a stern look. She relented with her bottom lip stuck out. The old-fashioned metal lawn chair creaked when I sat on it. The whispers and murmurs increased. This hadn't been what people expected.

"Do you need a cushion?" Cecil said into my ear. I shook my head. He took my hand, his swollen knuckles and sun-spotted skin a sharp contrast to my battle-scarred fists and smooth skin, still tan even in the winter. "You've given an old man hope for the future. You and me are gonna have some fun."

A camera flashed in front of us. I took my eyes off Cecil's, so like mine and like Memaw's, and saw Dillon backing away.

"I'll have that one printed up. Get a copy for both of you." She scooted back behind Cecil and me. Her lawn chair squeaked as she sat down.

I stared out into the assembly of people. This was the first good look I'd gotten at them and they at me. I recognized what they were, even if I only knew a few names. These were the kind of people I'd known growing up, the kind who wore dollar store shoes and didn't know the difference between a hotel and a motel.

They peered right back at me, taking in my new boots and my aggressive T-shirt. A woman about my age who had a little girl hugged to her legs smiled. I smiled back.

Someone tugged at my hand. I didn't have to look to know it was Zora. She climbed into my lap, giving her mother a triumphant grin. Poor Dillon. She had her hands full with this kid.

The feeling of someone's gaze heavy on us had me glancing around until I saw Wade Hill. He and Bradley flanked Jadine. She had a flush high on her cheekbones and a smile on her face. She waved in my direction. My black opal zinged at the magic of our minds meeting. Wade took a step away from Jadine and crossed his arms over his chest, staring at me with an unreadable expression. He gave me a barely perceptible nod. Did that mean he still had hot iron for me? I smiled at him. It wasn't over until it was over.

Finn stood from his chair and clapped his hands. People quit talking and watched him. "I, Finlay Gregg, call to order the winter tribunal of Sanctuary, begun by Iris and Filip Gregg on this very land in winter of 1959."

So that was why they came back here. We all need a home base, a place to go when the outside world threatened to take all we were and gnash it to bits. I was still looking for that place. Maybe I'd find it sometime or another.

"We only have a few items to cover, and then we'll get back to this party so we can pull out tomorrow morning." Finn gestured at Cecil, who gripped my shoulder and stood.

"I'd first like to say a few words in honor of Eric and Kitty Lyons. They died protecting my great-niece Zora and her brother Zander. They'll always be remembered in this community for their heroism and sacrifice. Let's bow our heads for a moment of silence." All the heads bowed. Cecil stood watching the group for several seconds, checked his cards, and spoke again.

"The next item of business is my announcement that I'm naming my great-niece, Peri Jean Mace, as my consultant and enforcer." Cecil paused while people talked among themselves. He'd have needed a bullhorn to be heard over them. He patted my arm as the talking died down and winked at me.

My heart thundered as my gaze ran over all the faces in front of me. I searched for signs of disbelief, disappointment, or disgust—all the things I figured people associated with me. None of those emotions stared back at me. Several of the women began clapping, and the rest of them joined in. I sat stunned at the display.

Cecil laughed. "The third item we need to discuss is Kenny's attempt to forcibly take this community from me. Incidents like this will be part of Peri Jean's duties, and I'll leave it with her." Cecil put one hand over my forearm.

I faced him and shook my head. This wasn't what we discussed. All I'd promised to do was use magic to keep a handle on things, to let people know Cecil had backup. He gave me a stern glare. I took a deep breath and tried to get Zora to get down. She whined and protested, so I stood, hitching her onto my hip, sure I looked ridiculous and not tough at all.

"Kenny and Anita Johnson." My voice rang over the silent pavilion. It sounded screechy, like the voice of someone who smoked too much. The thought of a cigarette made my fingers itch to hold one. I took a deep breath and reigned in my roving thoughts. "You campaigning against my uncle Cecil, taking a private vote, and then trying to enforce it at gunpoint could have ended with someone seriously hurt. Do you agree?"

Anita tossed her head, her face darkening. It was probably the only admission I'd get from her. I set my gaze on Kenny's creased face.

"Yes, ma'am." His voice trembled. He'd helped us dispose of the bodies from the Coachman's coven, his face shiny with fear sweat. When we got to Danielle, with her eyeballs blown out of her skull, he'd gasped and rolled his eyes fearfully at me. Maybe he figured he was next. He should have been, really, but I didn't want to start off like that. Besides, I had a feeling a man like this, one who owed me something, might come in handy at some point.

"Are you sorry? Would you do it again?" I ignored the mumble from the crowd and held up my hand when it threatened to get loud. They shut up immediately. Zora clapped her hands, and a few people giggled.

"No, ma'am. I've been in this community for going on fifteen years. I'm a convicted felon. Had a hard time getting started after I got out. All I want is to see Sanctuary keep going." He swallowed hard. If he'd had a hat, he'd have held it at waist level. "Thing's been getting kind of crazy the last year. I just got scared of losing it."

I nodded, thinking things over. *What would Priscilla do?* The mantle swirled inside me, locked into the deepest part of my soul, even this small measure more giant than I could have ever imagined.

"Well?" Anita Johnson glared at me. "What's our punishment?" She swallowed at that, eyes darting back and forth.

"Understand that what you did was strike one and two. There won't be any more chances." I sucked in a deep breath, concentrating on my magic. The black opal warmed on my chest. I narrowed my focus on Kenny and Anita. "If you betray us again, I will crawl all over you like an army of fire ants."

I aimed my magic at the couple and imagined red, livid fire ants crawling all over their bodies and biting. Kenny and Anita stood still, staring back at me with identical frowns of confusion stamped on their plain faces.

Then Anita rubbed at her neck and let out a little shriek. She grabbed for her leg and slapped at it. Kenny jerked his shirt away from his chest and stared down his hairy chest. He began to dance foot to foot, face contorted in fear. I waited until both of their cheeks turned red and swept my hand in front of my face, the same way I'd have brushed fire ants off a kitchen counter. The two relaxed and turned their sweat-sheened faces toward me.

"Do we understand each other?" Fatigue from the little show pounded in me, but I held myself straight, determined not to let it show. Kenny and Anita nodded.

Cecil gave me a pat and stood again. By now, I knew this was his way of telling me I'd done what he wanted. "This community is and always has been for people who are a little different. A safe place for people like us. We do allow those with no special talents to travel with us, but they will never lead this group. There's room enough for them in the outside world." Cecil nodded at Finn, who stood up.

"Meeting adjourned. Enjoy the barbecue and get a good night's sleep. We hit the trail at daybreak," he shouted.

The crowd dispersed. None of my family made any move to get up, so I stayed put too. Wade came over, shrugging into his leather jacket.

"I need to get moving." He kissed my cheek. I hugged him.

Cecil watched the exchange, glancing back at Jadine then at me. "We're opening our membership again, healer. You'd be welcome here. Be a good place for you to start again."

"I can't leave the Six Guns. I owe them my life." Wade held out his hand to shake. Cecil took it.

"Some debts beg to be paid and forgotten." Cecil gave Wade a smile I couldn't interpret.

Wade smiled and saluted Cecil. He walked away. I followed Wade to his motorcycle.

"This would be a better place with you in it." I watched him pull his gloves and riding glasses out of his saddlebag. "Even if you don't want to be with me." I thought of Wade flirting with Jadine and cringed.

Wade shook his head, his jaw set. "I'm not the kind of man to walk away from a debt like the one I owe the Six Guns."

He wasn't, but did King Tolliver share Wade's unflinching loyalty? He'd beaten Wade for coming here. Something bad was going on with King, and I hated to see

Wade go back to it. While I was thinking it over, Wade leaned close and spoke into my ear. "And Jadine's too young for me. I just like torturing Bradley." Our eyes locked, and that old, heady lust worked its way through me.

"When will I see you again?" I had to ask. Just couldn't help myself.

Wade winked at me. "You know me. I'll be around whenever you need me."

I stared at the healing bruises and cuts on his face. Fear and anger stirred around in my head. Was King's problem with me? He could drink a toilet water martini if so. I'd mash him flat.

"What're you thinking about?" Wade's grin made me think he knew more than he let on.

"Just about how much I'll miss you." I hugged my friend, still wishing he was my lover, and went back to my family. The day passed too quickly. Before I knew it, people began packing up and preparing to travel the next day.

"It's time to talk about the Coachman." Cecil's soft voice surprised me, and I nearly dropped the cigarette smoldering between my first and second fingers. "He's still alive, is he not? Trapped wherever he hid his soul?"

Finn and Dillon stopped playing with their kids and wandered over, wariness etched on both their faces.

"Yep. I sent him back to where he hid his soul." It had seemed like a cave of some sort, and the article I read about him had mentioned an underground river to hell.

"What's next?" Finn pulled up a lawn chair next to

mine. Jadine wandered over, her hand on Brad's arm. Once Wade left, the two of them glommed onto each other.

I thought it over. It was only a matter of time before someone else found a tile and the Coachman started whispering in their ear. There was no telling how many Samuel and Samantha missed or where the Coachman had hidden other runes. We needed to find the place where the Coachman hid his soul.

But the scar tissue keeping me from the mantle's power also needed my attention. I suspected I'd need way more of the mantle's power than I currently had in order to separate the Coachman's soul and banish it from the living plane. Finn's impatient sigh drew me out of my thoughts.

"We have both the Coachman's soul and the scar tissue spell to deal with." I glanced at Cecil, hoping he had more answers than I did right then.

"I have a contact in Central Texas I'd like to talk to about that spell," Cecil nearly whispered. "He's our best bet if we can find him."

"Meanwhile, I'll try to figure out what Samantha meant about using the disk and the runes to uncover the location of the Coachman's soul." I kept my voice low too.

"And we keep what we're doing quiet, right?" Dillon scooted a chair in front of us, her own cigarette burning between her fingers.

"Yes." Cecil nodded. "No need to alarm anybody. For all they know, we're traveling to Central Texas because of Kenny killing that stupid fence in Florida." Cecil's dark gaze found mine, and I murmured my agreement.

Another time, not very long before this one, I might

have argued with Cecil, told him his community needed to know everything. Now, after what I'd seen, I knew why we kept things even from the people we loved and wanted to protect. The truth was dangerous.

I drove home to Griff and Mysti's in the dark, the moonlight dancing through the tops of the pines. The concrete roads and heavy traffic overtook me soon enough. The mild sadness, the odd longing I'd felt since I came down here to live didn't come with them. I'd left the crossroads where I'd been trapped since the day of my father's murder and chosen my path.

This rutted, potholed road cut through the landscape of the rest of my life. Deadman's curves hid in shadowy valleys and had big, deadly trees in just the right spot to kill me if I misjudged my speed. Long stretches of straightaway lay in waiting, their shoulders full of hitchhikers with plans to make sure I didn't see another day.

But I had friends who'd sacrifice everything to help me. A new family who wanted me, for better or worse. Power beyond what most people could imagine.

Maybe I couldn't know the dangers waiting to trip me up. But those baddies had a surprise coming. Picking the wrong girl to mess with burns like hellfire.

Keep reading for a sample of the next book in Peri Jean Mace Ghost Thriller Series.

DEAD END EXCERPT

Chapter 1

Late afternoon sun streamed into the window of Gaslight City Title Company's conference room. It heated my jeans-clad leg to the point where I slid off my leather jacket and laid it over the back of my chair. For the billionth time, I asked myself if I was doing the right thing.

It didn't matter how long I waited to sell Memaw's property. It would never be easy to let it go. I'd considered keeping it, but knew I'd never live in Gaslight City again. My ugly past lurked around every corner. These city people had offered above market value for ten acres with a burned-out house and barn. I had to take it and move on.

The upside was I could see Hannah while I was in town. That would make all the unpleasantness worthwhile. We had spoken only a few words since the night I killed a man to rescue her. Things would never be as they were. But I couldn't just let her slip away, our friendship ending altogether. Maybe soon she'd answer one of the half-dozen messages I'd left her over the last week.

While the woman read from the infinite stack of closing papers, I stared out the window at the Easter decorations, eggs and bunnies in pastel colors, fluttering on the antique gaslights lining the street. A tall woman, sun glowing on her long, red hair, hurried down the street. She stopped to peer into the plate glass window of Purtlebaugh's General Store, where they still sold cups of coffee for five cents with purchase of a souvenir ceramic mug.

I sat up straighter, really alert for the first time since I sat down. *Hannah?* Perhaps she hadn't returned my call because she was coming to meet me here at the title company. My heart beat faster.

A little red-headed boy raced down the sidewalk and hugged the woman's legs. She bent to kiss his head, and I caught a direct look at her face. *Not Hannah.* I slumped in my seat and checked my phone to see if she'd returned my call since I set it to silent.

"Leave that alone." Rainey Bruce shoved a stack of papers at me to sign.

I shoved the phone in my pocket and signed the first paper. A sob crept up my throat. Relinquishing ownership of the land where Memaw raised me stabbed me right in the heart. I swiped at my face.

"You planning on staying in Houston?" asked the male half of the yuppie city couple buying the property. I finished signing and raised my head. The couple wore the kind of clothes they probably thought country people wore—pearl snap shirts, tight blue jeans, brand new cowboy boots. I pushed the stack back at Rainey.

"Still undecided." No need to bother telling him I no longer lived there. "What are you planning for Memaw's land?"

The woman showed me a mouthful of perfect teeth and pushed her phone across the table. "We're having this house built."

I glanced at the phone. A brick McMansion that looked like it belonged in Griff's subdivision back in The Woodlands. Deep sadness worked its way through me. Rainey passed me another stack of papers and gave me a warning glare. She needn't have worried. I was too numb to say much. I started signing again.

"We're going to get some cows and horses, maybe some chickens," the husband said. "Be modern-day farmers."

"Good luck with that." I had no reason to be angry at these nice people, but I was. Letting go of the last piece of my life here in Gaslight City stung like a bitch. I signed the last paper and pushed them back at Rainey.

She glanced through the forms. "If this is all Peri Jean needs to sign, we'll be on our way."

The title company lady, whose name I couldn't remember even though we went to school together, scowled but nodded.

I nodded at the yuppie couple and shook both their hands. Smooth as babies' butts. They sure had a rude awakening on the not-too-distant horizon.

Rainey and I walked out to her convertible Mercedes.

She popped the trunk and took a sheaf of papers out of the leather messenger bag she used as a briefcase.

"The last of the jewelry and gems from the Mace Treasure sold to an antiques collector in Austin." She passed me a sealed envelope with my name on it. "This is the final sum transferred into your bank account. As agreed, I cut checks for Hannah, Wade Hill, and me, set up the scholarship fund we talked about, and paid myself back what I loaned you to buy your Toyota sedan. Where is it, by the way?" She stared up and down the street.

"I made the drive in this." I patted the huge, white truck next to me. The car was in storage, and I was considering its sale. "It pulls the travel trailer better than my Toyota would."

Rainy made a face at the truck. "I can't believe you're traveling around with a bunch of grifters and living in a *camper*." She said the word with her lips puckered.

I ignored the barb. Rainey couldn't possibly understand how wonderful it was to be around people who shared both my gifts and my blood for the first time in my life. "Did you name the scholarship what I told you?"

She rolled her eyes. "The Chase Fischer Budding Musician scholarship."

I smiled, hoping some kid like Chase would be encouraged to go to college instead of hang around this town and waste away.

Rainey set out another sheaf of papers. "This is the paperwork for the trust you had me set up for your uncle Jesse. It'll be taken out of the property sale. Very good of you. It's what your memaw would have wanted."

"This needs to cover his legal counsel and drop the maximum in his commissary account each month." I glanced through the papers. The words didn't make sense. I was too rattled from letting go of my last tangible link to Memaw.

"You think I'm incompetent? I always get your uncle everything he needs." Rainey tapped the paper with one long, dragon lady nail to show me where to sign.

I scribbled my name. "This feels like a kiss-off. I wish we could get him out."

Rainey shook her head and stared down the street. It didn't hide the flush in her cheeks. She always got that flush when we talked about my uncle Jesse. I didn't dare ask what it was about. She might snatch me bald. I handed back her papers, and she stowed them in her trunk. When she turned back around, she had her lips pressed together and held a white envelope pinched between her thumb and forefinger.

"As you requested, I sent King Tolliver a check. He returned it un-cashed with this."

I opened the envelope. King had scribbled "void" on the check, which had been for a sizable amount. Especially since he didn't do a damn thing to help find the Mace Treasure.

The money had been a show of respect, one Wade strongly encouraged to keep King as a friend. Behind the check was a folded slip of paper. I withdrew it and read the typed words . My scalp tingled as sweat broke out.

The bill read "services rendered." The amount listed was easily five times the check I'd had Rainey send King.

"You want my professional advice?" The disdain on Rainey's face gave a good idea what she'd say.

"I don't guess it matters because I don't have this kind of money. Not after all the other stuff I did." I folded the invoice and put it back in the envelope, offering it to Rainey.

She waved it off. "King has no right to expect anything, especially not the amount of that invoice, from you." The cords in her neck tightened, and fury crossed her face. "No right at all." She shut the trunk of her car too hard. "Where are you and the rest of your con artist family camped?" She crossed her arms over her chest and squinted her eyes at me.

"Outside Shreveport." My family had flat out refused to cross into Burns County. Our mutual ancestor had been lynched in Gaslight City by a bunch of witch haters. Her descendants feared Burns County the way some folks fear boogeymen in closets. My great-uncle Cecil, who'd taken me in like a prodigal daughter, had expended considerable hot air trying to convince me to conduct the sale of Memaw's property online. But I'd come anyway in hopes of talking with Hannah, to see if I could salvage some part of our friendship.

"Get on out of the county before dark." Rainey settled her direct gaze on me. Something in her eyes chilled me, made me sort of want to leave.

I checked my phone and shoved it back into my pocket. "I want to see Hannah, but I can't get her to answer her phone."

Rainey sucked in a deep breath and stiffened. She'd

done that every time I mentioned Hannah. I didn't understand the problem. If Hannah wanted no more to do with me, why didn't Rainey just tell me? She'd never cared about hurting my feelings before.

The blat of a motorcycle echoed off the buildings. Before I turned away from Rainey, I saw her shoulders relax. What had her in such a twist? The old Rainey would have encouraged me to go out to Long Time Gone and eat King Tolliver a new asshole for sending that stupid invoice. She wouldn't have said get out of town before dark.

The motorcycle cruised toward us, sunlight winking off the iron horse's chrome. The driver's massive body came into view. Wade. My face stretched into a big, goofy smile, and I forgot about Rainey, stepped off the curb, and began waving.

Wade Hill pulled to the curb. I threw myself at him and hugged him as though it had been more than a couple of months since we last saw each other. He hugged me back, laughing into my hair.

I broke the hug and planted a kiss on his cheek. The part of his cheeks not covered by his gray-shot black beard reddened. "I thought you were tied up today with Six Gun Revolutionary business."

"I pulled a diva fit. Told King I was damn sure going to see you before you got out of town." Wade took off his sunglasses and tucked them into the neck of his leather jacket. The skin around his left eye was puffed out and beginning to bruise.

"King do that to you for coming to see me?" I didn't need Wade's confirmation. Not after seeing King's bill for services rendered. I had his services rendered. Sure did. I'd shove them right up his hairy old ass.

"Doesn't matter. We're together now." Wade glanced at Rainey, something moving behind his dark gaze. I followed it and saw something almost like fear cross Rainey's exotic features. She covered it quickly.

"I've got to prepare for court." She walked to her car and started climbing inside but stopped and turned back to speak to me. "If you need anything else, come by the office." She waved and drove off.

Wade watched, frowning. He caught me watching and plastered a smile on his face. It didn't reach his eyes. "New fried chicken place on your way out of town. Let's go get some food. I'm about to starve." Instead of giving me a chance to answer, Wade started his motorcycle. Shouting over the thing was impossible. I started my truck and did as he said.

———

Wade lied. The place we went to eat wasn't just a fried chicken place. They served a full country meal. I closed my eyes as I bit into my second piece of fried chicken. It actually had flavor.

"You act like you haven't eaten in a month." Wade scooped up a forkful of the creamiest mashed potatoes I'd had since Memaw died.

"You don't understand. You have to find a little hole in the wall town to get a meal like this. Restaurants in big cities have to cater to a diverse crowd. The majority of the food has about as much taste as—" I stopped speaking as a bony hand closed over my shoulder.

"Hey, girl." The nasally drawl came from behind me, but I didn't have to see Tubby Tubman to know his voice or the feel of his skinny hand. "I didn't know you's coming to town." Tubby sat in the extra chair without being invited and grinned like a little boy up to no good.

"Why would I tell you I'm coming to town?" I finished my chicken and started on my collard greens.

Tubby shrugged and reached one skinny, tattooed arm across the table. He snagged a cornbread muffin and set about putting honey on it. Wade glowered at him but said nothing.

"Might be I thought we'd renewed our friendship after I helped you find the Mace Treasure." He ate the cornbread and licked honey off his fingers.

I thought about it and nodded. "Okay. I'll buy that."

Tubby grinned again and slid his cold blue eyes over me. "Might be you still owe me a favor."

I rolled my eyes and ate another forkful of collards. "Why can't we just say we saved each other's asses and leave it there? I mean, if you really want to be friends again."

Tubby considered it and reached for another cornbread muffin.

Wade grabbed his arm and shoved it away. "What do you really want, Tubman?"

"Talk to Peri Jean." Tubby withdrew his arm. "Heard she might be in need of a friend right now."

"What's that mean?" Wade wiped his mouth, wadded the napkin, and threw it at the table.

"Heard Peri Jean's trying to get in touch with pretty Hannah Kessler." Tubby grabbed my iced tea and took a sip before I could stop him. Good thing I was finished with it.

"Who told you that?" Wade's voice sharpened in warning. He shifted in his chair, one hand gripping the edge of the table. I stopped shoving down my collard greens to watch Wade. If I didn't know better, I'd think I saw actual fear in his dark eyes. Tubby might annoy Wade, but scaring him was another matter.

Available now.
Order Dead End from your favorite bookseller.
ISBN: 978-1-947462-01-4

Visit Catie's website:
www.catierhodes.com

Find Catie on Facebook:
http://www.facebook.com/catierhodesauthor

Follow Catie on Book Bub.
https://www.bookbub.com/authors/catie-rhodes

Join Catie's email list:
http://smarturl.it/lrdenewsletter

ABOUT THE AUTHOR

Catie Rhodes writes southern-fried urban fantasy with a strong dose of horror and a side dish of humor.

She is the author of the Peri Jean Mace Ghost Thrillers. Her short stories have appeared in *Tales From The Mist, Let's Scare Cancer to Death, and Allegories of the Tarot.*

Catie was born and raised behind the pine curtain in East Texas. She comes from a family of world champion liars.

Their tall tales molded Catie into a purveyor of her own brand of lies and legends. One day, she found the courage to start writing down her stories. It changed her life forever.

Catie Rhodes lives steps from the Sam Houston National Forest with her long-suffering husband and her armpit terrorist of a little dog.

Find Catie online:
www.catierhodes.com